D1318050

DECEPTIONS

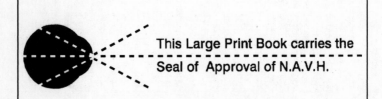

DECEPTIONS

A JAMESTOWN NOVEL

MARILYN J. CLAY

WHEELER PUBLISHING
A part of Gale, Cengage Learning

GALE
CENGAGE Learning

Detroit • New York • San Francisco • New Haven, Conn • Waterville, Maine • London

GALE
CENGAGE Learning

Copyright © 2010 by Marilyn Jean Clay.
Wheeler Publishing, a part of Gale, Cengage Learning.

LIBRARY OF CONGRESS CATALOGING-IN-PUBLICATION DATA

Clay, Marilyn.
  Deceptions : a Jamestown novel / by Marilyn J. Clay.
    p. cm.
  Includes bibliographical references.
  ISBN-13: 978-1-4104-3279-7
  ISBN-10: 1-4104-3279-3
    1. Virginia—History—Colonial period, ca. 1600–1775—Fiction.
  2. Jamestown (Va.)—History—17th century—Fiction. 3. Large
  type books. I. Title.
  PS3603.L3877D43 2010b
  813'.6—dc22   2010033792

Published in 2010 by arrangement with Tekno Books.

Printed in the United States of America
1 2 3 4 5 6 7 14 13 12 11 10

DECEPTIONS

CHAPTER 1

London, March 1617

The bright morning sun squinting through panes of wavy leaded glass scattered patches of bright light on the uneven floor of the small garret room. Furnished only with a narrow bed, a cupboard, chair and low washstand, the cramped space squeezed beneath the tiled roof of the otherwise elegant London townhome was not brightened even by the sun.

Light falling across her face awoke Catherine. With a low groan she turned toward the wall, at once aware of the same sense of dread and foreboding that had twisted her insides the entire past month. Blinking sleep from her eyes, she pulled herself upright and cast an anxious gaze about the tiny chamber she'd called home the past six years. The austere furnishings and low ceiling had always made her feel like a prisoner . . . and unless she could figure out a way to escape today, she would virtually become one, her future lost to her forever.

As usual this time of morning, the third floor of the sumptuous London townhome was silent as a tomb. The maidservants who occupied rooms on either side of Catherine arose far earlier than she in order to hurry below stairs and get about their duties.

Catherine had been a girl of ten and two years when, upon the death of her mother, she'd been sent up to London to live with the aristocratic Lord and Lady Montcrief, to whom she was told she had some connection, though no one had bothered to explain to the grief-stricken little girl what that connection might be. During the ensuing years, Catherine had tried to please her guardians. Still she knew they thought her foolish because she wanted the selfsame thing today that she wanted six years ago — to reunite with her father and brother and spend the rest of her life in the arms of her beloved.

Finding a way to escape the Montcrief household should be easier for a grown-up young lady of eighteen years. But thus far no opportunity had presented itself, and now, today, time had all but run out. If she did not find a way to escape today, all would be lost. She'd never see her father, or brother, or *him* again.

One month ago, two events transpired that not only disrupted Catherine's life but set the entire Montcrief household on its ear. The first was that Catherine had at last received the long-awaited letter from her father, forwarded to her here in London. Fortunately Lady Montcrief had been away from home that morning and, because a maidservant had delivered the missive straight to Catherine's door, not even Lucinda knew about the letter. Anything Catherine confided to Lucinda soon found its way to Lady Montcrief's ears; therefore Catherine had wisely decided to keep the contents of her letter to herself.

When she was alone in her room, however, she could hardly keep from laughing aloud, so jubilant was she to finally know that her father, brother, and Noah were actually alive. Six long years ago, the three men had sailed across the sea to a vast, unknown wilderness the English called the New World.

"As soon as we're settled," her father had said, "we'll send for you and yer mother."

Poor Papa, Catherine thought now. Neither he nor Adam knew that Mama, who'd suffered from a weak constitution, had passed away only a few short months after they departed. Catherine fervently hoped now that she would be able to deliver the sad news to her father and brother in person. In his letter Papa had enclosed a voucher good for passage to the New World. He said he'd send another one as soon as he could. All one had to do was present the voucher to the ship's captain.

Trouble was, how was Catherine to escape unnoticed from the Montcrief household and find her way to London's busy dockside the very day a ship was set to sail for the New World? Especially now — now that the second occurrence had suddenly rendered Catherine Parke the most important member of the Montcrief household.

Dragging herself from the narrow cot, Catherine dejectedly put on one of her two fustian frocks, the one she'd worked so hard to pretty up with a frilly edge of embroidered lace.

Though the hour was late when she entered the elegant dining chamber below stairs, she noted that Lady Montcrief and Lucinda had also just come down to break their fast.

"Good morning, Catherine," said Lady Montcrief. Not unkindly. Not warmly. Matter-of-factly, as she had done every morning since Catherine had come to live with the family. The fashionably attired matron then turned her full attention to her sixteen-year-old daughter Lucinda.

As Catherine nibbled on a buttered scone and swallowed a few bites of the coddled eggs placed before her by a liveried footman, she vaguely heard her companions discussing Lucinda's bright future. Not at all hungry, Catherine, who was rarely included in the conversation when Lady Montcrief was present, soon murmured her excuses and rose to leave the table.

Lady Montcrief glanced up. "You'd best pack your bag this morning, Catherine. By this time tomorrow you'll be a married woman. I expect Mr. Windmere will be eager to whisk you off to . . . somewhere." She paused, perhaps expecting Catherine to exhibit some show of enthusiasm over her impending nuptials.

"Yes, ma'am."

Lady Montcrief's lips pursed. "Ungrateful gel," she muttered. "We shall be making calls this afternoon. See you do not keep us waiting."

"No, ma'am."

Back in her bedchamber, Catherine obediently dragged her mother's well-worn valise from beneath the sagging cot.

A month ago, Catherine had accidentally

11

learned that not all was as it seemed in the Montcrief household. Apparently, as did many members of England's upper class, Lord and Lady Montcrief lived far beyond their means. Lord Montcrief was now in the embarrassing position of being head over ears in debt. The same day Catherine's father's letter arrived, a wealthy London merchant named Mr. Windmere, to whom Lord Montcrief owed thousands of pounds, had rapped at their door intent on collecting the enormous debt owed him.

On his way inside, Mr. Windmere happened to catch a glimpse of Catherine and Lucinda strolling in the garden. Drawn by the lovely face and figure of one of the young ladies, whom he assumed to be Montcrief's eldest daughter, he'd pointed out the girl to his lordship.

Vastly relieved that the man had not fixed on Lucinda, since to marry one's daughter off to a lowly tradesman, no matter the size of his purse, was not the done thing, Montcrief had seized the moment when Windmere declared all of Montcrief's debts would be cancelled — the amount owed Windmere as well as that owed every other tradesman in town, and a generous portion besides — in exchange for the hand in marriage of the auburn-haired beauty. The "generous portion besides" Montcrief decided would serve nicely as a handsome dowry for Lucinda, something on his own he couldn't hope to provide. His lordship wasted no time in orchestrating a match between his daughter and a wealthy earl, a widower without issue.

Quite by accident, Catherine had overheard her guardians discussing the convoluted arrangement.

"All my debts shall be canceled the very second the wedding vows are exchanged!"

"And the additional funds Windmere has promised?" asked Lady Montcrief. "When will he pay —"

"The selfsame day. I will immediately turn the funds over to Pembroke's man of business. When our Lucinda provides the earl with an heir we shall be set for life! Pembroke understands Lucinda to be a lass of tender years, and has agreed to delay the wedding a bit."

"We shan't want them to wait too very long," cautioned Lady Montcrief.

"Our daughter's wedding will take place just as soon as Catherine's is safely executed."

An execution is exactly what it felt like to Catherine. Even if she hadn't received a letter from her papa, she would not agree to marry Mr. Windmere, a man of greater years than her father and whose rotund belly reminded her of the puffed-up toads her brother and Noah used to catch from the pond on the land her father farmed.

It didn't matter to her that Windmere had deep pockets. Her heart belonged to another — a handsome young man with twinkling blue eyes and golden curls. She had loved Noah Colton as long as she could remember and he loved her.

Now, as Lady Montcrief had instructed, Catherine listlessly set about folding up her few garments and stuffing them into the tattered valise. The heartfelt words Noah had scribbled on the bottom of her father's letter — telling her how much he missed her and longed for her to join them in a far-off place he called Jamestown, Virginia — replayed over and over in her mind.

Would she ever see Jamestown? Would she ever see Noah?

Terrified that her much-longed-for future was fast slipping away from her, Catherine felt a rush of tears fill her eyes. How, how, how was she to travel to the New World when she could not even figure out how to escape from the Montcrief household? Neither she nor Lucinda were allowed to go freely about London. Always a maidservant or footman must be along. True, she'd be out of the house this very afternoon, but she could hardly fling herself from the carriage and outrun the horses on foot.

She had no money. Reaching to the bottom shelf of the wobbly old cupboard, she retrieved the small pasteboard box she'd hidden amongst the folds of an old bed rug. In the box she kept a few precious mementos — a miniature of her mother when she was a girl, her mother's sewing scissors, her grandmother's pestle and mortar, and a few faded paper notes, the value of which Catherine hadn't a clue. The few pieces of her mother's fine jewelry, which had been in her possession when she arrived here, had somehow vanished — sold, she believed, by Lord Montcrief. Fearing she'd be turned out without a farthing, Catherine had never said a word about her loss, since perhaps the money his lordship gained from the sale of her mother's jewels had helped defray the cost of keeping her.

But that was neither here nor there. *Now.* Today her father and Noah were awaiting her in the New World. And she simply had to find a way to reach them! Tomorrow would be too late. By then, she'd be wed to Mr. Windmere. For the rest of her days.

Though Lord and Lady Montcrief had

succeeded in bending Catherine to their will in many areas, this was the one time she was determined not to acquiesce to their wishes. Because they'd insisted she take lessons alongside Lucinda, Catherine now knew how to read Latin and French, was familiar with Greek mythology, knew how to cipher sums, and how to paint a pretty picture and sew a fine stitch. She was truly grateful for all that her guardians had done for her. But to their latest plan, she could not agree. She simply had to find a way to escape. *She had to!*

"Lady Tarkington has invited us to a reception this afternoon, girls, but we shall not stay overlong," Lady Montcrief declared as she and the young ladies climbed into the Montcrief carriage after a tedious visit at the mantua-maker where fittings had been taken for Lucinda's trousseau, the cost to be borne by the girl's unsuspecting bridegroom.

Seated across from them in the carriage, Catherine tried for the thousandth time that day to swallow past the lump of fear in her throat. Thus far today, she'd seen no viable means of escape.

"The reception is to honor that Indian woman," Lady Montcrief said. "Your father insisted I pay my respects. For the life of me, I cannot understand his interest in this New Virginia Company."

Virginia? Catherine's ears perked up.

"Papa says he stands to make a good deal of money investing in the New Virginia Company," Lucinda replied.

"Your father is atwitter to be able to invest in anything these days. At any rate, I am told the woman and her husband will leave for the New World on the morrow. Good riddance to them, I say."

Catherine could hardly believe her ears. *A ship was leaving for the New World on the morrow?*

"I thought you met the Indian woman at Lady Sandys's reception a twelvemonth ago," Lucinda said.

"Indeed. And I have seen her at countless balls and dinner parties since. She is rather attractive . . . in a foreign sort of way. The king was quite taken with her. Though on my life I cannot think why John Rolfe would marry a savage!"

"Perhaps there are not many women to choose from in the New World," Lucinda offered.

Seated across from them, Catherine was hanging onto every single word her companions exchanged. In recent years, she had

17

avidly read every notice printed in the weekly news pages about the New World. How the colonists were to ship back silk, sugar, grain and exotic woods to repay their debt to the investors, who, in turn, sold the goods for a profit here in England. How the prominent colonist John Rolfe had married an Indian woman, and not just any Indian woman, but the favorite daughter of the Emperor of the New World, the powerful chieftain Powhatan, who had thousands of warriors at his command. Catherine had been alarmed to read that before the Rolfes' marriage, the colonists had known virtually no peace or harmony with the Indians since the first settlers arrived back in 1607. Consequently, this marriage between an Englishman and an Indian woman was seen on this side of the Atlantic as a triumph. Except to King James, who feared the Indian princess might be planning to elevate herself to a position of power in direct opposition to him.

When Catherine had read nearly a year ago that, at the king's invitation, John Rolfe and his new wife had arrived in England and were to be presented at court, she had ached then to meet them. Mrs. Rolfe, she read, had embraced her husband's Christian religion and even spoke English. Perhaps, Catherine thought now, the Indian woman was acquainted with her father? Or Noah? The excitement within her grew.

"I shall be obliged to present both you girls to the savage," Lady Montcrief was saying, "though I confess I cannot recall her name. Something . . . foreign-sounding, a word no civilized person could pronounce and would not make sense to us anyhow."

"Pocahontas." Catherine was surprised to hear the sound of her own voice, it being the first word she'd uttered all afternoon.

"Well, I suppose it doesn't signify. Lady Tarkington will no doubt tell us her name and there'll be an end to it."

"Is her name Pocahontas?" Lucinda asked, a twinkle of mischief in her blue eyes as she grinned at Catherine.

"Why . . . yes, dear, that's it precisely! How clever of you!" Lady Montcrief patted her daughter's gloved hands, folded primly in her lap.

Lucinda shrugged an apology at Catherine, who said nothing. She was accustomed to being ignored by Lady Montcrief.

"You will not be expected to actually converse with her, sweetheart. I doubt she understands a word of English."

Again, Catherine was unable to hold her tongue. "I read where the princess has

19

delivered several speeches in Town and even addressed Parliament."

"Well, I doubt a one of them could understand a word she said either!" Both Lady Montcrief and Lucinda laughed at that. "At any rate" — Lady Montcrief turned a bored gaze from the carriage window — "we shall only stay the requisite quarter hour."

When the carriage rumbled to a halt, a footman flung open the door and let the steps down for the ladies to alight.

Catherine's spirits soared as the three of them were shown into Lady Tarkington's lovely drawing room. Catherine's alert green eyes traveled the length of the chamber to where the women were seated in a cluster at the far end. She strained to see past their elegantly coiffed heads for a glimpse of the celebrated Indian woman.

The Tarkington butler announced them and Lady Tarkington cried, "Do come in, my dears! We had about despaired of you!"

The three late arrivals headed toward their hostess who interrupted the flow of conversation to present them to her honored guest.

Catherine wasn't certain if etiquette demanded they bow to the Indian princess, as one most certainly would when presented to continental royalty. But instead of following Lady Montcrief's lead, who merely nodded her head, Catherine dropped into a respectful curtsy.

Hearing the tinkle of a laugh, she raised her head, and her eyes locked with those of the most beautiful woman she had ever seen. But this "woman" was little more than a girl! Her skin was a rich creamy brown. Her eyes were black as pitch, as was her long, shiny hair that hung like a curtain of silk about her shoulders. Her cheekbones were high, her nose small and straight. She was dressed in a buff-colored doeskin garment richly ornamented with colored beads sewn into a pattern of swirling lines. The fringed sleeves of the garment seemed to float when she moved her arms. On her feet were soft, suede boots also decorated with sparkling stones. Catherine had never seen such lovely clothing. She thought the princess looked breathtakingly beautiful.

"I am so happy to meet you," Catherine said, surprising herself by being the first of her party to speak up. "I hope you have had a wonderful stay in England." Catherine felt rather than saw her guardian's outraged look aimed straight at her back.

"Thank you, Miss Catherine," the princess replied in well-modulated English. "I happy to know you." She extended a small brown hand toward Catherine.

Who wrapped both her gloved hands about the princess's smaller one. "I do hope you will come to visit us again."

"I like to very much," the princess said with another tinkling laugh. She glanced expectantly toward Lady Montcrief but, hearing no welcoming words from her, did not extend her hand in greeting to either the older woman or her daughter. Instead, she patted a place beside her on the small settee where she was seated alone. "Come," she said, looking directly at Catherine, "sit beside me. I think you want to hear about New World, yes?"

"Oh, yes, indeed, I do!" Catherine slid onto the green velvet settee next to the beautiful princess. In her excitement, she took no notice where her companions were seated, nor did she care.

For the next quarter hour, Catherine sat mesmerized as the lovely dark-skinned Indian girl captivated her audience, excluding one, with tales of her life across the sea. Her black eyes danced as she described lush forests, beautiful flowers, and streams filled with all manner of fish. She spoke of plentiful game — deer and turkey, a fowl few Englishmen had tasted but which the princess declared was delicious when roasted.

She told of the four largest English colonies: Jamestown, Henricus, Charles City, and Kiccowtan — the only one that had retained its original Indian name. She said all were reached by waterways stretching inland from the Chesapeake Bay.

She said the settlers and Indians had lived side by side peacefully for many moons, trading goods such as grain and tools with one another. Jamestown had a lovely new church, and every settler now farmed his own land, as opposed to the communal farming method of earlier years.

In what seemed like no time, Catherine felt a sharp tug at her sleeve and glanced up into the stern countenance of her guardian. "We will take our leave now. Do forgive us, Lady Tarkington. We have several pressing engagements this afternoon."

The farewells were said, and in moments, the three women were once again seated inside the Montcrief carriage, skimming over the cobblestones toward home near the fashionable end of The Strand, since they did not, in fact, have any other engagements that afternoon, pressing or otherwise.

A disapproving scowl pinned Catherine. "Well, you certainly made a spectacle of yourself, young lady! Imagine, taking a seat next to her royal highness! People will think you've had no upbringing at all! I will not be unhappy to see you gone from my house-hold!"

"Mama!" cried Lucinda. When her mother merely tilted her chin up, Lucinda turned an apologetic gaze on Catherine. "I believe the princess quite liked you, Cat. She spoke directly to you again and again."

"Unseemly," muttered Lady Montcrief.

Catherine was far too thrilled over actually meeting the Princess Pocahontas to fret over what her guardian thought. Her only regret this afternoon was that the opportunity had never arisen for her to ask about her father or Noah. But that did not signify. A very bold plan was already taking shape in her mind.

That evening, Lord and Lady Montcrief set out for the opera and a dinner party afterward. Catherine knew they would not return home until the wee hours. As she and Lucinda lingered over their supper, Lucinda talked excitedly about her forthcoming marriage, but seemed to grow irritable when Catherine appeared lost in her own thoughts.

"Forgive me, Lucinda." Catherine tamped down the anxiety building within her. "I am despondent over the fact that I am to marry a man I do not know, or . . . love."

"Father says Mr. Windmere has a fine

24

home with many servants."

"But I know nothing of his character. Much of what the reverend spoke about yesterday served only to plant fear in my mind."

In preparation for marriage many young ladies received special instruction from the Church before repeating their vows. Because both Catherine and Lucinda's marriages were so *very* important, Lady Montcrief had taken the precaution of actually engaging the reverend to come to their home and address the girls privately. During his lengthy sermon, Lady Montcrief had remained seated in the room, nodding her head in apparent approval of all the minister said. Over dinner that night, she'd proudly declared to her husband that both girls were now duly prepared for marriage.

"I, too, have only just met Lord Pembroke," Lucinda said to Catherine, "but I am quite looking forward to marrying him. I shall have everything I want!"

"But are you not afraid he will . . . beat you?" The minister had spoken at length about a man's right to beat his wife and said that a woman must suffer in silence any such ill-treatment from her husband. Were she to marry Noah, Catherine knew she would never have to fear such a thing; he was so good-hearted, and their love for one another ran so deep, he would never raise a hand to her. Besides, as the son of a clergyman, Noah had no doubt heard many such Marriage Sermons delivered by his own father after marrying young couples in their parish; therefore Noah was also duly prepared for marriage and knew quite well how to treat a woman.

"I expect I shall rarely see him," Lucinda said flippantly. "The earl is a man of wealth and power, with many large estates. Besides he is . . . old."

"But what of love?" Catherine asked quietly. "Do you not think love important in a marriage?"

Lucinda grimaced. "Mama says love does not signify. Once I have done my duty and provided the earl with an heir, I shall be free to love any man I choose. It's the way of the world."

Not my world, Catherine thought. "I would sacrifice anything to be with the man I love."

"That's a very romantic notion, but Mama says it isn't at all wise or prudent." She studied her companion. "Do you not feel the least bit grateful that Mr. Windmere wishes to marry you?"

Catherine did not reply.

26

"Mama says that with no dowry or jointure you could not possibly hope to do better. You will not be nearly so rich as I, but you will be quite comfortable. It's what Mama has always wanted for you."

Catherine fidgeted with the corner of the linen napkin in her lap. Guilt pricked her when she realized her selfish actions would soon cause Lucinda heartache, but it could not be helped. Lord Montcrief's deplorable financial state was not her doing; therefore to rescue him from it was not her responsibility. Lucinda was young and not unattractive. She would have many suitors and receive many offers of marriage.

"I wish you every happiness, Lucinda, truly I do. I never meant to appear ungrateful . . . or heartless." Her appetite completely gone, she stood up. "Excuse me, please. I am not feeling at all well." It was not a lie.

Catherine raced to her bedchamber and shut the door behind her. Standing with her back pressed against the door, her body quaked with fear. The time to put her plan into action was upon her. This afternoon she'd heard the Princess Pocahontas say she and her entourage were staying at The White Swan Inn. She had also told them the New Virginia Company had arranged for ninety young ladies to travel to the New World to become wives to the settlers. Catherine meant to join them.

She had never left the house on her own before but this was her only chance to escape and she was not about to pass it up. Snatching up her cloak, she flung it about her shoulders. It would be hours before Lord and Lady Montcrief returned home and they would not miss her until morning when she did not come down for breakfast. Scooping up her father's letter, with the precious voucher tucked safely inside, she stuffed it into the pocket of her cloak, then pulled open her bedchamber door and cautiously stepped out. If she came upon Lucinda, she would simply say she needed some air. Which is exactly what she did.

"Where are you going at this hour, Cat?" Having finished her supper, Lucinda was now on her way to her own suite of rooms.

Catherine did not slow her pace. "I need to clear my head."

"I shall miss you dreadfully when you are gone! You are like the sister I never had. Shall I come with you now? Mama will never know we have gone out. I'll just get my —"

"No, thank you. I prefer to be alone. I've a great deal to think about."

Lucinda smiled. "Don't fret. Everything will turn out fine; you'll see."

Catherine managed a shaky smile and hurriedly descended the wide sweeping stairs to the ground floor. The lone footman dozing by the door stirred when she approached. Catherine thrust her chin up, affecting the imperious manner she'd observed when Lady Montcrief and Lucinda addressed the servants. "I need a chair and torch bearers, if you please."

"Very good, miss."

It being the first time Catherine had ever issued an order in the Montcrief household, she was somewhat surprised when the footman scurried to do her bidding. In minutes she was bouncing along in a covered sedan chair held aloft by four liveried footmen, each holding one end of the two long poles that ran beneath the chair. Two additional retainers ran ahead carrying lighted torches.

When they reached The White Swan Inn, Catherine alighted and instructed the footmen to wait until she returned.

The princess had said the Rolfes occupied the entire top floor of the Inn. Catherine's heart raced as she scampered up the steps inside the noisy tavern. Reaching the top floor, she caught sight of several dark-skinned women in the corridor, obviously carrying out last-minute instructions as the Rolfes prepared to leave on the morrow.

"Excuse me." Catherine hoped the Indian woman understood English. "I wish to speak with the Princess Pocahontas. Might you direct me to her, please?"

The native woman smiled, her white teeth a sharp contrast against her dark skin. "This way, miss."

Once inside the comfortable chamber, the woman led the way to where the princess sat in a ladder-backed chair before a blazing fire, her eyes closed, a blanket wrapped about her shoulders. In her arms she held a sleeping child. Because the room felt especially close to Catherine, she removed her wrap and draped it over one arm.

When the princess looked up, her lovely face relaxed into a warm smile. "Hallo, Miss Catherine. I not surprise to see you."

"Do forgive me for coming uninvited, but I had to come. I simply had to."

"You welcome to call without special invitation." The princess's small brown hand indicated the empty chair opposite hers. "My husband oversee packing." She shifted the sleeping child in her arms as Catherine sat down. "He say I am in way and for me to stay put." She laughed, the merry tinkle bringing to Catherine's mind an image of

30

water rippling over pebbles in a clear stream. "Husband say I overtired and must rest."

"I'm sure your trip has been very tiring. I admire you for coming to an unknown land amidst strangers. You are quite famous here."

"Perhaps. But I . . . have few friends in big city."

The princess's forlorn tone tugged at Catherine's heart. "I am your friend." She smiled warmly at the gentle Indian girl.

The princess's black eyes held hers for a long moment. "You and I be soul sisters. You feel kinship, too, yes?"

Catherine nodded tightly, the heartfelt words bringing a rush of moisture to her eyes.

"Your hair color of English fox," the princess mused. "You much pretty girl."

"Thank you. I think you are very beautiful. Is this your child?"

Pocahontas gazed lovingly upon the tousled head of the sleeping babe. "My son, Thomas. He soon be three summers."

Just then, another Indian woman, also in native dress, appeared so silently beside them that her sudden presence startled Catherine. Pocahontas put her boy into the woman's outstretched arms. "Sleep well, my little son. We go home tomorrow." Her

31

shining black eyes followed the woman until she disappeared from the chamber. "He be a good boy."

"He is very handsome," Catherine said.

"Someday he grow tall and strong like his father."

"And kind and gentle like his mother."

"You very kind, too, Miss Catherine. But I see you be troubled. What may I do to help, my sister?"

Catherine blinked back another rush of tears. "I do need your help. My father, my brother, and the man I am to marry have settled in Jamestown. I only just received a letter from my father."

"Ah-h." The Indian girl's expression grew grave. "Your father and brother go to New World . . . willingly?"

Catherine nodded. It was common knowledge that many colonists were convicts sentenced to transportation. She swiped at the tears trickling down her cheeks.

"What is it, my sister?" Pocahontas leaned forward, a look of concern in her dark eyes.

"I must go with you tomorrow!" Catherine blurted out. "My guardians do not know I am here. They have arranged for me to marry a man I do not know. But I am betrothed to another. We have loved one another since we were children. This after-

32

noon you spoke of the women who are to become wives to the settlers. I wish to join them. I have my passage voucher right here." She fumbled through the folds of her cloak for the letter in her pocket.

"No, no." Pocahontas reached to stop her. "You not understand. The ship with the women, it not leave for twelve moons, maybe more. They only just now get up list of ladies to come. You must wait."

"But I cannot wait! I must go now!"

"Why such rush?" Pocahontas smiled serenely. "New World still there in twelve moons. You come then. If your father or brother . . . no longer there, I give you home with me until you and your man wed."

"Thank you, but I cannot wait. I am to be married tomorrow! Once I am wed, I shall never be allowed to leave. Tonight is my only chance to escape!"

"Mmmm." A faraway look replaced the understanding in the Indian girl's eyes. "A long time ago, my father arrange a marriage for me. I was young girl then, only thirteen. My father strike bargain with chieftain of warring tribe. I forced to marry man I not love."

Catherine tried to listen patiently to her new friend's tale. "You were married before Mr. Rolfe?"

"Yes. I carry first husband's child, too. But they both die, then I run away. I loved . . . another."

When Pocahontas lowered her head and Catherine saw her black eyes squeeze shut, she knew the beautiful princess was sharing a secret hidden deep in her heart. A moment later, she looked back up and smiled. "But that be long time ago. Now, I have wonderful husband and beautiful little son. Perhaps when you marry this man you not know, you have child you love; then you forget your beloved and no longer wish to travel to New World."

"I cannot marry this man!" Catherine cried. "I love Noah with all my heart! And he loves me!"

Pocahontas fell silent, her dark eyes sad. "Life in New World not easy for woman." She reached for Catherine's hands and with one brown fingertip traced a circle in Catherine's palm. "Your hands very soft. Not accustomed to hard work."

Catherine drew her hands away. "It is true I live in a world of affluence, but I am used to making do with very little." She did not add that Lord and Lady Montcrief begrudged every cent they spent on her, that most of her gowns were castoffs of Lucinda's, and that Catherine herself had altered the garments to fit.

"I see you be very unhappy."

"I love Noah. I miss my father and my brother. They are all the family I have left." Catherine's spirits sank lower and lower. "My mother is gone. I thought the ship with the women was to leave tomorrow and that I could be on it." When despair threatened to engulf her, she gathered up her cloak to leave.

Pocahontas touched her arm. "In New World woman must work from sunup to sunset. Grow food. Make clothes. And clean. White man's houses dirty." Suddenly, she laughed. "White man's houses *very* dirty! White man's ship dirty! England smell bad! Not clean, like forest."

Despite her wrenching pain, Catherine managed a small smile. London did smell bad. Fine ladies carried scented handkerchiefs pressed to their noses when they went out. But when their shutters were flung open, the foul stench permeated their homes. There was no escaping it, just as for Catherine there seemed no escaping London.

"We clean entire inn before we move in here!" Pocahontas declared. "My people not live in filth! We bathe every day in stream."

Catherine had read in the news pages

about the Princess Pocahontas's odd habit of bathing daily, which must have seemed very queer to the king, who never bathed or even changed his clothes until they were worn to rags. "I know how to clean," she said hopefully, "and I could learn to grow food. I helped my mother tend her herb garden."

Pocahontas paused. "You know how to heal with plants and flowers?"

Catherine nodded. "My mother and grandmother were both naturalists. They taught me how to crush the leaves and flowers and to prepare simples and cures."

Pocahontas nodded slowly. "You know how to read and write, yes? You know numbers and many English words?"

"Yes," Catherine nodded eagerly.

"Well . . . then —" Pocahontas sat back. "You come to New World and teach my son Thomas." She threw off her blanket, hopped to her feet and hurried away. "I go tell John Rolfe I hire proper English tutor for our boy."

CHAPTER 2

Catherine could hardly believe her ears. Suddenly it dawned on her that if John Rolfe agreed to his wife's plan, she would have to leave for the New World with only the clothes on her back. With gossip rife amongst the servants, were she to tell the Montcrief footmen she would not be returning home, the entire household would know her whereabouts in minutes. When Lord Montcrief came home that night, he would instantly be told she was not there and also where she'd been taken. He would send someone to fetch her, or worse, come for her himself and drag her back.

She had no time to think further for, in seconds, Pocahontas returned with her husband. Catherine stood up as John Rolfe, a tall man with wavy brown hair, approached. The smile on his face was indulgent as he regarded his pretty little wife, talking animatedly beside him as she walked quickly in order to keep up with his long strides.

"M'wife tells me you are a teacher and that you wish to come to the New World."

"Yes, sir, I do!"

Pocahontas resumed her seat by the fire and pulled the warm blanket about her shoulders. Rolfe was momentarily distracted as he turned a concerned gaze on his wife. "I fear you may have taken a chill, my dear. Perhaps you should let your women get you to bed. It will be time to board the ship soon. The ocean voyage will not be kind."

Catherine gazed with concern at the lovely Indian girl, but with her brown skin, it was difficult to tell whether or not her cheeks were flushed.

In a flurry of activity several dark-skinned women rushed in, and soon Pocahontas had bidden both her husband and Catherine good night. To Catherine she said, "I see you on ship tomorrow, my sister." Then she was bundled off to bed.

Rolfe turned again to Catherine. "My wife and I considered leaving our boy behind to be educated in England, but he is such a mite, she cannot bear to part with him, nor can I. A proper English tutor is the perfect answer. Other children in the colonies need learning, so your talents may prove of value to many. Are you prepared to leave at once?"

Catherine's mind whirled. "Do I have time to return home and collect a few things?" she asked breathlessly.

"We leave at first light. I plan to work through the night, seeing that everything is loaded — our belongings and the supplies we are taking back to the colonists. You may take one of the carriages at our disposal, and when you are ready, board ship tonight. Our cabins are secured on the *George,* but there are three ships in the fleet. It may be you will be given a berth on one of the other barks." He moved to a small desk and bent to scribble a few words on a scrap of paper. "See that one of the ship's officers gets this."

Catherine could scarcely fathom her good fortune. Pulling her cloak tighter about her shoulders, she turned toward the door.

"Another item of import." From an inside pocket of his doublet, Rolfe withdrew what appeared to be a list. "I need your name for the ship's log." He dipped the quill into the inkwell and gazed up expectantly.

Catherine hesitated. The ship's log, containing the names of all the passengers on board ship, often appeared in the London news pages. "Catherine . . . Fielding." In a flash of inspiration, she blurted out her maternal grandmother's surname instead of her own. Were Lord Montcrief to scan the ship's log in the news pages, the name Fielding would not give him pause.

She heard Rolfe's pen scratching as he wrote.

"I have my passage voucher, sir." She fumbled through the folds of her cloak.

"Not necessary. You are now one of our party." Straightening, he glanced at her apparel. "I suggest you bring along warmer clothing, Miss Fielding. Heavy woolens, a snug bed rug, and" — his eyes flicked toward her feet, shod only in lightweight kid slippers — "a pair of sturdy boots. There are no shops in Jamestown to purchase things you will need."

"Indeed, sir. I am indebted to both you and your wife."

"We are indebted to you, Miss Fielding. May God grant us a safe voyage."

Once outside, Catherine bid her waiting footmen to go on ahead without her, telling them her friends would see her home. Moments later, she and two of the Rolfes' female servants climbed into a small closed carriage and headed for The Strand. Barely able to contain her excitement, Catherine forced her mind to think ahead to what she would need in order to survive harsh winters in the New World.

Nearing the Montcrief townhome, Catherine instructed the driver to halt the coach a bit away from the front entrance. Her thoughts raced ahead as she hurried along the footpath. She rang the bell so at least the footman who flung open the door could attest to the fact that she had, indeed, returned home that evening. Then she rushed up the steep stairs to her own chamber, intent on making quick work of what lay ahead. The most pressing problem was how to procure a pair of stout boots, something she had never owned in her life.

Fortunately, she had already packed her valise this morning, so that saved precious time. She stuffed in a heavy gray duroy coat, her hairbrush, her Bible, and her well-thumbed Anglican Prayer Book. She decided if she wore both of her lightweight fustian gowns beneath her cloak that would leave room for the heavy old bed rug folded up on the bottom shelf of the cupboard. With it inside, the satchel would just barely close. After finally getting the bag fastened, it was far too heavy to lift. And she still didn't have a pair of sturdy boots.

Her mind whirled. To leave the house and ask one of the Indian women who had accompanied her in the Rolfe carriage to come inside and help with the heavy bag would only rouse suspicion. Chewing fretfully on her lower lip, she sat down on the bed. When a fresh idea struck, she leapt to her feet and raced again to the cupboard.

Moments later, she slipped into the corridor carrying a pair of her prettiest slippers and the new silk stockings Lucinda had given her as a wedding gift. Glancing furtively about, she knocked lightly on the door adjacent to hers. Soon a sleepy-eyed girl about Catherine's age opened the door. Heftier in size, she spent her days lifting and toting heavy buckets of water and coal up and down the stairs.

"Nancy," Catherine whispered, "I need your help."

"What be the trouble, miss?" The servant girl yawned widely.

"I need a pair of stout boots." She held up the dainty slippers. "I'd be much obliged if you'd take these in exchange for the new boots you received last quarter day."

Coming more fully awake now, Nancy tilted her tousled head to one side. "Now what you be needing boots for, miss? Ye be going somewheres?"

Catherine flinched, but said nothing.

The servant girl didn't press for an answer, just snatched the slippers and stockings from Catherine's hands and disappeared into her darkened chamber. Catherine couldn't see a thing, but she heard muffled sounds and, in what seemed like an eternity, Nancy finally reappeared, fully clothed now and wearing her own new boots. In her hands were an identical pair.

"Here." She handed the boots to Catherine. "I put your slippers under Mary's side o' the bed. Her feet be more your size." She turned to scoop something else into her arms and stepped from the room. "I knows ye be a-goin' to the New World, miss, an' I be a-goin' with ye." She thrust her chin up. "I know's ye been unhappy here. I's heard ye a-cryin' into yer pillow. I's as unhappy here as you are. Now seems a good time for me to be a-leavin' too."

Catherine's eyes widened. "But, Nancy —" She gazed from the maidservant's determined face to the parcel she carried, but didn't argue, just turned and led the way to her own chamber. In moments the pair reemerged, Catherine carrying Nancy's smaller bundle, Nancy, not even breathing hard, toting Catherine's heavy bag. Both girls wore sturdy brown leather boots laced clean to the ankles.

As they tiptoed down the steep back stairs, Nancy paused when they reached the ground floor. "Wait here, miss." She set her

43

heavy burden down and disappeared again.

Catherine's eyes rolled skyward. They'd come this far without awakening or disturbing anyone in the household. What was Nancy up to now? In seconds the girl reappeared carrying yet another small parcel.

"Thought of sumthin' important we be a-needin', miss." She grinned mischievously as she tucked the package under one arm, then hefted Catherine's heavy bag off the floor.

The two girls noiselessly slipped from the rear of the house, and in no time, both were settled inside the dusty black carriage awaiting them a few yards down the cobbled street.

The vehicle sped through the night towards the busy quay at the mouth of the Thames. The dockside teemed with activity as sailors and journeymen scrambled to fill longboats with goods and supplies which were then loaded onto one of the three hulls rising like phantoms from the murky black water.

Once the four women — Catherine, a wide-eyed Nancy, and the two Rolfe servants who'd accompanied them — had been rowed to one of the ships and helped aboard, Catherine presented the note John Rolfe had given her to the first ship's officer she saw. All four women were ushered below the main deck into a cramped space on the starboard side of the ship. The cabin was far smaller than Catherine expected, and it contained no furniture. The oil lamp swinging from the midshipman's hand illuminated the tunnel-like room, lined on either side with a double row of what looked to be wooden troughs. The Indian women seemed to know the troughs were beds and claimed two by dropping their bundles of belongings onto them.

Catherine and Nancy exchanged puzzled looks, then selected a pair of side-by-side troughs and placed their possessions squarely in the middle. Elsewhere in the room, the Indian women unrolled their thick bed rugs, then, rolling themselves back up inside, promptly fell asleep. Catherine and Nancy fumbled in the darkness even as others of the Rolfes' female servants filtered into the cramped compartment, wordlessly selected their sleeping quarters and settled in for the night.

"I not be a'tall sleepy," Nancy whispered to Catherine.

"Nor am I," Catherine replied, still trying to peer through the darkness to inspect their surroundings.

"I think I shall have a walk-about," Nancy

announced importantly, which made both girls giggle.

"I'll stay here and guard our things," Catherine whispered back. "Be careful and don't get lost," she cautioned just as Nancy tripped over an empty trough on her way to the door.

It was only when Nancy disappeared that Catherine realized she'd brought along another person without express permission to do so, and that Nancy's name had not been added to the ship's log, or her passage paid. But, she assumed there would be plenty of time to straighten the matter out in the morning, and she would gladly forfeit her voucher to settle Nancy's account.

Early the next morning, a loud rap at the cabin door awakened both girls. Suddenly it flew wide open, and a midshipman stepped inside. In a flat, unemotional tone, the man delivered a terse message.

"Mistress John Rolfe, the Princess Pocahontas, is dead."

CHAPTER 3

Stunned, Catherine could only stare wide-eyed at the man. What could possibly have happened? True, the princess had not felt well the previous evening, but she had certainly not been at death's door! The news was so shocking as to be disbelieved. Catherine and Nancy could only blink with alarm at one another. Tears streamed down the faces of the Indian women, who had all slept soundly beside the two English girls. When the women began to keen and wail and chant prayers in their native tongue, Nancy flung a bewildered look at Catherine, who was now dabbing at the tears in her eyes as she tried to digest the horrible news.

"Perhaps we should go up on deck, miss," Nancy said, her tone fearful. "If the ship don't sail today, we may very well have to . . . well, I don't know what, miss."

Catherine could not speak. Nancy was right. If the ships didn't sail today, which

47

was highly likely given the circumstances, she and Nancy would have no choice but to return to the Montcrief household and face the consequences of their respective misdeeds. Her heart sank as she realized a fate far worse than punishment hung over her head.

Still clothed as they had been the night before, both girls scrambled to their feet. They'd neither one slept well; both had tossed and turned in a futile attempt to get comfortable on the hard wooden floor. The cramped cabin was cold and drafty, heated only by the bodies and breath of the dozen or so women who'd slept beside them, each wrapped tightly in a blanket of security that had now been cruelly snatched from them.

Nancy, with Catherine close on her heels, led the way through the ship's narrow passages and up a steep flight of steps to the main deck. Blinking into the daylight when their heads emerged from the hold, the girls joined the horde of humanity moving thither and yon on the upper deck, made somewhat slippery as a fine mist seeped through the thick morning fog swirling overhead. Everything felt wet and soggy to Catherine, as if the entire world wept over the death of a beloved daughter. She pulled her heavy cloak tighter about her trembling body.

Above them, the raw east wind whipped and snapped through the sails, the motion causing the heavy hulk to teeter this way and that in the choppy water.

A cacophony of noises assaulted them as they made their way to nowhere in particular. They passed several crewmen rolling heavy hogsheads, the large barrels noisily crashing into one another as the men worked to guide them across the listing deck. Several hastily constructed pens, erected right there on deck, held an assortment of farm animals. Cows mooed their displeasure as they, too, sought purchase on the uneven surface, the roiling motion causing their heavy bodies to slam against one another. Goats bleated annoyance. The squeal of frightened pigs contrasted with the raucous crow of roosters squeezed into rickety crates.

As the girls neared the gangplank, dozens of men, women and children clambered onto the ship, all talking loudly and excitedly, each carrying as many bags and bundles as they could manage. Above their chatter, the crew shouted orders, telling the new arrivals where to deposit their belongings and where the various parts of the ship were located. Soon, the men began to turn people back and send them to board the third ship anchored in the harbor. From their cries, Catherine determined the ship they'd boarded the night before was the *Inverness.*

Huddled together by the ship's railing, Catherine and Nancy watched the chaotic scene. Suddenly from out of the mayhem, a sturdy fellow, whose garb told them he was a ship's officer, headed straight toward them.

"Ye be Miss Fielding?" The man addressed Catherine. "With the Rolfe party?"

Unable to find her voice, she nodded tightly.

Beside her, Nancy piped up, "An' I be her maid, Miss Nancy Mills."

Catherine's head jerked around. Until now she hadn't realized Nancy had a surname, let alone known what it was.

"Follow me to the roundhouse, miss."

He set off, wending his way through the crowd though not leaving the ship. Icy fingers of fear raced up Catherine's spine as she hurried to keep pace. Had the Montcriefs already discovered them missing and this "roundhouse" was where they would be detained until Lord Montcrief came for them? Perhaps he was already here, spitting mad. The death of Pocahontas was already having far-reaching effects. It obviously meant the death of Catherine's dream for a new life. John Rolfe would certainly not be leaving England today, so there was no need for her to make the journey to the New World to tutor their boy. The plain truth was she and Nancy were to be put off the ship.

The officer led them to a spacious cabin secreted high above the quarterdeck. Once they'd stepped inside, Catherine was surprised to find not an incensed Lord Montcrief, but a dozen or so men gathered around a large oaken table, breaking their fast!

"Miss Fielding an' her maid, Capt'n."

Catching sight of the young ladies, the captain and several of the men leapt to their feet.

"Be seated, gentl'men," the captain said. A tattered napkin tucked in his collar, he stepped behind the men to approach the girls.

"Capt'n Phillips, at yer service, Miss Fielding."

Catherine nodded nervously.

The captain dismissed the midshipman and motioned for the girls to follow him into a small anteroom, which contained a massive desk, two chairs and various and sundry nautical devices. The captain shut

51

the door and turned to face the girls, their eyes round with fright.

"We was all deeply saddened by the news of Mrs. Rolfe's death, Miss Fielding. Mr. Rolfe tol' me to look after you and . . . ah . . . yer maid. Actually" — he directed a look at Nancy — "Mr. Rolfe dinna' mention ye was travelin' with a maid, but, I 'spect, in his grief, it were a mere oversight."

"Mmmm." A squeak of alarm escaped Catherine. She was so distraught at the moment that the matter of explaining Nancy's presence was far and away beyond her capability.

"In any event," Captain Phillips went on, "we be settin' sail today as planned, unless ye've decided not to travel with us." He paused, his eyes a question as he looked at Catherine.

"No — no, sir. Our plans have not changed, sir."

"Very well, then."

The captain told Catherine that while aboard ship she would take her meals with the other gentlewomen, whilst Nancy would be obliged to dine . . . ah . . . elsewhere. Relief flooded Catherine, and she relaxed a mite.

The captain led them back into the dining chamber, which in their absence, had thinned out somewhat . . . although, Catherine noted, there was still plenty of delicious-smelling food on the table! A growl of hunger escaped her midsection.

"Newell," the captain barked to one of the men, "show Miss Fielding and her maid to their cabin and 'ave some victuals brought 'round."

"Gor-r!" exclaimed Nancy, when they were left alone in a small, neatly furnished cabin tucked in a far corner of the quarterdeck. "I daresay we be right lucky, miss! I feared we was being brought up on charges, and all along we was becoming 'Important Persons.' At least, you was, miss!" The relief in her tone echoed that which Catherine felt.

They stood grinning at one another, and when a large wooden tray loaded with food — coddled eggs, thick slices of bacon, warm sourdough bread and mugs of steaming black coffee — was delivered to them, they dug in and ate like starved prisoners.

The high easterly wind that day was more than favorable, and in no time at all, two of the three filled-to-capacity barks put out to sea for the New World. The voyage to Virginia was estimated to take from sixty to eighty days. Near dockside, the *George* lingered behind. Word was there would be a funeral for the Princess Pocahontas at nearby Gravesend. Catherine realized how lucky she was to have been assigned to the *Inverness.*

Though the girls' snug little cabin featured a feather mattress atop a rope bed hanging from the wall, the room was just as cold and drafty as every other nook and cranny on the ship.

After the girls dressed for the day, each headed in different directions to break their fast. Initially, Catherine enjoyed the company of the other women she dined with. From their conversation, it was evident they all possessed some degree of education, as well as a passing knowledge of the social graces. However, Catherine's remark that her father and brother already had a thriving plantation in Jamestown and that she was to be married as soon as she arrived elicited cool replies.

"How nice for you, Miss Fielding, to already have a home awaiting you in the New World," said one, whose husband planned to establish an iron-ore company in the Virginia colony.

"The rest of us," said another, "will be obliged to remain aboard ship until our men folk can build a house — a task which can take weeks."

"Oh, my," Catherine murmured, "I had no idea."

That the other women began to regard her in a less-than-agreeable manner did not lessen Catherine's excitement a whit. Each and every day, she offered up a prayer of thanksgiving that, at long last, she was, indeed, on her way to her father and brother and . . . most of all, to Noah. She imagined how happy they would be, once wed and settled in their own home. She'd make the house pretty for him, for she loved beautiful things. In due time they'd have a child, with more babes to follow. They'd be a happy, loving family. Surely the good Lord had at last looked down and smiled upon her. Every dream in her heart was coming true.

Though conditions on board ship worsened as the voyage progressed, Catherine clung tenaciously to her dream to see her through what were surely the worst of times.

Eventually the supply of foodstuffs on board ship began to dwindle — the butter, cheese and fish grew rancid; cabbages, turnips, and onions wilted and spoiled. The only thing consistently fresh was the milk that came straight from the cows and goats, but it was generally given only to children and those few men who requested it. However, that too dwindled when the rations set aside to feed the livestock began to give out. Meals soon became no more than a simple pease porridge, or boiled mush served in wooden trenchers along with cold hardtack and brackish water, which grew to taste less and less like water and more and more like . . . Catherine became hard-pressed to say.

For Nancy and the rest of the common folk, meals were served anywhere one could find to sit or stand on deck. The women cooked over open "hearths" which consisted of bricks piled up beneath a tripod from which an iron kettle hung suspended over the flames. In rainy weather, when cooking on the open deck was impossible, lower-deck passengers were served cold victuals near a hatchway that opened onto the hold.

In inclement weather, Catherine chose to leave her private cabin only for meals. The filth and slime that accumulated on deck from the livestock made strolling there unpleasant, even hazardous. A sudden lurch of the ship and one could find oneself slipping and sliding in a mish-mash of foul-smelling dung and other murk and mire. The malodor soon permeated the entire ship and reminded Catherine of Pocahontas's comment about white man's ships being dirty. Dirty was putting it mildly, she thought. The ever-present stench from overflowing slop buckets and unwashed bodies soon became overpowering.

At times following a hard rain, the crew made an attempt to swab the deck, but all that effort really netted was to move the filth from one end of the ship to the other. Sewage and masses of dirty rainwater managed to filter through the rotting floorboards of the deck and finally end up in the bilge from which an intolerable and sickening odor emanated.

According to Nancy, who daily associated with the common folk at mealtime, the men and women, whose sleeping quarters were similar to one another's but located in separate parts of the ship, bunked two and in some cases, three and four to a narrow wooden trough. Both girls felt fortunate they'd been spared that inconvenience and insult to their privacy.

They were not spared all insults, however, as it wasn't long before the lice, fleas, bedbugs, mice, and rats that plagued both passengers and crew — some who slept in elevated hammocks on deck in an attempt to avoid the vermin — soon infested their secluded cabin. Both girls constantly scratched at red whelps all over their bodies.

"I'm beginning to see why Pocahontas insisted on bathing every day," Catherine remarked irritably as she strained to scratch a spot in the middle of her back.

"I don't believe that would help," Nancy said peevishly as she dug at a whelp on her arm.

"If only we had some cottonweed or fleabane."

"You know about simples and cures, miss?" Nancy asked with interest.

"A bit." Catherine nodded. "My mother and grandmother taught me how to make salves and potions from herbs and flowers."

"Perhaps your cures could have saved those souls already lost on our voyage." Lung ailments and ship fever had claimed several lives, their bodies slipped overboard into a watery grave. "At least we've not come down with anything."

"Thanks to you," Catherine replied, referring to the parcel of lemons Nancy had snatched at the last minute the night they fled London.

"If m'brothers hadn't been sailors, I wouldn't a'knowed that sucking lemons would keep ship fever at bay. Some men, women, too, got no teeth left. Their mouths and tongues so swelled up, their teeth all fell out!"

Catherine blanched.

"Course if I'd been a-caught stealing lemons from the Montcrief's, we'd a'both been hanged."

"Or transported," Catherine said on a laugh. "Which means we'd have ended up on our way to the New World anyhow."

Due to a lack of anything better to do, she and Nancy whiled away many long afternoons in relative comfort in their private cabin exchanging plans for their future, as well as telling stories from their respective pasts.

Catherine learned that Nancy Mills's three brothers were all sailors, and both her sisters had married fishermen who lived in villages dotting the southwesterly coast of England. The day the ship had sailed past that part of England, Nancy spent nearly that whole day up on deck, her gray eyes scanning the shoreline, no doubt thinking about the family she would likely never see again.

From Nancy, Catherine learned there were eighty passengers on board ship, most new settlers bound for Virginia and the promise of new lives. A number of convicts were also aboard, some released from debtors' prison, their only crime being an inability to pay their debts.

One night as the girls lay in bed quietly talking before they drifted off to sleep, Nancy asked Catherine about her particular status once they reached Virginia. "Seeing as how you done paid my passage, am I to become yer servant, indentured to you and Mr. Noah?"

Catherine considered. She had, indeed, given Captain Phillips her precious voucher for Nancy's passage and watched him add the name "Nancy Mills" to the ship's log. Though the girls had lived side-by-side on the third floor of the Montcrief townhome for as long as Catherine could remember, they'd never become acquainted. Now, she'd all but ceased to think of Nancy as a maidservant.

"No," she finally said. "That I took care of your passage shall be our secret. We shall begin our lives in the New World on an equal footing."

"But, what if I choose to hire on as yer housekeeper, or maid of all work?"

"I expect that would suit. Noah shouldn't object to my having a maid." She remembered Pocahontas saying that in the New World, a woman worked from sunup to sunset. "I shall surely require help."

"Then it be settled," Nancy concluded. "I shall be in the employ of Mistress Noah."

Catherine chuckled. "Mistress Colton."

She recalled how fervently Noah had wished them to wed before the men left for the New World. Though she was just a child of twelve then, he'd held her in his arms and told her how much he cared for her and how happy they'd one day be. Those fond memories and others from their shared childhood had sustained her throughout the years of heartache and loneliness she'd endured in London. And they kept her going now.

After a record sixty-eight days at sea, the two ships at last sailed into Chesapeake Bay. The day was bright and sunny, the sky overhead a clear, cornflower blue. Throughout the long journey, they'd never once set eyes on the *George,* the third ship in the fleet. Nor was it known whether or not the flagship had even left England.

Following the first cry of *"Land ahoy!"* the excitement on board ship was palpable. Nearly every last passenger, except the prisoners chained down in the hold, scrambled to get up on the main deck. Jockeying with one another for the best position at the crowded railing, all eyes strained to catch a glimpse of the land they would all soon call home.

Despite the horrendous conditions they'd

endured, the terrible food, and several frightening storms, they'd never once been thrown off course. Although a few passengers aboard the *Inverness* and quite possibly the second ship were still too ill to walk under their own power, they were all grateful to have made it to the New World alive.

Numerous soundings were taken as the two ships, only yards away from one another, drifted noiselessly into the bay; their progress slow as there was little to no wind that day. From the shore the tall ships must have looked like brightly painted ornaments silently perched on the shimmering flat surface of the sea.

That next morning, a strong wind pushed them toward the fort of Jamestown, the ship's hull creaking and straining as they sliced through the blue-green water toward the James River, one of several waterways that jutted off the bay.

At last, thought Catherine, they had reached their destination.

CHAPTER 4

Catherine and Nancy were amongst those passengers pushed up against the railing of the *Inverness,* their eyes stung from the wind as they gazed with excitement at each and every sight the ship sailed past.

Catherine had never beheld such tall trees as those lining both sides of the river — among them, oak, walnut, chestnut, pine, and elm. On the forest floor, crimson, gold, blue, and purple wildflowers contrasted sharply with the lush, green foliage. Catherine could hardly wait to explore the woods for flowers and wild herbs, which she meant to dig up and plant in her own garden, she told Nancy.

"You might become Jamestown's first lady physick," Nancy replied grinning, her gray eyes also taking in the wonders spread before them.

"Several times I assisted my mother with birthings in our village," Catherine added.

63

Their talk of healing herbs and plants brought to mind her conversation with Princess Pocahontas that fateful night in England. Although their time together had been brief, Catherine still ached over the great loss they'd all suffered by the Indian girl's death. Catherine had no idea what fatal illness had so quickly claimed Pocahontas's life, but due to her chills and possible fever, she suspected pneumonia, or perhaps even smallpox. If Pocahontas had lived and they'd made the crossing together, she was certain they'd now be fast friends. Her thoughts of the Indian princess were so strong, she imagined she could feel her gentle, loving spirit watching over them when, at long last, the two ships rounded a curve in the river and the fort of Jamestown came into view.

Exultant cheers and applause arose from those pressed against the loops of prickly hemp lining the ship's railing, although no one felt the rope's sting as the pain was overshadowed by joy and relief. From the quarterdeck, someone managed to shush the excited passengers in order to offer up a prayer of thanksgiving for their safe voyage.

Although not all of the passengers would go ashore, Catherine and Nancy fell in with a group of men and a few women who excitedly scrambled into the longboats to be rowed across the stretch of water still separating them from land. Those in town who had spotted the ships came running from the fort's palisaded walls to stand close to the water's edge, waving and shouting to the newcomers. Children jumped up and down as barking dogs ran in circles at their feet.

Catherine's excitement reached new heights as she breathlessly scanned the sea of faces on shore. Would her father, her brother, and Noah all be there to welcome her? Or would they still be at work in their fields, not even aware she had come all the way from England to join them?

When the shallop drew nearer the pier — for indeed Jamestown now had its own pier — the two men nearest the front of the longboat clambered onto the sturdy wooden planks to wrap lengths of rope around one of the tall poles jutting up from the muddy water. At last Catherine, with Nancy trailing a few steps behind her, began to shakily walk the length of the pier toward the sandy shore.

Suddenly spotting her brother standing just outside the timbered walls of the fort, Catherine let out a cry. *"Adam!"* She broke into a run, but in her haste to reach him, stumbled over a craggy rock. She scrambled to right herself, then, in her haste to reach her brother, dropped the bundle she carried and, finally finding her land legs, ran the rest of the way towards him. *"Adam!"*

"Cat? Is that you?" A tall, swarthy young man with the same rich, auburn-colored hair as Catherine's caught her up in his arms and swung her around and around. Setting her down, he held her at arm's length. "I can hardly believe m'eyes! My little sister, an' all grown up, I see!"

A plain-looking young woman with mousy brown hair and a somewhat weary smile stepped forward, and Adam introduced her to Catherine. "This is m'wife, Abigail."

"Your wife? Oh, Adam, you've married!"

"Just over a year now," he replied with obvious pride.

The two women embraced, but already Catherine's glittering green eyes were searching the crowd for the one familiar face she so longed to see.

"Where is No— ?"

And then she saw him.

He was looking right at her. *"Noah!"* she called, it not registering in her mind to question why he was not racing toward her.

She hiked up her long skirt and hastened to close the few yards that separated them.

"Noah! It's me, Catherine!"

Nearing him, their gazes locked. He was as handsome as ever, but. . . .

"Hello, Catherine." The handsome man made no move to embrace her. Just then, a pretty apple-cheeked girl with long blonde curls stepped closer to his side. Glaring at Catherine, she wrapped both arms possessively through one of his.

When Catherine's gaze dropped to the girl's belly, swollen huge with child, her heart plummeted to her feet.

Then everything went black.

"Put her in father's old room."

"Adam, fetch a trencher of water."

"You may put your things over there, Miss Mills."

"Nancy, my name be Nancy."

"Very well. How long has it been since she's eaten, Nancy?"

"There was victuals this mornin', sir, but rations been scant of late. We've 'ad nothin' t'eat since mornin'."

"That was hours ago! She's exhausted, poor thing."

"The sea voyage was simply too arduous for her."

"She feels feverish."

And a bit later someone said, "I think she

may be coming 'round."

But she wasn't coming around. How could she? Her soul felt numb, as if it had suffered a shock too horrible to bear. Her head throbbed with every beat of her heart. Her entire body trembled when she attempted to stand. How could she possibly go on living?

Sometime later, without speaking, Catherine let Adam's wife Abigail slide an arm beneath her shoulders and prop her up against a pillow to spoon some broth into her mouth. Later, Nancy helped her out of bed to use the chamber pot, but once back in bed, her head sank into the feather pillow and her eyes squeezed shut.

The truth was too dreadful to bear. Noah had married! *Why?* How could he have married when he knew she was coming? *They* were to be wed. *She* was the one meant to carry his child, not some girl he barely knew and who could not possibly love him as she did. Why? *Why?*

As she lay in the darkness that night, comforted only by the soothing sound of Nancy's even breathing from the pallet Abigail had prepared for her on the floor, Catherine could no longer hold back her tears. They streamed down her cheeks, soaking into the pillow beneath her head. Would the pain ever go away? If only she could rip out her heart, she might be able to bear this torment. As it was, she could not imagine what on God's green earth she would do now? She couldn't go back to England. She could *never* go back there. But . . . she also could not stay here. *Dear Lord, what was to become of her now?* When no answers came, she sank deeper and deeper into a seemingly bottomless pit of gloom and despair.

Early the next morning, Catherine's fitful slumber was disturbed by the sound of voices from another room in the house. From the muffled words that drifted toward her, she gleaned that the Jamestown settlers had learned that the Princess Pocahontas was dead. When it became known that Adam Parke's kinswoman had been friends with the Rolfes, Deputy-Governor Yeardley had sent a delegation to the Parke home to learn what they could from Mistress Fielding. Catherine crept to the door of her chamber and peeked through a crack to look and listen.

"I was unaware my sister was acquainted with the Rolfes," Adam told the men, standing solemnly inside the doorway of the small house. He turned to Nancy. "Perhaps Miss Mills can enlighten us."

Fully awake now, Catherine listened intently for Nancy's answer.

"I be happy to tell you what I know, sir. Miss Fielding met Mr. and Mistress Rolfe the night afore we set sail. They engaged 'er to tutor their boy."

"Ah . . . so, your sister is a Dame Teacher, is she?" one of the men asked.

"Um . . . yes. Yes, she is," Adam replied, not sounding terribly certain, but his answer was accepted. "A very fine one, I'm sure."

Nancy spoke up again. "We was to reside with the Rolfes when we arrived here, sir."

"May we speak with your sister?" the second man asked.

"She is too ill to receive visitors," Abigail said.

"Many of the women on board ship was too ill to come ashore, sir," Nancy added. "Miss Fielding should 'ave rested a bit afore she left her sickbed."

"She suffers from ship fever, does she?"

"Yes, sir. We ate lemons in the beginnin' but after a spell, they run out. All the food was near spoilt then. There wasn't much of anythin' left to eat."

Apparently satisfied with what little they'd learned, the delegation expressed their well wishes for Mistress Fielding's recovery and departed.

A puzzled look on his face, Adam turned to Nancy. "I am most curious why you refer to Catherine as 'Miss Fielding' when that is clearly not her name. And the delegation referred to her as *'Mistress'* Fielding. Has my sister married and is now a widow?"

"Umm . . . indeed, sir, that be the way of it. She wish now to make a fresh start in the New World," Nancy fabricated.

Catherine breathed a sigh of relief and crept back to bed. She could not have provided better answers to their questions than Nancy did. And she was most grateful to have been spared the trying ordeal.

During the second morning Catherine lay abed, she was aware that Nancy rose early to help Abigail prepare the morning meal. It surprised her that breakfast alone took close on two hours to prepare. Listening to the bustle coming from the other room, she surmised that her brother and his wife had a servant, who perhaps slept in an outbuilding, or in the loft. She assumed the house contained a loft, for she'd heard noises — creaking floorboards, a cough in the night, footsteps ascending and descending stairs somewhere. She'd heard Abigail address the fellow as "boy" or "lad" as she sent him for water, to milk the goat, feed the chickens, or bring in what eggs he could find.

That morning Catherine was alert enough to cast a curious gaze about the room where she lay. It was quite small, furnished with only the one bed, a roughly made washstand, and a simple, two-drawer chest. Overall it was not too terribly different from the tiny garret room where she'd lived in London. The ceiling was higher here but there was no real floor, just hard-packed earth covered by a sprinkling of rather soiled-looking straw. On the wall opposite the bed was a single window, covered with a wooden panel that looked as if it might slide back and forth. Everything she saw seemed bare and sparse, not at all what she'd expected.

But then, nothing thus far in the New World had been as she'd expected.

Later that day, when sleep eluded her and curiosity overcame her, she dragged herself to her feet and padded barefoot across the room. Noiselessly, she slid the wooden window covering aside and was surprised to find no glass in the window. Peering out, she saw that Adam's house stood some distance away from the one next to it. Craning her neck from the opening, she could see a dusty path in front of the row of houses, and beyond that, a wide grassy area

72

dotted with tall trees. On the other side of the greensward lay another dusty path fronting a row of identical-looking huts, all crudely constructed of rough-hewn timbers, the spaces between smeared with what appeared to be a hardened mixture of sand or clay. All the roofs were thatched, much like their old farmhouse in England. Most were high-pitched, with a single window near the top that bespoke a loft. Most had chimneys. Catherine watched thin curls of smoke drift lazily upward, then disappear into the thick treetops that sheltered the houses like canopies.

The bit of activity going on outdoors mildly interested her. Men called to one another as they crisscrossed the greensward, asking after the progress in one another's fields or just hailing a greeting. Some carried tools; one led a goat somewhere. She saw only a few womenfolk scurrying here and there, tending to their work without looking up or bothering to speak to the men, or even to each other.

Straining to see further up the wide grassy area that separated the two rows of huts, an odd-looking structure caught her eye. Dome-shaped, it was made of large, rounded stones. She watched two women carrying long-handled griddles of something they then slid into an opening on one side of the domed structure. A thin ribbon of smoke curled upward from the top, leading Catherine to surmise the odd building to be some sort of oven. Most women left their griddles stuck inside the opening before they hurried away.

The busy women brought to mind what Pocahontas had said: that women here worked from sunup to sunset. A sigh escaped Catherine. Apparently it was true. She had hardly seen either Abigail or Nancy that day, but she'd heard their voices coming from the other room as they told one another about a task just completed and another each was about to begin.

Catherine turned and headed back to the relative comfort of her bed. The primitiveness of the colonists' hovels surprised her. Those she'd seen from the window were cruder than the huts of the poorest peasants in England. She'd had no idea how her father and brother lived, what sort of home they had, or what their lives were truly like. A sob caught in her throat. How were she and Nancy to get on here . . . alone?

With the dream she'd clung to these many years now shattered and gone, she wondered if the emptiness inside her, the gaping hole in her heart, could ever be filled. Turning her back against the window, she closed her eyes to shut out the sights and sounds of this strange new world.

Sometime later, when the smell of the evening meal caused her empty stomach to growl, Catherine again pulled herself to her feet. She couldn't lie abed forever. Moving to where her dusty valise sat in a corner on the earthen floor, she pulled out a fresh gown and put it and her boots on. Because she'd had little to eat the past two days, weakness nearly overtook her as she headed toward the doorway that separated the tiny bedchamber from the room beyond.

Abigail glanced up when Catherine entered the common room. "Welcome, sister!" She smiled as she set a platter of sizzling roasted pork onto the planked wooden table at the far end of the room. "Come to join us for dinner, have ye?"

A wan smile lifted the corners of Catherine's mouth as she slowly headed toward the table. This room was a good deal larger than her bedchamber. A fireplace, large enough for one to actually walk into, took up one entire wall. A long-barreled fowling piece hung on the stone wall above the fireplace. That it was crossed by her father's sword made her wonder about him again. She'd seen no sign of her father since she arrived. Was he — ?

On the far side of the hearth she saw a crudely constructed ladder, which she assumed led to the loft. In a helter-skelter fashion, various cooking and cleaning implements leaned against the wall. Pegs holding an assortment of clothing littered all the walls of the room. The one small window here was located next to the door; it now stood ajar on wooden hinges.

"Where is Nancy?" Catherine asked, reaching the table, which consisted of two wide rough planks of wood supported by a pair of sawed-off tree trunks. A backless bench, supported by smaller tree blocks, fronted the table. Another gouged-out section of tree trunk had been turned into a serviceable chair that sat at one end of the planked-board table. A second backless bench skirted the other side.

"She'll be along," Abigail replied gaily. "She went to fetch my flatbread from the oven. I've prepared a feast, as you can see. Adam comes home from the field fair starvin' most days."

She motioned for Catherine to slide onto one of the benches, and soon after she'd settled herself, Adam, Nancy, and the servant boy all streamed into the house. The boy, who looked to be about twelve with a disheveled thatch of straw-colored hair, slid onto the bench right next to Catherine — which surprised her, as she was not accustomed to having stable boys dine with the family! It did not seem odd for Nancy to eat with them, of course, but Catherine had long ago ceased to think of her as a servant.

Nancy and Adam both expressed their pleasure at seeing her up and about, but cautioned her not to overexert herself. When the meal had concluded, which Catherine admitted was surprisingly tasty, Nancy jumped up to help Abigail clear the soiled trenchers while Adam turned to Catherine.

"Do you feel steady enough to walk a bit, sis?"

"I feel quite strong now." She smiled pleasantly. "The dinner was delicious, Abigail. I admit I was near famished. Do you need me to help wash up?"

"You go along with Adam. Nancy and I can manage. Boy, we be needing a bucket of freshwater; scoot now, afore it gets dark."

Adam turned a concerned look on Catherine. "Ye might need a shawl. Evenings are cool here. We'll not walk far. Wouldn't want you to catch a chill."

Nancy had already hurried to fetch Catherine's wrap, and helped to settle it about her shoulders before brother and sister set out for their walk.

Outdoors the sun had already dipped lower in the sky, the golden orb now completely obscured by the thick cover of tree leaves. The evening air felt crisp and the cool breeze promised a chilly night ahead, but to Catherine the fresh air smelled especially good. Despite the raw emotions still churning within her, the New World seemed quite peaceful now.

"A walk will do me good," she told Adam.

"Since you were . . . unconscious when we brought you here, I thought you'd like to see something of this end of Jamestown."

Before they reached the dusty path in front of the house, she glanced over one shoulder and noted that Adam's hut sat at the far end of the long street. From the window on the opposite side, where she'd looked out earlier, she'd been unable to see that the dense forest lay directly to the other side of the house.

"You're quite close to the woods," she remarked, falling into step beside him as they turned onto the dusty road.

"When Pa and I first came, there were no other houses this far out. Since then, more and more settlers have come. This end of town is completely built up now." Glancing at her feet, he grinned. "I'm glad to see you brought sensible shoes."

"Yes." She smiled. "Nancy and I both managed to get ourselves a pair of boots."

"Nancy seems a good sort. Was she indeed your maidservant in London?"

"The Montcrief household was full of servants. Nancy was one of many."

"I wonder that you would leave such opulence for . . . this." His tone sounded a trifle wistful.

Catherine bit her lip to keep from blurting out the real reason she had come and the immense disappointment over what she'd found here. "Tell me about Father. Neither you nor Abigail has mentioned him."

"Pa died last winter. Dysentery. He passed only a few days after the onset."

A wrenching sob caught in Catherine's throat. She had guessed her father was gone but hadn't wanted to believe it. Her chin began to tremble as tears of grief welled in her eyes. Her precious dream with Noah dead and gone, now here was yet one more death to mourn.

"There was no one here to bleed him," Adam went on. "In the end he was too weak to move, and couldn't speak."

"I brought our grandmother's pestle and

mortar," Catherine murmured, sniffing back tears.

"Pa worked hard. I watched him become an old man before my eyes. Life is not easy here, Cat."

"I'm beginning to see that."

Although darkness was nigh upon them, the few womenfolk Catherine saw were still toiling over their chores. One stood outdoors dousing wooden spoons and trenchers in a bucket of cloudy water. Another was on her knees attempting to break up clods of dirt at the side of her hut in preparation to plant a garden. A stoop-shouldered woman emerging from a ramshackle hut began to toss scraps over a rickety fence to a pair of grunting pigs. They came upon a white-capped girl of no more than ten or eleven sitting astride a stool, milking a goat. When Catherine and Adam passed by, the startled goat spun toward them. One of its legs kicked the bucket over. Luckily the girl caught it before all the milk spilled onto the ground.

"A number of settlers brought livestock with them on the ship," Catherine said, though she didn't think Adam heard her over the sounds of the milkmaid scolding the goat.

"Abby and I own a horse," he said

proudly.

"Do you?" Her interest was mildly aroused. "Where do you keep it?"

"In the lean-to behind the house. I ride back and forth to the plantation every day. I'm a real Virginia planter now. I own two hundred fifty acres of rich Virginia soil, and this year I've planted nearly four acres with tobacco."

"Only four? Why have you not planted more? I understand tobacco leaves are quite lucrative."

Adam laughed. "Virginia is a wilderness, sis. I've only managed to clear four acres. If a man did nothing else, it could take as long as a year to clear a single acre."

"How did you gain so much land?"

"We early settlers, those of us who settled at our own expense, were given fifty acres rent-free. When Pa died, I inherited his land and I've since paid the passage for two other men to help me work it. Under the New Headright System, for each indentured contract I buy, I get another fifty acres."

"That's wonderful, Adam." She was genuinely pleased for him. "You must be considered quite wealthy." She ached to ask how Noah fared. Although her dream of sharing in his success in the New World was now shattered and gone, she longed to know how he was getting on. Yet she feared if she were to speak openly of him, she'd burst into tears right here on the street.

"Tell me about Mother," Adam said. "You're the image of her now." He draped an arm about Catherine's shoulders and gave her a quick squeeze. "I've missed you, Cat."

She told him about their mother's death and being sent to London to live with their distant kin, Lord and Lady Montcrief, and a bit about her privileged life there.

"Doesn't sound as if you had it too bad off in London."

"I missed Mama terribly. And you and Papa and . . . Noah," she added in a whisper. "I only just received Papa's letter. I suspect now it was written some time ago."

"I don't recall when Pa wrote it. Can sometimes take years for a letter to reach its destination."

At the end of the street, they walked around the curve at the top and headed back down the opposite side.

Catherine still ached to know more about Noah. She knew she wouldn't rest until she knew why he hadn't waited for her, why he'd married another. Even if a tear did trickle down her cheek now, Adam wouldn't see it in the dusky light.

She inhaled a breath of courage. "Why didn't Noah wait for me, Adam? Why did he marry when he knew I was coming?"

"Well, it appears you didn't wait for him either, *Mistress Fielding!*"

She stared up at him, her eyes wide. "But I . . . I —" His allusion to her having married confused her, until she remembered what Nancy had said that morning.

"Who did you marry, and when?" he demanded.

"It was an arranged union —" she blurted out, borrowing from the truth of what would have transpired had she stayed in England. "More advantageous to Lord Montcrief than to me."

"Ah. With your husband's surname the same as our grandmother's, I assume he, too, was a kinsman?"

"Yes," she lied, her green eyes shuttered. She hated forwarding the deception she'd set in motion when she boarded the ship, but if the truth came out, she feared it was still possible for Lord Montcrief to track her down and demand she return to England. Especially now; now that she was not to be married here. "I expected Noah would wait for me," she murmured sadly.

"You wouldn't have wanted to marry him, Cat."

"But, I love him!" she cried. "I've always loved him. And he loves me."

Adam's tone hardened. "Noah's not the same man you knew in England. It takes a lot of hard toil to work this land. Not every man wants to do his share."

Nothing he said against Noah could change her mind about him. Of course hard work changed a man! Even Adam had changed. Despite what her brother said, she loved Noah as fiercely now as she ever had.

"I'll understand if you want to return to England."

"I cannot go back now," she said. "I'd pinned all my hopes on being with Noah. I thought once we were wed and had our own family, that — oh, Adam, I feel so . . . so. . . ." Another sob escaped her.

Drawing her into his arms, Adam murmured soothing words into the tangled mass of her hair. When her sobs subsided, they began again to walk.

"You and Nancy will get on very well here."

"But how? We cannot clear a field or . . . plant tobacco."

"No." He chuckled. "But Jamestown is full of young men in want of good wives."

"Noah and I should have wed before you left England."

84

"You were but a child then."

"And now it appears he has married a child. The girl can't be more than fifteen." Her tone hardened. "A child about to become mother to a child."

Adam said nothing further on the charged subject.

Catherine was also ready to abandon it. "You have grown thin, Adam."

"Everyone is thin here."

"Noah's wife is not thin."

He turned a surprised look on her. "I don't recall you having such a sharp tongue, Catherine."

"I have held my tongue for the past six years. Perhaps it is time I began to say what is on my mind."

They came upon a cluster of men talking together on the greensward. The light cast by the oil lantern one carried flickered across their faces. Adam exchanged a few words with the men, then introduced Catherine, telling them she was his sister just arrived from England.

She forced a small smile to her lips before they moved on.

"You just met a number of freemen. It will not be long before you and Nancy find husbands. Everything will be fine, you'll see."

He sounded so sure and confident, she almost believed him.

But, not quite. How could she possibly carry on as if nothing had happened? How could she marry another man when her heart lay broken in a million pieces and she was still deeply in love with the man who had broken it?

CHAPTER 5

Over the next few days, it became evident to Catherine that some sort of rift had sprung up between her brother and Noah, though for now, she didn't ask about it. She had enough on her plate trying to get past the hurt and betrayal she'd felt over seeing her beloved with a very pregnant wife by his side.

Stewing over her situation, she realized that although she would never understand the reason why, she and Noah Colton were apparently not meant to be husband and wife. At length she concluded that since she refused to go back to England, she had no choice but to get on with her life here the best way she could. There was certainly plenty to do every day.

Mornings, she arose at dawn along with the rest of the household and as cheerfully as she could set about helping Nancy and Abigail prepare the morning meal. After they'd eaten and Adam had left for the plantation, the servant boy slung the wooden yoke with empty buckets dangling from either side over his shoulders and headed into the woods for water.

Over breakfast one morning of that first week, Catherine asked Adam where his land was situated.

Without looking up from his trencher of *samp* — a dish the Indians taught the English to make from cornmeal and water — he jabbed a thumb over his shoulder in the direction of the forest. "About eight miles that way."

"And you travel there and back every day?"

"Doesn't take long." He paused to ask Abigail for another piece of flatbread. "Rolling road is still fairly clear."

"Rolling road?" Catherine grinned.

"A special road cut through the forest. Before I built my own pier, I had to roll my hogsheads of tobacco into town in order to load 'em onto the ship. Now the ship comes to me."

"How clever of you!"

"Every serious planter builds his own pier."

"I take it these houses lie outside the old fort?"

Not looking up, he nodded. "Meetin' house, storehouse, governor's chambers, the church, and a few older huts, are all that's left inside. Most of the early settlers have moved onto their own land."

"But why do you live here when you have your own lan— ?"

"We're building a house." He talked while he ate his breakfast. "Bigger." He glanced up and winked at his wife.

Taking his meaning, Catherine looked from one to the other. "Abigail, are you — ?"

A grin of pleasure made Abigail's coarse features look almost pretty.

"That is wonderful!" Catherine cried. "I'm to be an aunt!"

Abigail laughed as she brushed an errant lock of hair from her brow. "I'm only a few months along." Blushing, she turned to sternly address the servant boy. "When ye've finished eating, boy, we need more water. We wash today. Scoot, now."

When Adam had saddled up and headed his horse through the woods, Catherine and Nancy helped Abigail begin the daunting task of washing the bed linens and large pile of soiled clothing. Catherine had noticed the past few evenings that Adam came in looking as if he'd spent the day wallowing in the mud with the pigs. His loose-fitting white linen shirt and gray jerkin — which had probably once been black — and his breeches were always caked with dried mud and grime.

"How far are we from the river's edge?" Catherine asked, thinking the job might be easier if they simply doused the soiled garments in the river as she recalled her mother doing on washday at the farm. She helped Abigail heave two heavy buckets of water up to pour into a larger container that was simply a sawed-off wooden barrel.

"Water's salty. Can't drink it, can't wash clothes in it, unless you don't mind the grit."

Nancy appeared from inside the house with another load of soiled linen, and the three women worked in silence. It was not long before Catherine's forearms ached from the exertion. Overhead, the sun blazed down upon them.

"Does Adam ever return here for the midday meal?" Catherine asked.

Abigail shook her head. "He and the men generally eat something in the field. They've put up a fair-sized outbuilding where the bondsmen stay. Has its own hearth and oven. Menfolk can cook and fend for themselves when they have to." She chuckled. "When the weather's bad, Adam stays overnight there."

Catherine pressed both fists into the aching flesh of her lower back. "What do you plan to do with this house once you've removed to the new one?"

Abigail swiped at the beads of sweat on her brow. "Trade it for something, I 'spose. Every new settler come with you and Nancy be in need of a house. Adam can trade for new tools, perhaps another horse, maybe even a cow." She raised up from the tub of dirty water and looked back at the crude structure they called home. "This be a good house. Three rooms and a loft plenty big enough for a family."

"I think the house be quite nice," Nancy said. "Right and tight for a man and wife, and a babe or two."

The three women turned back to their work.

That night after Catherine and Nancy lay down to sleep, Nancy, still awake on the pallet on the floor, addressed her companion in a low tone. "I be wondering what you plan to do now, miss?"

"You mean now that I am not to be . . . married," Catherine replied sadly.

"I be so sorry how things turned out for ye, miss."

Catherine sighed. "I've no choice now but

to go on as best I can."

"Will ye be going back to London, then?"

"Never! Though you are free to do as you please, Nancy."

"I please to stay right here with you, miss."

Catherine smiled ruefully. She was grateful for the fierce loyalty that had sprung up between herself and Nancy. Odd that they had lived side-by-side in the Montcrief townhome but had never known one another existed. Now Catherine could not imagine her life without the congenial servant girl. "I think in future, Nancy, it would be best if you addressed me simply as Cat, or Catherine. You are not a maidservant here."

"Very well, miss . . . I mean, I shall try to remember."

They lay in the darkness a spell longer, neither speaking. Before retiring, Catherine had slid back the window covering to let in fresh air during the night. She stared hard at the thin shaft of moonlight that spilled through the opening.

"I've been thinking, Nancy. Since there is no saying when, or if, John Rolfe will return to Jamestown, or if he will bring his son back with him, I should not count on tutoring young Thomas. But, if I were to buy this house from Adam, you and I could live here together. We'd each have our own room, and the common room would serve nicely for a school. For the children of Jamestown. Would you consider helping me start a Dame School here in the New World, Nancy?"

"How could I be of help to ye? I caint read or write meself, miss, I mean . . . Catherine."

"Well, during the day, when the children are at their lessons, you could do the things for us, the cooking, the washing, that you are now doing for Abby. In the evenings, I could teach you to read and write."

Nancy paused. "That be a right good plan, miss." A moment later she added, "I expect the children will call ye Mistress Fielding, so perhaps that's what I should call ye."

Catherine grinned. Apparently, old habits were hard to break. "You may address me however you please, Nancy."

The next evening after the supper dishes had been cleared and Abigail had sent the boy for water to wash them, Catherine drew the one straight-backed chair in the room nearer to where Adam sat on a tree stump before the fire. Staring hard at the glowing embers, he thoughtfully smoked a pipe that looked to have been fashioned from a corn-cob.

"There's something I wish to speak with you about, Adam."

He blinked as if bringing his thoughts back around. "What's on your mind, sis?"

Catherine briefly told him of her idea to purchase the house from him and to start a school for the children of Jamestown.

"Well." He considered. "I cannot say how the idea of a school will be received."

"But surely no one could object to educating their children. Adam, there are now scores of grammar schools in England. Girls and boys alike are taught to read, and write, and to cipher. Of course, in smaller parishes, many young children still learn at their mothers' knees. Others attend a Dame School such as the one you and I and Noah attended when we were children. I thought to model my school on that order."

Adam nodded. "And what will you teach from? I know of no hornbooks in the entire colony."

"Since I have no copy of *The English Schoolmaster,* I thought to begin teaching from the Anglican Prayer Book. Every family should have one. Later, I could send for a copy of Mr. Cootes's text as well as other supplies — drawing paper, maps, French and Latin textbooks."

Adam shook his head. "Latin would be of no use to anyone here, Cat. A few boys may indeed be sons, or grandsons, of English gentlemen, but boys here are not educated in the old way."

"Well, then I shall begin with simple reading and writing, and, of course, ciphering. Every boy and girl should know how to read and write." Glancing over her shoulder, she lowered her voice. "Not even Nancy can read or write. I find that appalling. Surely the Jamestown leaders would agree that every child should possess the rudiments of education."

"Indeed, but again, how will you finance the venture? These 'supplies' you speak of will cost a good deal of money, and since you and Nancy cannot grow tobacco, I see no way you could earn the necessary funds to purchase what you'll need. Or purchase the house from me. You'd best give up your lofty notion, sis, and do the sensible thing."

"The sensible thing? And what would that be?"

"Get yourself another husband, of course. Have children, make a family."

"I have no intention of marrying just yet," Catherine replied firmly. "I am not ruling the possibility out, of course, but for now, marriage is not uppermost in my mind. Nor is it for Nancy."

He ignored her protest. "You could both be wed inside a fortnight. There are a dozen or more men to every woman in the settlement. And not a woman here as comely as you." He gazed sidelong at her. "You've become a real looker, Cat. Several unmarried men have remarked on your beauty."

Her lips pursed. "Thank you, Adam, but at present, I do not wish to marry."

He looked at her as if she'd gone daft.

"There'll soon be plenty of women in the colony for the unwed men to choose from," she added.

"How's that?"

"The New Virginia Company plans to send some ninety women to Jamestown for the express purpose of becoming wives to the settlers."

"And how did ye come to know this?"

"Pocahontas told me. My original plan was to be amongst them until the Rolfes engaged me to tutor their boy."

"Ah. One day ye'll have to tell me about your friendship with the esteemed Rolfes. For now, I know a good many men who'll be pleased to know when this shipload of women will arrive."

"In a twelvemonth, perhaps sooner. And"

— she thrust up her chin — "I was told even they shall be free to choose whether or not to marry. My wish at present is to not take a husband."

"Still as stubborn as when you were a girl."

"I am not being stubborn, Adam. I believe my plan to start a school for the children of Jamestown is a good and worthy one, and I shall not abandon it."

His jaw hardened. "You are being foolish, Cat. The cost is prohibitive and furthermore —"

She interrupted him as a fresh idea struck. "I could charge for lessons. A small sum for each pupil per term."

"Very few colonists have money, and those who do would deign to spend it on lessons!" His tone turned peevish.

"But . . . how do you manage without money?"

"We trade, with the Indians and amongst ourselves. Corn, tobacco, tools are money here. We trade," he repeated with emphasis.

"Very well, then. I shall trade lessons for provisions — food, meat, firewood. I intend to have a garden, so Nancy and I shall have plenty of fresh vegetables. I expect the forest is full of nuts and berries. Pocahontas said —"

"It is far more complicated than that." He tone grew hard. "Great stores of food must be put away for winter. The meat and fish salted, peas, corn, fruit dried and stored in a place the rats won't get at it. Two women alone couldn't manage. It won't work. You and Nancy will come live with us on the plantation, and there's an end to it. Abigail will need help once the baby comes."

Considering his stormy tone, Catherine chose to let the matter drop. For now. But not even her brother's refusal to listen, or help, was enough to cause her to abandon her plan.

"And another thing," Adam said out of the blue the next morning as they all sat around the table breaking their fast over trenchers of pease porridge and corn bread, "this house sits too near the forest."

Three women glanced up from their meal, but only one knew to whom he was speaking. "What does that have to say to anything?" Catherine demanded.

"Indians," Adam replied simply.

"I done seen four already this mornin'," put in the boy as he stretched a grubby hand past Catherine toward the last crumbs of cornbread on the platter.

"Exactly," Adam said with satisfaction.

"But I thought the Indians and settlers lived peacefully together. You said you trade with them, and Pocahontas said —"

"Peace with Indians is always tenuous. You never know what will overset one. One overset Indian can lead to an all-out uprising." Adam shoved his empty bowl aside.

"Adam's right," Abigail put in quietly. "The Indians live by their own rules. They've not yet learned our ways."

"And I doubt they ever will." Adam nearly toppled his dugout chair as he rose and stalked to where his jerkin and hat hung. He reached for the jerkin, then changed his mind and grabbed only his hat before yanking the door open. "Savages, the lot of 'em. I refuse to worry myself over two women living alone in town. You and Nancy will come live with us once the house is complete."

That afternoon, as Abigail was stirring a pot of ragout for their dinner, she asked Nancy and Catherine to each take a long-handled griddle of flatbread to the outdoor oven. "It's a bother, I know," she apologized, "but Adam never got around to building an indoor oven, and now that we'll be leaving soon, I doubt he will."

Once the two of them reached the domed building, Catherine asked Nancy if she'd mind watching the bread while she ventured up the street alone.

Nancy readily agreed and Catherine set out. Unable to get Adam's sharp words off her mind all day, she needed a few minutes to herself to think further on her plan. No matter what his arguments were, she was determined to see her idea through. Not only did she feel strongly that teaching the children of the colony to read and write was an excellent idea, but she had to latch onto something worthwhile to do with herself, and what better way to occupy her mind than with something as important and useful as teaching? Her father had always said if one wanted to be happy, one must find a need and fill it. To start a grammar school here in the New World would, indeed, make her feel as if she were contributing to the growth of a new nation. There was obviously a need here for a school. How could the colony hope to survive if the next generation could not read or write, or correctly figure sums?

It appeared to her that Adam's concerns were more for himself than for her and Nancy's safety. She could easily understand how he might worry about them living alone in town, but she and Nancy had managed to come through some pretty close scrapes on their own thus far. Adam wasn't aware of that, of course, but all they'd endured leaving London and getting here made Catherine believe very strongly in her own resourcefulness. In the few short months since she'd left England, she'd felt herself change inside. She'd grown more confident, and she rather liked that quality in herself. And Nancy had proven herself quite clever in a pinch.

As far as Indians went, Catherine had no fear of them. How could she after meeting Pocahontas and finding her such a kind and gentle soul? She simply did not believe, as Adam claimed, that all Indians were savages. Men very often jumped to conclusions when it suited them. She knew Adam had a great deal on his mind, making a go of the plantation and taking care of a growing family. And she admired him immensely for that. Adam had become a man.

But, she was also now a woman. And in order to get past her grief and disappointment over Noah's betrayal, she had to throw herself headlong into something. She also needed to prove to herself — and, yes, to Adam and to Noah — that she could succeed on her own.

Suddenly unwelcome thoughts of Noah flooded her mind. She wondered how she'd feel the next time she came face-to-face with him. She gazed from one side of the dusty road to the other as if she feared merely thinking about him would conjure him up. She wondered where he and his wife lived. Did the house Noah had built for his new wife resemble these crudely constructed huts, with a rickety pigpen in back and a couple of ramshackle outbuildings, or was he able to provide something finer?

The plainness of everything here offended Catherine's love of beauty. Not a single house or fence or outbuilding bore paint. No cheerful color anywhere broke up the ever-present and monotonous . . . brown. Everything looked crude, plain, and most of all, dirty.

A sigh escaped her. Pocahontas had said white men's houses were dirty. "Not clean like forest." Thinking about the forest caused Catherine to turn around and head back down the road. If she did convince Adam to let her and Nancy stay here in Jamestown, she'd ask him to cut a window in the common room on the forest side of the house so she and her pupils could see out. The sight of trees and greenery was comforting to her, and being able to see beyond the plain walls of the house whilst standing at the head of the room teaching would be a pleasant diversion. She'd also figure out how to hang wooden boxes beneath all the windows in the house and fill them with colorful wildflowers.

When she stepped back indoors, Adam was there.

"Where have you been?" he demanded as if she'd committed a serious infraction.

"I walked up the road and back."

He said nothing further, but it was clear he was displeased over . . . something.

"Can I do anything to help, Abigail?" Catherine asked pleasantly.

"No, thank you, sweetie, all done. Lad, take off your cap before you come to the table. We've a nice ragout tonight, Adam."

Nancy was busy placing pieces of warm griddle-bread alongside each trencher while Abigail poured ale into a wooden tankard for Adam. Everyone else's mug, made from gourd shells, contained fresh, cool water. After a quick prayer of thanksgiving for their food, the only sounds heard 'round the table were wooden spoons scraping against wooden trenchers. Adam was noticeably silent.

Presently, Abigail addressed him. "The weather was pleasant today; I expect the men got a good deal of work done on the house."

"House is coming along. Men have fallen behind transplanting the tobacco seedlings. Tobacco flies are swarmin'. Won't be anything left to harvest if nothing's tended." He continued speaking, his tone sullen. "Soon as the house is finished, there's the barn and new drying sheds to build. This year's crop will be far bigger than last year and we barely had room then to hang the leaves. I need more sheds."

Abigail began brightly, "Well, I don't know why the four of us" — her gaze took in the two other women and the boy — "couldn't come and sweep the seedlings for you."

Adam slammed his tankard onto the table. "I will not have you in the field this year, Abigail, not in your condition. I need men. Able-bodied men."

In the silence that followed, Catherine thought again how much Adam reminded her of her father, spouting off at anyone who happened to be nearby when something was bothering him. Thinking about her father brought tears to her eye. Despite his sometimes foul temper, she missed him terribly and wished with all her heart she could have seen him again at least once more before he died. She had often heard her father say that a woman's duty was to stay calm, keep silent, and do everything in her power to keep her menfolk comfortable and happy.

She was rather surprised when Nancy bravely spoke up.

"There was a goodly number of bond servants on our ship, and counting the other bark, there must be twice that number altogether."

Catherine addressed him in a cheerful tone. "Have all the new indentured contracts been purchased?"

Adam sulked. "I wouldn't know."

"Perhaps you could inquire," Abigail suggested. "We should have a good bit left from the sale of our tobacco leaves last fall. I see no reason why —"

"I haven't a farthing to my name!" Adam spat out.

Catherine smiled to herself, then said quietly, "Perhaps I can help."

CHAPTER 6

Later that evening, after Catherine and Nancy had retired to their room for the night, Catherine was sliding the window covering back to let in fresh air when a rap sounded at the door.

"Come in," she called, expecting it to be Abigail inquiring if they needed a fresh pine-knot candle or a clean chamber pot. She was surprised instead to hear her brother's voice.

"I'd rather you came out here."

She quickly threw on her wrapper and entered the common room where he stood sullenly staring into the low-burning fire. "What is it, Adam?"

"Last evening you mentioned 'purchasing' the house from me. I . . . ah . . . wondered what exactly you meant."

"Well, originally I thought to pay you from what I made teaching. I also have some English banknotes that might be worth something."

He glanced up. "Left to you by your late husband, I presume?"

"No. I discovered the notes amongst Mother's things after she died, so they are as much yours as mine."

"I'll have a look at them."

Catherine hurried to retrieve the paper money. Handing the notes to her brother, she watched as he turned them over and over, studying the faded print.

"Appear genuine to me. There's over twenty-five pounds here."

"Fifteen pounds would buy you three indentured contracts, correct?"

"Fifteen pounds is more than my share."

"Indeed, but I want more than just the house. I want the furnishings — chairs, beds, tools. And two more plank tables" — she glanced over one shoulder toward where the family took their meals — "with benches. And I want sufficient provisions to see Nancy and myself through two winters. I also want an indoor oven and a window cut in that wall so I can see through to the forest."

His gaze followed hers when she pointed to the opposite wall of the house. "I considered putting a window there," he mused, "but decided against it since the draft in winter is apt to put out the fire."

"Not if the window contains glass."

"Glass." His lips twitched, the first hint of a smile Catherine had seen on his face in two days. "There's not a pane of glass to be found in Jamestown, Cat, but I could manage some nice oiled cloth. You can roll it up during the day, and at night, it helps ward off the chill. I'd also fashion a sturdier bolt for the door and windows."

"Thank you."

"You strike a hard bargain, sis. I suppose you also want Lad. Despite what I can provide for you, ye'll still need someone to do the heavy work — chop wood, fetch water, the like. I'd feel a good deal better about leaving you and Nancy here if there were a male on the premises. Lad will suit."

Pleased with the way the negotiations were going, Catherine grinned up at him. "Does the boy have a real name, Adam?"

"Joseph. John. He answers well to 'Lad' or 'Boy.' "

"Hmm. So . . . it's settled?"

"This means a great deal to me, Cat." Folding three of the paper notes up, he stuffed them into his pocket and handed her the remaining two.

"I'm glad I was here to help, Adam."

Once back in her room, Catherine blew

out the pine-knot candle and climbed into bed. But she was far too excited to sleep. Instead, she lay awake making mental notes for Jamestown's first school for boys and girls.

On Sunday morning of Catherine's first week in Virginia, a bright sun peeked through the puffy white clouds overhead; a warm breeze drifted inland off the water.

Having arisen before dawn, the Parke household ate a hastily prepared cold meal, then disappeared to their respective bed-chambers to don clean, fresh-smelling garb. Lad, after several prompts from Abigail, managed to water down his unruly hair. When the church bells began to peal, calling the colonists to worship, they all set out to walk to the Anglican Church located inside the walls of Jamestown's fort.

Though Catherine's gown was a hand-me-down from Lucinda, it was one of her finest, and Catherine especially liked the soft blue linen with its stylish slashed sleeves. The gown showed off her figure to advantage, and she thought the pastel blue looked especially lovely with her red-gold hair. She'd brushed it to a sheen and it now hung in soft waves down her back.

"What a beautiful gown," Abigail remarked. "You'll be the finest dressed lady at services."

Casting his sister an appraising look, Adam nodded appreciatively. "Ye'll no doubt turn heads this morning, sis."

Catherine hadn't been entirely certain she wanted to attend services today, fearing a face-to-face meeting with Noah and his wife. At breakfast, she'd feebly complained of a headache. But Adam had declared that attendance at Sabbath services was mandatory for everyone in the colony.

"There are stiff consequences for anyone who refuses to obey the governor's mandate."

"But what if one is seriously ill?" she'd asked stubbornly.

"A life-threatening illness would of course excuse one. But, as ye well know, a megrim is hardly life threatening. You're lucky you were not here under Governor Dale's rule when we were obliged to attend services twice a day! Now, I expect ye both to be ready in a quarter hour," he added firmly.

As they drew near the walls of the old fort, Catherine worked to tamp down the apprehension that had beset her the minute she awoke this morning. She knew she would have to face Noah sooner or later, but she much preferred it be later — after she'd successfully set up her school and felt more confident of her position here in Jamestown. Now was still too soon, the wound to her heart still too fresh.

She glanced up shyly as other settlers joined their small party. Still, she saw no sign of Noah and his very pregnant wife.

As the church edifice came into view, Abigail motioned for Nancy to follow her. Both were carrying cloth-covered bowls of food they'd prepared the day before. Following services a colony-wide picnic would be held on the church green, mainly to benefit those new settlers who still lived aboard the ships anchored on the river. Catherine noted the long trestle tables loaded with bowls and wooden platters. Her stomach roiled not with hunger, but with anxiety over what lay ahead that afternoon. If not at services, she was certain to see Noah and his wife at the picnic.

As Abigail and Nancy hurried to deposit their offerings, the sight of Jamestown's impressive new church captured Catherine's attention. Though also built in the customary wattle-and-daub style, these timbers rested on a sturdy foundation of cobblestones, the first she'd seen since leaving London.

"Our original church burned to the

ground a few years back," Adam remarked as they all filed into the surprisingly spacious interior.

The elegance inside also surprised Catherine. With its polished pews and chancel of sweet-smelling cedar, it was the finest-looking structure she'd yet seen in the New World.

Before beginning to preach, Reverend Buck welcomed all the new settlers who'd joined the colony that week and issued a plea for those colonists who could to take in families who'd been living aboard the *Inverness,* as that ship was scheduled to sail for England on the morrow. Across the aisle from the ladies, on the gentlemen's side of the building, Adam, along with a score of other men, raised an arm to volunteer space.

Catherine glanced at Abigail to ascertain how she felt about taking on the burden of additional people in their tiny house, but a slight firming of the older woman's lips was all she detected. Catherine wondered if she or Nancy might already be acquainted with the family who'd come to live with them?

When the service got underway, she stood along with the congregation and joined in the singing and prayers. But she found it difficult to keep her mind on the reverend's sermon so anxious was she to turn around and crane her neck to scan the congregation for Noah's handsome face. Surely, she'd see him at the picnic. She also fervently wished to meet Deputy-Governor Yeardley for Adam had said she'd need his approval before she could move ahead with her school.

When the interminable service finally drew to a close, Catherine and Nancy joined those crowded around the trestle tables laden with delicious-smelling victuals. Those who'd lived the past week on the ships especially enjoyed the offerings: sliced pork and venison, roasted turkey, fried fish, pease porridge, beans and greens, and a goodly number of corn dishes. Catherine saw flatbread, bowls of spoon bread, and another sort of bread Abigail called "rye an' injun," as it was made from half rye and half cornmeal. For dessert, there were clotted-cream custards dotted with currants, and an assortment of berry pies and quince tarts.

As there were no benches or chairs, people stood in groups to eat, or sat in circles on the ground beneath the elm and oak trees. Not spotting Noah and his wife, Catherine's spirits sank lower and lower as the afternoon wore on. Except for the brief glimpse she'd had of him the day she arrived in

113

Jamestown, she essentially hadn't seen Noah since she was a child. Although she knew he now belonged to another, she couldn't stop herself from longing to gaze upon his handsome features.

Her attention strayed to her surroundings. A number of boys, Lad amongst them, and even some of the men had begun to play a spirited game of bowling on the green. Other men tossed quoits. It crossed her mind that there were very few children in the colony. Only a handful were running and playing, which meant the number of pupils in her school would be quite small. But that rather put her mind at ease, because the truth was that her experience as a teacher was . . . nil.

Adam introduced her to a number of colonists, who, despite the fact that he referred to her simply as "Catherine," insisted on addressing her as Mistress Fielding. Apparently the false name she'd given the night she boarded ship was now set in stone, and everyone, including her brother, believed her to have once been a married woman.

Mulling the oddity over, she decided that to try and put the matter to rights now would do more harm than good. After all, how many of these God-fearing folk would trust a woman who told lies with educating their children? Moreover, telling falsehoods most assuredly went against the strict moral code that governed the colony, and she feared it might give the governor sufficient reason to withhold his approval for her school. At the very least, he would demand to know why she fabricated the falsehood, and might even send her back to England thinking she had committed a serious infraction and was attempting to hide in the New World as a means of escaping punishment.

Her idle thoughts drifted to studying the few women in the colony. Most, like Abigail, wore simple homespun skirts of faded blue or red stuff with the sleeves tied in the plain white bodice. Most wore close-fitting white caps. Only a few wore chip bonnets, though tied with frayed ribbons. Men dressed in a fashion similar to Adam — brown or gray gathered breeches with matching doublets or sleeveless jerkins over white linen shirts.

By contrast, the important town leaders were all finely turned out in red or green satin puffed breeches. Their doublets sported gold buttons, and most wore wide-brimmed plumed hats. A few wore shoulder-length periwigs. In their colorful finery,

Catherine thought they looked like a handful of peacocks amongst a flock of brown geese.

When she saw two of the peacocks approach Adam and begin to speak with him, she thought he might be about to motion for her to join them, for surely one of the peacocks must be Deputy-Governor Yeardley. Watching the men, it occurred to her that the gentlemen seemed especially overwrought about something, making wide, sweeping gestures with their arms. At one point Adam did cast a gaze over one shoulder and looked directly at Catherine. She held her breath. He had promised to introduce her to Deputy-Governor Yeardley that afternoon.

Instead, her brother headed straight back to the family and announced it was time to leave. He told Abigail he was going aboard the *Inverness* to help retrieve the belongings of the family who'd be coming to live with them. He told her to put Lad's things in the shed.

Nancy and Abigail headed toward the trestle table to collect their empty bowls, and Adam gave a shout for Lad, who was still playing with the other boys not far off. To Catherine, he said, "I'll need a private word with you this evening, Cat."

His grave tone alarmed her. What could be the trouble? And why had Noah and his wife not been at Sabbath services since Adam had said church attendance was mandatory for the entire colony? And why had Adam gone back on his promise to introduce her to Deputy-Governor Yeardley?

That evening, she had to wait until everyone, including the new family — who, it turned out, neither she nor Nancy knew — had settled down in the loft for the night. As everyone had eaten their fill that afternoon, the womenfolk were spared the arduous task of preparing yet another meal that day.

When the house was finally quiet, Adam rapped softly at Catherine's door and asked her to join him in the common room.

"I was approached by two of Yeardley's councilmen this afternoon."

"I noticed. I also noticed you did not introduce me to Deputy-Governor Yeardley."

"The matter of your school will have to wait. A problem has arisen that is far more important. I need you to listen carefully, Catherine."

"Very well, what is it?"

"Apparently Pocahontas's father is grief-stricken over his favorite daughter's death. Rolfe's Indian women have told the chieftain what they know about Mrs. Rolfe's death, and he has sent word that he is satisfied with the explanation, but the emperor's brother, Opechancanough, who has a quick temper and is far more distrustful of the whites, has convinced Powhatan that not all is as it seems. It is his belief that John Rolfe purposely spirited his wife away to England and either killed her himself or had her killed."

"Oh!" Catherine sucked in her breath, her eyes wide with alarm. "That is not true, Adam!"

"I know that, but they now view the fact that Rolfe did not return to Virginia as an act of cowardice and, therefore, proof of his guilt."

"Well, someone will have to make them see the truth!"

"Indeed." Adam looked at his sister. "Yeardley believes the only person who can do that is you."

"Me?" Catherine cried. "Why, me?"

"Because you are the only person now in Jamestown who actually spoke with Pocahontas the night of her death."

"But I know nothing!"

"Lower your voice, Cat. I don't want to

overset the entire household."

She reached to drag up the chair. "I suddenly feel quite weak."

He sat down on the edge of the stump before the hearth. "This is a grave matter, Catherine. It must be handled with diplomacy. The safety and future of the entire colony is at stake. We've lived peacefully with the Indians since Rolfe married Pocahontas. When she converted to Christianity, there was little to no resistance from her father. But now the Indians, at least some of them, think it may have all been a sinister plot to undermine Powhatan and confiscate his empire. Yeardley is overset to the point he intends to reinstate regimental drills."

"Oh, my, this indeed sounds serious."

"It is. The Indians fear that upon Powhatan's death, Rolfe may claim that his child, Powhatan's grandson, is the rightful heir to the entire kingdom. Some years back, when Captain John Smith was here, there was speculation that he intended to marry Pocahontas so that he and his heirs might inherit all the tribal lands. There are over thirty tribes under Powhatan's rule, encompassing thousands of acres of land. It's a preposterous notion, but the Indians' fears must be put to rest or . . . there's no saying what might happen. In the not-too-distant past,

Indians have killed light-skins over far less provocation than this."

"Oh-h!" Catherine wrung her hands. "I do not know what to say."

"Well, you will have to think of something. A meeting has been arranged between you and Powhatan and his brother Opechancanough, in a few days' time. I expect there will be a good many other werowances there. And a good many angry warriors."

Catherine gasped. "You will be there, of course. Wh— what are wer-o-wan-ces?"

"I'm sorry. I forget you know nothing about the Indians. A 'werowance' is the Indian name for the chieftain of a tribe. Many tribes comprise the so-called Powhatan federation. The chieftains all have names, of course, but collectively, the leaders of all the different tribes are known as werowances. All the tribes comprising Powhatan's empire live in separate villages up and down the river or hidden deeply in the woods. Most are friendly and peaceful and willing to trade with us, but some, like the Chickahominy, aren't. Their warriors are fierce and stubborn."

"But you will attend this meeting with me."

"No." He shook his head. "I have no part in this, other than responsibility for you."

A pang of fear stabbed Catherine. "But, how can I manage without you there? I cannot do it, Adam! I cannot!"

"You have no choice, Cat. You have to do as Yeardley says. The safety of the entire colony is at stake. There are far more Indians than there are settlers; they could wipe us out on one rampage if they chose." He sighed. "I often wonder why they haven't. Every year, we encroach more and more upon their land, cut down trees, claim the land as our own, or trade useless trinkets for it. It's clear to anyone we're overrunning the Indians, driving them further and further inland, and still they do nothing to stop us. It makes no sense." He paused. "Of course, until now, no white man has been accused of murdering the emperor's daughter."

Catherine could hardly comprehend this turn of events. "And these other tribes, the unfriendly ones, their chieftains and warriors will also be present at the meeting?"

"They will no doubt be represented."

"The meeting will be right here in . . . in Jamestown, correct?" She hoped.

"No." He shook his head again. "You are to go to them."

"Where?" Her tone was horror-stricken.

"To Powhatan's old village, Werowocomoco, where he used to live. It's closer to Jamestown than Orapaks, where he now lives. He has agreed to meet you halfway. A group of white men will escort you. The chieftain understands a bit of English, but there will also be interpreters. I expect the Indians will ask questions and probe for answers until they are satisfied."

Panic seized Catherine. "And if I do not answer their questions satisfactorily?"

He shook his head. "I can't answer that one, Cat." In a weary tone, he said, "Just be truthful. Tell them all you know."

"Which is virtually nothing!" she cried. "The Indian women with Pocahontas the night she died know far more than I. Nancy and I were already on the ship."

"Then your testimony will serve to corroborate what the Indian women have said." He reached to squeeze her hand. "I'm sure it will turn out fine. But, between now and then, I advise you to pray to God for guidance. As I said, I won't be there . . . but you will have one friend along."

Her worried gaze became a question. "You mean Nancy is also to go?"

"No, Noah will be there."

CHAPTER 7

Noah would be there! The words echoed in her mind as she tried to fall asleep that night. Suddenly she sat straight up in bed. *Why would Noah be there? What did he have to say to anything?*

The next morning, Catherine reined in her questions until everyone had eaten their morning meal and their individual tasks had been decided upon for the day. "Everyone" now included the Morgan family: Robert, a tall, strong-looking man with a full black beard, his pleasant-faced wife Margaret, and their fifteen-year-old son Ethan. Since there was no real bed in the loft, Robert Morgan, who declared himself to be a carpenter, and his son Ethan decided to spend the day building themselves a pair of sturdy rope beds.

Over breakfast, Adam proposed that thereafter Robert and their boy accompany him to the plantation each day, as there was plenty of carpentry work to be done there. Margaret would assist Abigail with the household tasks.

When Adam donned his hat and headed toward the lean-to where his horse was stabled, Catherine followed close on his heels, determined to wrench answers from him before he disappeared for the day.

"Adam, I simply must know why Noah was chosen to escort me to the Indian chieftain's village. And, why were he and his wife not present at Sabbath services yesterday? I also want to know what the trouble is between you two. Something has marred your friendship and I want to know what it is."

"Whoa, there, sis." Adam grinned as he tossed a blanket over the back of his horse, then reached to remove the bucket of oats the mare had been nibbling from. "Indeed, there is bad blood between Noah and me. I suppose it best I tell you since he will no doubt remark upon it when you see him. Your trek through the woods will take a lengthy spell and you'll have plenty of time to talk." He paused to draw breath. "When we first came to Jamestown, the three of us set about building this house, then we — at least Pa and I — commenced to work in the communal fields, uprooting trees, planting, harvesting, the like. No one owned any land then; we all worked together for the good of the colony.

"Later, the Virginia Company decided to grant tracts of land to those settlers who'd come here at their own expense, and since Father had paid the passage for the three of us, he was given three tracts. Noah balked, declaring he was entitled to one of those shares, but Father didn't see it that way. I wasn't given a separate share either. Then Noah became even more incensed when I later inherited all of Father's shares. I'm sorry to tell you this, Cat, considering how you feel about him, but the truth is, Noah never did pull his own weight. He grew angry, moved out of the house, fell in with a group of freemen, some who worked, some who didn't. Noah wasn't the only shirker.

"Eventually, he took up with the traders, and, truth is, he's become quite good at negotiating with the Indians. He has a . . . way with them. There were times when Noah was the only white man some of the werowances would deal with. Which is why he was chosen to accompany you to Powhatan's village."

"When did he marry?" she demanded, which had nothing to say to anything, but as long as Adam was speaking freely, she wanted to know.

"Autumn last. His success with the Indians came to the attention of the governor's council, and he and Richard Benson, who's treasurer of the council, became friends. Benson owns a good bit of land and is a wealthy planter. Noah married his only daughter, Charity. So, you might say, the girl came well-dowered."

"Where do they live? I mean Noah and Charity. Do they live in town or on her father's plantation?"

"In town, in the house the Bensons occupied before they removed to the country. Same as Abigail and I mean to do."

"So, where was Noah yesterday? Why weren't he and Charity at services?"

Adam huffed with exasperation. "You ask too many questions, Cat. I have no idea why Noah and his wife were not at services. Considering his wife's condition, perhaps they elected to stay at home, or perhaps they are with Mrs. Benson on the plantation."

"Was Mr. Benson one of the men you spoke with yesterday . . . I mean, about me?"

He nodded.

"Will he be along, or just Noah?"

"I doubt Benson has ever met an Indian

face-to-face," he said with derision. "He's a fine gentleman. Not one to get his hands dirty. Forgive me for speakin' plainly, but there it is."

"Thank you for telling me the whole truth, Adam."

He turned to bridle his horse, then vaulted himself onto its back, *sans* saddle. "I wish you Godspeed, Catherine. It may be today; it may be tomorrow. You'll learn that Indian time is different from ours. They reckon by suns and moons and the length of a deer's antlers. I rather expect the party to escort you will simply appear at the door, and ye'll be whisked away with no warning. And, unfortunately . . . there's no saying when ye'll be back."

The resignation that had settled on Catherine's face turned to horror. "Adam!"

His heels had already spurred his horse into a gallop.

Her thoughts a tangle, Catherine trudged back to the house.

Two rainy, soggy days later, the knock came at the door. When Abigail flung it open, Noah Colton stepped inside.

"I've come for Catherine," he said simply.

"I'll get her. Cat," she called. "They've come for ya'."

Her heart thundering in her ears, Catherine entered the common room and stopped a few feet before reaching Noah, the man she'd loved as long as she could remember, the man she still loved. A smile trembled on her lips as their eyes met.

His were cold. "It's time to go."

His brusque manner caused her stomach to roil. But she said nothing, until she noted his unusual manner of dress. A shiny breastplate covered his broad chest. A short skirt of mail jingled over his gathered breeches. Tucked under one arm he carried a plumed helmet.

"Why are you dressed that way?" she demanded. "You look as if you're going into battle!"

He turned around. "One never knows about the Indians. It's always best to be prepared and . . . uh . . . protected."

"What about me? I have no armor!"

"Powhatan will likely want to adopt you to replace his daughter. He won't kill you."

"How can you be certain of that?" She folded her arms across her chest and refused to budge an inch. "I won't go."

An amused grin softened his features. "Still as stubborn as when you were a girl."

"Adam said the same thing," she muttered.

"Come, Catherine." His tone was indulgent. "We've a long walk through the woods, then a dugout will take us to —"

She thrust her chin up. "I refuse to go unless you tell me what this is all about! I mean, I know *why* I'm being summoned, I-I just don't know what is expected of me. I'm . . . afraid, Noah."

His handsome face relaxed into a genuine smile, and, spotting the familiar twinkle of affection in his blue eyes, she yearned to fling herself into his arms. He was far taller and more muscular than when last she saw him. His curly blond hair nearly reached his shoulders. He had always been the most handsome boy she'd ever seen, but now, with his bronzed skin and rugged features, Noah, the man, was more appealing than ever.

He seemed to be studying her as well. "You look beautiful, Catherine. But I always did think ye were the prettiest girl I'd ever seen. Ye still are."

She blinked back the sudden rush of moisture that sprang to her eyes. "Oh, Noah."

A shuttered look replaced the warmth in his eyes, and his tone again grew firm. "We've no time for reminiscing, Cat. We have to go. Powhatan's warriors are waiting for us on the shores of the Pamunkey. We've a long trek through the woods. We mustn't risk angering the Indians."

She took a tentative step forward.

"Ye'd best take a shawl. Evenings on the river are chilly. It may be late when we return."

Catherine turned to find Nancy a few feet behind her, carrying her warm woolen shawl. Her gray eyes were fearful as she regarded Catherine. "I'll wait up for ye." She directed a narrow look at Noah. "Ye take good care of her now."

He grinned. "She'll be fine. Powhatan is just an old man missing his daughter. I expect Catherine will charm him." His tone was tender as he spoke, his blue eyes fastened on Catherine. "As she does everyone."

Her cheeks flushed, she draped the shawl over one arm and followed Noah into the sunshine. The rain had subsided, and it was fast becoming another steamy day in Tidewater Virginia.

Two other Englishmen whom Noah introduced as Lieutenant Sharpe and Richard Tidwell were also to make the journey. Both were dressed in protective armor, each carrying somewhat bulky-looking packages.

"Gifts for Powhatan," Noah explained.

"Bribes, more like," muttered Sharpe.

Tidwell laughed.

The men's jibes irritated Catherine, but she held her tongue. Noah being there provided her with a modicum of relief.

The four set off on foot, picking their way along what had once been a well-worn path through the woods, now overgrown with new spring vegetation. They were headed in a northeasterly direction towards the shore-line of the Pamunkey River. Werowocomoco lay on the other side of the river, Noah said.

Today was the first time Catherine had ventured into the woods, but she was far too distracted now to take particular note of any of the plants on the forest floor, or the flowering vines that hugged the tall trees, all of which would have otherwise interested her deeply. She did notice the oc-casional splash of color provided by wild-flowers and the feathery white dogwood now in full bloom.

The foursome walked in silence for a spell, the only sounds being their footfalls crunch-ing the dry, brittle leaves not yet covered over with new growth. The sharp snap of a twig breaking or the shrill cry of a bird oc-casionally pierced the stillness, but other-wise the forest was ominously silent. As they moved deeper into the woods, Lieutenant Sharpe and Tidwell, tramping ahead of

Noah and Catherine, took to hacking away at the tangled undergrowth with hatchets.

With each step she took, Catherine grew more apprehensive. Unconsciously she began to slow her pace. She became aware that Noah, too, had slowed up a bit. She wondered if he could sense her fear, or did he think she might be growing tired and require his assistance?

When Sharpe and Tidwell's backs became mere shadows up ahead, Noah leaned closer to her. "Do ye think as children back home in England, we'd have thought that one day we'd be headed toward a face-off with a savage Indian chieftain in the New World?"

"I'd feel a good deal better about this if you'd refrain from referring to him as a 'savage'!" she snapped.

Noah laughed, reaching to help her over a fallen log in their path.

"Thank you," she murmured. "No, as children, our games ran toward more gentler topics, like love and marriage." She threw a challenging look up at him and was dismayed when his shoulders merely rose and fell in a shrug.

"You didn't wait for me; I didn't wait for you."

Thinking, or perhaps hoping, she'd detected a hint of dismay in his tone, she relished the prick of satisfaction she felt over inflicting on him a small measure of the pain she felt over his betrayal of her. She knew she'd feel sorry for the jab later, but for now, she clung to it.

"Who did you marry, Cat? Some fine Lon'non gen'leman?"

Her chin shot up. "Yes. Yes, he was quite fine. Very wealthy and very, *very* handsome." That her falsehood was working to her advantage now rather pleased her. "Mr. Fielding was the handsomest man I have ever met."

"Well, then what a shame he stuck his spoon in the wall and left you penniless."

"Who says I am penniless?" Her auburn head jerked up again. But when she saw the familiar twinkle of merriment in his blue eyes, her stubborn features relaxed into a smile. "I am not penniless. For your information, I have purchased Adam's house from him and I intend to start a school in Jamestown."

"Then you'd best be certain to say the right thing to His Savage Highness, otherwise you won't be coming back to Jamestown to teach anyone anything."

"Noah, you are frightening me," she fussed, then knew a stab of regret when she realized how quickly they'd fallen back into

133

the easy camaraderie they'd shared as children. Except the warmth between them now meant nothing. She could never be wed to him, which meant all the trials she and Nancy had endured to reach the New World had been for naught.

His tone turned serious. "I'd best teach you a few things, Cat." He dipped his head and spoke in a whisper. "About the Indians."

"Why are you whispering?"

He took her arm and drew her closer to his side. "Because I expect we are being watched. Indians are everywhere. I've no doubt one or two of them are following alongside us now. They keep a sharp eye on the Tassentasses."

"The what?"

"Englishmen. Tassentasse is the Indian word for Englishman." He threw a cautious glance over one shoulder. "We can't see them, but make no mistake, they see us, or smell us. Indians have a keen sense of smell and hearing. Where we might hear only a twig snap, or a bird chirp, it could be one Indian signaling to another. They put their ears to the ground and listen. They know the meaning of every sound in the forest. The naturals might seem like savages to us, simple and uneducated. But make no mistake; they are alert and cunning. They know far more about how to survive off this land than we do."

The deeper they penetrated the cool, dank woods, the graver his warnings grew. "Because we don't fully understand them, or they us, there are strict rules we must follow when we're around them. Don't speak until spoken to. Don't move quickly, or reach for a weapon —"

"I don't have a weapon!" she cried in an alarmed whisper. A quick glance at his side told her he had none either.

"We are on a peaceful mission." He leaned into her ear. "I'm carrying a pistol and a knife, and so are Sharpe and Tidwell."

"And I'm carrying *nothing*," she pointed out in an angry whisper.

He ignored her. "When we arrive, just stay calm, look mournful and, above all, speak in a respectful tone. Powhatan is their king. Some Indians understand a good deal more English than they let on, so if you have a question, ask me quietly. None of your stout refusals or cries of alarm."

"How did the Indians come to know so much of our language?"

He shrugged. "I expect your friend Pocahontas taught them. In the early days, she learned a good many words from Captain Smith."

"Her English was quite good."

"So, you did know her."

"Of course I did."

He switched topics. "I should also warn you that you will see a good many Indian braves rather . . . scantily clad, but, as a married woman, the sight of a man's bare limbs or naked buttocks shouldn't shock you."

His plain talk made her uncomfortable since, truth was, she'd never seen a man unclothed in her life. But she wasn't about to tell Noah that.

A bit further along, he asked, "So, you were well-acquainted with the Indian princess, eh? Probably met her at some fancy-dress ball or Lon'non dinner party."

"Yes, I did," she replied softly.

"Well, at least you've calmed down. One day ye'll have to tell me about your fine London life. I wonder what your society friends would think if they could see you now? Didn't that rich husband of yours have family who could take you in? One wonders why you chose to come here."

She glared up at him, thinking the answer to that question should be obvious. Was she the only one who remembered that she and

Noah Colton had been betrothed since childhood? Instead of answering his question, she replied, "I am far more concerned about getting safely back to Jamestown at the moment. Please tell me more about what to expect once we reach the Indian village."

But there was no more time for talk. They soon stepped out of the shadowy forest and onto a sunny stretch of sand where Catherine's eyes widened with fresh alarm at the sight that greeted them there.

Standing beside what looked to be a large tree trunk dragged up on shore were two tall, very-dark-skinned Indian braves wearing less clothing than Catherine had ever seen on a man. Their entire bodies, arms, legs and torso, were naked except for the scrap of leather covering their loins. Stripes of red and white paint decorated their muscular legs. Necklaces of colorful beads and bones hung down their hairless chests. Red and white paint streaked their foreheads and cheeks. Each brave carried a bow, and, peeking over their strong shoulders, Catherine spotted feathery tips of a dozen or more arrows.

The sight of their weapons caused her heart to hammer so loudly that if the natives' hearing was as acute as Noah had said, they could surely hear it.

Noah took her arm and drew her forward. "We're to go with the braves, now," he said gently.

As they drew nearer the tree trunk, Catherine could see that it was, in fact, a boat. About twelve feet long, the guts of the tree trunk had been scooped out and the inside walls rubbed smooth. She wondered if the thing would float; but, of course, the Indians had come to this side of the river in it.

They all climbed inside the dugout and sat down, one Indian fore, one aft. Each picked up a flat wooden oar. Catherine spent the next quarter hour studying the Indian seated ahead of her. His quiver of arrows had dropped to his waist, leaving the strong expanse of his muscular back exposed to full view. She grew fascinated watching the ripple of his muscles as he rhythmically moved the oar to and fro in the water. A light breeze ruffled his shiny black hair, shaved close to his head on the right side, hanging long and loose on the left. White feathers tied into his hair fluttered lightly on the breeze. An odd movement close to his right ear caught her eye and she leaned forward to better see, then drew back in horror when she saw that the brave was wearing a live green snake as an earring!

Nothing Pocahontas had told Catherine about her people had prepared her for this. She was beginning to understand why Adam and other Englishmen referred to the naturals as savages.

Once the small party reached the opposite shore, the braves silently escorted their captives, which is how Catherine now thought of herself and the traders, through the palisaded walls of Werowocomoco. The walls surrounding the village were built of sturdy upright tree trunks tied together with braided hemp. Inside the walls, Catherine was taken aback by the orderliness she saw there.

The village was filled with odd-looking domed-shaped huts, their outsides covered with woven grass mats. Beside each hut was a neat garden much like those she'd seen in Jamestown. Indian women tended the gardens. Here and there, laughing children ran and played together. She couldn't help noticing that the smallest children, girls and boys alike, wore nothing at all. The women's bodies were covered to the knees with smooth doeskin dresses, much like the one Pocahontas wore, though with far less ornamentation. Their long black hair hung loose or plaited in a braid down their backs.

They seemed happy and content as they silently went about their work.

Work that surprised Catherine. It was women, not men, she saw industriously building a new dome-shaped house, working in teams of two or three to bend the long poles of green wood that would form the arched frame. Others wove mats that would cover the walls.

Catherine was so caught up studying the Indians she was startled when suddenly, their guides whirled around and one cried, *"Sacani!"*

In plain English, the other said, "Wait here."

They stood in the hot sun for what seemed like an eternity. It was already past noon and Catherine was both hungry and thirsty. From somewhere, the delicious smell of roasting meat drifted toward them on the light breeze. Hearing her own stomach growl, she glanced at Noah. His face was calm and impassive. No one talked.

Finally, some sort of signal must have alerted the Indians because the one who spoke English said, "Inside now."

Reaching the longest of the domed houses at the far end of the clearing, one brave pulled aside the mat covering the entrance and they all filed in. Catherine blinked to accustom her eyes to the dim light.

They sat down on the ground, the men cross-legged, Catherine's long blue skirt covering her legs.

When she looked up, the great chieftain Powhatan had silently entered the structure, and was settling himself on a raised platform draped with skins and plush animal furs in the middle of the room. More fully clothed than his braves, a band of white feathers held his long gray hair back from his face. Many necklaces of shiny copper and brightly colored beads lay around his neck. That no war paint was smeared anywhere on his body gave Catherine some measure of relief.

However, her relief vanished when she caught sight of the two Indian braves standing on either side of him, especially the tallest, ugliest one, the one casting scowls of hatred at her. Their bodies were painted black as pitch, with stripes of red, white, and green paint on their legs, arms, and faces. Wads of black-tipped feathers attached to the tops of their heads made them seem even taller. One carried a spear, the other stood with his arms folded across his chest, assessing her and the other Tassentasses from the narrowed slits of his eyes.

Catherine's breath again grew short. On either side of the long domed structure, she spotted other groups of male Indians seated on the floor, but as they caused no distraction, she did no more than glance their direction.

Before the audience officially began, Lieutenant Sharpe was granted permission to approach Powhatan with his bag of "bribes" as Tidwell called them. Catherine watched with growing alarm as he withdrew hatchets, hammers, tomahawks, and steel-bladed knives from the bundles and spread them at the emperor's feet. To bring the Indians more weapons hardly seemed a wise course to her! However, nothing seemed to interest the chieftain until Sharpe drew forth a pouch of shiny copper pieces that could be cut into any shape Powhatan desired. For this gift, the lieutenant was rewarded with a nod of approval.

After the men had gestured and talked back and forth a bit, the tall, ugly Indian seemed to grow agitated.

"Talk stop! Bring *crenepo!*"

The two warriors who'd escorted them into the village approached Catherine. Each took one of her arms and fairly lifted her off the ground. Noah also rose to his feet and followed them to the chieftain's platform.

Catherine willed her pounding heart to remain calm as she faced the fearsome warriors and the mighty emperor. However, standing closer to Powhatan she saw no anger or malice in his faded watery eyes. She saw only sadness.

He too gazed intently at her. In a low mournful voice, he finally said, "Matoaka gone."

Beside her, Noah translated softly. "Matoaka was Pocahontas's given name. It means Little Snow Feather."

Catherine's chin trembled as tears of sadness filled her eyes. She lowered her head, but was unable to hold back a sob. Thoughts of the father she'd so recently lost filled her mind. At times, the losses she'd suffered since coming to the New World still seemed too much to bear. But she had no choice. Pushing through her tears, she tried to return her thoughts to her surroundings. She and the powerful Indian chieftain had much in common, both were grieving, she for her father, he over the loss of his beloved daughter. "Yes," she said. "Matoaka gone."

She watched a droplet of moisture spill from the old chieftain's eye and melt into the deep wrinkles of his leathery cheek. The two of them looked full at one another for a long moment.

"Crenepo love my daughter."

Catherine nodded solemnly. "I loved her

very much."

The old chieftain's knowledge of English now apparently exhausted, he turned to address the angriest brave in his own tongue. The brave spoke to the three Tassentasses in broken English mixed with Indian gibberish. Between them, they managed to translate the chieftain's questions to Catherine and relay her answers back to him.

Powhatan wanted to know many things about his beloved Pocahontas: was she happy, had she enjoyed her visit to the faraway land, had she had many adventures, how did her child fare, was the boy well and happy, and did John Rolfe treat her kindly?

Through his interpreters, the chieftain said he knew Catherine had been with his daughter the night she died. When she nodded, he wanted to know if his daughter had been very ill then. Catherine told him the princess was feverish, that she'd been wrapped in a blanket before a warm fire, and that before Catherine left them, Mr. Rolfe had had his wife's women put her to bed. Her husband knew she did not feel well and feared for her health.

She told the chieftain they had talked of the forest Pocahontas so dearly loved, about healing plants and herbs, and that she was to teach their boy once they arrived here.

Catherine said she believed Mr. Rolfe had not returned to the New World following his wife's sudden death because he was grief-stricken and could not bear to leave her alone in a strange land. She said she did not know when, or if, he would ever return.

When the audience drew to a close, the old chieftain rose to his feet and with slow deliberation drew an arrow from the quiver of the angry warrior, who Catherine later learned was Powhatan's brother Opechancanough. After speaking a few words, Powhatan snapped the arrow in two and cast the pieces on the ground. Noah whispered to her that for the Indians, a broken arrow signified peace.

"And then what happened?" demanded Margaret Morgan.

Catherine and her escorts had returned to Jamestown just after dusk, and she, her family, and the Morgans were all seated around the board table in the common room of the Parke cabin as Catherine hungrily ate from a trencher filled with thick vegetable stew.

"Powhatan bade us leave. I don't believe his brother, the tall angry Indian standing next to him, wanted us to go, but Powhatan waved him to silence every time he tried to speak. Powhatan wished us a safe journey,

145

then . . . we left."

"Did you eat all kinds of strange things?" asked Ethan Morgan, his eyes round.

"No." Catherine shook her head. "It was not a time for feasting. It was a time for mourning. Two Indian women bade us sit on a grass mat beneath an oak tree. They brought us fruit and bread and something tart to drink." Catherine scooped up another bite of stew. "I admit I was frightfully hungry by then, as I am now," she added with a laugh. "On the way back, we munched on wild berries and drank sweet water from a pretty spring."

"Well." Adam pushed up from the table. "It sounds as if you handled yourself very well, sis. I'm proud of you."

"Your first visit to a real Indian village," Nancy said with awe.

"It's time we all got to bed," Margaret declared. "Come along, Ethan, you've heard enough Indian tales for one night."

"I hope I see some real Indians soon!"

"I see them all the time," Lad boasted.

Catherine grinned at the boys. She was vastly relieved the dreaded ordeal was over and was now looking forward to a long night of rest. Tomorrow she was to meet with the deputy-governor and his councilmen to report on her visit with Powhatan. More importantly, she intended to bring up the matter of her new school.

CHAPTER 8

"From what you've told me, Mistress Fielding, it appears the danger we feared from the Indians has passed," Deputy-Governor Yeardley said. "Which is a considerable relief to all of us." He paused. "Now, I understand you have another matter to bring before the council."

"Yes, sir." She hesitated, noting there were only two of the seven council members present that afternoon. "I wonder if I need to approach *all* of the council members . . . or, if. . . ."

"Just apprise me of the nature of the matter, Mistress Fielding. If others of the council are required to give an opinion, they will be consulted. I expect our consideration will be sufficient for your . . . ah . . . little matter."

Though Yeardley's patronizing tone irritated Catherine, she had no choice but to proceed. With a shaky smile, she gazed at the three elderly gentlemen looking expectantly at her.

The Council House, situated inside the fort of Jamestown, sat opposite the church, facing the greensward where the village picnic had been held on Sunday last. Catherine had walked into the fort alone this afternoon, wondering if she would see Noah today. Thus far, she hadn't. Apparently he and the other men who'd escorted her to Werowocomoco had already delivered their report and departed.

"As you know, sir," she began, "I came to the New World for the express purpose of tutoring the Rolfe boy, but that is not to be. Therefore, I have decided, that is, sir, I very much wish to start a Dame School here in Jamestown, for the children." She rushed on. "I feel it is of extreme importance, sir, that all citizens, that is, the *future* citizens, of Jamestown know how to read and write. Education is very important to the survival of the colony, sir."

"Indeed, Mistress Fielding. However, a . . . school." Yeardley paused, as if considering how best to refuse her request.

Catherine noted that the other two councilmen, a Mr. Porter and a Mr. Weymouth, were both nodding their heads in apparent support of her proposal. She waited for the governor to go on. When he didn't, she took advantage of the long pause.

"I wondered if I needed to obtain a special charter from you before I began holding sessions, or . . . if I merely needed to apprise you of my plan."

"To apprise the council of your plans is indeed necessary, Mistress Fielding, but . . . I . . . we . . . have not yet considered the notion of a . . . school. The council treasurer will have to be consulted if you expect to receive any monetary aid —"

"Oh, no sir," Catherine interjected. "I am not requesting any funds, at least, not at present. Perhaps, once I am able to ascertain what my needs will be, I might require some financial aid, but, for now —"

"Without funds, how do you propose to finance your venture?" asked Mr. Weymouth, who seemed a kindly sort with a pleasant smile.

"I intend to barter with the parents of my students. Lessons in exchange for whatever they can spare — firewood, meat, corn, flour."

"Ah." Weymouth nodded but said nothing further.

Yeardley spoke next. "The main thrust of the Virginia Company, Mistress Fielding, is not to educate, but to make a profit for our stockholders in England. I, and the other councilmen, are educated men, and the shareholders have placed express trust in us to manage the affairs of the township and to ensure that the settlers do all in their power to use the natural resources of the region to produce useful commodities — lumber, clapboards, pitch, tar, and of course, tobacco, and also furs and skins, which we obtain from the Indians and which do, indeed, fetch quite a high price in England. All of the products that we, as a commonwealth, can export back to England are necessary and essential in order for us to alleviate the tremendous debt we owe to the stockholders who have placed their trust in us. For my part, Mistress Fielding. . . ."

Catherine listened intently to the governor, but eventually when it seemed he was merely droning on and on and saying nothing relevant, her thoughts began to wander. Did the governor truly believe education was unnecessary? From his ramblings, she had no idea what point, if any, he was attempting to make. Even when he appeared to have concluded his lengthy speech, she was unsure what his opinion of her idea truly was.

"Not to be disrespectful, sir, but Sir Edwin Sandys, who I understand was instrumental in forming the New Virginia Company, has very definite ideas about how to ensure the growth and future of this colony and others like it in the New World. One of his ideas involves bringing women here for the express purpose of marrying the men of Jamestown and forming families . . . with children, which will naturally further the growth of the settlement. I believe, sir, that any self-respecting and forward-thinking family will want to see their children educated at least to the point of being able to read and write. As I am sure you are aware, sir, there is now a grammar school in most every village of a size in England."

The governor cleared his throat but seemed to be growing impatient with her persistence. "Of a certainty, Mistress Fielding, of a certainty. But here in Jamestown, that eventuality is well in the future. At present, we have very few children and there is not a child in Jamestown who does not share in his or her familial duties, whether working the tobacco fields alongside the father, or if the child be female, helping the mother with chores and duties in the home. I hardly think any parent will want to do without the help provided by their children for any length of time, and certainly not for something as frivolous as learning how to read."

Catherine bristled. "But surely you agree, sir, that the ability to read and write, and correctly figure sums is important for the success and survival of the family and therefore the entire community."

Both Mr. Porter's and Mr. Weymouth's heads turned toward the deputy-governor.

Yeardley's lips thinned. "I believe if a man thinks it necessary that his son know how to read or write, the teaching of that lesson should fall to the mother."

"And if the mother is unable to read or write?"

The governor suddenly seemed to lose all patience. "Mistress Fielding," he huffed. "I can see you are determined to move ahead with this venture, whether or not I think it a sound idea."

Catherine was also losing patience with him. "Sir," she said in a firm tone, "we think the Indians are savage and uneducated, yet if we do not educate our own, what will set us apart from them? To bring the Indians to Christianity, which I understand is one of the foremost purposes of settling this land, will hardly be possible if the one doing the bringing cannot even read from his own prayer book!"

The governor appeared to have heard her at last. "Are you saying, madam, that you intend to educate Indian children in your school?"

"I — why, yes, of course, any child will be welcome."

"And you intend to teach the reading of the Anglican Prayer Book?"

"I do, indeed, sir, as I have nothing else to teach from."

The governor sat up straighter. "Well, why did you not say so at the outset? The establishment of an Anglican Missionary School in Jamestown will greatly impress the Virginia Company stockholders and the king! No doubt King James himself will issue a Royal Commendation!" His face beamed with pleasure as he turned toward Mr. Porter. "Porter, draft a letter at once to Sir Edwin Sandys apprising him of the establishment of Jamestown's Anglican Missionary School. Tell him the savages will be brought to Christianity and taught to be loyal subjects to His Majesty, the king! The stockholders will be very pleased, very pleased, indeed!" He turned to Catherine. "Are you certain you do not require any assistance, Mistress Fielding? Anything at all?"

"Now that I think on it, sir, I am in need of two additional tables and benches for the students. We've only one board table in our common room. I have purchased my brother's home to use for my Dame School. My — my assistant, Miss Mills and I will, of course, reside there."

"Consider it done! That and any other carpentry tasks you require. I am vastly pleased with your show of loyalty to the cause, Mistress Fielding. I can see why Mr. and Mrs. Rolfe placed such a great deal of confidence in you. I am vastly pleased, Mistress Fielding, vastly pleased, indeed."

Catherine left the deputy-governor's chamber in a daze, her thoughts awhirl as she set off across the greensward towards home. Though she hadn't noticed whilst in the meetinghouse, storm clouds had gathered outside. Strong winds blew in gusts off the sea. Again and again Catherine wondered how her simple idea to teach boys and girls to read and write had suddenly become a Missionary School to bring Indian children to Christianity. How Yeardley proposed to persuade Indian children to attend her school, she hadn't a clue. The notion of a commendation from the king was equally preposterous to consider.

She shuddered to think what would happen if it became common knowledge why she wished to start a grammar school. Or if it became known that she had begun her journey to the New World by giving John Rolfe a false name simply to escape her guardian and that she had clung to her deception simply because she had been scorned in love. The truth would make her the laughingstock of the New World — perhaps even a criminal! To put a very fine point on it, she and Nancy were both already criminals! The Newgate Prison was full of serving wenches who'd be hanged for far lesser crimes than pinching lemons!

Catherine knew she could trust Nancy. But she did not ever want Noah to know how deeply his betrayal had hurt. On the other hand, if the truth did come out and Mistress Fielding's Missionary School became a newsworthy item in London, that lofty accomplishment alone should free her from Lord Montcrief's censure. And now that she was an entire world away from him, his wrath probably no longer mattered anyhow.

Shaking her head to clear it as she stepped through the palisaded wall of the fort, a fierce gust of wind nearly hurled her back inside. The air, she realized, was pungent with the smell of impending rain. Suddenly over the noise of the wind, she heard a man's voice calling to her.

"Catherine! Catherine! *Come quick!*"

She whirled around and was astonished to see Noah running toward her. "What is it?" she called back.

Panting, he reached her side. "It's Charity. It's her time! She's frightful sick and screaming! I haven't a clue what to do for her."

"Where is her mother?"

"Not here." His eyes were as wild as the tempest of wind and leaves swirling about them. "Please, come, Catherine! Ye'll know what to do. *Please!*"

"Of course, I'll come, Noah." She fell into step beside him as he raced back the way he'd come. The wind at their backs whipped Catherine's long skirts around her and caused Noah's shirt and breeches to billow about him. "Are there not any other women in the village who are more experienced at this than I?" Catherine's tone was anxious.

He held onto his hat as he shouted back at her. "I remember back home when you and your mother assisted with birthings in the village."

The tiny hovel where Noah and his young wife lived was a mere bark-covered hut that looked so flimsy Catherine expected a single

157

gust of strong wind could topple it. Before they stepped inside, she could already see twigs and grass and bits of bark lifting upward from the low-slung roof as the wind swept past.

Inside, there was only one room with not even a wall or doorway to separate one section from another. A tattered curtain hanging from the low ceiling afforded some privacy to the girl writhing on the bed in the corner, but her loud wails could be heard long before Noah and Catherine entered the hovel.

Apparently Noah became aware of the rude look of their home for he said, "We'll be removing to the Benson plantation as soon as Charity and the babe are able."

Catherine was already across the room to ascertain the girl's condition, though with Charity's thrashing about on the bed, her exact condition was difficult to determine.

"Please, dear, do hold still," Catherine pleaded. "I cannot help if you do not lie still."

Charity ceased her screaming for a moment, but her blue eyes were wild as she gazed at the stranger.

"Sweetheart," Noah said, "this is Catherine, she's come to help with the birthing."

Recognition must have dawned for the

girl's screams began afresh. "No-o-o! Not her! No-o-o! She'll kill me!" She flung her arms at Catherine in an attempt to push her away. "Go away! Noah! Help me! Please, help me!" she sobbed.

Catherine glanced at Noah. "You'll need to tie her wrists if I'm to do any good."

"Tie her wrists?"

"To the bedpost. I need to feel her belly."

Noah glanced about the hut in search of a piece of rope. Spotting a length, he snatched it up and came back to the bed. "Sweetheart, the nice lady needs you to hold still so she can help you." His anxious eyes sought Catherine's for reassurance.

Together they managed to secure the girl's wrists. Noah moved to the bottom of the bed to hold her ankles in place while Catherine gently probed her distended belly.

Suddenly, Charity let out a long, deep wail, which caused Noah to let go of his hold on her and step back in alarm.

Catherine was also fearful. "I cannot do this alone. She is far too frightened. I fear she could harm herself and the babe. Is there not another woman who can help?"

"I . . . I do know someone, but —"

"Get her!"

Noah dashed from the hut and returned in only a few minutes. When he reentered the house, Catherine was indeed taken aback when she saw the woman with him was a dark-skinned natural. Her doeskin garment was soiled with soot and a dusting of flour or cornmeal. Her black hair hung in a single braid down her back.

"She cooks and keeps house for the freemen I used to live with. She's a widow-woman like yourself, but she has a passel of children, and I . . . I trust her."

The Indian woman had already assessed the situation. Pulling a small leather pouch from her pocket, she expertly pried Charity's mouth open and put a pinch of the contents beneath her tongue.

"For calm her." She turned to shoo Noah away. "Man no help."

Glad to obey, he backed away, making an attempt to tug the tattered curtain more closely around the three women.

The Indian woman gestured for Catherine to hold Charity's knees apart while she drew up the girl's skirt and began to work her magic between her legs. Charity's wails became mere drugged whimpers. Her brow wet with perspiration, blonde curls lay plastered to her damp cheeks. The Indian woman moved to heft Charity's body to a semi-sitting position and in English told her to push.

Charity silently obeyed as Catherine positioned herself at the foot of the bed to help the babe gain entry to the world. Minutes later, she drew the newborn infant upward and held it aloft.

"Hold heels," instructed the Indian woman. "Pat rump, make cry."

Catherine did so, and soon her pats on the baby's wet bottom produced a weak whimper, then a lusty wail.

Catherine laughed. Awe filled her as she realized she was holding Noah's child, and that while it was not also hers, it was part of him, and . . . she loved it dearly. Lost in her thoughts, she was unaware that the Indian woman had severed the cord with some sort of sharp tool. Catherine glanced about for something to wrap the baby in, but seeing nothing, she merely carried it covered in slime and blood, through the torn curtain to Noah. "I need a cloth to wrap your son in," she said, "and water to clean him."

"A son!" he cried, staring with wonder at the wriggling infant Catherine carried.

"I didn't do anything, really," Catherine protested later that evening as she relayed the events of the day to the Parke family. The torrential downpour had held off until she'd reached home, but the rain and wind had been howling outdoors ever since. "The Indian woman did it all. I never did learn her name."

"It was no doubt Tamiyah," said Abigail. "She comes to the village every day to cook and clean for the unmarried freemen."

"And Noah has a son," marveled Adam, who'd also managed to make it back home, though he and the Morgan men were soaked to the skin when they reached the house. "Perhaps we'll be so blessed." He turned a shining look on Abigail.

Who touched her swollen belly. "Perhaps we shall be, husband."

That night as Catherine lay abed going over the events of the day, she wondered about the herb the Indian woman had given to Charity. It was obviously something very powerful as it had had the immediate effect of calming her. Whatever it was, Catherine was thankful Tamiyah had been on hand to administer it and to assist. Without the Indian woman there, she feared what the outcome of the birthing might have been.

Suddenly, she recalled the final words the Indian woman uttered moments before Catherine left the house. Charity's parents had arrived by then, and a general hubbub had ensued. While Mrs. Benson cuddled the babe, she'd issued crisp orders to Tamiyah, who had already taken care of the afterbirth and, without being told, had begun changing the bed linens. But Catherine remembered hearing the Indian woman say to no one in particular: "Girl no have more babes."

Catherine wondered at the dire prediction.

The strong storm, which Adam called a hurricane, continued throughout the night and into the following day. Because neither Abigail nor Margaret Morgan expected the men to return to the house that night, they did not prepare a large evening meal, thinking that the four women and Lad could do with a simple vegetable broth and cold flatbread for dinner. Instead the men returned home, Adam wearing a grim expression on his face.

He said little until they'd all crowded around the board table, each trencher barely half full of the scanty offering. Catherine sensed something amiss but knew better than to ask. Adam would bring the matter up when he was ready.

Her curiosity heightened when, instead of folding his work-roughened hands on the table before him as was his custom when leading the family in their prayer before a meal, he reached to clasp the hands of the two sitting on either side of him, herself and Abigail. Before concluding his prayer, he added a postscript.

"Dear Lord, we ask that you be with the Benson family in their time of grief. Amen."

Both Catherine and Abigail's heads jerked up.

"What has happened?" Abigail demanded.

"You don't know?"

"We've not left the house today. The rain was too —"

"Figured you'd have heard." His gaze darted toward Catherine. "Last night, when the worst of the storm hit, the Coltons' old hut blew down. The babe was killed."

"Oh!" cried all the women in unison.

Adam gave Catherine's hand a squeeze. "The rest of the family is safe. They managed to get Charity to Yeardley's home last night. The family plans to return to the plantation as soon as the rain lets up and the roads clear. Except for Noah. He wants to sift through the rubble and salvage what he can, though I can't imagine what he could find of value there. I'm sure he's heartbroken over the loss of his son. We all are."

Catherine's appetite vanished as the pain in her heart threatened to engulf her. "Excuse me, I'm not the least bit hungry."

164

She slid from the bench and headed for the seclusion of her own bedchamber.

Falling to her knees beside the bed, she buried her face in her hands. *Dear God,* she prayed, *please be with Noah and his poor, dear child-bride. Help them to cope with their terrible loss.*

She sat on the floor a long while, thinking back on the innocent, sweet pride she'd beheld on Noah's face when she handed him his son. And now the babe was gone! How could God have dealt such a cruel blow? The child had lived less than one day.

The enormity of the tragedy was so intense she could not take it in. How would Noah and his little wife go on after this? She gave in to the tears that streamed down her cheeks.

After a time, she pulled herself to her feet and climbed into bed, drawing her knees to her chest. Remembering again the final words the Indian woman uttered — "Girl no have more babes" — fresh tears gathered in Catherine's eyes. *Dear God, please, please let the Indian woman be wrong.*

CHAPTER 9

The following day, Catherine considered walking back to where Noah's hut had once stood, thinking she might find Noah there and could perhaps say something to him that might be comforting. But what could she say? If she felt numb with the pain of his loss, she could only imagine how he must be feeling.

Instead, she decided it best to put the tragedy from mind and turn her attention to other things. For her to attempt to comfort Noah might be construed as over-stepping the bounds. After all, he was a married man. It was not her place to comfort him.

When the storm passed, the colonists on the Parke end of the peninsula began to emerge from their homes. They soon learned that Goodman Colton's hut was not the only one damaged from the storm. Two other bark houses located near the river had also toppled. Though there'd been no deaths, all five of the inhabitants had been injured, and both families had lost everything. The devastation left five more Jamestown settlers homeless.

A few days later, the *George,* the third ship in the fleet that should have left England along with the *Inverness* and the *Hampton,* at last limped into Jamestown's harbor. While at sea, it, too, had been struck by the hurricane and had lost ten more souls before the torrential fury subsided. Catherine learned that John Rolfe was indeed aboard the *George,* and that he had returned to Jamestown without his son, which meant he would not need her services. Word was, he retired at once to his plantation in Henricus, no doubt still mourning the death of his beloved Pocahontas. Catherine hoped their boy had not also been stricken and that his father had left him behind for some other reason. Aboard the *George,* several of the Indians in the Rolfe entourage had succumbed to the same illness that claimed their mistress. Though it had been several months, Catherine continued to mourn the death of the beautiful Princess Pocahontas.

The *George* brought a new deputy-governor to Jamestown's shores. Appointed by The New Virginia Company in London,

Captain Samuel Argall was to replace Deputy-Governor Yeardley, who'd known for some months now that he was serving an interim term until the new appointee arrived. Catherine hoped the new deputy-governor would honor Yeardley's decision to let her open her school. She decided that rather than ask afresh for permission, she'd simply move ahead as if she had all the permission she needed.

She was pleasantly surprised when, true to Yeardley's promise, a team of two house-wrights appeared on the doorstep one day, tools in hand, declaring they'd been commissioned to make whatever alterations she required to the house, in preparation to open her school.

Everything Catherine wanted — two board tables, complete with backless benches, a window cut into the wall in the common room, oiled cloth attached to all four windows in the house, new bolts on both doors and windows, and an indoor oven — were quickly and expertly constructed at no charge. At the last minute, Catherine mentioned to one of the men that she yearned for a pair of flower boxes, one for the new window in the side wall and the other for the front window of the house.

"Be my pleasure, ma'am," said the burly,

bewhiskered fellow. "An' if'n they's anythin' else ye'd like, just say the word an' I be happy to oblige."

Catherine rewarded the congenial fellow with a bright smile. "Thank you kindly, sir. You are a true gentleman."

As the work on the house neared completion, Adam and Abigail and the Morgans packed up their meager belongings to remove to the country. Moments before the two families were to depart, Adam drew Catherine aside.

"I want you to know I greatly admire your spirit in seeing this venture of yours through, sis. I've no doubt ye'll be successful. Still, I daresay leaving you here alone does continue to worry me. If anything should happen to you or Nancy, I'd never forgive myself. Promise me, if you ever encounter a problem with the men hereabouts, or, Heaven forbid, with the Indians, ye'll come straightaway to the plantation. You and Nancy are always welcome."

"Thank you, Adam." Catherine smiled. "Nancy and I both thank you for your kindness. I could never have imagined how full and busy my life would be once I left London and joined you here. I admit," she said with a rueful laugh, "nothing has been as I expected, but I'm confident that everything will work out for the best. I'm far happier and more content than I ever thought I could be the day I stepped off the boat."

"If the work ahead of you is more than you can bear, don't be too prideful to say so," he admonished. "Despite our simple upbringing, you are a gently bred young lady. Abby was accustomed to hard work when we married. She comes from hardy north-country stock and has worked hard all her life."

"You've never told me how you and Abigail met. What brought her to Jamestown?"

"She came with her parents a good many years back. She, a sister and a pair of brothers." He paused. "Entire family — save Abby — died during the starving time."

"Starving time?"

"Winter of oh-nine. Every settler in the colony lost several family members. Pa and I didn't arrive till two years later. Things weren't a great deal better then. Since the starving time, every family is required to always have a barrel of corn on hand and to grow either berries or grapes. Winters in Jamestown can be brutal and . . . you have yet to live through one."

"Nancy and I'll be fine. We survived many a cold night on the crossing." She glanced up at the rafters. "I haven't noticed the roof leaking. What with all the rain we've had, the thatch seems tight."

"For now. Lad needs to add another layer of brush. Wind takes off some every time it blows hard, especially during a storm like the one just past. Expect we lost a full layer then. I also need to remind him to fill the chinks in the walls with fresh daub and to build up a thick wall of mud outdoors come fall. Knee-high mud wall will keep the winter wind out and seal the heat in." He paused a moment, thinking. "I told Abby to leave what's left of the pine-knot candles for you and Nancy. I assume she did."

Catherine grinned. "Yes, she did. And she also showed us how to make them and where to find the narrowest pine sticks in the forest. You're a good brother and I love you dearly."

"I love you, too, sis. Abby and I are both glad you're here. Where I can keep an eye on you!" He glanced past her through the opened doorway to the grassy area in front. "I see everyone is ready and waitin' for me."

Catherine threw her arms about her brother's neck. He returned her warm embrace, then reached up to remove his long-barreled fowling piece from above the fireplace.

"Wish I had another one of these, or at least a pistol I could leave with you."

"Nancy and I won't be needing a pistol and we have one another for company, so we won't be alone, or even feel lonely, once my pupils are here every day."

She linked an arm through his as they walked toward those gathered out front.

"When does your school get underway?" Adam asked.

"My summer term starts next week. I tacked a note to the meetinghouse door yesterday asking parents to sign their child's name to the list. So far, I have three pupils."

"I expect ye'll soon have many more."

The following Sabbath, Reverend Buck announced that Mistress Fielding's Missionary School would open on Wednesday next, and those parents who wished their sons and daughters to attend should see Mistress Fielding following services.

By sunset, Catherine had spoken with three sets of parents who enrolled a total of four more pupils, three boys and one girl. That afternoon, one of the fathers brought over a cartload of firewood as payment for his child's lessons. A mother arrived with a bushel basket of dried apples and pears, which Nancy took to the loft to store with the rest of their food. Catherine didn't yet have a single Indian child amongst her pupils and, truth to tell, rather doubted she would.

Her plan was for school to stay in session until harvesttime, then close for six weeks and reopen for the winter term, which, weather permitting, would last until planting time in the spring. She knew illnesses and other circumstances would keep her pupils away from time to time, but she was determined that, except for those things that could not be helped, nothing would interfere with the steady progress of each term.

Evenings when she and Nancy sat up by candlelight, she worked out her lesson plans and began to teach Nancy her letters by drawing them in the ashes of the hearth with a stick.

On the day classes commenced, her first students arrived bright and early, not all of them eager to buckle down and actually learn something, but still curious since not a single one had ever attended a thing called a "school" before. All went well, despite the fact that two of the boys, aged five and six, were more interested in following Lad around than sitting quietly on a backless bench for hours at a stretch. The two little girls, Patience and Emily, proved model pupils and, Catherine hoped, shining examples of good comportment for the boys.

The first few weeks were somewhat difficult both in establishing discipline during the ever-worsening summer heat and in figuring out how to tailor lessons to the varying needs of pupils who displayed varying degrees of aptitude. She began holding classes outdoors, letting the children draw their letters and numbers in the sand, and at least once each day, taking the children for a walk into the cool interior of the forest where she pointed out the variety of flowers and plants and made mental notes to herself regarding what was growing where. Now that she had the leisure to explore the woods, she fell in love with it. Every time she walked amongst the tall trees, she felt the comforting presence of Pocahontas there with her.

Each day classes were dismissed soon after noon, the exact time being difficult to pin down since there was not a single clock in the entire settlement. That left Catherine a part of the long afternoon and a few evening hours to herself. Nancy and Lad stayed busy most all day taking care of household chores. Evenings, Catherine helped Nancy prepare a hot meal for their supper.

One late summer evening after supper, Catherine was behind the house pulling stray weeds from the nice-sized patch of herbs she'd transplanted from the forest floor. Pleased with the variety she'd collected, she spent several hours each day tending them. Some of the flowers and stems would soon be ready to pluck and dry, then, using her grandmother's pestle and mortar, she'd crush and pound them, label each herb and indicate what ailment it was good for. Lost in thought, she didn't hear the sound of someone approaching.

"So, there you are," came a male voice.

"Oh!" Catherine rose to her feet, surprised to see Noah Colton striding toward her. She hurriedly brushed bits of dirt and debris from her long blue skirt, then reached to tuck up beneath her cap the stray wisps of hair she'd felt tickling her cheeks.

He stood grinning down at her. "You look. . . ."

"A frump?" she finished for him.

"No, I was going to say you look fresh, and . . . pretty."

She smiled as she picked her way amongst the rows of plants. "What are you doing here? More importantly, how are you doing?" She hadn't seen him since the day his child had been born. Neither he nor Charity had attended a single Sabbath service since the one held at the church for their infant son.

Catherine linked an arm through his as they both walked around the forest side of the house toward the front door. It stood wide open as evenings in Jamestown were quite warm, and any breeze that happened to drift by was welcome indoors.

"I never told you how sorry I am about —"

"It's alright," he cut her off, his tone curt. "Charity and I are doing fine. We've settled in with the Bensons. Her mother likes the arrangement. Although —" he stopped abruptly.

Catherine looked up, saw that his blue eyes were shuttered, so politely changed the subject. "Shall we sit here and talk where it's cooler?"

Nodding, Noah stepped inside the house to retrieve the chairs. Catherine heard him exchange a friendly greeting with Nancy, who was busy with chores. Emerging with the two new ladder-backed chairs the workmen had built, he positioned them side by side on the patch of grass in front of the house.

Catherine had reached to snap a stray weed from amongst the lemon verbena growing in her flower box.

Grinning, Noah watched her. "Your flowers look nice. I expect we'll soon be able to tell which huts have a woman living there simply by whether or not there's a flower box."

Catherine smiled. "A bit of color is just what these drab little houses need. Goodwife Taylor and Goody Smithfield have already had their husbands build flower boxes for them." She tossed the weed aside and moved to take a seat beside him. "So, what brings you to our little village this fine evening?"

"I plan to leave at first light on a trading expedition. It's a long walk in from the Benson plantation; easier for me to stay the night in Jamestown with the other traders than make the walk into town on the morrow."

"Which tribe will you visit?"

"Chickahominies."

Her green eyes registered surprise. "But I thought they were our enemies!"

"We hope to persuade them otherwise. Now that Argall is back in office, we're hoping to reinstate the treaty he and Governor Dale made with the Chickahominy a few years back. Chicks refused to trade with us when Yeardley was here. Said they'd made their agreement with Dale, not Yeardley."

"I've heard their braves are very fierce."

"True. But back then they declared themselves loyal subjects of King James and even wanted his picture!" His head wagged from side to side.

Catherine had removed her cap and it now lay discarded in her lap. The setting sun on her auburn hair glistened like copper. "You find that amusing?"

"I find it quite amusing that a tribe of savages would want a portrait of the king of England, a man they will never see and who doesn't care a tinker's damn about them, except to see them subdued and eventually killed off."

She said nothing in reply, though she thought his remark rather coarse. "What do you plan to trade with them?"

"The usual. Axes, chisels, hoes, a few rifles."

"Rifles!" Catherine blanched. "Why would we want to give a potentially explosive tribe of Indians rifles?"

Noah remained calm. "Rifles are not real effective without shot."

She gazed at him curiously. "Don't you tell them the rifles need powder?"

He shrugged. "Not unless they ask."

"And what do you get in return from these poor, misguided Indians?"

"We hope to persuade them to honor their original agreement with Governor Dale, which was to bring two bushels of corn per man to Jamestown's storehouse. Seems we're running a trifle low."

Catherine shook her head. "You continue to amaze me, Noah."

He'd casually leant his chair back against the wall of the house, the fore legs off the ground. He leaned forward, an intent gaze on her. "Why is that, my dear?"

"You are so . . . nonchalant about what you do, as if meeting with a tribe of unfriendly Indians is mere child's play. It's like a game to you."

Again, his broad shoulders lifted and fell. "It is a game. Sometimes I win, sometimes I lose." Abruptly, he changed the subject. "Does your brother often come around here?"

"No. He and Abigail have not been here since they moved to the plantation. Abby is . . . increasing. I suppose you and Charity will soon be . . . ," her voice trailed off.

"Her parents hope she'll be in the family way soon. I sometimes think they only wanted me around to —" He paused.

Catherine studied him in the failing light. It was obvious a number of things were troubling him, but she didn't feel it was her place to invite his confidences, especially about something as personal as his relations with his wife.

He changed the subject. "I suppose you have several suitors by now. I hear a number of unmarried men are keen on you."

Blushing, Catherine looked down. "I am not interested in any one of them. Jonathan Reed has stopped by on occasion . . . mainly to ask if I need anything. He plowed up my garden for me. Actually" — her tone softened — "I think Nancy might be sweet on him."

"Nancy doesn't stand a chance against you."

Catherine said nothing. Glancing up the road, she caught sight of Lad and two other boys, playing some sort of game on the greensward with a stick and clods of dirt. "I'd best go in now. I usually work out my lesson plans of an evening."

"Forgive me." He stood up when she did, gallantly picking up both chairs to carry back inside. "I did not mean to impose."

"You are not imposing, Noah. I . . . always enjoy seeing you." Feeling self-conscious, she looked down. Then looked back up to drink in his rugged good looks one last time before he left — his twinkling blue eyes and curly blond hair, which she noticed he'd cut short for summer. There was no saying when she'd see him again and, as usual, being with him made her want to be with him all the more. "God go with you tomorrow."

An easy grin on his handsome face, Noah touched the brim of his flat beret. "Good night, my lovely Catherine. Perhaps I shall see you again soon, if . . . that would be all right."

She sucked in her breath but did not reply. Just stood on the doorstep watching him walk away, both hands jammed into the side pockets of his wine-colored breeches. When she finally turned away, the sound of the jaunty tune he was whistling drifted back to her on the light evening breeze.

Catherine exhaled a long sigh. Would the day ever come when the mere sight of Noah Colton did not set her heart pounding?

CHAPTER 10

It was especially hot the following afternoon, and when school let out, Catherine spent a few hours outdoors in the sweltering sun helping Nancy wash the bed linens and drape the heavy lengths of fabric over the bushes to dry. They sent Lad to the spring for more water to rinse the last of the laundry. When he returned, Catherine noted his sandy-colored hair was dripping wet. No doubt he'd taken a quick dip in the cool water, something she'd considered doing these hot summer days.

Although not common practice for young ladies to bathe outdoors, she recalled as a girl she'd more than once stripped down to her chemise and waded into the pool of cool, clear water in the meadow. She remembered how delightful the water felt rippling over her nearly naked body and how free and clean she'd felt when she lay back on the grassy shore.

"Water felt good, eh, Lad?" she teased as he slipped the buckets from the yoke around his neck.

"Yes, 'um, sure did." He grinned.

"Just be careful you don't step on a snake. Snakes also like to cool off in the water."

"Snakes don't bother me none, ma'am. It's Injuns I watch out for."

Catherine didn't reply; she'd already turned to speak to Nancy. "If you can get along without me a bit, I spotted a patch of comfrey in the woods I'd like to dig up."

"You go along, miss. I be nearly done here. I may rest a while m'self afore I start our supper."

In no time, Catherine found the comfrey she'd seen when she'd been there earlier with her pupils. She'd only just squatted to her knees when she heard a rustling sound coming from near the ground. Her first thought, perhaps because she'd just been speaking of them to Lad, was that it might be a snake.

She raised her head to listen, but decided the noise was far too loud to have been made by a mere snake. She considered what to do, tiptoe over and investigate, or continue digging, when suddenly up popped the face of a dark-skinned boy.

Unafraid of a child, Catherine smiled

brightly. "Hello, what's your name?"

The boy, who looked to be about five or six, bravely stepped from his hiding place and stood staring at her, his black eyes round.

Like the Indian braves she'd seen in Werowocomoco, the boy was naked except for a scanty scrap of leather covering his loins. However, she saw no war paint smeared on his body, and he wore no feathers in his hair, which . . . was not black! Nor was it straight and silky and did not hang long and loose about his shoulders. Instead, his light-brown hair lay in soft curls close to his head.

Dismissing the oddity, she gestured to herself. "My name is Catherine. What is your name?" She extended a hand toward him.

The boy, his large black eyes never leaving her face, seemed to be considering whether or not to speak. Which gave Catherine additional time to study him. With his small button nose, it struck her that his features looked nothing like any Indian she'd ever seen. His cheekbones were not high or prominent, yet his skin was nut brown.

Suddenly, another Indian child, this one a girl, rushed into the clearing and began to scold the boy. *Nummacha! Nummacha!* The girl's features looked as unlike his as they did Catherine's. She snatched up the boy's hand and attempted to drag him away.

"No!" he cried in plain English. *"Sacani!"*

Catherine's ears perked up. She'd heard that word before. In Werowocomoco. One of the Indian guides had used the word, and Noah later told her it meant "stop" or "wait."

Before the two Indian children scampered away, she decided to try it. *"Sacani!"*

Both children stared at her, their black eyes wide with surprise.

Catherine was again startled when an Indian woman stepped into the clearing. Catherine rose to her feet, leaving the spade on the ground lest the woman think it was a weapon. When she tramped closer, Catherine was relieved to realize she recognized her.

"Tamiyah? Do you remember me? I am Noah's friend, Catherine. I was there when his baby was born."

The Indian woman studied her a second, then her features relaxed. "How you know my name?"

"My sister-in-law Abigail Parke told me. Abigail is married to my brother Adam. I am Catherine," she said again.

"Cat-a-wren."

"Yes. Are these your children?"

Tamiyah nodded. "Boy, Pamoac. Girl, Tonkee."

Catherine turned another smile on the children. "They are beautiful."

The four stood in awkward silence for a moment, then Catherine glanced down. "I found this patch of comfrey and wished to dig up some for my garden."

Tamiyah seemed to understand. "For many ills, good." She pointed the opposite direction. "Wighscan. Root for snakebite good."

"Oh, thank you for showing me! I was just telling our boy, Lad, to watch out for snakes. I should like some of that, as well. What did you call it? Wighscan?"

Tamiyah pointed out another herb she simply called "medicine plant." But Catherine recognized it as yarrow and knew that a tea made from either fresh or dried blossoms relieved fever, stomach aches, and a woman's monthly discomforts. She was especially glad to have some.

In the next half hour, Tamiyah showed Catherine where to find several other herbs, and Catherine gratefully dug up her new treasures. The children seemed to forget the grown-ups and began to laugh with one another as they played hide-and-seek amongst the trees and bushes.

When Catherine's basket was full of greenery and roots, she thanked Tamiyah again for showing her where to find the new plants.

"I have learned so much from you today, Tamiyah, how can I thank you?" Suddenly, an idea struck. "Your children seem to know a number of English words. Would you let them come to my house for a few hours each day to learn more? I have begun a Dame School for boys and girls. The children could all learn from one another!"

Tamiyah considered. "I think about. Maybe one day come."

"Splendid! My house is just —"

"I know where Cat-a-wren live."

"Oh. Well, then, I hope you'll let the children come. I would love to have them."

Over supper that evening, Catherine excitedly told Nancy about her chance meeting with Tamiyah and her little boy and girl in the forest. Of late, Lad had taken to filling his trencher and taking it outdoors to eat where it was cooler. Sometimes he sat on the doorstep; sometimes he sat on the ground in front of the lean-to in back, an area nicely shaded by tall trees. Catherine enjoyed having only herself and Nancy at the table in the evening, as they felt freer to openly converse with one another.

"Were the children . . . clothed?" Nancy asked.

Catherine laughed. "Partly."

"Goody Smithfield told me when Tamiyah first began bringin' her little ones to the village, the boy an' girl never wore anything. Someone finally told her that if she continued to bring 'em, they had to wear clothes. From what I understand, it's common practice for Indian children to wear nothing at all until they're 'round ten years old."

"I do recall seeing a number of little ones running around Werowocomoco without clothes."

"At least half a dozen Indian women come to Jamestown every day now," Nancy said. "I 'spect all the unwed men in town need help."

"I think it quite a good sign that the naturals feel comfortable enough to move freely amongst us. The races should mingle and learn from one another. I do hope Tamiyah will allow her children to come to school. It would benefit all the children."

Later that evening, while Nancy was busy outdoors washing the soiled trenchers, and Lad had gone off somewhere, Catherine busied herself indoors crushing the stems and flowers of a pennyroyal plant. She'd just begun to scatter the herb onto the straw at her feet when a long shadow fell across the floor.

She glanced up and was surprised to see Noah standing in the doorway.

"Noah, how nice to see you again."

"May I come in?"

"Certainly." She set the trencher on the table. "I was just spreading pennyroyal on the floor to ward off fleas."

He grinned. "Still the little naturalist, I see."

She brushed her palms on the skirt of her apron, untied it and let it fall to the bench. It was then she noticed he was carrying a small bundle. She gazed up at him, her eyes a question.

"I . . . wondered if I might leave this here?" He indicated the bundle. "It's a few things I'll need for my next expedition. No need to cart it home, then turn around and bring it back. If it's no trouble."

"No trouble at all," Catherine replied, pleased that his leaving something with her would mean she'd get to see him again when he came to retrieve it. "Where would you like to put it? In my chamber, or . . . in the loft, perhaps?"

Noah glanced furtively about. "Does the boy still sleep in the loft?"

"No, for now, he prefers sleeping in the lean-to. With Adam's horse no longer here, or a goat or chickens, the lean-to has rather become Lad's domain." She chuckled. "He says it's much cooler sleeping outdoors at night. I wouldn't be surprised if he wants to enclose it for winter."

Noah didn't appear interested in Lad's doings. "I'll just put it in the loft." Already he was climbing the ladder in the far corner. "No need for you to come up. I'll find a safe place."

When he returned, Catherine was anxious to take him outdoors and show him the new plants she'd found in the forest that day. On the way around the house, she told him about seeing Tamiyah and inviting her two children to her school.

"Do you think that a good idea?"

"I believe Deputy-Governor Argall will think so. Or at least, Yeardley would have. It was he who leapt on the idea of my school becoming a missionary academy to bring Indian children to Christianity."

Noah chuckled. "To my way of thinking, bringing the Indians to Christianity is not a likely prospect. The Indians believe in their own gods, with strange rituals and whatnot."

"I see. How did your trading with the Chickahominies go?" Catherine asked with genuine interest.

"Better than expected."

"They liked the rifles, then?"

"Indeed. Not a one asked about shot. The guns are all loaded, but they'll only fire once."

"When the Indians discover they need powder, are you not afraid they'll accuse you of misdealing?"

He shrugged. "I'll just say they broke them."

Catherine worried her lower lip. "Seems to me you are taking quite a risk, Noah. The Chickahominies could accuse you of being dishonest."

"And, you, my dear, are being naive." He sounded amused. "The Indians are almost never honest in their dealings with us. They go back on their word every day."

She abandoned the subject as they walked back around to the front of the house. Catherine heard Nancy moving about indoors, and she spotted Lad up the way with a couple of other boys.

A pang struck her. Noah stopping by these past two evenings had been a pleasant surprise. Although she knew his visits were odd occurrences, and she could not expect to see him every evening, talking so easily to him about the events of their day made it seem much like they were . . . well, married.

She looked up at him now, standing beside her in the lowering light. The long shadows falling across his face made him appear all the more handsome, even mysterious now that he was a man. The tug of attraction she'd always felt for Noah now made her skin tingle with an odd excitement. Suddenly, a need to tell him how she felt bubbled up like a hot spring inside her and before she knew it, the heartfelt words spilled from her lips.

"I've missed you terribly, Noah."

A smile softened the angles of his face. "And, I you, Catherine."

"If you had known I was coming, would you have waited for me?" she asked softly.

He laughed aloud. "How can you ask that of me when you married another?"

At the mention of her perfidy, she felt her cheeks burn with fire. "It was not my doing," she muttered irritably.

He took a step away from her, then looked back. "I don't think it's a good idea for Tamiyah's children to attend your school."

Before she had a chance to reply, he'd headed off down the path. This time he was not whistling.

CHAPTER 11

Two evenings later, Noah again appeared on Catherine's doorstep. He told her he had a trading expedition the following day and had come to retrieve the package he'd left in the loft.

As usual she was pleased to see him and stood breathlessly awaiting him on the ground as he climbed the ladder to the loft, then came back down.

"Do you have time to sit and visit a spell?" she asked, an expectant look on her face.

"Shall we sit outdoors?"

She nodded, and they each picked up one of the ladder-back chairs and carried it to the grassy patch in front. Nancy was just rounding the corner from the garden holding her apron up like a basket, it full of green beans and a few carrots she'd just picked.

Noah greeted her. "Looks as if you have tomorrow night's supper planned."

Both girls laughed.

"We don't have much to eat in our little garden," Catherine said, "but what's there is quite tasty."

Nancy went inside the house and Catherine and Noah sat down.

"How is your school?" Noah asked with interest.

"The children had a surprise today when Tamiyah's little boy and girl joined us."

"So. You decided to take them in. Did Tamiyah mention anything . . . particular about them?"

"No, nothing. She left the children and came back for them a few hours later. I was a bit apprehensive, but as it turned out, I had nothing to fear. The children took to one another at once. The little boy, Pamoac, is adorable. I could hardly keep from throwing my arms about him. The oddest thing is, he doesn't look at all like an Indian."

"Meaning?"

"He has light-brown hair, curly, like yours; and his features do not look . . . Indian."

Noah shrugged. "I've seen all manner of oddities amongst the Indians. A Paspahegh squaw has hair as red as yours. There are light-skinned Indians and Indians with skin as dark as Negroes. One Weanoc brave has sky-blue eyes. I admit that rather startled me the first time I saw him."

"I expect so. But what could account for such. . . ."

"You are indeed naive, Catherine," he teased. "The Spaniards and French were both here long before we came to these shores. Apparently there has been a good deal of . . . crossbreeding."

"Oh." She looked down. Obviously he thought that speaking so plainly about things of a carnal nature would not shock her since he believed she'd once been a married woman. But plain talk, even with Noah, from whom she'd never, until now, kept secrets, still put her to the blush. "I hadn't thought of that," she murmured. "At any rate, the children all got on very well together."

He said nothing else on the matter, but a moment later returned to it. "Have you heard anything . . . untoward about Tamiyah?"

"I have not discussed her with anyone, save you." She gazed at him quizzically. "Is there something I should know?"

As if considering how to begin, he pulled a small pipe from his pocket and began to fill it from a pouch of finely ground tobacco.

Catherine watched the process with interest as it was not something she'd observed many times before. "I'll get a pine-knot candle for you." She rose to her feet and disappeared inside.

When she came back out, she carefully handed the flaming reed to him. He lit the pipe and after a long, slow draw, exhaled the aromatic smoke.

"What does it taste like?" she asked curiously.

"Would you like to see for yourself?"

"No." She shook her head, then quickly said, "Yes, I believe I would."

He handed her the small pipe, and she drew in a tentative breath and instantly coughed it right back out. "Oh! I hadn't expected it to be so . . . smoky!"

He laughed. "I believe that's why it's called smoking."

Still coughing, she handed the pipe back to him. "I can see why King James calls tobacco hateful to the lungs."

"The king isn't trying to scratch out a living in this godforsaken land." His tone sounded scornful.

"Noah, hush! Someone might hear you!"

"Who would hear me? There are no king's soldiers here."

"Well, I shouldn't wish to see you hanged for treason."

"We are not in England, sweetheart, and

there's not been a hanging in Jamestown in over a year, not since Governor Dale left."

Catherine's eyes widened with horror. "What crime could a colonist commit so heinous it would result in his hanging?"

"According to Dale, any number of things. Thievery for one. Some years back, a man was caught stealing from the communal storehouse and hanged for his crime. Another, who'd only stolen a few kernels of corn, was tied to a tree and allowed to starve to death."

"Oh!" Catherine sucked in her breath.

"There are severe penalties for sins of a carnal nature, of course, and then there's desertion. I recall a few years ago a number of colonists thought they'd fare better living with the Indians. Dale had them captured and brought back. Two were hanged, a couple more burned at the stake, and one was shot to death. Back in oh-nine, the man who ate his wife was sentenced to death."

Catherine shuddered. "Adam told me about the starving time. I'm so glad you and he and Father waited until later to make the crossing."

Noah grew pensive. "I sometimes wish I'd never come."

"But you appear to be doing very well for yourself. You . . . married well."

Noah did not reply. After a pause, he said, "I expect I'd best be going. We leave at first light on the morrow."

"Which tribe are you trading with this time?"

"The Quiyoughcohanocks. Down river."

Rising to her feet, Catherine laughed. "However do you learn to pronounce those odd-sounding names? Or remember them?"

"It's in my best interests to remember tribal names."

What he did next took Catherine completely by surprise. In an easy, natural manner, he leaned over and kissed her lightly on the cheek. Startled, her hand flew to the place on her cheek where his lips had been. She was so taken aback she could not speak. Just stood staring at him as he sauntered away.

"Good night, my sweet Catherine."

Later that evening, as Catherine and Nancy puttered around the common room, Catherine was still thinking about the unexpected kiss, wondering what it meant.

"Nancy . . . ," she began, feeling she had to tell someone. "Noah kissed me."

Catherine had just placed three clean trenchers and spoons on the table in preparation for their breakfast the following morning. She walked back across the room and slid onto a chair opposite Nancy, who sat slicing carrots and green beans into a pot on her lap.

Without looking up, Nancy replied. "I should warn you, miss, there's been a bit o' talk about you and Noah."

Catherine looked puzzled. "What sort of talk? The house across the road is so far away, the identity of a man on our doorstep could hardly be discerned from such a distance. Noah never stays long. And when he is here, we are in plain sight in front of the house."

"And tonight, in plain sight in front of the house, he kissed you."

Catherine flinched. "I am certain it meant nothing. Just a simple parting of friends. What more could it be?"

Nancy cast a sidelong look at her companion. "What more indeed?"

Alone in her bed that night, Catherine reluctantly admitted that Nancy might be right. Noah's visits, however short, were happening now with greater regularity. Thoughts of seeing him, and looking forward to seeing him, constantly filled her mind. At odd moments throughout the long days, while she was with the children, walking in the forest, or tending her herb garden, she found herself thinking about Noah . . . thinking about things to tell him when next she saw him, wondering what he was doing, wondering if he was thinking about her.

And tonight, he kissed her.

In the darkness, she touched her cheek and imagined again the feel of his smooth lips on her skin. The gesture had surprised her so, that only now did she realize she hadn't said good-bye, or wished him luck with . . . whichever tribe he was off to see tomorrow.

She exhaled a troubled sigh. Life here was indeed hard. Having Noah come around was the one small pleasure she had at the end of a long, difficult day. Were his days equally as long and burdensome? Despite the terrible disappointment she'd suffered when she first came here, her love for Noah ran deep. The few precious moments she spent with him now meant a great deal to her. She could not bear to give that up. It appeared Noah felt the same. Still, that Nancy had said there had been talk about the two of them *did* disturb her. As a teacher, she knew she was expected to conduct herself in a respectable manner. To have her pupils pulled from her school because of her misconduct would be too shameful to bear. Yet, she knew she would continue to take the risk, for she could not give up her precious moments with Noah. Not now, not ever.

The following morning, with thoughts of Noah still uppermost in her mind, she was taken by surprise when only three of the English boys and one of the little girls showed up for classes. However, both Indian children were there bright and early, their little hands folded before them in eagerness for whatever the day might bring.

"Emily, has Patience fallen ill?" A good many cases of something called swamp fever had struck many colonists that summer, resulting in an alarming number of deaths. Catherine had been saddened to learn there were as many deaths in Jamestown during the sweltering summer months as there were during the harsh winter ones.

"No, Mistress Fielding. Her mama, and David's mama, too, don't want them. . . ." The little girl's eyes cut toward Pamoac and Tonkee. "It's because of . . . *them*," she said.

Catherine was stunned. The parents of two of her students had withdrawn their children from school because there were now Indian children present! And after Reverend Buck had announced from the pulpit that one of the primary goals of her school was to bring the Indian children to Christianity!

Though her breath quickened with anger, she managed to listen to the English children recite the letters of the alphabet. When the lesson was done, she moved straight into another one. Holding up one finger, then two fingers, she attempted to teach Pamoac and Tonkee their numbers, at least one through five, all the while her worry and agitation increasing over the consequences of the presence of the Indian children.

When it appeared Tonkee was having difficulty understanding what the word "three" meant, Pamoac finally turned to his sister and said, *"Nus!"*

In a flash of inspiration, Catherine decided the English children should learn to say their numbers in the Powhatan language. She motioned for Pamoac to come stand beside her. After a good bit of gesturing and repeating, she was rewarded by the appearance of the deep dimples in his cheeks when he finally understood what she wanted him to do.

Proudly holding up one finger, he said, *"Nekut."*

Catherine instructed her English pupils to repeat that word again and again, until Pamoac giggled with delight. Again, she could hardly resist hugging him.

After the children had mastered "nekut," she had Pamoac hold up two fingers and tell them what the Indian word for "two" was. At length, they had all learned to count one through five in both English and Powhatan.

"Tomorrow," she announced triumphantly, "we shall learn how to count in French."

Before the children left for the day, she called Emily aside and told her to be sure and tell Patience's mama what she had learned at school that day. "Tell her that when you grow up, you will be able to converse with your Indian neighbors, or if your mama ever has an Indian servant, you will be able to communicate with her, whereas Patience will not."

"I've no idea what the outcome of this will be," Catherine told Nancy that evening over their supper. "But you should have seen the proud look on Pamoac's little face when he realized he'd taught the English children to count in his language."

"He is a darling child," Nancy agreed, smiling. "But don't you wonder who his father might be?"

"I broached that very topic with Noah just last evening."

Nancy's gaze cut 'round. "What did he say?"

Catherine didn't look up from her trencher of green beans, carrots, and "scrapple" — a dish Goody Smithfield had told Nancy how to make from pork scraps and cornmeal. After the mixture dried, one sliced and fried it. Both girls and Lad, who had already gobbled up his share and disappeared, declared it quite tasty.

"He said there had been a good bit of crossbreeding with the Indians when the French and Spanish were here. They came to these shores long before we did, you know."

"Ah. Well, I've heard a few . . . interesting things about Tamiyah."

Catherine recalled that last evening Noah had been about to tell her something about Tamiyah, only they'd become distracted smoking his pipe. Perhaps it was of no consequence. She didn't care what anyone said about the Indian woman. She liked Tamiyah, and she loved her children, especially Pamoac. She had never been one to listen to gossip and she had no intention of doing so now. Furthermore, she was not about to let the prejudices of a few narrow-minded Jamestown citizens prevent her from teaching those two sweet Indian children how to read and write.

Finishing up her meal, she rose to her feet. "I don't care to hear what anyone says about Tamiyah." She walked briskly toward the doorway, carrying her soiled trencher and spoon, which she meant to dip in the bucket of freshwater outside. "And I care even less to know what people are saying about Noah and myself."

CHAPTER 12

August 1617

The following Sabbath was sunny and hot. Catherine, Nancy, and Lad set out for services a good half hour before the church bells summoned the settlers to worship. Catherine wished to arrive early in order to speak privately with Reverend Buck in regard to the matter of the English children no longer attending classes due to the presence of the Indian boy and girl.

She was disappointed, however, to find a notice posted on the meetinghouse door saying Reverend Buck had fallen ill, and an interim minister would be delivering the sermon.

"I do hope we will not lose Reverend Buck to the fever," Nancy murmured.

"I had no idea swamp fever was so very treacherous or prevalent. Thank the Lord our entire family has escaped it these last months."

They soon met up with Adam and Abigail and the Morgans, who came into Jamestown now via the river. When everyone was seated, the service commenced. As was customary before the reverend delivered his sermon, prayers were offered up for the family members of those colonists who'd succumbed to illness the past week. That only three Jamestown settlers had recently perished gave them all reason to rejoice.

"Perhaps the pestilence is near over," intoned Reverend Giles. "We thank our dear Lord for sparing so many of us during these blistering days of illness and fever."

Even though the church house shutters and front door stood wide open, many of those seated in the congregation began to fan themselves with their prayer books. Some used leaves plucked from the trees outdoors as fans. Apparently the whooshing sounds began to annoy the reverend, for as his face grew redder from the heat, his voice grew louder. Suddenly, he announced it was time for the closing song and prayer.

Following the final amen, he hurriedly said, "If there are no further announcements, I —"

From her pew, Catherine leapt to her feet, her quick action startling those around her. "I have something to say, Reverend Giles, if you please."

"Uh . . . indeed. And, you are?"

"Mistress Fielding, sir."

The congregation grew as silent as a tomb as all eyes focused on Catherine, everyone wondering what the attractive young lady had to say.

In somewhat of a daze herself over her boldness, Catherine skirted past both Abigail and Margaret Morgan and hastened to the platform so she might stand facing the parishioners.

"As you recall," she began, in a rather shaky voice, "when Reverend Buck first announced the opening of my . . . Missionary School, he and, at that time, Deputy-Governor Yeardley were both greatly pleased that there was now a place where Jamestown's boys and girls might learn to read and write. In addition" — her voice grew more steady as she progressed — "I also recall Reverend Buck mentioning that our close neighbors, the *Indians*" — she put special emphasis on that word — "were to be invited to send their children to learn as well from our Anglican Prayer Book. This week, I welcomed my first Indian pupils, a boy and a girl."

A rustling noise from the back of the building interrupted Catherine.

"Who come to school naked!" cried a woman.

Amidst gasps of alarm, Catherine recognized little Patience Riverton's mother.

"That is not entirely true, Goodwife Riverton. The boy is naked only from the waist up and the girl is quite properly clothed. However, if the child's nakedness, as you call it, is your only concern, then may I appeal to the generous natures of the good citizens of Jamestown for the donation of a shirt for a bright little boy who has already learned nearly all his ABC's and has taught my other pupils to count in his native tongue." She paused, and when no one said a word, she added, "My lesson plans for next week include the memorizing of the Ten Commandments."

Unable to think of anything further to say, she turned toward the reverend, who was staring dumbfounded at her from behind the pulpit.

"That is all I have to say, sir."

"Very well, then." When she'd left the platform and Reverend Giles had regained his composure, he addressed the congregation. "As Mistress Fielding has so eloquently reminded us, the Indians are our neighbors, and as we have been taught to love our neighbors as ourselves, might I inquire who amongst you has a small boy's shirt you'd be willing to donate to . . . uh, Mistress Fielding's pupil?"

"I daresay you set the colony on its ear this morning, sis," Adam said as the family stood clustered together on the green.

Catherine thrust her chin up. "That, dear brother, was precisely my intention."

"How many shirts were donated?" Abigail asked, a grin of amusement on her face, rounder now as her pregnancy progressed.

"Three. Lad is on his way even now to collect them."

"Which reminds me," Adam said, "I mean to have a talk with Lad. I hope he has done as I asked and added another layer of rushes to your roof."

"No." Catherine sighed. "He has not. Truth to tell, Lad has become somewhat unruly of late, going off on his own for long periods. I sometimes haven't a clue where he is."

"I feared it might come to that. As soon as tobacco cutting is done, I'll have a talk with him."

"Thank you, Adam." Catherine glanced around and realized then that not only was Lad not there, but neither was Nancy. However, spotting Noah and his little wife

210

Charity conversing with her parents a few yards away, Catherine's breath caught in her throat. Noah was looking straight at her. Their eyes locked for a long moment before Catherine grew flustered and looked away.

Just then, Nancy returned accompanied by two young men, neither of whom Catherine recognized.

"Catherine," Nancy began in a confident tone, which startled Catherine as it was the first time Nancy had ever used her given name in public without "miss" attached to it. "I should like to introduce you to two of Jamestown's newest colonists. This," she said, indicating the taller of the men, who had nut-brown hair and smiling brown eyes, "is Jack Lancaster. And this," she said, turning to the other fellow, who had wavy black hair and blue eyes, "is Victor Covington. They arrived a few months ago on the *George*."

Before Catherine said a single word, she cast a quick glance toward Noah to see if he might still be looking her way. Noting that he was, a ripple of pleasure coursed through her. Holding her auburn head at a tilt, she smiled sweetly. "Welcome to Jamestown, gentlemen. I am very happy to meet both of you."

The men nodded but Victor edged closer

to her. "So, you are Jamestown's Dame Teacher?"

"Yes, I am." He had a pleasant smile and was really quite handsome. Though not as tall and lean as Jack, he stood a good head and shoulders taller than she and had a sturdy, muscular build.

Adam stepped up to introduce himself and to present his wife and the Morgans to the men. "You fellows must be settled in by now."

"Indeed, we built a cottage down by the river." Jack jabbed a thumb over one shoulder.

"And cleared a piece of land to plant a few rows of corn," Victor added. "Might be too late in the season for a decent crop, but. . . ."

"Not necessarily." Adam shook his head. "If the heat holds, which it easily could on into October, ye'll likely get a bushel or more for your efforts. Which will satisfy the governor's mandate. We're cutting tobacco leaves in my fields now. Men are working into the night to hang what they cut during the day. Could take us another month or so. I could use some help if ye'd be interested."

Both men brightened and in seconds a deal was struck.

When the sunshine became too hot on their backs, her brother and his wife turned to go. But not before Catherine overheard Margaret telling Abigail she thought it was simply wonderful that little Charity Colton was again with child.

A pang of jealousy shot through Catherine. Her blood pounded against her temples, and she became so upset and preoccupied over the news she was hardly aware when the two men fell into step beside her and Nancy as they all set off for home.

Though she chastised herself for having such impure thoughts, and although she knew she had no right to begrudge Noah pleasure in his marriage, she had thought, nay, *hoped,* that perhaps he had grown tired of his child-bride, and perhaps that was why he'd been coming to see her. Obviously that was not the case.

Thinking over the events of the day as she lay in bed that night, she realized she didn't recall anything anyone said on the walk home that afternoon. She knew she was being silly, but she hoped Noah had at least seen the gentlemen walking beside her and Nancy.

The following morning, although she was still upset over the news regarding Charity,

Catherine knew a moment's satisfaction when not only little Patience Riverton returned to school, but David Shores also showed up.

She watched for Tamiyah and hurried out to meet her before her children entered the house. Handing the Indian woman two of the three shirts that had been donated after Sabbath services, she asked that Pamoac be allowed to wear a shirt when he came to school. Without a word, the Indian woman draped the somewhat faded garment over the boy's small shoulders, and he shrugged into it, turning a bright smile on Catherine as she bent to fasten the buttons. Catherine had decided to hold onto the other one in case another Indian boy showed up for classes one day and might need it.

That night over their evening meal, Nancy surprised Catherine by mentioning a supper that the two of them would be hosting for Jack Lancaster and Victor Covington on Wednesday night.

Catherine looked quizzical. "When did this come about?"

"Ye don't recall?" Nancy returned Catherine's quizzical look. "Yesterday, just before the gentlemen departed, I turned to you and asked if Wednesday would suit, and you said, 'Certainly.' Ye don't recall?" she asked again.

Catherine sighed. "Forgive me, Nancy. I expect I was still thinking about what had happened at services. The loss of two of my students had quite overset me. But" — she smiled — "it has all worked out splendidly. So, we invited the gentlemen to dinner, and they agreed to come, did they?"

"Indeed." Nancy's pleasure was evident. "They said they'd be delighted. I thought I'd prepare scrapple again, since we all liked it so well. And for dessert, if ye don't mind, I'd like to use the last of the dried apples and pears for a nice apple cobbler. I don't think the addition of pears will spoil the taste, do you?"

Again Catherine wasn't listening. When she realized Nancy had asked her another question, she said, "I'm certain whatever you prepare will be well-received, Nancy. You've become quite an accomplished cook."

Nancy appeared to warm to the compliment. "I am very happy here, Catherine." She grinned. "You see, I've even learned to address ye by yer given name."

Catherine smiled. "I daresay it's about time."

They laughed and, rising from the table,

picked up their soiled wooden bowls and spoons and took them outdoors to wash in the bucket of freshwater Lad had set by the doorstep for that very purpose. He, by now, was nowhere to be seen.

On Wednesday evening, Victor and Jack arrived just as Nancy was pulling the long-handled griddle out of the new fireplace oven that the deputy-governor's men had constructed. Sitting atop the griddle was Nancy's hot apple cobbler.

"My, that smells delicious," said Jack, reaching to take the contraption from Nancy's hands before the sizzling cobbler slid into the ashes. "Where shall I set it?"

Nancy pointed to one of the empty board tables at the far end of the room. On another, she had laid out four clean trenchers, spoons, and the platter containing the fried scrapple. A gouged-out gourd contained steamed corn kernels and another held hot greens and bacon bits.

Hearing voices, Catherine entered the common room from her bedchamber. She had just come in from weeding her herb garden and needed to tidy up before the gentlemen arrived. She greeted the men, thinking they looked fresh in their white linen shirts, puffed breeches, dark hose, and buckled shoes.

She and Victor slid onto one of the backless benches with Nancy and Jack on the opposite side. In moments, Lad burst into the house. "Smells good in here! What'd ye fix tonight, Nan?"

Nancy picked up a trencher at her elbow, which she'd already filled with scrapple and corn and handed it to him. "Here's your supper, Lad. Take it out to the lean-to. As ye can see, Mistress Fielding and I have guests."

Catherine smothered a grin, thinking Nancy had the situation well in hand.

Lad took the trencher, but continued to cast longing looks at the apple cobbler, the aroma of which was making everyone's mouth water. "But . . ." — he glanced down at his plate — "where's m' . . . what about the — ?"

"If there's any left after we've eaten, ye may have a piece. Scoot now."

Catherine laughed aloud as Lad grudgingly obeyed. "You've got the boy better trained than Adam and Abigail ever did."

"He needs a strong hand, that one."

The four of them fell to talking about one thing and another, the men telling tales of their crossing, which was still fresh in their minds, and Nancy and Catherine chiming

217

in with reminiscences of their own shipboard journey.

When the meal concluded, they decided to continue their conversation outdoors where it was considerably cooler. They were all laughing aloud at a tale Victor was telling when Catherine looked up and saw Noah approaching.

She rose to her feet as he turned into the short path that led to her front door. "Excuse me, I'll just be a moment," she murmured.

Noah walked straight into the house as if he lived there, getting Catherine's back up. That he was carrying a small bundle told her why he had come and where he was headed.

"You might have waited to be invited in," she said peevishly, following him into the house.

He had already gained the ladder. "I won't bother you for long, sweetheart. Just need to —" The rest of his words were lost as he reached the loft and stepped onto the loose floorboards there.

Catherine was waiting for him when he came back down, both hands parked on her hips. "So, I hear your little wife is again with child." Her auburn head sat at a tilt.

"Indeed. Although I fail to see where that

is any of your concern."

Her lips thinned with annoyance. Despite her anger over the fact that he'd not given up being with his wife in *that* way, she still found him attractive to a fault. Her nostrils flared as she glared up at him.

His long gaze strayed beyond her to the soiled dishes littering the board table. "Did those two jackanapes eat supper with you and Nancy?"

"They are not jackanapes!"

"Well, they've no business here that I can see."

"And that is none of your concern!"

"I don't want you associating with —"

"I will associate with whomever I please!" she retorted.

Holding her angry gaze, he said nothing more; instead, he took a step closer to her and, sliding one strong arm around her trim waist, pulled her to him. His free hand reached to cup the back of her head as his mouth came down hard on hers, his tongue parting her lips to roughly explore the inside of her mouth.

Catherine's breath quickened as fire shot through her veins. She'd been kissed before by Noah, but not like this! She'd been only twelve then. Now, she wanted only to melt into his embrace and for this delicious moment never to end. But, it had to end! She pushed against his strong chest with both fists until at last he flung her from him.

His smoldering gaze bored into hers as his own breath came in ragged gasps. "You belong to me, Catherine, and don't you forget it."

He stalked from the house and, without addressing the other three people seated near the doorway, strode off down the dusty road.

Catherine stood rooted to the spot where she stood, her nostrils a-flare, her breasts rising and falling with pent-up rage and desire.

For the rest of that evening, she did not hear a single word Victor or anyone else said. Noah's kiss had possessed her very soul. A fact that terrified her.

When the men finally got up to leave, she and Nancy returned indoors to straighten up.

"Is something troubling you, Catherine? You've not been yourself since Noah was here."

Catherine willed herself to remain calm. With a shaky smile, she said, "I have decided I shall not see Noah Colton again."

CHAPTER 13

A decision she knew she could not keep. The next time Noah stopped by, she was glad both Nancy and Lad were home. He did not stay long and he did not say much. He merely climbed the ladder to the loft, retrieved the bundle he'd hidden there and, after speaking only a few curt words to Catherine, left.

However, one night during the following week, he reappeared. This time, Nancy and Jack had just quitted the house for a walk. Lad was up the street playing a rowdy game on the green with two other boys.

"So, we are alone," Noah said, a smoldering gaze pinning her.

Catherine's breath grew ragged. Despite her resolve to not see Noah again, with all her heart she knew the longing she felt for him matched what he felt for her. Apprehension over what might happen between them had kept her stomach tied in knots for days.

She'd never lain with a man before but something told her that was all about to change. Fidgeting with the frayed hem of her apron, her anxious gaze fluttered down, then up, then back down again.

Her nervousness increased when, without taking his determined gaze from her, he walked back to the front door and shut it. When he threw the bolt, Catherine opened her mouth to protest, but her fitful breath prevented words from coming out. She also said nothing when he scooped up her hand and led her into the chamber where she slept. And latched that door.

Apprehension arose within Catherine, but she quickly thrust it aside. Since Noah's kiss the other night, she'd been on fire for him. More than anything, she wished to be alone with him, at least once. Since the day as children when they'd pledged their love to one another, she'd thought of herself as his wife. She did belong to him. She always had. She always would. He loved her as deeply as she loved him, else why did he keep coming to see her, *after* he'd married another?

Prepared to give herself to him fully, Catherine stood submissively beside her bed, gazing adoringly up at the man she loved with all her heart.

"There's no one here but us, Catherine." His tone was seductive.

Her lashes fluttered nervously against her flushed cheeks. "It's . . . almost as if it were meant to be."

"My thoughts exactly." He grinned wickedly.

Though she knew she could never have him all to herself, this moment may never come again. She smiled as he reached to unlace her bodice and flung it to the floor. He untied the strings at the neck of her blouse and with two fingers loosened the gathers. When he shoved the thin fabric from her shoulders, an involuntary purr of pleasure escaped her. Arching her back, she thrust her bare breasts upward.

His gaze dropped to devour them with his eyes. Lowering his head he began to trace slow, sensuous circles around each pink nipple with his tongue, leaving a trail of cool wetness on her skin.

"Oh-h-h," she murmured, her breasts rising and falling as tingles of delight began to course through her.

"You like that, do you?" Taking one nipple in his mouth, he licked it to hardness.

"Oh-h, Noah." The delicious sensations swirling within her drove all reason from her mind.

She reached to fumble with the cords at the neck of his shirt. When she was unable to undo them, he did so, then yanked the shirt over his head and tossed it aside. They stood before one another naked now from the waist up. When he pulled her against his bare chest, she melted into his embrace, standing on tiptoe to twine her arms around his neck. Years and years of pent-up longing for Noah brought tears of joy to her eyes.

"Oh, Noah," she breathed. "I have waited so very long for this moment."

He reached behind her back to unfasten her skirt, and she obediently stepped from it and her petticoat. She kicked off her shoes and, still looking worshipfully up at him, slid her stockings down and discarded them. Though he was gazing deeply into her eyes, his hands were busy removing his breeches and tossing them and his own footwear aside. They were both completely unclothed now. His arousal was complete, and when he again pulled her to him, she was acutely aware of that hard part of his body pressed intimately against her belly. Molding her soft flesh to his muscled hardness, the longing inside her intensified.

"Noah, please," she gasped, "take me now."

He bent to bury his face in the tangled

mass of her copper-colored curls. "In a moment, my sweet." His breath was raspy with desire. "I'm as hungry for you as you are for me."

Picking her up, he laid her gently on the bed. Lowering his body over hers, he began to rub his lean hips and his hardness against and around and between her bare thighs. Arching her back, Catherine wrapped her legs around him, aware of the prickly feel of the hair on his chest as it grazed against her soft skin. For a girl who had never been with a man before, she marveled at how easily the motions of lovemaking came to her.

His fingers found the moist place between her legs, and lifting himself up and off her a bit, he began to slowly massage her there, a finger going around and around and around, then, cupping that intimate part of her completely with the palm of one hand.

"Oh-h-h," she moaned. Never in all her life had she felt anything so exquisite. How desperately she loved this man!

"You want me?" When she made no reply, he asked again, "Do you want me, Catherine?"

She tightened her arms around his neck. "Oh, Noah, yes! Yes, I want you. More than life itself!" Her eyes squeezed shut as gasps of pure pleasure escaped her.

Abruptly, he pulled away. "Then, this is how I shall leave you," he said coldly.

Stunned, her eyes sprang open. He clambered off the bed and stood gazing coolly down at her as she lay panting before him. The question in her eyes turned to hurt as she watched him reach for his breeches and put them on. *What was he doing?*

After he'd pulled his shirt over his head, he sat down on the bed to draw on his hose and shoes. His blue eyes were hard as he looked at her. "If I ever catch you with another man, Catherine" — his eyes narrowed — "the bastard will not live to see another day."

She stared at him with disbelief. "What . . . what are you saying? I thought you . . . loved me. I thought you wanted to —"

Fully clothed now, he roughly pulled her into his arms and buried his face in the tangled mass of her auburn hair. "I will make love to you one day. Just not tonight. Tonight, I merely wanted you to know how much you want me. If another man touches you, I know you won't be thinking of him, you'll be thinking of me, you'll be wanting me. Now, put your clothes on, sweetheart, and walk with me to the street. Darkness has not yet fallen. If anyone saw me come in, I want them to see me leave . . . with you standing beside me, fully clothed."

Stunned into submission, Catherine wordlessly obeyed. She walked with him to the street as he'd ordered but she was far too overset to speak.

Long, long into that night, she lay awake, still thinking about what had *not* happened between them. It was clear that Noah was jealous of Victor. The clergyman in London who had spoken with her and Lucinda had referred to God as being jealous, did that mean love was akin to jealousy? Was Noah's jealousy and then his refusal to complete the act they both so ardently desired yet one more way he was showing her he truly cared? But, it seemed so cruel! He knew how much she loved him, how desperately she wished to make love with him; why had he refused? Why?

Perhaps because there was always the possibility she could conceive his child. A fact she could never hide in a township as small as Jamestown. Surely that was it. Noah did love her, but he was far too honorable a man to break his marriage vows and risk bringing shame upon her. And she could not fault him for that.

And yet, she also could not halt the tears

of anguish that ran down her cheeks and melted into the pillow. It had been sheer agony to have him wrenched from her at the height of their passion. Every part of her body still ached for him. Seeing Noah these past weeks had served only to open the horrible wound she'd felt the day she arrived in Jamestown and learned he had married. Now, once again, her emotions felt tortured and raw.

How, how, how was she to get through each and every long, dreary day now . . . when all she truly wanted was to be with Noah Colton forevermore?

CHAPTER 14

Several hours later, Catherine was awakened from a troubled sleep by a scratching noise that seemed to be coming from outside her window. Sitting up, she cocked her head to listen just as the noise sounded again. Coming more fully awake, she slipped from her bed and crept across the room to peek out. And drew back with alarm when in the dim glow of moonlight she saw what appeared to be a figure pressed against the outside wall of the house.

"Catherine, it's me, let me in!"

She thrust her head out the small opening. "Noah?"

"Let me in," came his whispered reply.

Moments later, he was standing in her room, hurriedly peeling off his clothes. "I couldn't sleep for thinking of you. I must have you."

Catherine's heart leapt with joy as she hastily tore off her night rail, the thrill of seeing him again so intense there was no room left in her mind for recriminations. Winding her arms around his neck, for the second time that night she drew him into her bed. "I am so glad you came back, my darling. I thought I would die from wanting you."

"My beautiful Catherine," he murmured between kisses, "I am yours, and you are mine. Naught can change that."

Wave after wave of pleasure washed over her as his hands skimmed over the curves and valleys of her body. He kissed her eyes, her lips, her neck, her breasts. She gave herself up to each delightful sensation though a part of her wished he might go slower so she could savor each moment to the fullest. In only minutes, he rolled on top of her and she knew he meant to enter her.

"Noah," she said with some urgency. She must tell him she'd never lain with a man before. "Noah, I've never. . . . *Oh-h!*"

But he had already thrust inside her, the knife-like pain so sharp it caused a cry of alarm to escape her. Her stomach muscles clenched as the wrenching pain replaced every ounce of pleasure she'd been feeling. "Noah, *please,* I —"

"Be still, Cat, we mustn't be heard."

His thrusting motions quickened. In seconds, he'd reached the apex of his own pleasure, and with a low moan, his movements ceased, and he fell limp upon her, a sheen of perspiration covering his back and chest.

Though she had not shared with him that final moment of their joining, her arms were still wrapped around him, and she was keenly aware of his hardness still buried deep within her. She was also keenly aware of the pain smarting between her legs and the pool of moisture that had spilled onto the bed linen. She wondered if it was his seed or her own blood that had flowed when his impatient thrusts pierced her maidenhead.

But she said nothing. His longing for her had been so great he had not heard her when she tried to speak of her virginity, but it didn't matter. She loved him, and she truly belonged to him now, and he to her.

Suddenly his weight atop her seemed to grow heavier. It surprised her when his breathing deepened, and he became as limp as a rag. Had he fallen asleep?

"Noah," she whispered, her lips close to his ear.

He didn't move.

She tried to squirm from beneath him,

but atop her, he was far too heavy. "Noah," she said, a bit louder. "You are hurting me."

"Hmmm," came a guttural noise from his throat.

Squirming in earnest now, her struggle to extricate herself from beneath him finally woke him. At once, he was alert.

"I have to go." He sprang to his feet and in the darkness began to fumble on the floor for his shirt and breeches.

Catherine sat up, hurt in her eyes and her tone. "It won't be daylight for hours, Noah. Please stay a bit longer."

He hopped on one foot as he pulled his hose onto the other. "I have to go," he said insistently. "It wouldn't do for me to be seen here at this hour."

Fighting back a sob, Catherine watched from the bed as he buttoned his breeches, the long tangled locks of her hair the only covering on her body.

While tying the cords at the throat of his shirt, he bent to drop a quick kiss on her forehead. "Don't worry, Cat. I'll come back again soon."

She scrambled to her feet and hurriedly pulled on her night rail, hoping for at least one last embrace before he departed, but he had already quit the room. By the time she darted after him into the adjoining chamber, he was gone, leaving the door standing ajar behind him.

Aware of the scratchy feel of the straw beneath her bare feet, Catherine raced to the door after him, but caught only a glimpse of his shadowy form as he disappeared into the night.

With a disappointed sigh, she pulled the door shut and, as quietly as she could, dropped the latch and bolted it. Her shoulders sagged as she slowly returned to bed, acutely aware of how empty and alone she felt.

Tears of despair overtook her as she realized that her previous rationale over Noah being too honorable to break his marriage vows now seemed foolish. But she could not lay all the blame for her hurt and disappointment at his feet. She should have made a more valiant effort to tell him she was a virgin. As it was he thought her a widow and therefore as experienced as he beneath the bedcovers.

The truth was, she had no idea what to expect in the bedchamber, but suddenly she recalled the words of the clergyman who'd spoken with her and Lucinda. With a somewhat red face, the man had haltingly said that to obtain harmony in the bedchamber often required a good bit of . . . practice;

that due to inexperience, a husband and wife must learn how to pleasure the other. If she had told Noah the truth, she was certain he would have taken greater care not to cause her pain.

Thoughts of the clergyman also made her realize that she and Noah had indeed committed a serious crime. He was now an adulterer, and she a fornicator. Men were hanged for committing adultery. She did not know what would happen to her, except if their crime were uncovered, she'd be declared unfit to become any man's wife. Fear and guilt spread through her like a fire gone out of control.

She buried her face in her pillow as tears of shame and remorse streamed down her cheeks. Just as painful was the fact that he had not held her close afterwards, had not kissed her again, not properly — for the quick peck on her forehead didn't count. Did his haste to leave mean that . . . no, no; it did not mean that he did not love her. It meant that he, too, knew they had committed a crime; that if he lingered, their sin might be uncovered, and they could both be publicly shamed and severely punished.

Suddenly she recalled with horror something else the reverend had said, that more than one father whose daughter had come to the marriage bed unchaste had slit his daughter's throat in shame! Oh! How grateful she was that neither of her parents would ever know of her shame. Burying her face in her pillow, she sobbed out her sorrow, her pain, her confusion, her regret.

Much, much later, she climbed out of bed and moved silently across the room to slide the window covering shut, and to fasten the bolt. She could not undo what had happened tonight, but she solemnly vowed it would never, *ever* happen again.

The next morning, after Lad headed to the stream for water, Nancy gazed across the board table at Catherine, staring into her bowl of corn mush, cold now as she'd eaten no more than a spoonful.

"I . . . heard noises last night," Nancy said quietly.

Catherine didn't look up. She knew this moment was coming and she had no intention of keeping secrets from Nancy. "Noah was here. Perhaps you . . . heard him come in, or . . . leave. He did not stay long."

"Ah. I thought the disturbance came from . . . in here." Her tone was not the least accusing.

Nancy's kindness caused tears of remorse to again well in Catherine's eyes. When her anguish became an all-out sob, she buried her face in her hands. "Oh, Nancy, I've done something terrible."

Nancy moved from her side of the table to slide onto the bench beside Catherine. Putting an arm around her friend's shoulders, she drew her close. "Did he . . . force you?"

"No." Catherine laid her head on the older girl's shoulder, relishing the comfort she so desperately craved. "I wished it as much as he. I . . . made only a feeble attempt to tell him . . . he would have been gentler with me if he had known the whole truth. I should have told him that day in the woods that I have never been married, that I am *not* a widow. Noah is not a cruel man, he would not have taken me if he had known the whole truth."

She sniffed back her tears and sat up. "He is jealous of my friendship with Victor. But . . . I am also jealous of Charity. I clung to my silly falsehood about having been married, because I wished to hurt Noah the same way he had hurt me."

Nancy's tone softened. "But he does have a wife, Catherine. And ye will only be hurt further if ye continue to see him."

Catherine thrust her chin up with firm resolve. "I shall never see him again. Not ever."

"There's a good girl." Nancy grinned as she rose to clear the table. "Although you did say the selfsame thing last week."

"But I mean it this time." She touched Nancy's arm. "You'll not tell anyone, will you, Nan?"

The older girl shook her head. "Ye've done such a great deal for me, Catherine, I would never betray you." Nancy ceased gathering up the soiled utensils and gazed at her friend. "Without you, I would still be a serving wench in a rich man's house, hauling coal up and down them back stairs till my bones ached from weariness. Then when I thought my back would break in two, her ladyship'd want hot water for her bath. Now, I have a new life. I am my own person. I, too, can marry one day and have my own home. You have made all that possible for me. Never fear for one instant that I would betray you."

"I do trust you, Nancy. I did not mean to imply —" Catherine tamped down her fear and confusion. "I will always love Noah, but . . . what happened between us was wrong. I-I just hope he —" Tears again swam in her eyes. "Oh, Nancy, what will I do if he got a babe on me?"

Nancy exhaled a sigh. "We will manage. But, surely you know of some posset or root you could chew on that would make it go away."

"Oh!" Catherine sat up straighter. "Why did I not think of that?"

"Because you are distraught, pea-goose."

Catherine grinned sheepishly. "I am being a silly goose." Swiping at the tears still glistening on her lashes, she scrambled to her feet. "I'd best get myself together before the children arrive for their lessons." She reached to help Nancy gather up the rest of the soiled things. "Classes will be over this week. Harvest is upon us, and I, for one, will be glad to have the house to ourselves for a spell."

The subject of Catherine's transgression came up again that night after Lad had quitted the house, and she and Nancy were once again alone. Although evenings in Jamestown were at last becoming cooler, Lad still preferred to bed down in the lean-to. Nancy was busy banking the fire for the night while Catherine folded the last of the clean linens they'd earlier brought in from the shrubbery.

Her task completed, Nancy propped the straw broom in a corner of the room far enough away from the hearth that it would not catch fire. Wiping her hands on her apron, she turned to Catherine.

"I hope you won't think I'm speaking out of turn, but I think I may have a solution to your problem."

Catherine's lips pursed. "And which problem would that be?" All day, she'd stewed over the fix she'd got herself into. If it turned out she were with child, she knew she could never bring herself to destroy it. But, what other choice did she have? She couldn't have it, not here, not in Jamestown. She'd considered the possibility of returning to London, but what good would that do? She couldn't support herself *and* a babe there. And she refused to throw herself again on the mercy of the Montcriefs. Because no viable answer had come to mind, her only hope was that she had not been fertile last night. But that did not solve her other problem: what to do the next time Noah came around hot to bed her? Despite her staunch resolve to the contrary, she was terrified she'd be as unable to refuse him the next time as she had been last night. Her stomach was still tied in knots, as it had been all day.

Nancy drew up a chair and sank wearily into it. "Do come and sit down, Mistress Fielding."

Catherine grimaced. "My, it appears I'm

to be taken to task over something." Still, she gladly abandoned the pile of rumpled linens to join her friend by the fire.

"I've been thinking," Nancy said, no longer the least bit timid around Catherine. "And I believe the answer to your problem is quite clear."

Catherine squirmed. She knew that whatever Nancy said was well meant, and that, as a friend, she wished only to help.

"It is time ye married." She held up a hand as if to forestall the many objections she believed would be forthcoming. "It would solve all your problems."

Catherine chewed fretfully on her lower lip. "Go on."

Nancy looked down, her cheeks flushed. "As ye well know, everyone here believes ye to be a widow —"

"Oh-h-h," Catherine groaned. "My pesky falsehood again. I never meant any harm when I gave Mr. Rolfe a wrong name. I was simply terrified that Lord Montcrief would discover me missing and guess where I'd gone. He would have dragged me back, and you, too, sure as we're sitting here!"

"Indeed, he would have," Nancy agreed.

The two had never fully discussed the matter, though Catherine was curious as to what Nancy knew of Lord Montcrief's nature. "Did you know about the marriage contract?"

Nancy laughed. "Servants know ever'thin'. I told you the night we left that I knew how unhappy you were with the Montcriefs. Believe me, I quite understand yer reasons for wantin' to leave his high-and-mighty lordship. But . . . as I was saying, since the whole of Jamestown thinks ye're a widow, the fact that ye are no longer —" Her gaze dropped to her lap. "What I mean is —"

Catherine brightened. "My husband will not expect me to be chaste! I hadn't thought of that!"

Nancy shrugged. "Seems logical. For fear of punishment, Noah will not say anything about what he's done and if you say nothing, then —"

"No one's to know!"

"If the truth came out," Nancy said gravely, "there'd be serious consequences . . . for both of you."

Catherine sighed. "My deceptions seem to be piling one on top of another. It all began with such a small misdeed and look where it's led." She paused. "If I'd told Noah the truth, I'm certain he would not have. . . . Yet, on the other hand, if I had told the whole truth when I arrived here, oh-h-h —" Her eyes squeezed shut as she shook her head. "So much has happened. And so many things would have been different if I'd only told the truth."

"To be fair, a good bit of the blame is mine. It was I who told your brother ye'd been widowed and had come to the New World to make a fresh start."

"But I said nothing to the contrary. And I cannot confess to a falsehood at this late date, for that would brand me a liar and bring an end to my school. Who would trust a liar to teach their children?"

"It has become complicated. But I cannot fault you, Catherine. How could I when I am as guilty as you? It was I who nabbed the lemons." She grinned. "In England I'd 'a been hanged for that."

"In the New World, you'd have been shot to death! We are both criminals." After a pause, Catherine asked, "What do you suppose happened when the Montcriefs discovered us missing?"

Nancy shrugged. "In your case, I expect the authorities fished some poor girl out of the Thames and convinced his nibs it was you. Me? I just became one more runaway servin' wench what got tired of being tol' what to do."

"You are quite clever, Nancy Mills. The plain and simple answer to my dilemma is indeed to get myself a husband. It would change my surname yet again, though by an honest means this time. By the by, is Mills truly your name?"

Nancy's gray eyes became mischievous, and for answer, she simply turned both palms upward.

"You slyboots." Catherine laughed.

Nancy joined in. "Well, I couldn't risk his nibs comin' after me either! Though I doubt he would; runaway servants are a common lot."

Catherine sighed. "We're a pair, we are. If the truth were known, there's likely not a man around who'd have either of us."

"You could marry any man you choose!" Nancy protested. "You are the prettiest girl in Jamestown, nay, in all the New World!"

"I've seen many a young man tip his cap at you!"

Nancy blushed. "Perhaps, but there's only one I'd care to share my bed with."

"Jack?"

"I rather think he will ask me one day."

"What is stopping him now?"

"He says he wouldna' ask me to live in that rude hut he and Victor built down by the river. They call it a cottage, but it's only a bark hut and will likely blow over come the next high wind."

"I see no reason why you and Jack could not live here."

Nancy's eyes widened. "You mean it truly?"

"Of course, I do! Jack is working with Adam now. The walk would be no longer from here to the plantation than it is from where he and Victor live. And by water, even quicker."

"Oh, my. I don't know what to say. I don't know that he'd agree to it, but . . . he might, if it is what I want."

"Well, it seems a good plan to me," Catherine concluded. "Now, we have settled your problem, what about mine? Whom shall I marry?"

"Victor Covington is top-over-tail in love with you. But, he thinks ye don't care a fig for him."

"I think Victor is a very nice man. He is kind and caring and . . . exactly the sort of man any girl would be proud to marry."

Catherine thought the notion over. Suddenly it all made perfect sense. In her heart, she would always love Noah Colton, nothing would change that, but she could plainly see that the only way to remove the temptation he presented was for her to wed another man. She liked Victor well enough. She was not in love with him, but she did not believe

244

she would ever be in love with anyone save Noah, so what did it matter whom she married?

At length, she said, "I expect I shall just have to make Victor Covington think otherwise, shan't I? But, don't put a bug in his ear, Nancy. I would like Victor to think our marrying is his idea."

"I won't say a word. But if ye are with child, the sooner ye let Victor know ye'd be receptive to his suit, the better."

"Oh-h," Catherine groaned, there was still that to worry about.

CHAPTER 15

When Deputy-Governor Argall decreed that Jamestown's fife-and-drum corps would resume weekly drill practice as had formerly been their habit, Catherine and Nancy, along with most colonists, walked into the fort to watch the colorful spectacle. Some corpsmen wore full armor; others wore only breastplates over their linen shirts. Most sported helmets with bright red plumes. Nearly every man carried a fowling piece or musket. To conserve shot, the guns were never fired, but, nonetheless, the sound of the fife and the beat of the drums were thrilling to hear.

Catherine's eyes scanned the military lines for Noah's tall form, but not seeing him, she reminded herself that searching out Noah was no longer a concern. That morning she and Nancy had prepared a surprise for the two men they had come especially to see. Nancy carried the cloth bundle filled with crisp apples, fresh rye bread, and the last jug of spiced ale left in the loft.

When the corps was dismissed, the girls approached Jack and Victor as the men were shrugging out of their heavy breastplates and removing their helmets. Delighted to see the ladies, the four set out to walk the short distance to the men's hut. After they'd deposited their armor, the foursome walked along the river's edge in search of a shady spot for their picnic.

Settled on the grass, Nancy handed out the meager but tasty offerings. They passed the jug of ale between them till every last drop was gone. By then, they all felt in a good humor.

Making an effort to draw Victor out, Catherine learned he hailed from Shropshire where a few years ago, he'd taken over his father's mill. When the mill burned to the ground and his father was killed in the fire, Victor joined up with his chum Jack Lancaster, who was headed for the New World to seek his fortune.

"Rumor had it," said Victor a bit sheepishly, "there was gold and silver here for the taking."

Jack laughed aloud. "We was foolish to believe such rubbish. But believe it we did, and here we are."

"Doesn't matter now," Victor said, his adoring blue eyes never leaving Catherine's.

"What do you plan to do now there's no gold?" she asked him.

"We understand that since we paid our own passage over, we'll each be allotted a piece of land to do with as we please."

"Indeed, that is true. Adam has quite a large tract and receives even more when he purchases additional indentures."

"I won't require near what your brother has."

"You have a plan?" Catherine asked, genuinely interested to know what the good-natured young man had in mind.

"To run a mill, of course. There isn't one hereabouts and with the grain every settler grows, a mill should prove both useful and profitable."

Catherine smiled. "I'm sure you will be very successful at whatever you do, Victor." She genuinely meant it and was glad to know he had ambition. She liked that in a man.

The foursome spent a pleasant afternoon talking and laughing. Catherine thoroughly enjoyed the diversion despite the fact that she was still agonizing over the possibility she might be with child. Still, she was determined to marry Victor Covington. That she might have to deceive him in the process, she chose not to examine too closely.

The next morning at Sabbath services, she made no attempt whatever to seek out Noah's handsome face. Instead, the minute services concluded and churchgoers began streaming onto the green, she and Nancy sought out the two men in whose company they'd spent the previous afternoon. This time it was Catherine who issued the invitation for the gentlemen to join them for supper.

Again, it was a pleasant time the four friends spent together. There was a good deal of ribbing between the men and much laughter before the evening drew to a close.

Catherine did enjoy being with Victor. That night as she lay in bed going over the events of the past two days, she tried to imagine how their life might be as man and wife. Victor and Jack still worked with Adam every day. They said the tobacco cutting was complete, and the leaves hung in the sheds to dry, and that, last week, Adam had his crew begin clearing another acre of land, where they'd plant tobacco come spring. But Victor didn't expect to be there then. Once he received the wages Adam owed him, he meant to build his own mill on his own land.

Catherine could easily imagine herself and Nancy saying farewell to their husbands each morning as they set off for their day's labor. For now, Adam had lent the men his dugout, which they rowed to and from the plantation each day, although in inclement weather, both men stayed the night on the plantation.

Once married, Catherine imagined her and Nancy's days would not be much different from what they were now. She'd continue with her school every morning and afternoons help Nancy with the chores. They got on well together, and neither had voiced any objection to continuing with things as they were. The men would fill the long evening hours with talk about their work and matters of import to men — politics, news from England, the governor's latest mandates, and whatnot. Then, they'd all bid one another good night and adjourn to their respective bedchambers. With her days and nights full, she'd have no time to miss Noah, or even think about him.

She would always love him, of course, but she could not be with him the way she wanted — as his wife, and she would not be with him the way he seemed to want — as his mistress — so that left no choice but to seek out a husband for herself. Preferably one she loved, or one with whom a union held the promise of love in the years to come.

She could tell from the way Victor looked at her that he was thinking about marriage. Jack, too. The only difference between the two couples was that Nancy and Jack were truly in love, and for now, it was more a one-sided affair between her and Victor. But, if Lady Montcrief had been correct — that regard often blossomed after marriage — then Catherine might one day grow to love him. If overall her life with Victor was pleasant and not unhappy, she'd be wise to count her blessings and agree to marry him when he asked.

In the next weeks, she agreed to see Victor whenever he wished. One afternoon they walked a mile beyond the fort to a new glass manufacturing plant where Catherine purchased a dozen glass jars in which to store her dried herbs and powders. Coming back, Victor pointed out the location of his fifty-acre grant where he planned to build his mill. The land conveniently fronted the water's edge. Perfect, Victor said, for the huge waterwheel needed to operate the mill. Catherine was pleased when he politely asked her what she thought of the location and of his plans. Several afternoons, they took long walks into the forest where Victor expressed his awe over her knowledge of plants and trees. One day they followed bear tracks in order to pick berries, and laughed when they also found a hive full of precious honey!

"Apparently the animals know where to find much that is good to eat," Catherine marveled.

Another evening when the two couples had set out for a leisurely stroll along the stretch of sandy beach fronting the river, Noah came to the house in their absence. Catherine learned of his visit later that evening from Lad.

"He come by lookin' for ya', miss. I tol' him ye and Nan was out with yer gentl'men friends. He 'ad a bundle 'e said it'd be all right wi' you ifen 'e left."

"Did he go into the house, or did you take it in for him?" Catherine did not like Noah poking around in the house when no one but Lad was there.

"He tuk it in hisself, mum."

Catherine's lips pursed. "In future, I don't want anyone going inside the house when neither Nancy nor I are here, do you understand?"

Lad nodded, the forelock of his straw-colored hair falling over his eyes. A grubby hand reached to fling it aside. "Yes, um."

That Noah had once again left a package here meant she'd be obliged to see him at least one more time. It surprised her that the prospect actually filled her with dread.

The next afternoon, exhausted after working an especially long time in her herb garden, Catherine entered the house with an apron-full of fresh cuttings to be hung and dried. When sufficiently dry, she'd crush the brittle leaves and stems into a fine powder to be used later in a healing tisane or tea. The rafters in every room on the ground floor were thick with cuttings she'd already hung up to dry. She and Nancy loved the aroma indoors and often commented to one another on the fragrance.

"I daresay we have the nicest-smelling house in Jamestown," Nancy said laughing.

Since there was no more space below to hang anything, Catherine saw nothing for it but to climb the steep steps to the loft. She rarely ventured there as the height made her dizzy. She'd been glad to find Nancy had no qualms about scampering up and down the rickety ladder to retrieve goods they stored there.

Climbing slowly, Catherine at last reached the top rung and stepped onto the relative solidity of the loose wooden planks that comprised the loft floor. The floorboards had been left loose a-purpose, Adam said, so they could be taken up when one needed to hoist heavy barrels of fresh foodstuffs into the loft using a rope and pulley mechanism.

Having not been up here in a spell, Catherine noticed now that a goodly number of barrels were close on empty. Which reminded her of one of the conditions of her purchase agreement with Adam — two winters' worth of provisions for her and Nancy. Beginning to tie her cuttings to strings already dangling from the rafters, she made a mental note to remind Adam of their agreement the next time she saw him. How nice it would be for her and Nancy to begin their married lives with plenty to eat!

At length she completed her task, but before venturing back down the ladder, she moved to a crate, which she knew contained only bits and pieces of fabric. She and Nancy used the rags to absorb their monthly flow, and since Catherine knew her time was near and was fervently hoping it would indeed come on schedule, she decided to take a handful of rags back down with her now. Reaching into the crate, she was surprised instead to feel something hard and lumpy.

So, she thought, carefully drawing out the bundle, she'd inadvertently discovered Noah's hiding place. Without meaning to pry, but unable to curb her curiosity, she undid the package to see what it contained. Inside were several scraps of copper, a few knives, four or five ax blades, and a quantity of blue and violet glass beads — an odd item, she thought. She knew he meant to trade the goods with the Indians, but why did he feel the need to conceal them?

Rather than put his stash back where she found it, she decided to take the package downstairs. She had every intention of telling Noah when he came to retrieve this bundle that he could no longer hide his things here, and that in future, she no longer wished to see him at all.

Ready to go downstairs, she hesitated a bit before beginning her descent. Confusion always set in at this juncture, as she never knew whether to back down the rungs, or step down frontward as if descending a stairwell. Today, the fact that both her hands were full made it all the more confusing. Finally, she decided to back down, but before beginning, she pulled her apron up and placed Noah's bundle and the handful of rags into it, which left one hand free to grasp the edge of the rung above her as she descended. Still, it was an awkward maneuver, and although she tackled it slowly, midway down, she lost her footing and with a cry of alarm, toppled backward off the ladder and landed with a thud on the hard-packed earthen floor.

Her cry brought Nancy running into the house. "Catherine!" Nancy knelt beside her. "Are you hurt?"

"I misstepped coming down. I don't believe I'm injured. It was just . . . a jolt."

Nancy helped her up. "Ye'd best lie down."

"I am uninjured," Catherine protested. Already she was on her feet, testing to see if her ankle could bear weight. Everything felt all right, so she bent to gather up the items that scattered when she fell.

Nancy reached to help. "What's this?" She held up a knife, then an ax blade. "What do ye mean to do with these?"

"They belong to Noah. He's been leaving things here that he trades with the Indians."

"Oh."

"I mean to tell him he can no longer use our loft. I don't want him coming around once Jack and Victor are here."

Nancy smiled. "It pleases me to know ye're in earnest where Victor is concerned."

"I'm pleased to see that Victor does,

indeed, seem to care for me."

"Of course, he does!"

As for Noah, Catherine knew he would be far from pleased once he learned she intended to marry another man and no longer wished to see him.

CHAPTER 16

The next morning, when Catherine awoke, she was thrilled to discover her menses had come during the night. She was unsure if the fall had brought on her flow, or if she had indeed been with child and the fall had caused her to miscarry. If she had been pregnant, a part of her regretted losing the only part of Noah Colton she might ever possess. Yet she felt vastly relieved that she would not now have to deceive Victor when they married.

A few evenings later, both she and Nancy were below stairs when a rap sounded at the door. A cold wind had been blowing hard for several days, and both girls had been glad to stay indoors in the evenings where it was considerably warmer. When Catherine opened the door, swirling red and gold leaves accompanied Noah Colton inside. She hurried to shut out the cold wind and turned toward him.

"I suppose you've come for your package."

He nodded, flicking a sullen gaze toward Nancy, seated before the fire stitching patches onto one of Lad's old shirts. The boy had torn it nearly to shreds that day whilst up on the roof attempting to add another layer of rushes before the harsh winter months set in. Worn out from his exertion, he was already fast asleep in the loft, it being too cold now to sleep in the open-air lean-to.

Still with no greeting or attempt at polite conversation, Noah merely advanced toward the ladder but stopped abruptly when he saw that it did not look the same as he remembered.

Glancing up, Nancy said, "Victor built us a new ladder . . . with a nice, sturdy railing."

"Your things are right here, Noah," Catherine said. "Lad's already asleep in the loft."

Noah glanced at Catherine as she walked toward one of the board tables no longer in use since her school sessions had ceased.

"You brought it down here?" Disapproval marred his handsome features.

Catherine was not the least bit frightened of an angry outburst from him; in fact, she fully expected one when he learned not all of his items were there.

"I was in the loft a few days ago and quite by accident discovered where'd you put your package. As you can see, Nancy needed some rags to patch Lad's shirt and I required some myself." She didn't elaborate on why she required rags; he was a married man, he knew about a woman's monthly needs.

He snatched the package up. And apparently thinking it didn't feel quite right, set it down again. Flinging angry glances at Catherine, he yanked the loose ends apart. "Where are the — ?"

"Beads? I accidentally dropped your bundle on my way back down. Unfortunately the beads rolled all over the —" Her gaze dropped to the straw-strewn floor. "Nancy and I managed to find a few, but I'm afraid the bulk of them disappeared beneath the straw. It was an accident, Noah."

He jammed the bundle beneath his doublet. "I should have known I could no longer trust you. I suppose you've told your new friend Victor about this."

She was taken aback. "I haven't said a word to anyone. Only Nancy and I know what was there. She helped me pick up the things I dropped. Lad, of course, knows you left a bundle here since he was here the night you brought it." She went on. "I hardly see why it would matter to anyone what's in your package, everyone in Jamestown knows you're a trader."

Because he kept flinging irritable glances at Nancy, it occurred to Catherine he did not want to say anything further whilst she was in the room.

Angry strides carried him to the door. "When you change the rushes, I'd appreciate it if ye'd gather up the beads and return them to me. They're mine."

"They appear to be only worthless glass."

"Worthless to you, perhaps, but as you pointed out, I'm a trader. I don't own hundreds of acres of land like your brother. To the Indians, those worthless pieces of glass are money, and they belong to me!"

Her lips pursed. "Very well, Noah. I'll be sure to save them for you. In future, I'd rather you didn't —"

"No matter." He yanked open the door. "I have no intention of returning. You are free of me, Mistress Fielding, or should I say Goodwife Covington?"

"I am not yet Goodwife Covington," she replied evenly.

"But I expect ye soon will be."

"If Victor asks me to become his wife, I intend to say yes."

261

On an unseasonably warm November day, puffy white clouds dotted the blue sky, and a slight breeze wafted through the treetops, now completely bare of leaves. Victor came for Catherine early that morning, and the two walked to the river's edge and climbed into the small dugout bobbing in the blue-green water. It was the first time Catherine had been on the river since she'd disembarked from the ship that brought her to Jamestown some seven months earlier.

Today, Victor was taking her upriver to see her brother and his wife and their newborn baby. Jack and Victor had relayed the good news to the girls a few days ago that Adam was now the proud father of a healthy baby boy. Catherine was elated for she knew her brother had always wanted a son.

"Has he named the baby yet?" she asked Victor as he helped her into the small shallop where she sat down on one of the backless wooden benches.

Having shrugged off his doublet, Victor was now rolling up his shirtsleeves. The sun also warm on her back, Catherine let her shawl drop to her waist.

"Elijah," he said, picking up the oars and plunging them into the water. "After your father. They call the little fellow Eli."

Smiling her pleasure, Catherine noted the corners of Victor's eyes crinkling in his sun-browned face as he grinned back at her.

"Ye look beautiful today, Catherine, but, then . . . ye always do. If all goes as I plan," he murmured, "there's something I mean to ask ye later."

Catherine gazed into his adoring blue eyes, the color of which matched the sky. She fully expected he meant to ask Adam for her hand in marriage today. This was the first time Victor had even remotely broached the topic, although she knew it had been on his mind of late, for she'd caught him looking longingly at her a number of times the past month. Although he had squeezed her hand warmly on several occasions when they parted, he'd never attempted to kiss her.

Once they reached the pier that jutted into the water only yards from the new clapboard house where Adam and his family now lived, Victor clambered out of the boat and tied it to a post. He helped Catherine step onto the wide-planked pier, which teetered a bit in the water as they made their way to shore.

"My," she exclaimed as they stepped onto solid ground and she gazed up at the two-story house perched on a small rise over-looking the water, "Adam's new home is lovely. Much bigger than I expected."

"You've not been here before?"

"No." Catherine shook her head. The sun glancing off her long auburn hair, hanging loose down her back, gleamed with splashes of red and gold.

Walking beside her, apparently Victor couldn't resist touching a wavy lock. "Your hair feels like silk," he said, feasting his eyes on the thick mass that swayed sensuously when she walked.

A smile on her lips, Catherine slanted a look up at him. "I washed it in lavender water."

Lifting a curl, he brought it to his nose and drank in the glorious scent, which made Catherine laugh.

Thusly engaged, they didn't see Abigail watching them from the wide verandah that fronted the house.

"Hallo!" she called as they drew nearer. "Welcome to Harvest Hill."

"You've named the plantation!" Catherine gaily called back. "Harvest Hill is beautiful."

Her plain face beaming, Abby held the

264

door open for them. "There's someone I'm dying for you to meet."

In moments, Catherine and Victor were gazing down into a small wooden crib, admiring the new baby. Gurgling happily, it stretched one tiny hand upward.

"With that red hair, he looks just like Adam!" Catherine gushed.

They all laughed as Abigail reached to tuck a small piecework quilt firmly about the baby's plump body. She carried the crib into the parlor at the front of the house where she could keep an eye on the infant while they visited.

The spacious house was bright and airy. Though plainly furnished, it had a real wooden floor, and the windows had shutters that could be closed to keep out the cold wind in winter. The furniture was all new and more finely made than the coarse pieces in their old home in Jamestown. In the last weeks of her pregnancy, Abigail had industriously stitched cushions for the chairs and even made knotted rag rugs for the floors.

"Everything looks beautiful, Abigail," Catherine enthused.

"We mean to paint the clapboards both inside and out come spring. In back, I've a real kitchen attached to the house and a room for eating that's separate from the kitchen," she added proudly.

"Oh, my!" Catherine gazed at the many wonders. "You must be very comfortable here."

"Indeed, we are. The Morgans have a cozy cottage on the plantation as well. Margaret helped me these last weeks, but since she has her own home to look after, Adam found a nice Indian woman to help me every day. She does most of the cooking and the hard labor."

"How nice," Catherine murmured.

"On the whole, my lying-in was quite restful. It feels secluded and peaceful this far out from town."

Catherine could see how happy her sister-in-law was, and it pleased her that her brother had married such a good woman, and they now had a fine home and a beautiful baby.

Later, when Adam came into the house, they all sat down to a sumptuous feast of roasted venison, steamed turnips, and ears of corn dripping with butter. The meal was topped off with blackberry pie and scoops of fresh clotted cream. Everyone remarked on how delicious everything tasted.

Adam was glad to see Catherine and, as they ate, told her what was going on at the plantation, that the men were now pressing the dried tobacco leaves into hogsheads, which he explained were wooden casks about four feet high and two feet wide.

"A hogshead stuffed full of dried tobacco leaves can weigh as much as thirteen hundred pounds," he said. "When the casks are full, we merely roll them down to the pier and load 'em onto one of the tobacco ships enroute for England. Considerably easier than in years past when we had to get the cumbersome things from here to Jamestown."

"On the rolling roads," Catherine said with a grin. "I remember you telling me about that."

"Every planter needs his own pier," Adam said with conviction.

"What will you do once tobacco season ends?" Catherine asked with interest.

"Oh, there's always plenty to do." He laughed. "Firewood to cut, fences to build, trees to girdle."

"Girdle? What's that?" Catherine asked, grinning. She had never heard of such a thing.

"Well, first you cut notches in the bark all around the tree, then when you pull the bark off, it gives it the look of a girdle . . . hence the name. After that, the tree will no longer sprout, and in a year or two, when the treetops decay, sunlight can more easily filter through the withered branches. You can then plant beneath the tree without having to dig out the stump. 'Tis a far quicker method of clearing a field than the old way."

"How clever you are!" Catherine exclaimed.

"We'll soon be slaughtering hogs," Abigail put in, "— and you know the saying: we use every part of the pig except the squeal."

"How's that?" asked Victor. "I thought you just ate the pork and threw the rest away."

"No." Abigail laughed. "Nothing goes to waste. Intestines are good for sausage skin, the bladder for holding lard, and, of course, the hair from the tail, being stiff and strong, is perfect for sewing buckskin."

"Ah." Victor nodded appreciatively.

"Meat from four good-sized hogs can carry a family through the winter," Adam said. "We'll be drying hundreds of pounds of peas and corn. I'll also kill as many deer as I can, then we'll smoke the meat."

Catherine seized the moment. "You haven't forgotten your promise to me."

"I remember. I'm to provide provisions to see you and Nancy through the winter," Adam replied good-naturedly.

"And the next one," Catherine reminded him.

"She drove a hard bargain," he told Victor.

They all laughed, and when the meal concluded, the men headed outdoors while Catherine stayed inside with Abigail and the baby. They visited while Abigail nursed the infant, and when the men returned, Catherine couldn't help noticing both were wearing secretive smiles, which told her her name had likely come up in their conversation.

When the afternoon shadows lengthened, Victor said he thought they should be heading back. The four made their way to the verandah, and when Adam put an arm about Catherine's shoulders, she fell into step beside him as they all strolled down to the water's edge.

"Victor Covington is a fine man, Cat," he said speaking quietly to her. "He's honest and hardworking. I know how ye feel about Noah, but ye'd be wise to settle your affections elsewhere."

Catherine looked up at him. "I do agree with you, and I care for Victor, but —"

She was interrupted by Victor's voice hailing her from the pier. "Sun's beginning to set, Catherine. We'd best head back."

Catherine hurried to join him. She

thanked Abigail and her brother for the delightful day and let Victor assist her into the dugout. On the way downriver, they both remarked on the beautiful sunset unfolding before them. Catherine watched as long fingers of gold, pink, and purple spread across the sky, then silently become a soothing panorama of dusky rose.

"The setting sun from this aspect is beautiful," she exclaimed. "We rarely see the sun set from the house. The trees are far too thick inland."

"Jack and I watch the sun rise every morning. We generally row back about now every evening. We've seen a good many things of interest from here." He grinned at Catherine. "One night last week, we saw four or five Indians on horseback in that clearing over there." He motioned toward shore with his head as both arms were engaged with the oars.

"Indians on horseback?" Catherine turned to gaze that direction. "I've never heard of Indians riding horses before."

"Herds of wild horses roam hereabouts. Jack and I could hardly believe our eyes the day we saw twenty or thirty horses galloping across that clearing. Folks say white men can't catch 'em, but appears the Indians can. They tame 'em, too."

"I wonder how the Indians catch them?" Catherine mused, still gazing across the glassy water toward the pretty meadow surrounded by tall trees.

"I wonder how the Indians do a lot of things," Victor said. "They're smart, I'll give 'em that."

Catherine turned back around. "I often wonder how long they've lived on this land. I think it rather sad that we English are so bent on disrupting their simple way of life. They seem so peaceful just as they are."

"You have a tender heart, Catherine. I don't know a great deal about the Indians. I didn't even know when I came here how close they live to the English." With darkness closing in on them, he began to row a bit faster. "I'm loath to admit it, but it makes me a tad bit nervous. I don't know how far an Indian's arrow flies, but I sure don't want one of 'em using me for target practice."

Catherine laughed softly. "We've nothing to fear, Victor. We're just rowing down the river. I don't believe the Indians would view that as threatening."

"Perhaps." But he didn't slow his pace any.

"Adam said there was trouble between the Indians and the English in the early years, but we've lived peacefully together for some time now."

"You're not the least bit afraid of them, are you?"

"No. All the Indians I've met, save one, have been gentle and kind."

"Well, it only takes one bad apple to spoil the bunch."

"I don't believe we have anything to fear," she said again, a serene smile on her lips.

The fort of Jamestown soon came into view, and Victor headed the small boat toward the shoreline fronting the men's bark hut. Once he tied up the boat, they set out to walk to Catherine's home.

The night air being cool, she drew her shawl closer about her. Victor edged a bit closer, and when he did so, she became aware of the warmth emanating from his strong body. Neither had said much since they began walking. Catherine wondered if he meant to propose to her tonight?

"It was a lovely day, Victor." She looked up at him. "Thank you for taking me."

"Was kind of Adam to grant me freedom for the day. Rather like being on holiday."

"It did seem like a holiday." Catherine smiled.

They fell silent. The smell of smoke rising up the chimneys swirled about them on the cool night air. Walking past the tidy houses,

Catherine could see lights flickering through cracks in the window coverings and chinks in the walls. She imagined folks sitting by the hearth or moving about indoors by candlelight. She imagined herself and Victor snug inside on a cold winter night, eating their supper or just talking together as they warmed themselves before the fire.

"Jamestown always seems peaceful to me at night," she murmured.

"I'm more content here than I ever expected to be," Victor said.

Catherine heard him inhale a long breath and wondered if he meant now to say something to her and was simply trying to pluck up the courage.

She waited, and when he said nothing, she attempted to help him along. "Did you and Adam talk about . . . anything particular?"

He cleared his throat. "As a matter of fact, we did."

Still, he didn't elaborate.

Catherine began softly, "Adam thinks you are an honest and hardworking man. I'm glad he likes you."

After a pause, Victor asked, "What about you, Catherine. Do you like me?"

She cast a sidelong look up at his rugged profile, which looked quite appealing in the shadows. He had a high brow, straight nose, and a strong, square jaw. His lips were thin, though well-shaped. "I like you a great deal, Victor." It pleased her that not a single word she'd said was untrue.

"I like you as well, Catherine. Very much."

He paused again. Catherine feared he was growing more nervous and flustered than ever, though she couldn't imagine why. She'd given him no reason to doubt what her answer would be when he finally posed the question.

At length, he said, "In all my life, I've never met a woman more beautiful than you, Catherine. To be sure, ye put every female in Jamestown to shame. You could have your pick of any man in the New World."

She waited, then when she realized he did not mean to say anything more, she said, "Thank you, Victor. I think you are a hand-some man, as well." She almost said she thought they'd make beautiful children together but caught herself before the words flew out of her mouth. He hadn't yet asked her to become his wife. To mention children at this juncture would likely frighten him for good and all.

"Damme, Catherine." He stopped and, turning toward her, gathered both her hands in his large, square ones. "What I'm trying to say and making such a muddle of is . . . will ye marry me? Will ye become my wife? Your brother gave his blessing. So, will ye?"

Catherine could not help smiling both at the length of his proposal when he finally got it out, but from relief over the fact that he had. "Yes, Victor. I will marry you. I will be happy to become your wife . . . and to bear your children." Well, it was on her mind. Having just spent the better part of the day gazing into the cherubic face of Adam's precious newborn had made her want one of her own. She may not yet love Victor Covington, but she knew she would love their child with all her heart.

That he did not take her into his arms did not surprise her. He merely nodded and, with determined satisfaction and a wide grin on his face, linked her arm through his and covered her slim fingers, curled over the crook of his arm, with his callused ones.

"When shall we do it?" he asked as they commenced to walk. "The sooner the better, I'm persuaded."

By week's end, the banns had been posted on the meetinghouse door, which merely stated a couple's intent to marry and allowed anyone with reason to protest the match ample time in which to do so.

No one came forward to protest the marriage between Victor Covington and Catherine Fielding, publicly, that is. But Noah Colton managed to make his protest known to one of the pair.

Catherine was surprised to meet up with him one cold afternoon in the forest where she'd gone to gather nuts. The walnuts, pecans, and chestnuts that blanketed some parts of the forest floor were delicious in apple crisps, custards, and bread. She and Nancy also enjoyed roasting them on a cold winter night before the fire.

Catherine had just about filled her bucket when she glanced up to find Noah striding toward her. As usual, the mere sight of him caused her breath to quicken. He looked especially appealing today wearing buckskin breeches and tall leather boots. His hair had grown long; his golden curls now grazed his shoulders. In an effort to stay calm, she inhaled a deep breath but that merely filled her nostrils with the fresh outdoorsy scent of the handsome man headed toward her. She worked to tamp down her reaction to him; after all, she was soon to become a married woman, and the only man for whom she wished her pulse to quicken was her husband.

As if reading her thoughts, Noah said by way of greeting, "So, ye're to be married, or perhaps ye've already repeated your vows?"

Flustered, she looked down. "The banns were only published last week. We've a bit longer to wait before we meet with the reverend."

"Well, for whatever difference it makes, I heartily protest the match."

Thinking his tone sounded decidedly cool, her head jerked up. "Don't be that way, Noah. Don't begrudge me the happiness you've found in marriage."

He pulled a face. "Who says I've found happiness in marriage? Why do ye think I kept comin' to see you?"

Her heart thumped in her breast. "I . . . wondered why you persisted in coming around."

His blue eyes twinkled. "Because ye belong to me, pea-goose. Ye always have, ye always will. Ye were willing to marry me once."

Her gaze softened. "I thought you'd forgotten the promise we made to one another as children."

"I remember how lovely I thought you were. But I'll not stand in yer way now."

"I'm a woman alone now, Noah. I need help. I expected that help to come from you

277

once I arrived in Jamestown."

He shrugged. "I also expected things would be different when I came here. We've no choice now but to play the hand we're dealt."

An anguished look dimmed the light in Catherine's eyes. "I'll always love you, Noah," she murmured.

He grinned. "I know."

She fought the urge to fling her arms around his neck, but instead reminded herself that all she and Noah could share now was the past.

"We shall always be friends," she said, doing nothing to conceal the longing in her eyes as she gazed up at the one man she'd loved for as long as she could remember.

He nodded, but the odd look she saw in his eyes was unfathomable.

At length, Catherine dropped her gaze. When she glanced back up, she noticed that he was carrying a bow and peeking over his shoulder was a quiver full of arrows.

"Where did you get that?" Her gaze indicated the bow. "And what do you intend doing with it?"

"Traded an ax blade for it. Been practicing m' aim this afternoon. Would ya' like to see?" Raising the bow into position, he reached over his shoulder and skillfully slid an arrow from the quiver.

"No!" Still, she edged closer. "I've never seen a real arrow before." She reached to touch the sharp point. "It's so small."

"It's a Powhatan arrow. Every tribe's arrowheads are different. Powhatan arrowheads are small and sharp. Chickahominies are large and wide, though every bit as lethal."

"Please tell me you've not killed anything with that!"

"Nothing of consequence, save this hare." He let the bow fall slack and reached behind his back for the dead rabbit attached to his belt with a leather tong. "Here" — he extended it toward her — "you take it. You and Nancy can have a nice rabbit stew."

Though Catherine hated to think of any living thing being felled by an arrow, she knew the Indians lived off what they hunted and killed in the forest. She reached for the hare, then drew her hand back. "I'd rather you give it to Nancy yourself."

Grinning at her squeamishness, he glanced toward her bucket on the ground, it nearly full of nuts. "Are you ready to go?"

When she nodded, he gallantly picked up the heavy bucket, and they set out, their footfalls crunching on the dry leaves as they trekked back through the tangled woods.

"Nancy and Jack are also to wed," she remarked in a conversational tone.

"Do the four of you plan to share the house, then?"

"For a while. Quite a number of families share homes, you know."

"Charity and I live with her parents. She has no objection to the arrangement."

"But you do?"

"I wasn't consulted. Benson home is plenty large and . . . with a babe on the way . . . ," his voice trailed off.

Catherine willed a bright smile to her face. "I think it's wonderful that you will soon be a father again, Noah. I predict when the baby comes, you will be very happy," she concluded sweetly.

He made no reply at once, then, in a low tone, said, "I hoped I'd got a babe on you."

"Noah!" Catherine's eyes widened. "You mustn't say such a thing!" She flung a wild gaze over her shoulder as if she feared the forest had ears.

"We could try again," he teased.

"Absolutely not! What we did was wrong, and none but the two of us must ever know of it." She ducked her head, fearful even of speaking about such things in broad daylight. "We sinned against God and the

Church, and you broke your marriage vows."

He grinned. "I've broken nearly all the Lord's commandments."

"I don't believe that." She directed an alarmed gaze up at him. "I daresay you're lying even now."

"There, I've broken them all!"

She couldn't help laughing. "Well, at any rate, you mustn't ever say a word about . . . what we did. Promise me you won't."

"I promise, Catherine; on my honor, which" — his tone again turned teasing — "isn't worth a damn."

She rolled her eyes. "You are incorrigible."

"So," he began afresh, "the four of you mean to share the house?"

"Yes; as I was saying, I don't know how long Nancy and Jack will remain in town. Adam has asked Jack to become his foreman, and I expect they will remove to Harvest Hill once he and Nan marry."

She heard his snort of derision. "Adam's taken to calling his swampland Harvest Hill, has he? Sounds rather pretentious to me."

Catherine frowned. "Adam is quite proud of all he's accomplished. You'll have a turn one day at managing a large estate."

"Not until Charity's father is dead and gone."

"No-ah! I'm sure you were all very thankful when your father-in-law survived the fever this past summer."

"Strong as an old ox, that one."

"I would expect he'd want you beside him now. To learn about things, and . . . whatnot."

"Benson says I'm more valuable to the colony as a trader. Jamestown's future is of paramount importance to him. He's refused to relinquish his seat on the council a number of times, despite my mother-in-law's protests."

"Perhaps you'll take a seat on the council yourself one day," Catherine suggested brightly.

He grimaced. "Not likely. Truth to tell, my father-in-law thinks I'm a bit of a ne'er-do-well."

"You just said he thinks you're a successful trader."

"I strongly suspect he allowed his only daughter to marry me because she's the apple of his eye, and he can deny her nothing."

They trudged on in silence for a spell, each lost in their own thoughts. Again, Catherine marveled over how easily she and Noah talked, as if there'd been no harsh words or recent animosity between them.

282

They seemed to easily put it all aside and pick back up in a friendly manner.

Presently, she said, "You're too hard on yourself, Noah. I think you are very talented."

He flashed an impish grin. "Still sweet on me, eh, love?"

She laughed. "You're a charming rogue, Noah Colton, I'll give you that."

He winked at her. "Ye'd give me more than that, ye saucy wench, if ye weren't about to wed another man!"

"You reprobate!" she said, laughing

Reaching home, Nancy was tickled to death to get the hare and declared she'd make a delicious rabbit pie for their supper the following evening.

"I'll invite Jack and Victor over!" she declared to Catherine, who winced when she saw the hurt look on Noah's handsome face. But he merely tipped his cap and sauntered off.

Later that night, as Catherine lay abed reflecting on her unexpected encounter with Noah in the forest, she relished the warm feeling his teasing banter had brought forth within her. She hated quarreling with him. Noah had been a part of her life for so very long, it hurt her deeply when they were at odds. Though loath to admit it, she still longed to lie with him again, to feel his arms wrapped around her and his lips pressed to hers. It warmed her to know that, despite her plans to marry another, he still cared for her. She only hoped that once she and Victor were wed and he'd bedded her, she could at long last put away her craving for Noah. She must. For how else could she make a go of her marriage to Victor? She would always cherish her shared past with Noah, but the harsh truth was, there was no future for them, and she had no choice but to accept that. With a sigh, she resolved afresh to put all thoughts of her handsome, loveable rogue from mind. Still, she could not quiet the niggling fear beneath her resolve that told her she was attempting the impossible, that her deep hunger for Noah Colton would never go away. And that fact troubled her deeply.

CHAPTER 17

A week before the wedding ceremony, Adam and two of his men poled their way down the river on a flat barge loaded with a dozen barrels of dried peas, corn, turnips, apples and pears, salted pork, and venison.

Once they arrived in Jamestown, Adam enlisted Victor and Jack's help. The five men spent a long afternoon hoisting the heavy barrels into the loft of Catherine's house. Once the task was completed, Adam told Catherine he was taking Lad back with him to the plantation.

"Boy's not done nearly so well here as I intended. Thatch on the roof is still too thin; chinks in the walls aren't filled. Guess he plain forgot to shore up a mud wall 'round the outside of the house."

"He has been difficult to manage," Catherine admitted. The two stood watching the men haul the last of the empty barrels down from the loft.

"Boy's growing up fast," Adam went on. "He needs a strong hand, or there's no saying what will become of him. I've plenty for him to do on the plantation. Jack and Victor will take up the slack once they move in."

Catherine nodded. "Both men are hard workers."

The muffled sound of Jack's voice from above their heads interrupted them. "What about this last one?" he called down. "Less than one eighth full of . . . something."

Catherine laughed. "That's soap, Jack."

"Which ye'll be needing to make more of come spring," her brother reminded her.

Catherine heaved a sigh as she watched the men herd the empty barrels outdoors to roll them toward the river where Adam had moored the barge. She was grateful her brother had made good on his word and thankful their larder was now full of food, but, as Adam said, there was still plenty to be done around the place before winter set in.

Because both she and Nancy wanted new gowns in which to be married, Catherine had earlier given Adam money to purchase lengths of frieze or fustian, whichever was available, from the ship's merchant when he loaded his hogsheads of tobacco onto the bark enroute for England. Today, he'd

286

brought the fabric to her.

Fingering the green, Nancy declared it her favorite, which pleased Catherine since she preferred the blue. So, whilst the men tended to the work still to be done on the roof and outside walls, the ladies stayed inside where it was warm, cutting and stitching their new gowns. Catherine ripped some black braid off an old frock to trim the skirts of their new dresses. The effect was pleasing, although they laughed about looking a bit like twins.

Two days before they were to repeat their marriage vows, the temperature plummeted and a thick sheet of ice formed on the river. Catherine didn't expect Adam and Abigail to make it into town for the wedding ceremony.

That morning snow began to fall, but as planned, Reverend Buck and two other freemen — Victor and Jack's friends who had agreed to stand as witnesses — arrived at the house just after noon. The simple ceremony was over quickly, and after the reverend had blessed the newly married pairs, he delivered the customary (though, in this instance, quite short) Marriage Sermon, placing particular emphasis on the wives being obedient to their husbands and reminding both partners that if temperamental difficulties arose in the marriage, they must be faced and not run away from; that they were to answer impatient words kindly, gently, and with loving consideration, and above all, never carry resentment. He reminded the ladies that they must never contradict their husbands, deride them, or desert them. Instead, they were to cherish and comfort their men; study their moods and manners until they became the rule of her life. Thereafter, the good reverend quickly took his leave, wishing to make it across town to his own warm hearth before the falling snow became an all-out blizzard. The freemen lingered, unable to pass up the opportunity to gorge themselves on the warm currant pie Nancy had made to mark the occasion, and to wash it down with mugs of stout ale.

When their guests finally departed, leaving the newlyweds at last alone, Victor set the small bundle he'd brought with him on one of the board tables. He removed from the bundle a few items of clothing, then proudly set out the remainder of his worldly goods: two tin cups and one small earthen pipkin, which Nancy exclaimed over.

"A serving dish! How I've wished for one!"

Her new husband's face fell. "I brought ye a shovel and a warm bed rug, love."

They all laughed at the hurt tone in his voice.

"Where's your bed rug?" Jack asked Victor.

He scratched his head.

"Not to worry, my dear," Catherine said sweetly, "I have a warm bed rug plenty big enough for both of us."

And it was.

As November gave way to December, the days grew shorter and colder. Although the newly married couples remained content and happy with their living arrangements, they knew that come planting time, Jack and Nancy would be removing to Harvest Hill where Jack would take up his duties as Adam's new foreman. For now, both men stayed busy from dawn to dusk in Jamestown doing whatever was needed at home. In addition to hauling water several times a day, fresh logs had to be split daily since the small supply Lad had chopped and stacked had dwindled to near nothing.

After felling some trees along the forest's edge, they used the branches and twigs for kindling; the cleared land would be used later to grow corn and squash. On one less frigid day, the men enclosed the lean-to. Though it was still a makeshift affair, it now had a thatched roof and a door that opened and closed. Other days they fished in the river, often bringing home a nice sturgeon or mess of herring. Jack had a fowling piece, and the men even attempted to hunt, though that venture proved less fruitful than their efforts on the river. The most they brought home from an entire day of hunting was the occasional rabbit and once a possum, which neither Nancy nor Catherine knew what to do with. Still, the foursome always had plenty to eat and for the most part, remained cheerful and in good spirits.

When Christmastide came, they bundled up as warmly as they could and trudged through the snow to the meetinghouse for a special service. Afterward, the four feasted on roasted turkey and corn. Jack had felled one of the wild birds from the large herds that freely roamed the countryside. After eating their fill, they sat around the table and took turns telling stories of Christmases spent with their families back in England. Catherine grew misty-eyed recalling the happy times she'd shared with both Adam and Noah on the farm. Even the Christmas celebrations she and Nancy remembered with the Montcriefs in London, when small gifts were distributed amongst the servants, were a source of remembered pleasure.

A week later, they toasted in the New Year of 1618 with mugs of hot apple cider. Gathered around their warm hearth on the eve of the New Year, they merrily sang songs recalled from their youth. As the weeks passed, Catherine grew to admire and respect her industrious, hardworking husband, who after working hard all day, spent his evening hours making plans for the mill he intended to build come spring.

During those early weeks after they married, Catherine willingly allowed Victor to gather her into his arms at night, but after their first few tentative times together, more often than not he merely laid his weary head on her shoulder and quickly fell asleep. Although Catherine knew he was worn out from his hard day's labor, still, she realized she didn't really mind, for good and kind as he was, his touch did not quicken her pulse, or set her blood afire.

On the other side of the house, however, Jack could hardly keep his hands off Nancy and vice versa. One could not walk past the other without stopping to pat, tweak, or embrace his, or her, beloved. Catherine knew the warmth between their housemates did not escape Victor's notice, for more than once, she'd caught a fleeting look of sadness flicker across his face as the lovebirds again pecked one another on the cheek or giggled their delight at being together. At times, after witnessing such a display, Victor would quietly move to stand nearer Catherine, or drag his chair closer to hers and shyly drape an arm across her shoulder to fondle her hair.

Though neither spoke of it, Catherine suspected he rather thought her aloof and unresponsive, and perhaps she was, though she didn't mean to be. It did dismay her that instead of growing to love him as she'd fully expected, her feelings for her new husband merely remained steady and constant. But she couldn't help herself. She cared for him; she even felt affection for him, but after two full months of marriage, the truth was, she cared neither more nor less for him than the day they wed.

It began to gnaw at her that her reticence to be openly affectionate with Victor might cause him to stop loving her. Oddly enough, that did distress her. Victor was a good man, and she felt lucky to have such a fine, thoughtful husband . . . but she did not love him and now feared she might never.

She wondered if her inability to love him was because she'd already given her whole heart to another man, and there was nothing left for Victor. If that were the case, then there was nothing to be done for it. She could not change her feelings just because she wanted to. Because she stayed busy each and every day, she rarely had spare moments to think about Noah; still, the deep love in her heart for him had not diminished a whit. She doubted now that anything would be powerful enough to dislodge it. And although she clearly recalled the London clergyman telling Lucinda and herself that a woman's purpose in life was to multiply her kind, it didn't surprise her that she was not soon with child. Nancy, on the other hand, was another story.

"Never in all me life did I think I'd be so happy," she confided to Catherine one cold January day as the girls sat huddled indoors before a warm fire — Nancy stirring the pot of spoon meat she was making for supper, Catherine mending yet another pair of breeches her hardworking husband had ripped apart the day before.

Catherine didn't look up from her work.

"It's a bit soon yet," Nancy went on, a merry lilt to her tone, "but I think my Jack may have already got a babe on me."

Catherine's head jerked up. "Nancy, how wonderful!" She smiled widely. "Have you told him?"

"Not yet." Nancy laughed. "But I couldna'

keep it to meself a minute longer!"

"I'm so happy for you. Truly I am!"

The girls chatted about how lucky they were to have landed such kind and dependable husbands. At length, a faraway look stole into Catherine's eyes. "My, when we left England less than a year ago, would we have believed such good fortune would befall us?"

"Not I!" Nancy shook her head, causing wisps of brown hair to escape the confines of her tattered white cap. "What do ye think his lord and ladyship would say if they could see us now, both married and snug in our own little house?"

"I've often wished I could get word to Lucinda to tell her I'm all right and that you're here with me, but I guess that's a silly notion." A sigh escaped Catherine as she turned back to her mending.

"Our midnight escape truly turned into a grand adventure!" Nancy enthused.

The girls sat in companionable silence for another quarter hour, then suddenly the door flew open, and on a gust of frigid air, a stricken-faced Jack burst into the room.

Nancy looked up. "What is it, love?"

"Something terrible has happened," Jack replied, but he wasn't looking at Nancy when the anguished words tumbled from his mouth.

CHAPTER 18

Panic gripped Catherine as she sprang to her feet, the mending in her lap falling unheeded to the floor.

"Something's happened to Victor." Her voice quaked.

From the doorway, Jack stepped aside as two men charged into the house, carrying a third man prone between them.

Cries of alarm escaped both girls.

"Straight through there." Jack directed the men toward the proper bedchamber, both Catherine and Nancy close on their heels.

"What happened?" Catherine asked.

"Took an arrow to a leg, another to his shoulder." Jack brushed past her into the room.

"Indians?" Catherine repeated in a daze, a part of her mind recalling Victor's fear of being used for target practice by the naturals. She pushed past the men to her husband's side to assess his condition for herself.

"I done pulled out the arrows," Jack said. "Tried to bind up the wounds afore I run back to town for help. Didn't know then if he was dead or alive."

Bending over Victor, Catherine was already peeling back the makeshift dressing Jack had applied to his leg . . . and drew back in horror when she saw the raw, gaping hole the arrowhead had torn into his thigh. Bright red blood oozed from the wound.

Wincing, she moved to inspect the assault to his shoulder and was relieved to find it not nearly so bad as the leg. Thus far, Victor hadn't moved or made a sound, but when his wife's soft fingers gently touched the feverish skin surrounding the fiery wound to his shoulder, a low moan escaped him.

"You're home now, sweeting. Lie still. I shall take good care of you."

Catherine felt Nancy hovering nearby. "Which of yer remedies do ye want?" she asked in a low tone.

Catherine looked up, her face ashen, her eyes fearful. Instead of answering the question, she silently herded everyone from the room. Once she closed the door to the bedchamber, she sent Nancy to the loft to fetch jars of powders, telling her which ones to brew into a tea and to bring the others to her straightaway.

Though Jack was engrossed in retelling the other two men what had transpired in the forest, Catherine interrupted him. "Do you have the arrows?"

"Didn't bring 'em. Just jerked 'em out and threw 'em on the ground. Why, do ye want 'em?"

"Yes. The arrowheads will tell us which tribe the Indian is from who shot him. Each tribe uses a different type of arrow."

Jack's brow puckered. "Never heard the like."

"Did you see the Indian? Were there several, or . . . what?"

"Didn't see a thing. Just of a sudden, I heard a swooshing noise and then another, and next thing I knowed, Victor was on the ground. Never saw nothin'." He scratched his head. "I'll fetch the arrows if ye want 'em."

"Search party is already forming," said one of the men. "I'll get my musket."

"I'll fetch my pistol," said the other.

"Jack!" cried Nancy, just then returning from the loft. "You're not goin' back out there!" She flung a desperate look from her husband to Catherine.

"Don't worry none about me, love." Jack

gave his frightened wife a quick hug. "Indians don't stand a chance against muskets and pistols."

"But you don't have a pistol!" Nancy protested.

"I have to go, woman," Jack said, in a tone that brooked no objection. "I'll take my fowling piece if it'll make ye feel better."

"Oh, Jack, do be careful!" Tears of anguish welled in Nancy's eyes. "I couldna' live if something happened to ye."

While the men were gone, Catherine tended Victor as best she could — holding his head up with one hand while coaxing a soothing herbal tea into his mouth with the other. When he'd quieted down, she smeared onto his shoulder a precious healing oil she'd brought with her from England. As the hole in his leg continued to bleed, she decided not to waste the oil there, since mixing it with his sticky blood would render it useless. She put Nancy to dapping at the flow while she stirred up a pasty mixture of herbs that would thicken and congeal his blood.

When Victor began to thrash about on the bed, she administered a dose of opium made from bright red poppies she'd found in the forest. When he fell into a deep slumber, she continued to work on his leg, picking out bone fragments and even a few shards of metal. She finished by winding a clean bandage of rags around his leg. At length, she returned to the hearth where Nancy was again stirring their supper in the iron pot over the fire. Wiping her bloodied hands on her apron, Catherine wearily dropped into a chair beside her friend.

"Ye think he'll heal up right and tight?" Nancy asked anxiously.

"His shoulder may heal, but the wound to his leg is far worse. I fear the bone has shattered. I picked out a number of fragments, far too many to count." Her chin began to tremble. As the gravity of her husband's condition sank in, her head dropped to her chest and she began to weep.

Laying her wooden spoon aside, Nancy knelt to wrap her arms about her friend. "Victor's strong. He'll be up an' about in no time, you'll see."

Catherine's sniffed back her tears. "I don't know what else to do for him, and with no doctor in Jamestown —"

"Dare we ask Tamiyah?" Nancy suggested.

"I don't know. I don't know if Victor would let an Indian come near him now."

Later that evening, Nancy was overjoyed when Jack returned with the arrows he'd found in the forest. Along with him were Deputy-Governor Argall and a freeman named John Fuller, who'd also taken part in the search that afternoon.

"This is a serious matter," Argall began, helping himself to a seat near the fire. A large bull of a man, about forty-five, he'd not bothered to properly greet Nancy when he came in. She hurried to fetch Catherine as the deputy-governor drew off his gloves and held up his icy hands before the flames.

When Catherine entered the room, he belatedly asked, "How does Goodman Covington fare?"

"He is no better, sir," Catherine replied a bit crossly. She turned to Jack. "May I see the arrows, please?"

He rose to retrieve them from where he'd set them just inside the door.

"We need to determine if some tribe has a fresh grievance with us," the deputy-governor said, "or if this was just an unfortunate accident. Could be you men just strayed onto one of their 'private' hunting grounds. Damn Indians think they own the entire country."

Overhearing Argall's remark, Catherine bristled but said nothing, instead turning her attention to examining the arrowheads. Noting that both were stained with Victor's

301

blood, she pushed down the bile that rose in her throat as she searched for some sort of mark that might indicate from which Indian tribe the arrowheads came. It puzzled her that they were distinctly different from one another. One was small with a needle-sharp tip, much like the one she'd seen in Noah's quiver. The other was larger and heavier. The larger one, she assumed, had done the extensive damage to Victor's leg.

Based on what Noah had said, she expected the arrowheads to be of a similar size and shape, meaning they belonged to one brave, or at least to Indians from the same tribe. She attempted to reason the puzzle out. If all the Indians in the region fell under Powhatan's rule, or were part of his so-called federation then wouldn't all the Indians technically be Powhatans? So, why were some of them called Pamunkeys, or Mattaponys, or Weanocs? Not clearly understanding the significance of anything at this juncture, she decided the men would have to sort the matter out. All she knew for certain was that her husband had been gravely injured by arrowheads belonging to one or more Indians from one or more tribes, and it fell to her to tend the horrific wounds. Still holding the arrows in her hand, she turned to head across the room to where the four men sat clustered around the hearth.

"Perhaps when Goodman Colton arrives," the deputy-governor said, rising to stand upright to warm his backside before the flames, "he can shed some light on the matter."

Catherine's head jerked up. *Noah was coming? Why?* She paused to listen.

"I don't know what to make of it," Jack said again, his brown head shaking from side to side as he again relived the terrible event. "One minute we was jes' walkin' along, the next minute, Victor was laying on the ground moaning."

"And with no snow on the ground, there were no prints laid down and, therefore, nothing for us to follow or track," put in John Fuller, his tone equally as frustrated as Jack's.

"And ye're certain ye was precisely at the juncture of the old rolling road and the stream?" Argall asked.

At that moment, a rap sounded at the door. Catherine, still clutching the arrows, walked back toward the door, knowing full well with whom she was about to come face-to-face.

Flinging open the door, Noah stepped

inside, his cap and shoulders dusted with snowflakes that had only moments ago begun to fall. His blue eyes fell at once to the arrows in her hand. "Is Victor — ?"

"Take these." Catherine thrust the arrows towards him. "The men want to quiz you about them."

"I wasn't anywhere near the stream!"

Not wanting to look at him, Catherine hurried away. As she brushed past the other men, she heard Argall say, "Could use something hot to warm me gullet, Mistress Covington."

Catherine made no response as she swept past the men.

"Good-looking wench," the deputy-governor said in an undertone. "Won't be long afore she finds herself another husband, eh, John?"

Catherine heard the crude remark but resisted the urge to whirl around and deliver the set-down the elder man deserved. How dare he say such a thing of a woman whose husband lay dying in the next room! Instead, she entered the chamber where Nancy was keeping a silent vigil at Victor's bedside.

"The men want some hot cider," she said irritably. "Noah has come. Apparently they think he can sort this out." She slid onto the chair Nancy hurriedly vacated. "Please see the door is kept tightly shut, Nan."

The men talked for quite a spell, but were unable to draw a definitive conclusion. Nancy, who'd stayed in the room listening closely to the discussion as she kept the men's tankards full of hot ale, later told Catherine the bulk of what she'd heard.

"Deputy-Governor Argall said unless there are similar incidents in the next few days, he'd have no choice but to declare it an accident . . . an unfortunate happenstance, he called it. Said Victor must have simply stepped into the path of the arrows. Noah said in wintertime the woods are full of Indians huntin' game."

"But, what about the arrowheads being different sizes and therefore belonging to different tribes? What did Noah say about that?"

Nancy shrugged. "Said it was not a hard-and-fast rule. Said in wintertime it was not unlikely for braves from neighboring tribes to hunt together." She rubbed her eyes sleepily. The hour was late and Jack had already taken to his bed. "I brought you a fresh pine-knot." She crossed the room to replace the one on the windowsill, now burnt to little more than a flicker. Nancy turned and glanced at Victor, lying on the bed with his eyes closed. Her gaze shifted to Catherine, sitting rigidly upright on the hard-back chair. "Ye really should try to sleep, Catherine."

"Perhaps I shall climb into bed beside Victor. The bed would be warmer, and perhaps my presence will comfort him. But I won't sleep."

Four days later when the deep puncture wound to Victor's leg showed no signs of healing, he still clung stubbornly to life. Catherine was heartened by the improvement to his shoulder, but the leg was another matter. The open wound had festered with fiery-red fingers of inflammation shooting as far up as his torso and as far down as his toes. In lucid moments, he said the leg ached, or it burned; at times it itched, or felt numb. He complained of stabbing pains that struck his chest and his head.

"You'll be up and about in no time, love." Catherine did her best to comfort him, but in her heart, she knew she was telling a falsehood.

Several times a day, she cleaned the gaping wound. Although his blood had indeed thickened, she found it impossible to halt the foul-smelling pus that soaked through the rags mere seconds after she'd tied them around his leg. More than once, the stench rising from the wound caused her to retch as soon as she left the bedchamber.

As each day passed, Catherine grew more and more frustrated over the leg's failure to heal. She'd exhausted all the remedies she knew, and, with no doctor to consult, she began to fear that if Victor were to survive the injury to his leg, it would have to go.

She decided to send Jack to the plantation for Adam and gave him firm instructions to relay how very grave the situation was. She hoped Adam would know of someone who could perform the amputation.

In the meantime, she knew she had to prepare Victor for what was to come.

As expected, he balked.

"I'll not be half a man!" His face contorted as Catherine haltingly told him what she feared would happen if the leg refused to heal. As if to prove that he could, Victor struggled to push himself up off the bed.

"No!" Catherine cried, pressing against his chest with both hands. "The leg will not hold! Please, Victor, lie back. Adam is on his way."

When Adam arrived, he went at once to the bedchamber, which reeked of rotting flesh.

"Took a couple of arrows, did you?" he began, hardly daring to breathe.

"No more'n a scratch," Victor said, struggling afresh to sit up. "M'wife's unduly alarmed. You know how women are."

"Victor, please, lie still," Catherine pleaded from where she stood at the foot of the bed. "Let Adam look at your leg and tell us what he thinks."

His features grim, Victor's head fell back onto the pillow. He looked away as if to shield himself from the ugly sight of his own leg.

"Do you not agree?" Catherine asked her brother a quarter hour later when they returned to the common room where Nancy and Jack, both wearing grave looks on their faces, sat before the fire.

Adam slowly nodded. "The wound is clearly infectious and doesn't appear to be healing. I'm sure you've tried all your salves and potions." He gazed at Catherine.

"Nothing has worked."

"Smells awful in there." Nancy shook her head sadly.

"Whole house smells putrid," Jack muttered.

The foursome continued to discuss Victor's condition until Adam began recounting the number of settlers who had perished from arrow wounds. "One man came stumbling into the fort with six arrows still sticking from his body. Lived eight days. And back in oh-seven, the first fatality in Jamestown was a fifteen-year-old boy who took an arrow to his leg. Boy's buried right outside the old fort."

"And how many have *lived?*" cried Catherine.

Following her outburst, the conversation turned to other things.

"I realize it's sooner than I first said, Jack, but I need you now at Harvest Hill. We may still get more snow this winter, but the worst of the bad weather is past and there are things I need to show you before we begin planting."

"We cannot leave Catherine to manage alone," Nancy protested, a look of concern on her face.

"We've no choice, love." Jack patted his wife's shoulder.

"I'll be fine. I plan to start up my school again." Catherine tried for a cheerful tone. "Now that the weather's turning, the children will be able to get here. I feared for their safety with snow and ice on the ground. School will give me something fresh to think about each day."

Adam reached to squeeze his sister's

hand. "I know you don't wish to speak of it, Cat, but the bald truth is you will very likely become a widow again soon. I don't believe amputating Victor's leg will help. And, I don't believe ye'd be able to convince him it would."

Feeling her chest constrict, Catherine tried to swallow past the lump of anguish in her throat. "What will I do once Victor has — ?"

"You will come to Harvest Hill, of course."

"We will all go," said Nancy, her tone soothing. "There will be plenty to keep you busy there, what with Abigail's new baby. And mine," she added, flicking a self-conscious grin at her beaming husband.

Adam had already congratulated Jack on the good news as they made their way into town. "Nancy's right," Adam said. "Harvest Hill is your only choice. In the meantime, I can ask Abby's woman if she knows of someone from her tribe." He paused, one hand stroking his chin thoughtfully. "I don't recall ever hearing what tribe the Indian woman is from, but she's a congenial sort and has been a big help to Abby. Anyhow, you'll need someone to help you until . . . ," his voice trailed off.

"I don't know how Victor will take to an Indian in the house. Not after. . . ."

"It can't be helped, sis. Nancy has no choice but to go with her husband. You and Victor are welcome to come, but the trip would be futile as far as he is concerned. An Indian woman to help you nurse him here until . . . the end, is the only answer. I doubt it will be for long," he concluded sadly. "And then ye'll come to us."

That night as Catherine slipped into bed, being careful not to disturb her sleeping husband, she lay awake in the darkness thinking over all that Adam had said. It had been nearly a fortnight since the accident and although Victor's shoulder did seem to be healing, his leg looked far, far worse. She realized she'd become so caught up in her obsession to bring him back to health that she'd become unable to accurately assess his condition. She turned her head on the pillow to listen for the sound of his even breathing, which in the short time they'd been married had become a source of comfort to her in the dark of night. Now, when she knew Victor was asleep, her comfort came from the knowledge that he was not in pain. Her heart ached for the strong, handsome man she'd so recently married and whose life was slowly ebbing away. He'd been as excited about his plans for the new mill as he was over their bright future together. Now she knew she'd never have a child with him, and they'd never become a real family.

Tears of grief slid down her cheeks. She thought back to that afternoon, which seemed so very long ago now, when she and Nancy sat before the fire talking about how pleased and happy they were with their new lives. Nancy had only just told her she was with child when Jack burst into the house and they brought Victor in. And, then . . . everything changed.

It seemed unfair. More so for Victor than herself, of course, but once again, she thought, through no fault of her own, her future had been cruelly snatched from her. Victor's death, when it came, would indeed make her a widow. It was almost as if her earlier deception, however inadvertent, had now become a self-fulfilling prophecy.

CHAPTER 19

February 1618

On the day Jack and Nancy left for Harvest Hill, a pretty young Indian girl of about fifteen or sixteen years, with long, shiny black hair and black doe eyes, arrived at Catherine's door. The girl spoke little English, but managed to tell Catherine she was called Lanneika. Catherine took to her at once, realizing she felt much the same kinship with Lanneika as she'd felt when she met Pocahontas.

Though she hated to, she had no choice but to put Lanneika to work at once washing the soiled bandages that had accumulated in a pile outside the front door. In the beginning, Catherine had not saved the soiled rags she'd used for Victor's bandages, but her entire store of fabric scraps was now gone, and she saw nothing for it but to wash and reuse those that remained.

That morning, she left Victor alone long

enough to walk to the stream with Lanneika, as much to show her where the stream was located as to help her carry back the heavy buckets of water to begin the arduous task of washing not only the stained rags, but a mountain of soiled linen.

Entering the forest with Lanneika, Catherine realized she'd not been outdoors since the accident. Glancing up, she was surprised to find the treetops still bare of leaves. She'd been cooped up in the house so long, she thought it must be spring by now, and she'd find bright green leaves on the trees, or at least the promise of them in the form of tiny new buds. But no — she pulled her shawl closer about her shoulders — the air felt quite chilly. Was it still January, or had February come? She couldn't say for certain. Despite the cold and the leafless trees, she became enthralled by the fresh, clean smell of the air and drew in one long deep breath after another. The fragrant scent of wet leaves and the cool damp earth beneath her feet also served to revitalize her.

Back at the house, she chastised herself for enjoying the short respite and hurried again to Victor's side.

Cleansing his wounds, applying her healing tinctures and ointments, and helping Lanneika prepare their meals were all that mattered now, and for days on end, it was all that occupied Catherine's mind. She and Lanneika stayed busy from early morn till sundown when the soft-spoken Indian girl silently vanished for the day, only to quietly return the following morning. Catherine was grateful for her gentle presence but made a special point of keeping her from the sick room lest her dark-skinned presence upset Victor.

In those early weeks after Nancy and Jack left, one or another of the goodwives, who lived within hailing distance and who had to pass by Catherine's door on their way to the stream for water, would rap at hers to ask after Victor.

"How does Goodman Covington fare today?" asked Goody Smithfield several days in a row.

One day after Catherine's answer had remained the same for close on a week, Goody Smithfield replied, "Well, don't ye worry none, missy, ye won't be alone for long. With your looks, ye'll have a new husband in no time."

Though upset by the woman's insensitive remark, Catherine's murmured reply hid her true feelings. Thereafter, she instructed Lanneika not to disturb her when Goody Smithfield knocked at the door.

Another of her frequent visitors was John Fuller, who in the beginning seemed to profess a genuine interest in Victor's welfare. But when Victor showed no signs of improving, Catherine began to suspect John was stopping by more to see her than to inquire after Victor. Oddly enough, she didn't mind John's visits as much as she did Goody Smithfield's. It was comforting to have someone to talk to during those long evenings she sat alone before the fire, jumping up every few minutes to check on Victor when she heard his low moan coming from the next room.

"Victor is a lucky man," John said on more than one occasion. "I can see ye've been a fine wife to him."

"I am still a fine wife to him," Catherine replied firmly the first time he said it.

She hadn't known John before the day of the accident when he'd arrived with Deputy-Governor Argall after the men had searched the woods for clues. She hadn't forgotten, or forgiven, Argall's thoughtless remark, directed to John, she recalled, about how quickly she'd find herself a new husband when Victor passed away. But, after coming to know John, she realized there was no malice in him. He was a kind man and always asked before he left if she needed help with anything.

"No, thank you, John," she always said, her voice tight and weary sounding, even to herself.

There were mornings when Lanneika arrived before Catherine was awake and the Indian girl quietly set about preparing something for them to eat. Many times, Catherine had no idea what was in the concoctions Lanneika prepared, she just shoved the food into her mouth and in a daze carried a trencher of it into Victor, only to spend an hour or more urging spoonfuls into his mouth. On those mornings when he ate something, she was pleased; most days, he barely swallowed more than a bite or two. In no time, his once muscular frame diminished to little more than a skeleton. It broke Catherine's heart to watch the life drain out of the strong, vital young man she'd married only a few short months before.

Yet, she refused to give up. Despite the fact that there were warmish days when the sun shone brightly but Victor lay inside shaking violently from chills, and nights when the blustery wind blew icy cold yet he lay in bed delirious and convulsing with feverish tremors, she persevered. She grew so weary tending him, she more than once nodded off when, long after sundown, she'd sit before the fire eating spoonfuls straight from the pot of whatever Lanneika had left for her to eat.

As the days passed, she found that even with Lanneika's help there was so much to do every day, she decided to delay the opening of her school another while longer. Besides, she reasoned, despite the fact that she and Lanneika had already scattered clean rushes on the floor several times over, the house still reeked with the malodor that emanated from Victor's leg, and the smell would no doubt repulse the children.

The only good thing to come of replacing the soiled straw on the floor was that she and Lanneika discovered the hiding places of dozens of the blue and purple glass beads Catherine had dropped when she fell from the ladder that day on her way down from the loft. Catherine recalled Noah telling her the beads were valuable to the Indians, and although Lanneika gathered up dozens of them, she quickly handed them over to Catherine rather than attempt to stuff them into her own pockets. Catherine began doling them back out to her as payment for her services. Lanneika seemed pleased with her reward and never asked for anything more from her employer.

On those rare days when Catherine's ointments seemed to keep Victor's pain at bay, she felt encouraged with his progress. When his mind seemed fairly lucid, she would sit beside him and listen to him talk, mostly about his plans for the new mill. She'd nod and smile hoping to lift his spirits, hoping that by doing so, it might help heal his wounds. But as the weeks passed, she knew in her heart that even though his words were positive and the dream in his mind still alive and well, the veil of sadness that always dropped over his eyes told her he knew as well as she that nothing he spoke of would ever come to pass, that his days on earth were fast drawing to an end.

As one long day blurred into another, she began to wonder how Victor managed still to cling to life. Each day she awoke fearful she would turn over to find her husband lying motionless by her side, the shooting pains he'd so often complained of having at last stilled his heart. He was a strong man and determined to survive, but in the end, the lethal arrow wounds finally claimed his life.

Catherine was at her husband's side the morning he died. She'd just brought in a bowl of warm broth and was holding the spoon to feed him when, of a sudden, his eyes sprang open. He gazed full at her; then a small smile appeared on his face, his head fell to one side, and Catherine knew he was gone.

Because she didn't know what else to do, she sent Lanneika for Reverend Buck, who came at once. When he arrived it was decided to remove Victor's body straight-away, rather than lay him out at home. There were no flowers to place beside the body, and her supply of pine-knot candles had dwindled to near nothing. The English custom of burning candles for three or more days and nights, said the reverend, was viewed in Jamestown more as a waste than a tribute to the loved one.

"Best to have done and get on with your life," the reverend concluded sadly. But he did say a prayer for Victor's soul and also one for Catherine, which comforted her.

Still, once Victor's body had been taken away, a fog of gloom settled about her. Inside, she felt numb and sick at heart. It was almost a relief when weariness overtook her long before that day drew to an end, and without thinking she crawled back into bed, some part of her believing that if she took a short nap, she'd wake up and find everything returned again to normal. Nancy, with her quick smile and merry chatter, would be there and also Jack, with his twinkling brown eyes and hearty laughter. And Victor. They were all going to services the next day, weren't they? They'd leave the instant the church bells pealed.

As she drifted off to sleep, Catherine was vaguely aware of Lanneika closing the window covering in her bedchamber, but only seconds later it seemed, vivid images of Victor's bloody, pus-filled wound jarred her awake. Alarmed, she sat bolt upright in bed. How could she have fallen asleep when surely Victor needed — ? But where was he? Suddenly she realized it was pitch dark both inside the house and out. And there was no one in bed beside her.

She spent the remainder of that long night huddled before the low-burning fire in the hearth, her bed rug drawn tightly about her shoulders as she sat staring into the flames, her eyes feeling as red-rimmed as the embers. Was the nightmare over, she wondered, or was she still dreaming?

In a daze when the sun came up the next morning and Lanneika reappeared, Catherine ate the corn porridge the Indian girl set before her, then put on the fresh gown Lanneika laid out for her on the bed. Seated again before the hearth, she wordlessly allowed the Indian girl to brush the tangles from her thick, copper-colored curls.

When Adam and Abigail, Nancy and Jack, and the Morgans all arrived, she walked silently alongside them to the church on the green. It was an especially cold day, and, although Catherine didn't particularly feel the chill, she noticed little puffs of air coming from everyone's mouths as they spoke in hushed tones. She had no idea why the patterns made by the feathery white puffs fascinated her so, but it kept her mind occupied, so she didn't fight it.

Upon entering the dank-smelling building, it surprised Catherine that the church was nearly full, but Abigail leaned over to tell her that Victor was not the only Jamestown colonist being eulogized that day. Influenza and lung fever had claimed the lives of three other settlers. All would be laid to rest that day in the stretch of land recently designated as Jamestown's cemetery.

When the short service concluded and the four pine coffins were carried from the building, Abigail turned to Catherine.

"While Adam and the other men take the coffins to the cemetery, I thought we women could help you pack your belongings. Adam thinks it best you return to Harvest Hill with us today." Her tone sounded as if she were speaking to a child.

Catherine felt like a child, hurt, bewildered, not knowing which way to turn or what to do with herself now that Victor was gone. It still seemed as if the horrible ordeal was not yet over, the long days and endless nights a hazy blur that would never end. But . . . it had ended, hadn't it? So why did she feel so tired and listless, as if all the life had been drained also from her body?

"Catherine," Abigail said. "Did you hear me, sweetie?"

"Hmmm? Yes, of course. Whatever you and Adam think best."

"Well, then —" Abigail said briskly. "We'll just go and get your things and be ready when Adam and the men come for us." She glanced around for Margaret and Nancy and upon spotting them standing a few yards away, said to Catherine, "Wait right here for me, dear."

Catherine said nothing. Her head felt as heavy as lead. Nothing about this nightmare was real. She heard other voices around her, but nothing anyone said made sense. None of their words penetrated the dark fog that filled every corner of her mind. She wished they would all go away and leave her alone. Yet, she didn't want to be alone. She was afraid to be alone. Not realizing what she was doing, she edged closer to a group of women standing nearby talking quietly amongst themselves.

"Well, I suppose we shall all gather here again in a day or two," one woman said, her bonneted head shaking sadly. "I only just learned Richard Benson's little daughter Charity passed away this morning. And her new babe not yet one week old."

Catherine blinked. The woman's words seemed to jog something in her mind. She edged a few steps closer.

"They say her husband is beside himself with grief. Such a handsome young man."

"I suppose Charity's mama will raise the babe. Was it a boy or girl?"

"A precious little girl. You know her first one, a boy, was killed in that awful hurricane we had last spring."

"I'd forgotten that. What a terrible shame. Charity was a taking little thing with her blonde curls and big blue eyes."

Catherine stopped listening. Suddenly, her breath grew short and her heart began to thunder like a drum in her chest. Suddenly, she felt fully awake and aware. *Dear God, in Heaven, was it true? Noah's wife Charity was dead?*

And Victor also gone.

She didn't stop breathing hard until long

after she and the other women had reached her front door. Upon entering the house, Abigail walked straight through to Catherine's bedchamber and knelt down to draw her valise from beneath the bed.

"Catherine, dear, you'll need to tell me what you'd like to bring with you." Abigail's voice sounded muffled from her position on the straw-strewn floor. Suddenly she sat back on her heels, sniffed and pulled a face. "My, I daresay we need to open the window in here."

Catherine was already across the room flinging the window casing aside. A gust of fresh cold air swept in and she filled her lungs to capacity. Turning to face her sister-in-law, she said, in quite a steady tone, "I've changed my mind, Abigail. I intend to stay right here."

Chapter 20

It took some tall talking, but eventually Catherine managed to convince everyone she would be just fine right there in Jamestown. That with Lanneika's help, she could manage quite well on her own. Her school had been in recess long enough. Why, the children had probably forgotten all she'd taught them last year. It was time now to get on with their lessons. Yes, yes, it was. Why, only this morning the reverend had said to let the dead bury the dead and that the living must turn their minds to other things. Well, that was exactly what she intended to do. She was not the least bit tired, not at all. In fact, she felt full of energy; truly she did. Though every last one maintained she looked thinner and more wan than they'd ever seen her, she completely disagreed. No, no she didn't. She was not at all tired, or afraid to be alone. Not at all.

Because, she told herself, after everyone had done precisely as she asked and left her alone, she would not be alone for long. Noah would soon be there. She did not know how long he would wait to come to her, but she had no doubt that he would. They were meant for one another. Had they not pledged their love for one another before God, even as they were children and did not know what "love" or "marriage" meant? God knew they loved one another, and now, at long last, He, in His infinite wisdom, had found a way for them to be together. So, until Noah came to her, she could, and would, manage very well on her own.

However, fearing she would reveal her uplifted spirits when she came face-to-face with Noah, she did choose not to attend the funeral services held two days later for Charity. But considering her grim circumstances, she knew her absence would be excused, if not expected.

The following week her great expectations for her bright future gave her all the energy she needed to spring from bed every morning ready to face the day. She posted a notice on the meetinghouse door stating that school would resume immediately. On the designated day, she was delighted when all her pupils, save one, returned, and that was because the little boy himself had succumbed to illness that past winter. But his younger brother was there to take his place, so she still had five English boys and two little girls. The Indian children had not yet shown up. But she hadn't yet gotten word to Tamiyah to tell her to bring them.

During the next few weeks, it amused her that when the children were there, Lanneika managed always to find something to do indoors. It finally dawned on her that the shy Indian girl was absorbing everything Catherine was attempting to teach the children. A few days after she'd reviewed numbers and sums, Lanneika began to refer to "two" of this and "three" of that. Lanneika, Catherine realized, was a quick study and in no time at all began to correctly use more and more English words, though she often arranged them in an odd, even comical way, which always made Catherine laugh.

Lanneika, in turn, seemed pleased to explain the meanings of many Indian words. The Powhatan word for water, she told Catherine, was *suckquahan*. The word *powhatan*, she said, simply meant falling water, or waterfall, which Lanneika demonstrated by dumping a bucket of water on the ground. *Keshowse* meant sun and a dog was *attemous*. When Lanneika tried to teach Catherine the Indian word for apple, she simply scampered to the loft and came back down carrying one, which she called a *maracah*. The Indian girl's mischievous nature and her humor amused Catherine. She genuinely liked Lanneika and enjoyed her presence more and more.

In addition to the feeling of satisfaction she felt over Lanneika's progress, the children's sweet faces and lively antics also helped to keep her spirits up as she patiently waited for Noah to knock at her door.

Attending Sabbath services on the third Sunday following Victor's death, she was happy as always to see her brother and Nancy, but dismayed to find that Noah was not present, nor any member of his family. She so wished to see him and his new baby, whom she assumed she would one day mother, since, of course, he would bring his infant daughter with him to his new marriage.

That day, she made her way back home, though not alone, as John Fuller made it a habit now to escort her home from services. As she walked, she assured herself she would see Noah again one day. She knew what her future held now, and that knowledge filled her heart to overflowing. The good Lord had smiled on them at last and she and Noah would soon be together as man and wife. The pair of them would then do exactly as the reverend had said at Victor's funeral; turn their minds to the living. Marrying Noah and becoming his wife had been her lifelong dream, and once again, the fulfillment of her dream was within easy grasp.

It did not occur to her that her good spirits might be misinterpreted by John, or any one of the other three men who'd begun to show her attention — Thomas York, who also worked for Adam at Harvest Hill; Ed Henley, a freeman who farmed his own fifty acres; and Jonathan Reed, who'd courted her before she'd wed Victor and who still hadn't found a bride of his own.

Still, on those days when her joy seemed to mount uncontrollably, she'd chastise herself for letting her imagination run away with her. Her own husband in the ground barely a month and in her thoughts she was already wed to another man! Surely God would punish her . . . but how could He? God Himself had plucked both Victor and Charity from this earth. She had done all in her power to keep Victor alive, but God's will was God's will, and no mere human was powerful enough to change that.

Yet, as the days grew longer and warmer, and still Noah did not come, it took every last ounce of her fortitude to continue on without him. How long would it be before he came, she demanded of the Heavens? How long would they have to wait to marry? Would the whole town turn against them if they married long before the accepted time of mourning had passed? But how could she wait a full year to become Noah's wife? She couldn't! She doubted he could wait that long either. On the other hand, judging from the increased attention she was receiving from other unmarried men in Jamestown, apparently it was perfectly acceptable for a young widow to remarry right away.

Both Jonathan and Ed had already made veiled attempts to propose marriage. John Fuller seemed a bit reticent, but perhaps it was because he'd been around during Victor's final days and believed it was too early yet for her to think of marrying again. She'd made a point of voicing her feelings about that to him on several occasions.

"I've only just become a widow, John. It would not be proper for me to entertain thoughts of marrying again so soon." She felt a bit guilty for speaking in direct opposition to what was in her heart, but it couldn't be helped. She had no intention of marrying anyone save Noah Colton, but she couldn't proclaim that truth aloud!

Many nights she lay alone in bed, sleep eluding her as her mind raced on unchecked with plans for their bright future together. They would live here, of course. Noah would continue with his trading, and she with her school. With his little daughter on her hip, they would already be a real family. Her own belly would soon be swollen with child, she knew it. Lanneika would stay on, as Catherine would need help with a husband and two small children to look after. She'd have a son — an adorable little boy with twinkling blue eyes and curly hair, like the little Indian boy, Pamoac's. Odd, she laughed aloud at her own musings. Why would she suddenly think of Pamoac? She hastened to push the image aside and finally drifted off to sleep thinking how happy she'd be to have Noah in bed beside her every night and to soon feel his child quickening within her belly.

The next afternoon, as she mindlessly patted the bed rug back into place on her bed after Lanneika had spent a good two hours beating the dust from it, her thoughts once again ran away with her. This time a vivid reminder of the first time she and Noah had lain together, the night he left, only to return to her later, filled her mind. Chills raced up her spine as she remembered the delicious feel of his lips pressed to hers, his strong chest crushed to her breasts, his caresses, the feel of his hardness against her stomach and her bare legs wrapped around him, then the rapturous moment when she realized he'd spent his seed within her. She dreamily lay down onto the bed as shudders of remembered pleasure rippled through her.

Stop! She shook herself, blushing at her own wantonness as she scrambled to her feet. She shouldn't be thinking such shameful thoughts!

She hurried from her bedchamber and went outdoors in search of Lanneika. Outside, she noted the shadows lengthening. Perhaps Lanneika had already gone for the day. But, no, Catherine found her behind the shed struggling to balance several heavy logs she'd pulled from what remained of the stack of firewood Jack had left for her.

"Let me help you!" Catherine cried, hurrying toward the smaller girl.

Grinning, Lanneika glanced up. "I strong. I carry."

"You are not as strong as I." Catherine

333

knelt to tug at an especially heavy log. But found it wouldn't budge. She stood back with a frown on her face, realizing that despite her earlier protests to the contrary, she *did* need a man around, if for nothing more than to do the heavy lifting and toting. Heaving a frustrated sigh, she looked about for a smaller piece of wood to take in for the night.

Lanneika had already taken her load inside and was now hurrying back outdoors. "One more I get."

"Very well." Catherine cast a last glance at the sparse pieces of wood scattered about on the ground before she also turned to go back inside.

How soon would it be before all the firewood Jack had chopped was gone, she wondered? She supposed she could say something to him or Adam when she saw them next Sabbath. They always asked how she fared, and Adam and Abigail always renewed their invitation for her to join them at Harvest Hill. Or . . . she could say something to John Fuller, as he was always asking if she needed anything, but she hated to take advantage of his good nature, or for him to get in the habit of taking care of her since she had no intention of making that a permanent arrangement. It dawned on her then that her high spirits about Noah were beginning to sag. How much longer before he appeared at her door, she wondered irritably? Didn't he know she needed his help right now?

The next afternoon, after the children had gone for the day, Catherine wearily decided to spend the few remaining hours of daylight turning over the soil in her garden. It would be time to plant soon, and, with the wide stretch of land Victor and Jack had cleared at the edge of the woods, she would be able to have a much larger garden this year. She had hoped Noah would be here to till the soil for her, but as he had not yet appeared, that grueling task still lay undone at her feet.

She made her way into the shed in search of the battered old hoe Adam had left behind. Finding it, she headed back out, her eyes on the ground as she thought ahead to the backbreaking work before her. Nearing the garden gate, she at last glanced up only to stop dead in her tracks when she saw the huge pile of neatly stacked firewood rising before her. Firewood, which had not been there the night before!

Dropping the hoe, she turned and ran back into the house where she knew Lanneika was busy stirring up another of her concoctions for Catherine's supper that night.

"Lanneika! Lanneika!" She jerked open the front door. "Where did all the firewood come from?"

Lanneika looked up. "I not know. It there this morning when I come."

Catherine's brow puckered. "If it was there this morning, that means . . . someone must have brought it during the night or very early this morning. Did you not see anyone when you arrived today?"

The Indian girl shook her head, then turned back to stirring whatever was in the pot suspended over the flames.

Confusion still etched on her face, Catherine retraced her steps back outdoors. It must have been Noah, she decided, her spirits lifting a mite. Perhaps he had come by late last night. Perhaps he had hidden one of his packages in the shed and noticed she was nearly out of firewood. How very like him to want to help her! Perhaps it was quite late when he came, and he had not knocked on her door because he hadn't seen a light. That was it. Noah had been here, dear, sweet, thoughtful Noah. He had come at last!

She picked up the hoe she'd dropped and moved toward the stretch of treeless land

336

where Jack and Victor had meant to plant corn and squash this year. And with a lighter heart set about the difficult task of breaking up the clods of hard dirt, pausing on occasion to toss aside a pebble or misplaced piece of shell. One long hour into her work, she straightened, her blue-green eyes gazing out across the large area still to be turned over. There were days when it seemed the work would never end, and yet, it would soon be easier, she told herself. When Noah was there to help her, every task would seem lighter. His teasing banter would cheer her, his merry laughter carry her through the day.

She turned with fresh resolve to her task and worked until again the shadows lengthened, and the sun began to dip lower in the sky. The tempting scent of whatever it was Lanneika was preparing for her dinner drifted toward her on the breeze, which was also beginning to turn chilly.

Lanneika would be leaving soon, and once more she would return to her empty house and eat her meal in silence, her heart aching for the company of the one man she truly loved and had longed to be with her entire life. Though it had been just over a month since they'd buried Victor, at times she felt guilty that she had almost ceased to think of him. Noah becoming her husband was all that filled her thoughts and dreams now. She should still be mourning Victor, but how could she make herself feel something she did not?

Dear God, her worrisome thoughts turned heavenward as she sank to her knees right where she was. *Dear Lord,* she prayed, her eyes squeezed shut, her hands folded before her, *please, please forgive me for no longer mourning my husband Victor, but dear Lord, please, please let nothing keep Noah from me! Not now, not after all we've been through. We deserve to be together and to be happy at last; truly we do.*

Please make haste to send him to me soon, dear Lord. I need him now. Thank you for your many blessings, Lord. I beseech you to enfold Victor and Charity in your arms forevermore. Amen. Oh, and, please, dear Lord, help me to rein in my wanton thoughts and to behave in a seemly manner when I am out amongst the townsfolk . . . at least until Noah and I become man and wife. Thank you, Lord.

When the aching muscles in Catherine's shoulders relaxed, and her thoughts and mind settled again into stillness, she opened her eyes but was at once startled to see some yards away from her at the edge of the forest what she at first thought was a vision. A vision of an Indian sitting astride an enormous white stallion!

Not taking her eyes from the image, she slowly stood up. She raised a hand to shield her gaze from the long rays of the setting sun that shone around the vision like a halo. Even in the glare, she could see that the Indian brave atop the horse was an especially tall man. His long muscular legs were covered with doeskin breeches. His powerfully sculpted chest and arms were bare except for the animal skin that lay draped across his back. She felt her breath quicken with a mixture of fear and alarm. What did the Indian want?

Something seemed to draw her toward him, but fear kept her rooted to the spot where she stood. Because the glaring sunlight shone so brightly in her eyes, she could not clearly see the Indian's features, but she could plainly see that his piercing black eyes were looking straight at her.

Suddenly the spell was broken when Lanneika ran from the front of the house toward the Indian brave sitting astride the enormous white horse. Catherine watched as the powerful man stretched one strong arm down to encircle the girl's lithe body, and in a single swift motion, lifted her up and settled her in front of him on the horse.

Then he pressed his heel into the beast's side. The mighty steed whirled around, and in a flash of flowing white mane and tail the vision disappeared into the woods.

Catherine stood transfixed. Who might the Indian brave be? Lanneika's beloved? Her brother, or perhaps, a friend from her village come to fetch her? Whoever he was, she decided, blinking herself back to her surroundings, he was magnificent. And the sight she'd witnessed between the pair of them just now struck her as breathtakingly beautiful.

The following morning, Catherine arose unusually early. Still fresh in her mind was the memory of the magnificent Indian brave sitting astride his enormous white stallion. For some reason, she had to know who the man was. She was up, dressed, and waiting for Lanneika when the girl quietly let herself into the house.

"Oh!" said Lanneika, surprise evident in her tone when she spotted Catherine busily stirring something in the pot over the flames. "You early up."

Catherine grinned. Lanneika's manner of speaking continued to bring a smile to her lips. "Yes, I am early up. Come, I have already made our breakfast." She filled two trenchers with steaming hot oatmeal, then led the way to the board table where she'd already laid out two wooden spoons.

Lanneika hesitantly slid onto one of the backless benches, no doubt feeling somewhat ill-at-ease over being served by her employer instead of the other way around.

Catherine took her place at the table and began to eat. "I thought we might talk a bit before the children come this morning," she began pleasantly.

Chewing small bites of oatmeal, Lanneika's dark eyes remained fixed on Catherine's face.

Catherine wasn't quite sure how to begin. She'd never asked the girl any questions of a personal nature before. "Is . . . your village close by?"

Lanneika shook her head, then, shrugged. "Sometime close, sometime long way. Not long way when I come on horse."

"Did you come on horseback this morning?"

Lanneika nodded.

"I don't believe you've ever told me the name of your tribe."

"My tribe Warrastanundas."

"Oh." Catherine didn't attempt to pronounce the convoluted name. "Do you have brothers and sisters?"

"Many brothers, many sisters."

"I see." Catherine hesitated, the one question she longed to ask burning like a flame in her mind. Why she felt she had to know the answer seemed quite silly to her, yet for some reason, she fervently wanted to know. "Well, I . . . happened to see you leave last evening with an Indian brave. Was he, perhaps . . . one of your brothers?"

Lanneika's face brightened. "Phyrahawque. He brother."

Catherine leaned forward. "Farea-huck?"

Lanneika laughed at Catherine's pronunciation of the odd name. "Phy-ra-haw-que." The girl tried to sound out the word as Catherine often did with her.

Catherine's brow furrowed. It appeared Lanneika was saying a word that sounded very like 'Fire-hawk,' although she knew that could not be right. Still, she tried it. "Phy-ra-hawk?"

Lanneika's shiny dark head nodded vigorously. "Phyrahawque!" Her dark eyes twinkled merrily.

"Phyrahawque." Catherine repeated, more strongly this time. "The name suits him," she said, thinking to herself that, indeed, it did. She'd never seen a more arresting, powerful-appearing man in her life. Why, if she were a young Indian maid, Lanneika's magnificent brother Phyrahawque would be the very man she'd set her cap for!

Chapter 21

"Was the firewood I left sufficient for your needs?" John Fuller asked when he stopped by the following Sabbath to escort Catherine to services.

John's question startled her, it having never occurred to her that her benefactor might be him. "Yes, it was . . . or, rather, is. Thank you, John. I had no idea who had done me such a kindness." She smiled up into his warm brown eyes as they set out to walk to the meetinghouse. It had also surprised her when he rapped so early that morning at her door. Typically, he only walked her *home* from services, not to.

After Reverend Buck had intoned his final amen that day, Catherine's entire family — Adam and Abigail, the Morgans, Nancy and Jack, and John — all made the return walk home to her small house. Once there, the men took chairs outdoors to smoke and talk, while the women set about preparing a late afternoon meal. It was an especially warm March day, and everyone was enjoying the balmy breeze and sunny sky.

"I see you and John Fuller have become a couple," said Abigail, smiling her approval.

Catherine ducked her head. Why did everyone, including John Fuller, seem bent on linking her with him?

"How 'bout it, missy?" Margaret teased as she floured her hands in preparation to pound a lump of dough into a sheet of flatbread.

Nancy directed a speaking look at Catherine, then said quietly to the others, "Our Catherine is not one to talk openly of her feelin's."

Catherine rewarded her friend with a look of gratitude, then to escape further questions headed bravely up the ladder Victor had built to the loft. Nancy would need apples for the pie she was making.

Nancy hurried up the steps behind her. "You remarrying is a topic of much concern these days," she said in a low tone.

"Well, I've no intention of marrying John Fuller," Catherine whispered. The two made sufficient noise as they dug in the barrels of foodstuffs to conceal the sound of their voices.

"I know you are waiting for Noah to appear at your door," Nancy said, not in an accusing way.

"I am certain he will come, Nancy."

"You know Adam has no use for Noah. In fact, he is dead set against you marrying him. He means to forward Tom York's suit." Nancy glanced at Catherine as if to gauge her reaction to this. "Tom is a good man; he and Jack get along very well."

"Nancy, please. You know I have eyes for no one but Noah. Now that we are both free, surely Adam cannot think I would be receptive to anyone save Noah."

"Have you seen him?"

They walked to a barrel of dried peas, into which Nancy dipped the empty gourd she carried.

"No. But, he will come. I am certain of it."

Nancy straightened. "In the meantime, you appear to be encouraging John Fuller and Jonathan Reed. And we've also heard talk about Ed —"

Catherine took umbrage. "I am *not* encouraging them! They just . . . appear at my door, and I . . . let them in. I am not encouraging them!" She turned and fled across the room, the loose floorboards creaking beneath her feet.

Once the meal was finally ready, the men

pulled two of the long board tables together and they all gathered around to eat their fill of the tasty pork-and-vegetable stew and top it off with Nancy's delicious apple pie. The talk was lively, and, though Catherine was growing increasingly agitated over the state of her affairs, she managed to join in with the others and enjoy the company and laughter, which she had sorely missed of late. Most especially, she enjoyed hearing Abigail talk about little Eli. How she longed for a babe of her own.

Before the meal concluded, a rap sounded at the door. When Adam rose to answer the summons, Ed Henley stepped inside.

Awkward silence filled the room until Adam invited the somewhat embarrassed young man to join them. "You're welcome to join us, Ed! Ethan," he addressed the Morgan boy, "scoot over and make room at your end."

"Please, do join us." Catherine remembered her manners. She rose to fetch another trencher, but Abby was closer to the shelf that held them, so she handled the task.

Finding himself seated on the bench directly opposite John Fuller seemed to distress Ed. To put him at ease, Adam drew him into conversation, asking if he'd yet started his tobacco seedlings this year.

"Coming up nicely," the young man replied, his gray eyes darting from Catherine to John Fuller and back again.

"Be sure to cover your new plants with brush to protect 'em from a late frost," Adam instructed. "Not unusual to get a snowfall as late as April 'round here."

"Here you are, Ed." Abigail set a trencher full of steaming hot stew before him. "Adam, send the flatbread to this end of the table."

The newcomer wasted no time digging into the food, and, in mere seconds, his presence was no longer noticed. Except by Catherine. And probably John. And Adam.

When the meal concluded, the men again gathered outdoors to smoke and sip the last of their ale while the women cleared away the table and scoured the soiled trenchers. When Catherine stepped outdoors, a nod of Adam's head indicated he'd like a private word with her.

They walked past the men toward the shed in back. Adam made a favorable comment in regard to the lean-to, which he hadn't seen since Jack and Victor enclosed it.

"We call it a shed now," Catherine replied, grinning. The setting sun glancing off her auburn hair sparkled with glints of gold. The excitement of the day had brought a becoming blush to her cheeks.

"Your beauty has returned, Cat," Adam said. "I confess Abby and I were reluctant to leave you here alone after Victor was gone." He paused, directing a long gaze out over the stretch of land his sister had begun to till. "But, you appear to be faring well enough."

Catherine looked up at her brother. She was especially thankful he was here with her in the New World — a frightening and unpredictable land where healthy young men could be felled by arrows, where houses were tossed about by strong winds and newborn babies struck dead. She wondered if she would ever grow accustomed to the wilderness life, or if some part of her would always remain anxious and afraid; or perhaps she simply needed Noah with her to calm her fears and keep her safe. "I'm settling in," she murmured.

"You cannot remain alone forever, Cat. You must remarry. You've a good-sized house here, with only you in it. Rather surprises me Argall hasn't insisted you take in another family now that Jack and Nancy are gone."

"No one has said anything about that to

me. Perhaps because I run the only school in Jamestown and require additional space."

"Perhaps."

"To my knowledge," she added, "no ships full of homeless settlers has recently docked."

"New settlers typically arrive in the spring," Adam said authoritatively. "Living alone goes against God and nature. You must remarry."

Becoming annoyed by her brother's patronizing tone, Catherine thrust her chin up. "I have every intention of remarrying, Adam."

"Ah? And is the lucky fellow amongst us today? You seem to be drawing suitors like moths to a flame. I daresay either John or Ed would suit, as well as Tom York. Which young man has stolen the fair Catherine's heart?"

She looked down, nervously drawing a circle on the ground with the toe of her boot. "You know where my affections lie."

"So," his tone hardened, "you think to marry Noah now that he is free." It was not a question.

So she didn't answer.

His tone grew even harder. "To marry Noah would be a grave mistake, Catherine. There are two fine young men here today

350

who'd make excellent husbands for you, and others to choose from, make no mistake."

Her lips pursed. "Who I choose to marry is my concern, Adam."

"That's where you are wrong!" he shot back. "Noah Colton is even now, today, even as we speak, forwarding the deception that he is heartbroken over the death of his wife. And do you know why he is behaving in so shameless a manner? Do you?" he demanded.

Catherine frowned up at him. "How dare you speak in so disparaging a fashion of —"

"Noah Colton wants one thing and one thing only," he cut her off. "Land. He thinks that by making Richard Benson believe he is grieving Charity's death that Benson will sign over his vast estate to his heartsick young son-in-law. What Noah doesn't know is that he is deceiving no one. Not even Richard Benson."

"I don't believe you!" She folded her arms across her chest. "Noah hasn't a devious bone in his body." Catherine glared up at him. "And what's more, he loves me. And I have never stopped loving him. Noah's suit is the only one I will entertain, or accept."

Adam snorted his contempt. "Then you are more foolish than I thought, little sister. Mark my words, you will live to regret the day you marry that scoundrel. He should have been the one shot by an arrow that day in the woods, not Victor."

"Noah wasn't in the woods that day!"

His eyes narrowed. "Can you be certain of that? It wouldn't surprise me to learn that he —"

"Hush! I will not listen to one more word said against him!" She picked up her skirts and ran back toward the house, tears of hurt and anger swimming in her eyes, her heart pounding in her breast.

That night as she lay alone in her bed, the house at last devoid of people, she could not halt the tears of longing that spilled down her cheeks and soaked into the pillow. Turning to bury her head in her arms, she began to weep. Her sobs of anguish became so loud she almost didn't hear the rap-rap-rapping at her door.

When the noise did penetrate her consciousness, she swiped her tears on the sleeve of her night rail and sat up to listen. Hearing the rapping sound again, she let out a joyous cry, and sprang from her bed to run barefoot to the door.

"Noah!" she cried when she flung open the door and saw that it was he. "At last, you've come!"

CHAPTER 22

She flung herself into his arms and, burying her face in his shoulder, drank in his familiar scent. "I am bereft without you. Please say we can now be wed."

He pushed her from him as he barged into the house. "There are things I must take care of before I marry again."

"What things?" she cried. "You are free, I am free, what can possibly stand in our way now?"

"Plenty." He sat down on the stump before the low-burning fire.

"I don't understand." She stood before him wringing her hands.

"Benson is making it impossible for me to marry again."

Catherine sucked in her breath. "How can he do such a thing?"

Noah snorted. "Benson can do anything he pleases."

Tears sprang to Catherine's eyes. "But

surely you can do something, Noah."

"Don't fret, sweeting. We can be together, we just cannot be . . . married."

"Noah, what are you suggesting? Tell me what's wrong. Why can we not be married at once?"

He inhaled a long breath and finally spoke. "When Charity and I married, her father promised to deed a hundred and fifty acres of land to me. I was already established as a trader, and Benson could see that my efforts on that head were of benefit to the colony. He never made good on his word about the land."

"But, why won't he give it to you now?"

"According to Benson, his daughter's death puts a different complexion on things. He says if I marry again, he'll not give me the land at all. He fears when I die, it would pass to my new family, who won't be in any way connected to him. The only way he'll deed the land to me now is if I agree to remain unmarried; in other words, if I stay on with them and raise my child, then he can be certain the land will pass in a direct line to Charity's daughter's husband. In fact, he says the only person he'll deed the land to now is Livvy."

"Livvy?"

"We named the baby Elizabeth, after

Charity's grandmother. They call her Livvy."

"I'd love to see your daughter." Catherine's tone softened. "Does she look like — ?"

"Yellow hair, blue eyes."

His words seemed oddly devoid of emotion, but Catherine took it more as a sign of his distress than lack of love for his newborn child, or grief over the death of his wife. Poor Noah, his heart was probably as heavy as hers when she first came here and learned that Noah was married and that her father was also gone. Suddenly she remembered Tamiyah's dire prediction of a year ago that Charity would have no more babes. She wondered now if what Tamiyah really meant was that Charity would not survive another birthing.

"How did . . . Charity die?" she asked softly.

He shrugged. "It was a hard birth. At first they thought the child was stillborn, then someone heard it whimper, though weakly. Baby's still not strong. Afterward, Charity never left her bed. Just grew weaker and weaker. Another pregnancy was simply too much for her. The Bensons blame me, of course." He paused again. "And now they think I'm being cold and calculating by wanting what they promised when we married."

"But couldn't you promise not to leave the land to anyone save Livvy?"

"I've mentioned that. Benson doesn't trust me to do it."

"How dare they mistrust you!"

"How dare Benson not make good on his word and in the same breath say he doesn't trust me!"

Catherine sank onto the chair opposite him, her head shaking sorrowfully. "We have waited so very long to be together. There must be a way."

"There is," he said.

Her head jerked up, her gaze trusting as she regarded the man she loved with all her heart.

"I could continue to come to you whenever I can, just as I have tonight. I could have come sooner, but —"

"No!" She drew back in horror. "I refuse to be your mistress, Noah! I want a real home, with children, and you as my husband. I will not settle for stolen moments in the dead of night. I will not!"

He shrugged. "Then I don't know what to say, Cat."

"Is possessing your own land that important to you?"

He sprang to his feet and began to pace.

"Land is what the New World is all about. I did not come here to be a common laborer, to toil in some field, or to serve another man! God knows I can't be a trader forever. A man must have a quick wit and be even quicker on his feet to remain alive in my business. I cannot be a trader forever!"

"Oh, Noah." Catherine also rose and attempted to wind her arms about his neck. But he'd have none of it.

"I suppose Jack is gloating over his elevated status as Adam's foreman." The anger in his tone increased.

"They were all here today. We had a nice family dinner."

"I saw who was here today," he growled.

"You . . . saw?" She resumed her seat. It was far warmer to stay close to the fire than to stand in the draft with Noah as he paced.

He inhaled a sharp breath. "I've learned a few tricks from the Indians. Such as how to 'see' without being seen." He paused to cast an angry glance at the door, as if he thought he could see straight through it. "I've seen all the men hanging after you — Reed, Fuller, Ed Henley — knocking at your door at all hours, early of a morning, leaving late at night." He whirled to face her. "What do you do with them?"

"What do you mean what do I do with

them? I don't do anything with them. They have all made their intentions known to me and I suppose I shall have to settle on one of them now, since you won't —"

He hurried to her side. "Catherine, you know I want you. I've always wanted you."

"And I want you, Noah." When he knelt before her, she reached to tenderly hold his handsome face between her hands. "Why is owning a piece of Benson's land of such importance to you, my darling?"

"Because it is!" He jerked from her grasp and resumed his agitated pacing.

"But why can you not purchase your own land?"

"With what?" He scowled. "Beads? Trade the Indians a few scraps of copper for a little plot of land hidden somewhere deep in the woods?"

She waited, hoping his anger would subside. "I wouldn't mind where we lived, Noah. I just want to be with you."

A frustrated sigh escaped him. "And I want to be with you. At least if I married you, I'd have something other men wanted. Right now I have nothing."

"It doesn't matter to me what other men want. I'm yours, and you're mine, that's all that matters."

He knelt before her again, his eyes hard.

"You are mine, Cat. I've said it before, and I'll say it again. I'll kill any man who touches you."

She drew back in horror. "Don't say that, Noah. Not after Victor —"

"Oh, I . . . I don't mean I would actually —"

She smiled shakily. "I know you would never kill anyone. I know you are as distraught as I that we cannot be together now. But surely you have something of value you could trade with the Indians for a piece of land? You must have something."

"It wouldn't matter if I did. The king, the governor, the Crown doesn't recognize that the Indians own this land. The only way for me to get any land is through a bona fide Virginia Company land grant."

Catherine thought a long moment. She knew about the Virginia Company Head-right System; it was how Adam had come by his land. She had paid Nancy's passage over. Shouldn't that entitle *her* to a fifty-acre grant?

"Noah, are women allowed to own land?"

"Of course they are." He resumed pacing. "Benson is threatening to leave my hundred and fifty acres to my daughter."

"I paid Nancy's passage over. Shouldn't that entitle me to fifty acres?"

He stopped dead in his tracks. "You own fifty acres?"

"Not yet. I've told no one I paid her passage. Nancy was a servant in London. So we could begin here on an equal footing, I promised her I would say nothing. But I can't see why it would matter now."

His features alight with interest, he sat down again. "Do you have a written record of the transaction?"

"No-o." She shook her head slowly. "But Nancy would attest to it. And, if Captain Phillips were to sail into Jamestown again, I'm sure he would verify that I gave him a five-pound voucher, and he wrote Nancy's name in the ship's log."

"Fifty acres." He nodded, apparently considering this new turn.

"Do you not have any money at all, Noah?"

Still deep in thought, he shook his head. "Only a bit."

"I still have a bit of what I brought with me."

"You have money?" Again his interest rose. "English pounds?"

She nodded. "Perhaps there would be enough to purchase another fifty acres, or —"

360

"Where is your money? I suppose Adam has it," he spat out.

"No." She stood up. "I have it here." She skirted past him into her bedchamber and quickly returned carrying a small leather pouch.

Noah's eyes fixed on her delicate hands while she withdrew the two faded five-pound notes and handed them to him. The pouch still jingled with a few coins. "There's a bit more here. How much land could you buy with ten pounds?"

He threw his head back and laughed aloud. "At least a hundred acres!"

"But how could you work that much alone, Noah? Wouldn't it be better to buy two indentured contracts? Then you'd not only have the land, you'd also have two men to help you work it."

He stopped, a sly grin lifting the corners of his mouth. "You are a rare find, Catherine, my girl!" He excitedly reached to pull her to her feet. As he did so, the notes slipped from his grasp and fluttered down, down, down toward the bed of red-hot embers.

Catherine's sharp eyes saw where the notes landed. She jerked away from him and, dropping to her knees, scooped up the notes mere seconds before they burst into flames.

"I think I'd best keep these!" she declared, waving the slightly scorched papers in the air, then stuffing them back into her pouch.

He continued to laugh. "You have made me a happy man, my love!" He grasped her around the waist and danced her about the dimly lit room, both laughing happily.

Less than a quarter hour later, Noah slipped from her door into the darkened street. Catherine was so thrilled he had come that it didn't occur to her to ask when they could be married, or even when he'd take her to meet with the reverend to have the banns posted.

She crawled back into bed, realizing only then that if Noah had wanted to make love to her that night she would have willingly let him. They already knew one another in the Biblical sense, so as far as she was concerned, they were indeed already married. But it didn't matter. They had a lifetime ahead of them to snuggle beneath the bed rug and to fall asleep in one another's arms. She closed her eyes and drifted off to sleep, for the first time in a long time with a smile on her face.

But she awoke the next morning realizing

she was indeed annoyed over the fact that she had no idea when she and Noah would be wed. He'd been so pleased that she could give him what he wanted, a hundred and fifty acres of land, that he'd made no definite decision regarding *when* they could marry. And, as usual, she had no idea when she'd see him again for he'd said nothing further on that head either.

Aware of muffled noises coming from the common room where Lanneika was busy preparing her morning meal, Catherine's brow furrowed as she dressed. Advancing into that room, she was startled to find Ed Henley seated at the board table, enjoying a hearty portion of Lanneika's hot corn pudding and fried journey cakes.

"Mornin', Miss Catherine," he looked up, a shy smile on his sun-lined face, "ye look lovely today."

"Thank you, Edward, but . . . what are you doing here, so . . . early?" She recalled Noah's remark last night regarding her gentleman callers arriving at all hours. "Do you . . . require something?"

"No, ma'am, Miss Lanneika fixed me up right good." He drove his spoon into the corn pudding again.

"He plow field," Lanneika said, a grin on her face as she set another trencher down

363

on the table for Catherine.

"What field?"

Ed motioned over his shoulder with his wooden spoon. "Yeste'dey I saw yer little plot was only jes' barely turned up. Thought I'd finish the job for ye. Brung my ox and plow."

"Oh, so you mean to till my garden for me?"

"Done it already."

"Well, thank you kindly, Ed. I truly appreciate your thoughtfulness." Except now she had to find a way to tell Noah and hope he would not be too terribly jealous, or angry.

A few days later, Catherine still hadn't seen Noah's handsome face, so she thought she'd plant her field with corn, which would have the effect of obscuring the ruts laid down by Ed Henley's plow. Perhaps she wouldn't have to tell Noah who tilled the land up for her after all. If Noah thought it was his place to perform that task, he should have been on hand to do it.

After lessons were over, and the children had gone for the day, Catherine rummaged around in the loft for the kernels of corn she'd set aside for planting. Finding them, she hastened outdoors, set the basket of corn on the ground and was walking back toward the shed for the hoe when Lanneika came running around the corner of the house.

"What you do now, Miss Cat-e-wren?"

"I intend to plant my corn now the ground's tilled up."

"No plant now!" Lanneika's dark head shook vigorously, her black eyes round.

Catherine looked at the girl as if she had taken leave of her senses. "Why must I not plant my corn today?" she demanded, both hands on her hips.

"Snow more come. Must wait."

One eyebrow lifted. "You are telling me more snow is coming?" She directed a pointed gaze up at the sunny blue sky. The past several days had been quite warm, complete with balmy breezes. "I believe winter is long past, Lanneika, and I mean to plant my corn today." She turned with decision toward the shed.

"No! Must wait! Come, I show you when time plant."

Catherine could see the girl would not be put off, so with a sigh, she let Lanneika lead the way into the woods. In moments the girl stopped and pointed overhead to a white oak tree upon whose branches tiny green buds peeked through.

Puzzled, Catherine looked up at the tree then back at her young guide, now shuffling through piles of dead leaves at the base of the tree in search of . . . something. At length, Lanneika snatched up a long stick, dropped to her knees and with the stick drew an outline of . . . something on the ground. When she finished, she gazed up at Catherine, a look of satisfaction on her pretty face.

"See?" Lanneika pointed to the picture she'd drawn, which looked to be some sort of . . . animal.

"A squirrel?" Catherine guessed.

"No!" Lanneika giggled. Using the stick she tapped at the animal's long, slim tail.

"A mouse?"

Lanneika nodded, her dark eyes twinkling merrily. "Plant corn when" — she pointed up at the tree — "leaf big as mo . . . ma . . . mause ear." She tugged at her own ear. "Snow no more come."

Catherine began to laugh. Lanneika always managed to find a unique way of getting her point across. "So . . . you are quite certain another snowstorm is on the way, and I simply cannot plant my corn today."

"No have *nammais*."

"Nam-ma-is?" Catherine repeated hesitantly, not at all certain she wanted to know what that was.

As they headed back through the forest, Lanneika did her best to demonstrate the meaning of the new word with hand motions that looked like a fish swimming in water.

By the time they reached the house, the only thing swimming was Catherine's head. She decided to heed Lanneika's advice and plant her corn another day.

And was glad she'd done so. Two days later, she awoke to find a blanket of snow had covered the ground during the night. Lanneika didn't have to say "I told you so" when she arrived that morning. An impish grin and the twinkle in her black eyes adequately conveyed the sentiment. For three days afterward, icy wind blew the frosty snowflakes inside the house every time Catherine opened the door.

Late one night, she finally flung it open to admit the one person she'd waited all week to see.

"Noah! Come in out of the cold."

He stepped into the house, stamping snow from his boots before hurrying toward the hearth where a warm fire blazed.

"Where have you been? I've so many things to ask you, I —"

"I'm here now." A curt tone cut her off.

She patted a chair for him to sit and sat down on the one opposite. "What's kept you?" she couldn't help asking, but willed her voice to sound a trifle less impatient.

"I'd have come sooner, but this freakish snowstorm kept me on the Benson farm the entire week. Benson put me to work covering the tobacco seedlings. Now he fears he may have lost a good many due to the ice."

"Oh, dear," Catherine murmured, hoping the same fate hadn't befallen Adam's young plants.

"At any rate, I finally managed to escape."

Catherine was pleased then to see Noah's familiar easy grin return to his face.

"When are we to marry, Noah?" she asked in a soft voice.

The grin disappeared. "As soon as ye've a land grant in your pocket, sweetheart. By my reckoning, that could take a while." He turned to hold his hands up before the fire.

"Are you saying we must wait until —"

"Exactly what I'm saying, my dear. Right now, I've only got promises from both you and Benson. As soon as you show me the fifty-acre grant you're entitled to for Nancy's passage, we'll summon the parson."

"But, Noah, I —" Her crestfallen tone matched the supreme disappointment on her face.

"Can't be helped, sweetheart. I'll not exchange one promise for another. I need proof. I want the land grant in my hand this time before I say 'I do.' "

Catherine had no choice but to abandon the charged subject. Though she was disappointed, she decided that perhaps Noah was not being unreasonable; after all, he had been disappointed before, so it was understandable for him to be mistrustful now. Later, when he suggested they warm one another beneath the bedcovers, she meekly followed him into her bedchamber.

He took her that night, but Catherine's heart wasn't in it. His stubborn refusal to trust her, or to set a date for them to marry, had cut her to the quick.

The following morning it dawned on Catherine that as Victor's widow she was already in possession of the fifty acres he'd been granted for paying his passage over. He'd shown her the land the day they walked to the glass manufacturing plant. And after they married, he'd also shown her the actual Virginia Company land grant.

Trouble was, she had no idea where he'd put the piece of paper. And, even if and when she had the legal document in her hands, she'd still have to wait until the next time Noah dropped by to show it to him.

But surely it would serve to hasten their walk down the aisle. Surely.

CHAPTER 23

By mid-afternoon, Catherine had located the document and tucked it into her valise next to the leather pouch with the five-pound notes. Now all she had to do was present it to Noah . . . the next time he appeared at her door. Although his stubbornness in the matter of their marrying both annoyed and dismayed her, she concluded that her ten pounds and the fifty acres of land could in a way be likened to her dowry, which was generally surrendered before the actual wedding ceremony took place.

That week all traces of the snowstorm finally disappeared, and it seemed spring had come at last. One sunny morning Catherine was pleased to find Tamiyah at her door bringing both Tonkee and Pamoac to school again.

Catherine invited the children in, noting that today both were properly clothed — Tonkee in a simple one-piece garment, Pamoac wearing a doeskin shirt over his breeches. Because the little Indian boy had grown taller over the winter months, his arms and legs now appearing somewhat gangly, she assumed the shirt she had given him last summer no longer fit.

As usual, the sight of Pamoac brought a smile to Catherine's lips. With his curly brown hair and the merry twinkle in his black eyes, he was such an adorable child she could hardly take her eyes from him. Suddenly, it struck her there was something about Pamoac that reminded her of . . . well, he reminded her of Noah, who'd been only a few years older than Pamoac the first time she caught sight of him playing in the meadow with Adam. As a little girl, she thought Noah was the most handsome boy she'd ever seen.

Later that afternoon Lanneika brought in a bundle of fresh pine-knot candles she'd spent the bulk of the day making. After depositing them in the loft, she came back downstairs.

"Indian boy and girl here today," she remarked to Catherine, busily sweeping ashes from the edge of the hearth into the fire.

"Yes, Tamiyah's children, Tonkee and Pamoac."

"Pamoac trader-man's boy."

At first Lanneika's words didn't register with Catherine. When they did, she nearly dropped her broom into the fire. "W-what did you say?"

"Pamoac's father light-skin. Trader-man."

Stunned, Catherine felt so light-headed she had to fumble behind her for the chair in order to sit down before she fell down. "Are — are you certain of that?" No matter what the girl said, Catherine knew it was true. She didn't even have to ask *which* trader-man. There was only one white man in all of Jamestown who could have fathered Pamoac.

Lanneika eyed her employer. "You not well, Miss Cat-e-wren? Need *suckquahan?*"

"No, thank you, Lanneika. I don't need water. I-I'm just a bit tired."

Catherine's mind was still reeling as she ate her supper alone that night. She recalled the conversation she'd had with Noah after she first met Tamiyah in the forest and invited her children to come to school. Now she knew why Noah had so vehemently opposed the idea.

He obviously knew Tamiyah, since she was the very woman he'd fetched the day Charity gave birth. Thinking further, she decided it best to say nothing to him. More than likely Noah would only angrily point out that it happened long before she came to Jamestown and it had nothing to do with her.

Besides, she had heard rumors about the Indians actually offering their women to Englishmen who stayed overnight in their villages. This was likely not the first time a child had resulted from such a union. Seven years ago, Noah was unmarried, so lying with Tamiyah was not violating any vow he'd made. Yet the London clergyman had spoken also of the importance of a man coming to the marriage bed chaste. Apparently, that had not been the case with Noah either.

Still . . . now that she knew the truth, she found it difficult to digest. What saddened her most was the fact that Noah knew Pamoac was his son and, so far as she could see, he took no interest whatever in the precious little boy.

Perhaps it was because he didn't want to be reminded of his sin. Life here was hard — it was no wonder Noah had succumbed to baser needs when so few pleasures were available. When they were married, she would help him see the world anew, including the beauty of his sweet child.

"You continue to surprise me, my love!" Noah exclaimed when she told him she was currently in possession of fifty acres of land, then handed him the actual Virginia Company land grant.

He strutted around the room, his chest puffed out. "I can hardly wait to see the look on your brother's face, and Benson's, the day I roll my barrels of fine Virginia tobacco down to the pier. And collect my fortune when I sell it to the captain. Do you suppose King James himself will deign to smoke my tobacco leaves?"

Catherine laughed, pleased to see Noah so happy. But she did wonder at his plans. According to Adam, it could take a man an entire year to clear even one acre of land in readiness to plant. Noah, she feared, didn't have the least notion what it took to plant, or harvest, a tobacco crop. But she supposed he would learn. There were plenty of successful planters in Jamestown who would gladly answer his questions. Perhaps even Adam would come around. She'd hate for the animosity between the two of them to continue once she and Noah were wed.

The next day Catherine was giddy with happiness when Noah came and took her to meet with Reverend Buck. The following

Sabbath, their banns were read from the pulpit, then posted on the meetinghouse door.

A fortnight later, she put on her favorite rose-colored padusay gown, and gazing dreamily up at Noah, standing beside her in the church on the green, she at last became Goodwife Colton. Adam and Abigail were not present to witness the nuptials, but Jack and Nancy stood up with them and both signed their names as witnesses in the church registry. Although Catherine regretted that her mother could not have been present, as she had also loved Noah and many times expressed her desire to see the two of them wed, her joy over at last being united in holy matrimony with Noah Colton was nonetheless complete and unfettered.

It was the second time Reverend Buck had performed marriage ceremonies for both Noah and Catherine, the second time in less than a twelvemonth for Catherine. She was a bit disappointed that, after their vows had been exchanged, the reverend did not deliver the customary Marriage Sermon, no doubt believing that since this was not a first marriage for either, they both knew what they were getting into and, if trouble arose, how to deal with it. Instead, he murmured, "May God grant you both good health and . . . long lives." Then he took himself off, leaving the foursome to make their way home and conduct whatever celebration they had planned to mark the occasion. The lack of special words from the minister made the beautiful occasion seem a bit rushed, but not even that omission could dim Catherine's joy.

On the way home from the church, the men gravitated to one another and walked together ahead of the ladies. Catherine took advantage of the opportunity to speak privately with Nancy.

"I hope you will not be displeased with me," she began in a low tone, "but I was obliged to tell Noah that I paid your passage to the New World. He insists now that I apply for the fifty acres of land I am entitled to."

It was a moment before Nancy responded solemnly. "I understand. If that is what your husband wishes, then ye have no choice in the matter. I have learned that is the way of it when a woman is married."

Catherine nodded. "Thank you for understanding, Nancy."

"It's just that here in Jamestown, I feel as if I am like everyone else, even above some."

"Indeed, you are, Nan. You have changed a great deal since we arrived — your bearing, your manner of speaking. Everyone believes you to be a refined young lady. Your transformation quite pleases me."

"I owe my fine new life to you, Catherine. You were brave to escape the Montcriefs as you did."

Catherine laughed. "And you were brave to follow me."

Smiling serenely, Catherine slipped her arm through her companion's. "You and Jack being here today means a great deal to me. I love you like the sister I never had."

Nancy patted her friend's hand. "And I love you, Catherine. I hope you and Noah will be as happy as my Jack and I are."

"I've no doubt that we shall be," Catherine replied.

That night, after she and Noah had spent an enjoyable interlude in one another's arms, Catherine fell asleep with her head resting on her new husband's shoulder, a small smile of happiness on her lips. There was no doubt in her mind that she and Noah were now the happiest married couple in the world and always would be.

If Catherine and Noah's lack of observing a proper mourning period following the deaths of their respective spouses could have raised any eyebrows, or been cause for gossip or speculation amongst the colonists, their hasty marriage was overshadowed by the sudden and shocking news that the powerful Indian chieftain Powhatan was dead, his body found in the forest. Because there were no visible wounds or obvious cause of death, it was believed the elderly chieftain, emperor of the federation from which he took his name, had never recovered from the death of his beloved daughter Pocahontas and that the grieving father had simply died of a broken heart. Of late, he had been observed wandering aimlessly from village to village, at times babbling incoherently. One day, he simply laid down on a bed of leaves in the forest and exhaled the last breath of air from his body.

Anxiety amongst the colonists ran high. Who would succeed Powhatan? Would the new chieftain carry on with the late emperor's desire for peaceful relations between themselves and the light-skins . . . or was peace between the English and the naturals now a thing of the past? What this new turn of events meant for every colonist up and down the James River became a matter of grave concern, particularly amongst those who'd settled in Henricus, located further upriver. That small township was surrounded on all sides by Indian villages.

Overnight, Noah Colton's consequence, and that of the other two traders, John Sharpe and Richard Tidwell, was substantially elevated. The three men, who for the past six or seven years had regularly visited most of the Indian villages under Powhatan's rule and were personally acquainted with a great many of the hundred or so werowances, were now being consulted by citizens and planters alike, all fearful for the safety of their land and families. Those planters who lived on the fringes of the tidewater area and whose land was the least protected were most especially troubled.

Because nothing was more important than the safety of the New World settlements, the recognized leaders of the community, the deputy-governor and his councilmen, were looked to for decisions on how best to handle the matter.

An emergency meeting was called, and Deputy-Governor Argall and all seven councilmen, including Noah's former father-in-law Richard Benson, filed into Noah Colton's home one evening. Catherine opened the door to admit the men. She remembered meeting both Mr. Porter and Mr. Weymouth the day she delivered her report to Deputy-Governor Yeardley those many months ago following her visit with

Powhatan at Werowocomoco. The five other councilmen she had only seen on occasion at Sabbath services. While the men talked, Catherine was allowed to remain in the room, but for one reason only: to keep the gentlemen's mugs full of hot apple cider. Beyond a murmured greeting when they arrived, no further remarks were addressed to Catherine. But as she moved quietly from one to the other filling their mugs, she kept her ears open and managed to hear plenty.

The first item of business on the agenda was the reinstatement of weekly drill practices. Attendance was mandatory with stiff fines levied for those who shirked their duty, although under the circumstances no one thought that would be an issue.

Rebuilding the old fort's outer walls was mentioned, but it was quickly decided that a twenty-four-hour guard on watch duty would be sufficient for now, since to rebuild the fort would first involve tearing it down, leaving the meetinghouse, storehouse, and other important offices unprotected for days and nights at a time.

Catherine was proud to hear Noah speak up to remind the others that it was especially important to keep closely trimmed the high grass around the outer walls of the fort.

"It was the Indians themselves who told

Captain John Smith over a decade ago that our high grass made it easy for them to sneak up and launch a surprise attack on us," Noah said.

"Good point, Colton." Argall motioned for Mr. Porter, the council secretary, to jot the item down on the list he was keeping as the meeting progressed. "You men need to resume your trading expeditions at once," he instructed the traders.

"And trade what?" Noah demanded. "Not a ship has docked in Jamestown the past half year. We've nothing of value to trade. No tools, copper, beads, nothing."

Argall rubbed his chin thoughtfully. "What about liquor? The Indians are quite fond of our 'firewater,' as they call it."

"Thought there was an ordinance against giving the Indians firewater," Tidwell remarked.

There were nods all around. Still, after some discussion, a list of men known to brew their own stout ale was drawn up. One name Catherine recognized was Ed Henley. Of him, it was noted that after a long day's labor in his tobacco and barley fields, he habitually drank himself into a stupor. She suspected Adam did not know Henley was a tippler, otherwise he would not have pushed for her to consider him as a prospective husband.

"Of course, the main purpose of resuming your trade expeditions," the deputy-governor went on, "is not so much to trade, but to see which way the wind blows in regard to what the Indians are planning."

"Certainly." The traders agreed.

Argall unfolded a map of the tidewater area and spread it on the table. A good bit of discussion followed as to which Indian villages should be visited first. At length it was decided to begin midway up the Pamunkey River, a good fifty miles away from Jamestown, then work their way back home, stopping at as many villages as possible along the way.

"You men may be gone quite a spell," Argall said.

Catherine, who happened at that moment to be hovering near Noah's elbow, could not hold back a cry of alarm. "But why must they go so far away?"

Stunned silence followed her outburst, then Argall cleared his throat. "We are every last one of us in grave danger, Goodwife Colton." He held up his half-empty cup, which she knew was more to point out her purpose for being there than to fill it.

She obediently poured additional ale into the governor's tin cup, one of the pair Victor had so proudly brought to their marriage. Still, she couldn't help adding, "I only just lost one husband to an Indian's arrow, sir. I don't relish the thought of losing another."

"You have made your point, madam," Argall replied, his sharp tone silencing her. "So, Colton, Sharpe, Tidwell, you will head out by river to Henricus, then move overland to Orapaks."

The men nodded. Tidwell said, "Since Orapaks is Powhatan's most recent home, might I suggest we take along something of special significance as a condolence for the old chieftain's family?"

"And which wife would ye present it to?" Noah said on a laugh, which brought a burst of levity all around. Catherine's lips thinned with annoyance.

The talk turned to speculation on who might succeed Powhatan. As each Indian chieftain's name came up, the traders imparted their opinion of that particular werowance's temperament.

"Wochinchopunck already calls himself King of the Paspaheghs," said Sharpe.

"He was the last holdout as far as agreeing to trade with us," Tidwell reminded them. "It won't be Wochinchopunck. War would instantly break out between the Massawomekes and the Susquehannas if a

Paspahegh assumed power."

"I believe Powhatan's brother Opechancanough is the more likely candidate," Noah said. "And if that's the case, we might all be in hot water."

Everyone agreed, since each was already acquainted with that warrior's foul temper. Even Catherine clearly recalled the tall, scowling warrior who grew agitated and insisted she be brought forth and questioned during her interview with Powhatan.

Other names were mentioned, but when Catherine again heard a familiar one, her ears perked up.

"Phyrahawque."

"Possible," Noah said. "Unfortunately, not a one of us has met him."

"Why is that?" demanded Richard Benson, who until now had remained silent throughout the meeting.

"He's somewhat a recluse. Doesn't often show hisself," Tidwell replied. "Appears to be a legend amongst the Indians, said to be the tallest, strongest, most powerful, most feared —"

"He's godlike to every Indian in the area," explained Sharpe.

From the shadows, Catherine listened raptly. Apparently, she was the only one in the room who had actually seen the powerful warrior Phyrahawque, and not one single thing they'd said about him was untrue.

"I doubt Phyrahawque would take on the task. Though in my estimation," Noah maintained, "he'd make a damn good chieftain."

"You men should meet with him," Benson declared, refusing to let the matter drop.

All three traders stared at Noah's former father-in-law. Finally, Noah said, "Unfortunately, sir, we don't know where he lives."

For some reason, that struck all the men seated at the table as highly amusing. Everyone guffawed. It was on the tip of Catherine's tongue to tell them she was well acquainted with Phyrahawque's younger sister and that she had actually seen the mighty warrior. But . . . since Argall had made it quite clear that her comments were unwelcome, she decided to keep her remarks to herself. The men wouldn't believe her anyway. How could she, a mere female, have seen this elusive paragon when the more experienced traders, and most Indians, had not?

"Well, find out where he lives!" Benson bellowed. "Surely you know the name of his tribe, that should give you some indication of the name of his village, since they are very often one and the same."

Apparently embarrassed, Noah fell to studying the amber-colored liquid in his tankard.

"We've heard he frequently moves his tribe from place to place," Tidwell muttered.

Benson frowned.

Catherine was still listening raptly. Tidwell's comment corresponded with the answer Lanneika had given her in regard to how far away her village was. Lanneika said her village was sometimes far and sometimes near, which made no sense to Catherine at the time. Now it did.

"Legend has it Phyrahawque rides an enormous white stallion and the horse can . . . fly," Sharpe said.

Again, the men seated at the board table burst into laughter.

Mr. Weymouth, a good deal older and apparently a good deal more educated than his counterparts, spoke up. "This Phyrahawque sounds like a figure from Greek mythology, a powerful Indian warrior whose huge white steed flies across the sky."

Argall rapped on the table with his mug. "Gentlemen, we have other business to discuss."

Catherine returned to the hearth to stir the pot of cider. Eventually the men grew weary of their talk and one by one began to take their leave. At length only Benson and the council secretary, who'd managed to dribble black ink onto the board table as he scribbled notes with a scratchy quill, and the other two traders remained.

As the four men drifted toward the door, Noah turned to address his former father-in-law. "I've another matter to take up with the council, sir."

Benson was drawing on his gloves. "And what would that be, Colton?"

Noah glanced over his shoulder at Catherine. "M'wife and I would like to apply for a fifty-acre land grant, sir."

Benson's eyes narrowed. "And on what basis are you making this outrageous claim, boy?"

Lifting his chin, Noah said, "On the basis that a year ago my wife paid the passage for her servant, Nancy Mills, who has since married Jack Lancaster . . . of Harvest Hill," he added.

After a pause, Benson said, "I see." For the first time all evening, he directed a gaze at Catherine. "Is this true, Goodwife Colton?"

Catherine moved to stand beside her husband. "Indeed, it is, sir."

"One might ask why you have waited until

now, a full year later, to make this . . . ah . . . claim?"

"My wife only now has a need for the land. She has occupied herself the past year running Jamestown's Dame School and . . . until now has not had a need for land."

Benson cocked a brow.

"One other thing, sir," Noah continued, sounding quite pleased with himself. "I have selected the land that adjoins my wife's late husband's fifty acres."

"And your late husband was — ?" Benson looked at Catherine.

"Victor Covington. He recently perished from an arrow wound," she said pointedly.

"I see. So, with the new grant, the pair of you would be in possession of . . . one hundred acres."

Noah nodded, a smug smile on his face.

Benson cleared his throat. "The proper procedure, Goodwife Colton, is for you to file your application at Jamestown's land office. We will, of course, need Goodwife . . . Lancaster, you say . . . to also sign the application, as well as her husband to . . . ah . . . verify your claim."

"Since the Lancasters reside a good distance away, sir, might I take the application to them to obtain their signatures?" Catherine asked.

"The land agent must witness the signatures," Benson said by way of denying her request.

"Very well, sir. My husband and I shall visit the land office on the morrow."

Before taking his leave, Benson flung a disgruntled look at Noah. Tidwell, Sharpe and Mr. Porter followed the council treasurer into the street.

When Noah had closed the door behind them, Catherine cried, "Noah, why did you bring up the matter of our claim in the presence of so many?"

"Three reasons, my love." He slipped his arms about her trim waist and drew her toward him. "Firstly, to goad Benson; secondly, to boast of my good fortune; thirdly, to force him to be civil."

Winding her arms around his neck, Catherine laughed up into his twinkling blue eyes. "People will now say you married me for my land."

He gave her lips a quick peck. "Well, people will not be wrong."

"Noah, you are telling another falsehood!"

"I can't very well tell the truth."

"And what would that be?" She grinned up at him, her auburn head at a tilt.

"Come with me, ye saucy wench, and I'll show you the truth."

Their lovemaking that night was more playful than usual. Afterward, they lay in one another's arms, and Catherine voiced her concern for his safety as he and the traders ventured so deeply into Indian Territory.

"If you encounter trouble, Noah, how am I to know of it? You will simply vanish and I will never know what has happened to you."

"Don't worry, love. I have no fear of the Indians. I am their friend. They trust me. They shouldn't, of course." He laughed. "But they do."

In the darkness, Catherine did not return his smile. His duplicitous remark had added to the niggling fear growing in the back of her mind over Noah's true nature. But when he again gathered her into his arms and murmured into her ear that he thought her beautiful, she thrust the worrisome thought aside.

Chapter 24

The following week was a whirlwind of activity. Noah's fellow traders were at the house for such long periods every day Catherine began to feel she'd married three men instead of one. The traders appeared in the early morn and did not depart until late at night. Even Lanneika's sweet temper was tested as the men ordered her about as if she were a slave. More than once, when one or another of them, including Noah, issued a particularly stern order to the girl, Lanneika flung a helpless gaze at Catherine, who knew the girl didn't understand exactly what had been asked of her.

"I'll take care of it, Lanneika. You may go to the stream for more water."

The traders' loud talking as they argued over their itinerary also interfered with her attempt to hear the children recite their lessons. By mid-week, Catherine insisted the men take their rowdy discussions outdoors.

"Catherine, you are being rude to Sharpe and Tidwell," Noah accused late one night after the men had finally taken their leave and he'd joined Catherine in their bed-chamber where she was already tucked into bed.

"I don't understand why you cannot meet at one of their homes. Neither are married and there would be no one to disturb." She patted the bedclothes about her irritably. "It is quite disconcerting to have the children reciting verses from the Anglican Prayer Book while across the room three grown men are cursing at one another!"

"You could give up your school!" He removed his doublet and hung it on a peg. "You have a husband to take care of now."

"Don't be cross, Noah."

"Truth is, I'm not that fond of children."

In the dim light, Catherine stared at her husband with disbelief. "Mayhap that is why you did not bring little Livvy with you?"

"Livvy belongs to the Bensons. I hardly consider her my child."

Catherine sniffed. "Well, I hope that will not be the case with our child."

He crawled into bed beside her. "Of course not. I've always wanted to get a babe on you. Though when the time comes," his tone grew stern, "I'm counting on you to give me a son."

"I will do my best to please you, Noah," she replied coolly.

He reached to pull her toward him, somewhat roughly, saying, "You may begin by pleasing me now, wench."

She did not struggle as he tugged her night rail above her thighs, though a part of her recoiled at the moniker he used so frequently when addressing her. "I am not your wench," she murmured crossly. "I am your wife."

His mouth came down hard on hers. Drawing away, he muttered, "Yer all wenches to me."

The following morning as they broke their fast at the board table, he announced, "We leave in two days' time."

"Oh, Noah." Catherine looked up from her trencher of corn pudding. "How long will you be away?"

"Hard to say with so many uncertainties. We'll spend today and tomorrow gathering what we can from the planters in order to have something to trade."

Later that morning, Noah was away when Ed Henley appeared at the door. The man looked as unkempt as ever, Catherine thought, as she hurried from where the children were reciting their lessons to speak to the man hovering on the threshold.

"I done brung what yer husband wonted."

Looking past him into the street, Catherine saw his ox hitched to a flatbed wagon loaded with jugs of what she assumed was his home-brewed ale.

"I . . . suppose you can put it in the shed . . . or, perhaps, Noah needed the use of your ox and wagon to take the . . . *it* to the dugout." Noah had not apprised her of his plans so she didn't know how he meant to transport the firewater.

"I'll jes tie ole Zeke up out back and yer husband can use m' ox and wagon." He turned to go.

A few minutes later, Ed surprised Catherine by actually entering the house. Again occupied with the children, she turned expectantly toward the man.

"Was there . . . something else?"

"You tell yer husband ta' bring back m' empty jugs! I tole him ta' tell them Indians they had ta' pour the ale in they own jars cuz I wont my containers back."

Keeping her tone civil, Catherine replied, "I'll tell him, Ed." When he departed, her eyes rolled heavenward. *Dear Lord, what would the children say to their parents about this?*

■ ■ ■ ■

"It was simply dreadful, Noah!" she exclaimed when he returned to the house that afternoon. "He was all but shouting in front of the children that he wanted his empty ale jugs back, and for me to remind you to tell the Indians they had to use their own containers!"

Noah, busy polishing his breastplate, didn't look up. "I can't tell the Indians that."

"Did you tell Ed you would bring his empty ale jugs back?"

He nodded. "He wouldn't give me the ale unless I promised to return the empties to him. But I can't very well tell the Indians they have to pour the ale into another container before they drink it!"

Despite the fact that she'd caught her husband in yet another lie, Catherine couldn't help grinning over the silliness of this matter. Her grin soon became a giggle.

Noah looked up. "What do you find so amusing?"

"Do you ever tell the truth, Noah?"

His grin turned cocky. "When it suits me."

That night, she snuggled against his strong chest, wanting to relish the comforting feel of his warm body next to hers. Despite the chaos that had ensued the past week readying him for his journey, she knew she'd sorely miss him the many long nights he was away.

And nights did prove the worst, for after she'd managed to get through the long days alone, at night she could not help wondering if Noah and the other traders were not bedded down somewhere in the forest with a pretty Indian maid to keep them warm. She would never ask Noah since she knew he'd most likely deny it. Or become angry. At some point, she meant to bring up the subject of Pamoac's paternity, but for now she felt unsure how to talk to him about such a sensitive topic.

One day Lanneika boldly asked about it. "Trader-man not know Pamoac his boy?"

The two were outdoors spreading wet linens over the shrubbery to dry.

Catherine didn't look up. "I don't know, Lanneika."

She had often wondered herself if Pamoac had been told his father was a light-skin. She had noticed the boy's dark eyes following Noah's tall form as he walked here and there about the house, most especially the day the men left. All three traders were finely turned out in their shiny breastplates, tall black leather boots and helmets with bright red plumes. Noah's breastplate sported a fringe of mail that jingled when he walked. Catherine thought he'd looked especially handsome as well, so it may have merely been the tall Tassentasse's striking appearance that arrested the Indian boy's notice.

"I no tell brother you marry trader-man," Lanneika said now.

Catherine's head jerked up. "Why ever not?"

Lanneika pulled one of Noah's white linen shirts from the pile. "Phyrahawque not like trader-man," she said quietly.

"I . . . didn't realize they knew one another."

"Phyrahawque say trader-man *sassaco-muwah*."

Catherine smiled tightly. "I don't know what that word means, Lanneika." And she wasn't certain she wanted to.

Her black eyes somber, the pretty Indian girl dropped to her knees and, with the edge of one brown hand, traced a wavy in-and-out pattern in the grass.

Her meaning was clear, and it pierced Catherine's heart like a sword. And heightened her worry over her new husband's safety. Although, she told herself, it shouldn't surprise her that her charming,

398

good-looking husband had made enemies amongst the Indians. No one liked a man who habitually misled them or told falsehoods. One more thing to speak with Noah about . . . eventually.

One evening before Lanneika left for the day, she told Catherine it was now time to plant corn, and she'd help with the task the following morning.

Catherine agreed, thinking that as it turned out, she'd had nothing to fear from Noah regarding who tilled up her cornfield. Since the night of the meeting with the governor and councilmen, Noah hadn't said another word about land, or tobacco, or planting anything. And with all the confusion and chaos of getting ready for his expedition, Catherine had forgotten to mention that Ed had helped her weeks ago by tilling up the field. She doubted they'd ever see Ed Henley again once he learned he wouldn't be getting his empty ale jugs back.

The next morning, Lanneika surprised Catherine by bringing a smelly, cloth-covered basket with her when she arrived for the day.

"What do you have in there?" Catherine asked, pinching her nostrils together.

Lanneika giggled. "Nammais. For plant corn."

Catherine still didn't know what the word meant, but by lifting the corner of the cloth she found out. Fish. For the nonce, she decided not to inquire why fish were necessary for planting corn.

By the time Lanneika was finished with her morning chores, it was also near time for the children to depart, so after they'd gone for the day, she and Lanneika hurriedly ate a bite, then headed toward the cleared plot of land that fronted the forest.

Lanneika seemed to enjoy being the authority in the matter and showing Catherine how to perform a new task. She placed the basket of fish on the ground beside Catherine's container of corn kernels. Both fell to their knees, and Lanneika demonstrated how much soil to scoop into a mound, how to punch a hole in the top and drop in precisely five kernels of corn. Before covering the kernels with soil, she also laid one small fish alongside the corn.

Catherine still wasn't certain what part the fish played in the ritual, but rather than try to understand what she expected would be a lengthy explanation from Lanneika given, or acted out, in her own language, she simply went along. However, the mystery was cleared up when Goody Smithfield stopped by.

"Ye putting in five kernels, are ye?" The older woman peered over Catherine's shoulder.

Catherine looked up and replied in a friendly manner. "Indeed, we are."

"One for the blackbird, one for the crow, one for the cutworm, and two to grow," the woman sang gaily.

"I confess I'm not certain what the fish is for," Catherine admitted.

"Fertilizer. Makes the cornstalks grow tall and straight." Goody Smithfield leaned over and inspected the remaining fish in the basket. "Herring." She nodded approval. "Your girl has showed you a-right. Stalks should shoot up straight and tall in a fortnight. Now, when they get about this tall" — she marked a place in the air about three feet high — "it'll be time to plant yer squash and yer beans. Cornstalks make good beanpoles, don't ye know?"

"Ah." Catherine turned back to her task.

"Yer husband gone, has he?"

"He and the other traders left some time ago."

"Well, I wish 'em Godspeed. Important we get this Indian business sorted out."

"Indeed. Thank you for stopping by,

401

Goody Smithfield."

With no more interruptions that long afternoon, by sundown the planting was nearly done. As the shadows lengthened, Catherine finally looked up and was startled to find that she and Lanneika were being watched. At precisely the same spot where she'd first seen him, Lanneika's brother Phyrahawque was sitting astride his huge white stallion, neither horse nor rider moving, neither making a sound. Though she was some distance away from the handsome brave, Catherine could see the Indian's piercing black eyes were aimed straight at her.

"Lanneika," she said softly. "Your brother is here."

"I know. I tell him *sacani.*"

Catherine blinked. *"Sacani?"*

"I tell him wait."

Catherine looked back at Phyrahawque. She hadn't heard the girl utter a single word. Were brother and sister able to communicate without speaking?

A few minutes later, Lanneika brushed the loose dirt from her hands and skirt, scooped up the empty fish basket and scampered toward her brother, who still sat unmoving atop his white horse. Catherine also rose, but made no move to return to the house.

Instead, she stood watching the pair. When the pretty Indian girl turned to look back at her, she waved good-bye. The next thing that happened both surprised and amazed her.

After Phyrahawque had lifted his sister onto the horse and settled her in front of him, the Indian brave turned full around, looked straight at Catherine, and . . . nodded. Then, he dug his heels into the steed's side, and the enormous white stallion sprang into action, disappearing like a streak of lightning into the woods.

As Catherine walked back toward the house, she marveled over what she'd witnessed. It was apparent Phyrahawque both loved and felt protective of his younger sister. Lanneika had a sweet temperament and was bright and playful. Catherine imagined her to be much like Pocahontas at that age, enjoying a simple, peaceful life with her family in the forest.

It worried her what Phyrahawque would do when he learned his enemy, the hated trader-man, now resided in the same house where his beloved little sister spent every day.

On one especially warm May morning, Lanneika arrived wearing her shiny black hair in a single thick braid hanging down the middle of her back.

By noon, in an attempt to cool off, Catherine had untied and removed the sleeves of her bodice. She also twisted her own long hair up and tried to stuff it under the tidy white cap she wore. But, as she and Lanneika pulled weeds from the garden, her auburn tresses continued to escape the confines of her soft white cap. Which began to make Lanneika giggle.

Eventually, she said, "Come. I fix."

Grinning mischievously, the Indian girl motioned for Catherine to follow her into the house. So, Catherine did.

Lanneika led the way into Catherine's bedchamber and, positioning the one ladder-backed chair in the room before the opened window, indicated for Catherine to sit. They had left the front door open so any breeze that might waft through the house would drift toward the opened window in the bedchamber.

Lanneika snatched up Catherine's hairbrush and, after removing her cap, began to brush her long, red-gold hair. Enjoying the feel of having her hair brushed, Catherine lowered her head and closed her eyes.

"Phyrahawque say you beautiful. He say your hair like sun-flame."

Catherine's eyes sprang open. "Oh. That was . . . nice of him." She wasn't certain how to respond to a compliment from an Indian brave, especially considering she was now a married woman. "I did not realize your brother knew English words." Perhaps Phyrahawque hadn't conveyed *exactly* that sentiment.

"He know plenty words. He learn when boy. He now know numbers. I teach. He know you name Cat-e-wren. He say Cat-e-wren beautiful. Like flower."

Catherine inhaled sharply. Were she to express her true feelings, she would have to say she thought Phyrahawque beautiful as well. Instead, she thought she and Lanneika should talk of other things. "Do you . . . have a garden at your home? With flowers? And corn?"

"Much corn." Lanneika nodded. "When corn ripe, I show how make —" Moving to stand in front of Catherine, she began to pound one fist into the palm of her other hand.

Watching, Catherine prompted, "How to pound the corn into meal?"

Lanneika nodded. "Pa-paund corn."

Catherine grinned as Lanneika resumed brushing her hair. Soon, she felt the gentle touch of the Indian girl's hands as she

405

began to lift sections of Catherine's long hair and fold it over and under into a single braid to hang down the middle of her back in the same fashion Lanneika's hair was dressed. Relaxing, Catherine again closed her eyes.

The weight of her hair lifted from her neck did feel cooler. Believing Lanneika nearly finished, Catherine opened her eyes. Of a sudden, from the corner of one eye she spotted a long shadow fall across the floor. Perhaps Noah had returned home from his travels! Catherine spun around, but it was not Noah she saw standing there.

The tall Indian warrior Phyrahawque completely filled the doorway. Catherine sucked in her breath as fear and alarm raced through her. This close to him, the Indian looked far more muscular than she remembered. His chest, arms, and legs were bare; his only clothing was a doeskin breechcloth stretched across his loins. His shoulders were the broadest she'd ever seen.

Lanneika had also turned around. *"Sacani!"*

His piercing black gaze fixed on Catherine, Phyrahawque nodded, but didn't move. Growing less frightened of the fierce warrior, she boldly held his gaze, then very slowly, the corners of her mouth lifted into a smile.

His penetrating gaze seemed to grow less guarded, and Catherine was certain she saw the hint of a smile soften the sharp angles of his face. The proud Indian brave was undeniably handsome, she thought, openly studying him as he, too, conducted an unabashed study of her. His forehead was high and smooth, his nose long and straight. His mouth was beautifully shaped with full sensuous lips. The sharp planes and angles of his face looked to have been carved from granite.

Her curious gaze dropped to his hairless chest. Fascinated, she watched the strong mounds rise and fall with each breath he drew. She thought the rich, golden bronze of his skin beautiful. Suddenly growing self-conscious for staring so openly at him, she blinked and lowered her gaze. A split-second later when she glanced back up, he was gone. She had not heard him leave.

Her task now complete, Lanneika reached for Catherine's looking glass. "See?"

Catherine looked at her own image in the mirror but grew embarrassed at the sight of her glittering eyes and the flush of color on her cheeks. She thrust the mirror aside.

"Thank you for dressing my hair, Lanneika." She stood up. "I believe your brother is waiting for you."

A quarter hour later, Catherine was busy preparing her supper over the hearth, but her thoughts were fixed elsewhere. Suddenly the sound of men's voices coming from outside roused her from her reverie. *Noah!* Her husband had been away far longer than she expected, and she'd begun to worry that something dreadful had happened to him.

She couldn't hold back the joyful smile that lit up her face the moment she caught sight of him bidding the other traders good night.

"You're home!" she cried, flinging herself into his arms before he'd even entered the house.

"I'm home and I'm hungry." He thrust her aside and led the way into the house.

"I've a nice venison stew boiling in the pot." She followed him inside.

"I need a mug of stout ale."

Indoors, Catherine hurried to do his bidding. Long strides carried Noah across the common room. However, midway, he stopped abruptly.

"What's this?" he demanded, bending to pick up something at his feet.

Catherine spun about, her face a question. Spotting what he held in his hand, a wave of fear shot through her. The long, black-tipped white feather her husband held in his hand belonged to Phyrahawque. She had seen several of them hanging here and there in his silky black hair.

"It's . . . a feather," she said.

"I can see it's a feather. Where did it come from?"

She turned palms up. "I suppose it belongs to Lanneika. She brought a basket of fish the other day. It may have been attached to the basket."

"Fish?" He looked skeptical.

She shrugged. "Perhaps it belongs to Pamoac. The boy often brings things to show the other children. He once brought a toy drum. He looked so adora—"

"A child would not play with this." He turned it over in his hand. "This came from the headdress of a high-ranking warrior."

Alarm rose within Catherine, and her heart began to pound like a drum. She forced her voice to remain calm. "Surely it belongs to Lanneika."

Noah was still studying the feather. "I've never seen anything like this before."

Shaking off her fear, Catherine lost patience. "It's only a feather, Noah."

"It's more than that. Look." He strode toward her pointing to a small circular emblem fashioned from tiny red and white beads stitched onto a round piece of leather. The emblem was attached to the base of the feather with thin leather thongs dangling from it like ribbons.

Noah's eyes narrowed. "Who's been here, Catherine? And don't lie to me!"

His accusing words made her temper flare. "How dare you accuse *me* of lying!" She walked back to the hearth. She would not let him intimidate her. Snatching up a piece of cloth, she folded it over and over to protect her hands as she lifted the lid of the pot hanging over the flames.

Noah followed her to the hearth, the mail around the edge of his breastplate jingling. "What tribe is Lanneika from?"

Catherine lifted her chin stubbornly. "You know very well I am not proficient in remembering those complicated Indian names. If Lanneika has told me the name of her tribe, I cannot recall it, and even if I did, I could not pronounce it."

Noah continued to study the emblem.

Catherine flung an impatient look at him. "Put the feather on the shelf by the door, Noah. I will give it to Lanneika when she arrives tomorrow."

His lips tight, he reluctantly moved to do as she bid.

Catherine worked to lighten her tone. "I shall have your dinner ready soon, sweetheart. I am anxious to hear all about your journey." She hated that she'd picked up her husband's habit of fabricating lies to cover the truth, but this was one instance where deceiving him seemed the wisest course. After hearing how the men talked about Phyrahawque, she didn't want to reveal that she knew him. She feared for both him and Lanneika, who had shown her nothing but kindness. She began to slowly stir the contents of the pot and was glad when she heard Noah's footfalls heading toward the second bedchamber where he stored his bulky things: breastplate, boots, helmet, musket.

Over their dinner that night, Noah told her that Powhatan's brother Opitchapan, instead of Opechancanough as everyone thought, had assumed the position of supreme power amongst the tribes of Powhatan's federation.

"So, unless some renegade warrior like Nantaquas or Wochinchopunck, or even Phyrahawque —"

At the mention of Phyrahawque's name, fear again shot through Catherine. She drew in long, deliberate breaths to calm herself. Though she was genuinely interested in what her husband had to say, she had to force herself to ask question after question in order to divert his attention from the black-and-white feather that lay like a smoking gun on the shelf by the door.

She noticed that during the meal he often flung sharp looks at it before returning to the tale he was telling. She also noticed that he drank several more mugs of ale than was his usual custom.

While she stood cleaning the soiled trenchers, he even left the house only to return minutes later with a fresh jug, which she recognized as belonging to Ed Henley. She flung perturbed glances at him as he lounged at the table gulping down mug after mug of the stout brew. But she chose not to remark on the matter as it was apparent her husband was in an ill frame tonight, and she did not wish to provoke him further.

Once in bed, Noah wasted no time pulling her to him. He took her roughly and quickly. Which Catherine realized sadly was becoming the norm. When the uncomfortable ordeal was over, he wordlessly rolled off her. Sighing, she turned over, looking ahead to the welcome relief sleep would bring. Until she heard him growl, "I mean to have a word with Lanneika on the morrow."

CHAPTER 25

When Lanneika had not arrived by mid-morning the next day, Catherine knew the Indian girl was not coming. She assumed Phyrahawque and his sister had seen Noah and the other traders returning to the house last evening; only a few minutes had elapsed from the time brother and sister departed and Noah and the men arrived. It saddened her to think she might never see Lanneika, or Phyrahawque, again. She had grown fond of Lanneika and would greatly miss her and her help every day.

"What's keeping the Indian?" Noah demanded, standing alert in the doorway as Catherine moved past him to lead the children outdoors to work their sums on the ground with pebbles.

"I'm busy, Noah."

"And I'm hungry. It's time to take care of me now."

She hurried to conclude the children's lessons and, after giving the matter only a cursory amount of thought, told the children there would be no classes the following week. With Noah underfoot, she would have all she could handle just looking after him.

"I have suspended classes for a week," she announced as she hurried to warm up the venison stew left over from last night. She spooned it into wooden trenchers and set it along with pieces of cold flatbread on the table. "I'll now be able to spend more time with you."

He began to eat. "I have a meeting with Deputy-Governor Argall this afternoon," he announced sullenly.

They ate in silence for a spell. When Catherine was nearly finished, she addressed her husband in a gentle tone. "Noah, I would like you to consider giving up trading. You could apprise the governor of your decision this afternoon. You could tell him you have decided to become a planter. We now have a hundred acres of land. In your absence, I received the new land grant. It's too late now to plant tobacco this year, but the land needs to be cleared, and you could —"

"You don't expect me to cut down trees and clear away brush, do you?" he de-

414

manded angrily.

"But you wanted the land dearly! That's why you delayed our vows. And the land must be cleared before you can plant. Adam says —"

"I don't care a fig what Adam says!"

Folding her hands before her, Catherine inhaled a calming breath. Perhaps she had chosen the wrong time to broach the topic, but she feared that by evening, her husband would be too full of Ed Henley's firewater to think or speak rationally. "Noah, I . . . I am afraid for you —"

"You don't think I can take care of myself?"

"No, it isn't that at all." Her stomach tightened with frustration. "When we married, before we married, your greatest wish was to become a planter. We have plenty of land now, and —"

"You are busy with your school," he spat out.

"I will give up my school if that would make you happy."

A brow lifted. "Indeed, it would. You have a husband now, and by all rights, you should be breeding. Though I am not particularly looking forward to that," he added sourly.

"What do you mean? I thought you wanted to get a babe on me."

He didn't look up from his trencher. "Been my experience that when a woman finds herself with child she suddenly becomes weak and fragile to the point she makes herself unappealing. I would not like to see you behave in so foolish a manner."

"I see." Catherine digested that. "I will certainly try not to displease you, although I believe it natural for a woman to want to protect her unborn child."

"I especially don't like those Indian brats in my house."

Catherine flinched. *He was referring to his own son!* "Very well. I will give up my school . . . if you will give up trading."

His face a thundercloud, he sprang to his feet. "How dare you attempt to bully me! You are my wife, and I tell you what to do, Mistress Colton!"

Mere seconds after Noah stormed out of the house, Catherine snatched up an empty basket, which she planned to fill with herbs, and bolted into the woods. Longing for the serenity she always found there, anguished tears streamed down her cheeks as she tried in vain to shake off the sting of Noah's angry words.

Dear Lord, how had things come to this pass? More and more, she was seeing a dark side of Noah she had never known existed. Why was he so angry with her? The Noah she knew was lighthearted and carefree; a man who bantered and teased and laughed easily. What had changed him? And what could she do to bring back the man she loved and had wished to be with as long as she could remember?

Worrying over her problem, she walked and walked, blindly stepping over fallen logs and ducking through underbrush. At last, she looked up and realized she was not at all certain where her unguided footsteps had taken her. Turning around and around, she saw nothing that looked familiar. In her anguish, she must have wandered further afield than she planned.

Thinking she was heading back the same way she came, she stepped through a particularly thick stand of tall trees and emerged into a small clearing. Straight ahead lay a sparkling pool of clear water. This was not the spring where she and Lanneika came to draw water. She took a few tentative steps forward, her feet sinking into a luxurious carpet of thick green moss. Gazing about, she noted flowering vines wound around the trunks of many of the tall oak trees that sheltered the cove. Sweet-smelling pink and purple blossoms, along with frothy white dogwood, grew in abundance.

Drawing in breath after breath of the heady fragrance, she walked to the edge of the pool and, looking across the glassy expanse, noted tiny bubbles gurgling up at the center. The pool must be the result of an underground spring, alive and breathing here in the forest. She reached to trail one hand in the cool, clear water. Scooping up a handful, she brought the sweet liquid to her face and washed away all traces of her tears.

Straightening, she slowly turned around and around, awed by the silent beauty that surrounded her. She moved towards a tall tree and sank down onto the moss-covered earth before it, her eyes gazing up . . . up . . . upward toward the brilliant specks of sunlight filtering through the treetops. She had never beheld such a beautiful place in all her life.

The day was especially warm, and, although the shade beneath the canopy of thick, green leaves felt refreshing, Catherine began to cast longing glances at the sparkling cool water. As a child, she'd often stripped off her shoes and stockings and waded into the stream that ran through her father's farm. She smiled now, remembering several times when she and Noah had waded into the running water together. He'd always insisted on holding her hand

418

lest she stumble and be swept away by the swift current lapping over jagged rocks in the middle of the stream.

There were no rocks here and no current. Except for the gurgling center, the water lay like a sheet of clear blue glass. Patches of sunlight through the treetops scattered glittering jewels onto the surface. Catherine drank in the stillness. Sitting beneath the tree, the only sounds she heard were the melodic chirruping of birds. Occasionally one, or a pair, would dart past her, or swoop low over the water, their bright orange beaks disturbing the glassy surface as they dipped low for a drink.

Watching the birds frolic and play brought a smile to her lips. Drawing in deep calming breaths, she relished the sense of peace that soon filled her. She was reminded of the comforting psalm that spoke of the Lord leading one beside still waters. She closed her eyes. In her darkest hours, she must remember to trust that God was taking care of both her and Noah, whether he be a trader or a planter. Her eyes still closed, she murmured a silent prayer of gratitude for being shown the error of her ways and for being reminded to always trust in the care of their Heavenly Father.

Upon opening her eyes, she thought she

detected a slight noise, like a twig snapping, coming from . . . she glanced about, she wasn't certain where the sound came from, but once more, she realized she had no idea where in the woods she had wandered. She cast another longing gaze at the water, but instead of venturing closer, or stripping off her boots and stockings and wading in, she picked up her still-empty basket and exited the clearing the same way she'd come in. Perhaps she'd be able to retrace her footsteps and find her way back home before the sun dipped behind the trees.

With only a few false turns, she finally managed to find her way out of the woods but along the way made mental notes so she might find again what she was already referring to as her Secret Place.

"Where have you been?" Noah demanded when at last she walked up the path to the house, the basket in her hand still empty.

"I went into the woods to dig up some herbs."

His eyes narrowed as he gazed at her empty basket. "Appears you didn't find any."

Catherine thrust her chin up as she skirted past him. "I became a trifle lost, if you must know."

He followed her into the house. "Argall

has called a town meeting for tonight. Seems all of Jamestown is eager to know what transpired with the Indians."

The meeting that night was held in the church sanctuary, but instead of Reverend Buck officiating, Deputy-Governor Argall stood behind the pulpit. Three chairs on the platform behind the podium were each occupied by one of Jamestown's respected trader-men.

Word of the meeting had quickly spread throughout the tidewater area and nearly every single man, and many women, had gathered to hear what the traders had to say. Both Adam and Jack had ridden into town. Because Catherine saw her brother so infrequently, and because Noah was seated on the platform, she chose to sit beside Adam.

"You look beautiful, Cat." He smiled. "How are you and Noah getting on?"

"Well enough." She looked down. "I am glad he is home safe."

"How long was he away?"

"Close on three weeks."

"Ah, so ye have a bit of catchin' up to do."

A shaky smile wavered across her lips.

The low buzz of several hundred voices talking at once grew silent the moment

Deputy-Governor Argall called the meeting to order. After he'd made the announcement they had all come to hear, that Powhatan's brother Opitchapan was now the new chieftain of the Indian tribes, he turned the meeting over to the traders. One by one they stepped up to deliver short summations of their recent visits with the settlers' closest neighbors, the Indians.

Overall the meeting proved uneventful until after Noah delivered his short talk. Not leaving the podium at once, he instead reached inside his doublet . . . and withdrew a feather.

Catching sight of it, Catherine inhaled a sharp breath, so audible that Adam's head jerked around.

"Is something amiss?"

Willing her heart to cease its wild pounding, she tightly shook her head.

"I have a few questions to pose to the congregation." Noah held up the feather. "I assume the majority of you would recognize this as being a mere feather. But . . . upon closer inspection, one would see an odd symbol attached to the base of it. It is this symbol that puzzles me."

"Why is that?" asked one of the men seated near the front.

"Because in all my years of dealing with

the Indians, I have never before seen this particular emblem."

Noah's pronouncement was followed by alarmed exclamations from the audience. Many exchanged frightened looks with one another before turning to gaze back up at him.

"Where'd you find it?" asked another man.

Catherine held her breath.

"Near my home."

Catherine heard a rustling noise as someone in the back stood up.

"I saw somethin' mighty strange down there t'other day."

Recognizing Goody Smithfield's voice, Catherine's eyes rolled skyward.

"What did you see, Goodwife Smithfield?"

"Well . . . yer wife and her Indian girl was a-plantin' corn in that little field what fronts the woods when I happened by. Then later, when I looked back down there, I saw a Indian on a huge horse, jes' sittin' there watchin'."

Hushed silence followed before Noah asked, "What color was the horse?"

"White!" Goody Smithfield shouted. "And big! Suddenly, yer wife's Indian girl run and got up on that horse with the Indian, and I swear, that horse tuk off like lightnin', like it was flyin'!"

Noisy eruptions and even a few screams from the ladies disrupted the meeting. The exultations grew so loud Deputy-Governor Argall had to step to the podium and call for the colonists, men and women alike, to settle down.

"Thank you for yer observation, Goodwife Smithfield," Argall said, "but I daresay there's no cause for alarm, isn't that right, Colton?"

Even from where she sat in the audience, Catherine thought her husband's face had become several shades redder. He knew the identity of the Indian on the white horse, and she knew he would not rest until he'd wrenched a satisfactory explanation from her.

CHAPTER 26

Catherine was glad Noah had the decency to wait until they returned home before he began to question her.

"Why didn't you tell me Lanneika was with Phyrahawque? And don't tell me you haven't known all along who that savage is! Perhaps you met him in the forest this very afternoon!" he accused. "You have a lot to learn about deception, my dear. You could have at least tucked a few weeds into your basket!"

Listening quietly to his tirade, Catherine removed her bonnet and hung it on a peg. Turning to face him, inspiration struck when she spotted something caught amongst the rushes on the floor. Stooping, she picked up a crusty brown leaf. "What do you call this, Noah?"

His lips pursed irritably. "Well, it's a leaf, of course. But what does that have to say to —"

"How do you suppose it got here?"

His tone sounded impatient. "I suppose it blew in the opened doorway!"

"As could a feather!" she ground out, sailing past him into their bedchamber.

He followed her. "You don't get off that easy! I demand an explanation from you or I shall —"

She whirled to face him. "Or you shall what?" she challenged.

His nostrils flared. "If you've been lifting your skirts for that greasy savage, I'll kill him, and then I'll kill. . . ."

His threat hung in the air.

"Kill me?" She removed her bodice and hung it on a peg. Reaching behind her back to undo her skirt, she held his steady gaze as she stepped from it.

"You whoring hussy!" He came at her like a man crazed. Grasping her bare arms, he shook her till her teeth rattled. Pressing her against the wall, his face contorted with rage. "You have cuckolded me with an Indian!"

She didn't struggle. Instead she lifted her chin stubbornly. "I have not betrayed you, Noah. But I wonder what term one uses when a married man beds an Indian maid, or several of them?"

He thrust her from him. "A man has a

right to seek whatever pleasure he wishes," he growled.

Standing with her back to him, she removed her undergarments and drew on her night rail before she turned to face him.

"I have never lain with an Indian, Noah. You are my husband, and you are the only man I wish to lie with."

She sat down on the bed and although at the moment she did not mean what she said, she thought it best to say it. "Come to bed. You are my husband, and I wish to lie with you."

Though Catherine was only going through the motions, she did her best to pleasure her husband that night and for several nights following. It occurred to her that with both of her husbands, lovemaking was a rather rushed affair. Victor seemed to have had less experience at it than Noah, but neither man said much before, during or after, when both quickly fell fast asleep. Despite the pleasure she remembered from those first few stolen moments with Noah, all in all she didn't see much to recommend the experience. Lovemaking seemed designed more to pleasure a man than a woman. Perhaps the pleasure for a woman was meant to come from the babe the act produced. Looking back on that night when

Noah left her, even as she so desperately wanted him, now seemed deliberately cruel of him. But now that she knew more of Noah's true personality, there was much about him that seemed cruel . . . something she would never have thought to be true of him.

The following morning, when her husband announced that he and the other two traders would be leaving on another expedition in a few days' time, she knew the first moments of relief she'd felt since he'd returned to Jamestown the week previous.

With Noah again gone, she felt especially alone now that Lanneika was no longer coming. The children were also no longer there as Noah had insisted the day before he left that she give up her school and be a proper wife to him. It was just as well, she told herself, for without help from anyone, she had plenty to do every day with the cooking, cleaning, washing, and pulling the hardy weeds that threatened to strangle not only her knee-high corn stalks, but the tender young herbs in her herb garden . . . and the pretty flowers in her window box.

She consulted Goody Smithfield as to exactly when to plant beans and squash beneath her cornstalks, and, when told that any day now would be fine, she busied herself with that chore.

One day she decided it was again time to remove the soiled rushes on the floor and replace them with fresh-smelling straw. In the process, she came across a dozen or so more of the blue glass beads she'd dropped the day she stumbled and fell from the rickety ladder. She gathered up the beads and placed them in the center of the board table. If Lanneika did return one day, she would give them to her.

Another day, on her way back from the spring, she met up with Goody Smithfield. Catherine lowered the heavy wooden yoke resting on her shoulders to speak with the woman, who seemed excited about something.

"Ship's comin'! Ship's comin'! M' husband said he seen two barks on the horizon! A hundred hungry settlers'll be descendin' on us any day now!"

Catherine smiled at the woman. "That is exciting news. Most like, they'll all be needing homes, too."

"Oh, my yes! M' husband and I always takes some in. You and yer man should too. You've got plenty o' room at yer place."

"Indeed we do," Catherine murmured, turning to go.

"I mean to make soap tomorrow," Goodwife Smithfield called after her. "If'n ye'd like ta' help, I can share with ye."

"Thank you. My supply is about gone."

"Mine, too!" The older woman laughed gaily. "Which is why my apron is such a sight!"

The more Catherine thought about inviting a couple to share their home, the more she liked the idea. Additional people in the house would serve more than the obvious purpose, which was to provide shelter to those who had none. It might also make Noah less likely to vent his wrath upon her over some trifling matter, plus another woman would be a great help to her. Surely Noah would not object since he was so seldom here.

When he was home, he would enjoy having another man to converse with, which might also restore his good humor. She also expected Noah would be eager to purchase one or two indentured contracts, since it would net him more land. The bondservants, she reasoned, could stay in a hastily constructed bark hut on the land. Noah could put the men to work clearing an acre in order to be ready to plant their first tobacco crop come next spring.

Once again, all would be well between them. Of late, she'd wished she had Noah's little daughter to take care of, thereby completing their family, but since he'd only mentioned his baby that one time, she never brought the matter up again.

Recently, however, she had begun to suspect she might be with child. Her moon cycle, as Lanneika called it, had been interrupted, so there was a good chance she was, although she felt exceptionally well every day with no sickness whatever. She hoped the news would please Noah, despite his remark that he cared little for children, or for a woman carrying one.

Still, the thought pleased her, and she felt in an exceptionally good humor that afternoon as she set about clearing the second bedchamber in readiness for the new family. Those items which Noah did not often use, she would store in the loft. The rest she'd find space for in the common room. With her school closed now, she decided they could give away the extra board tables to new settlers who didn't yet have furniture or they could break them down and stand them up in the shed. That would free up plenty of space for Noah's bulky breastplate, musket, helmet, and other things in an unused corner of the common room.

Humming to herself, she made several trips back and forth between the two rooms, carrying items of his clothing to hang on empty pegs lining the wall in their bedchamber. He'd worn his armor and carried his musket, so that meant she now only had to find room for his bow and quiver of arrows, which he seldom used. In fact, she hadn't seen him so much as pick up either since they married. Deciding to take them to the loft, she slung the quiver over her back as she'd seen the Indians do, and headed up the ladder, one hand tightly grasping the bow, the other clinging to the sturdy rail of the ladder.

Once above stairs, she glanced about in search of a place to put them. Spotting an empty corner, she headed that direction but had to bend over to move a small keg. When she bent over, all the arrows tumbled out of the quiver, falling helter-skelter to the floor. Smiling at her own clumsiness, she squatted down to gather up the arrows and put them back in the quiver, feather-end up as they'd been before, but suddenly, something odd caught her eye. Picking up several arrows, one after another, she noted that nearly every last arrow in Noah's collection had a different-sized arrowhead.

The head on the arrow she now held was tiny, no bigger than her thumbnail, with a needle-sharp point. She remembered Noah telling her that day in the forest that the smallest arrowhead was a Powhatan arrow. She picked up another one. Its head was twice as large, relatively flat, and the tip of the arrowhead, though equally as sharp, was wider, much like the one Jack had pulled from Victor's leg; the one that shattered the bone and left shards of metal in his flesh.

She inspected the rest of the arrows. Though some were similar, there were no two exactly alike. The shafts also had different markings, odd drawings, or symbols, not unlike the emblem on the base of the feather that had so arrested Noah's attention.

She thought back to the night of Victor's accident when she'd opened the door to admit Noah. She'd thrust both of the arrows at him and told him the men wished to question him. She clearly recalled Noah instantly declaring he hadn't been anywhere near the stream that day.

Stunned by what was swirling in her head, she sat back on her heels, her heart pounding wildly in her ears.

What, she wondered now, had Noah been told when Argall summoned him? Had he been told exactly *where* the accident took place? If not, how would he have known it was near the stream?

Feeling as if the blood in her veins was on fire, she shook herself. How could she be thinking such horrible thoughts about her own husband? Certainly Noah had nothing to do with Victor's death. She stuffed the rest of the arrows into the quiver and hastened back downstairs.

But he had threatened more than once to kill any man who touched her, a small voice in her head reminded her.

Stop! She put both hands over her ears to shut out the nagging thoughts. Noah was a man of strong passions. It was one of the reasons why she had loved him so. When he spoke of killing any man who touched her, it had surely been his way of expressing the depth of his love!

With fresh resolve, she determined to never think about the arrowheads or the awful events of that night ever again!

Catherine spent the entire next day in Goody Smithfield's yard learning how to make soap. It was a lengthy process using the grease one had accumulated throughout the year along with half a dozen bushels of ashes collected and saved from the hearth. Catherine had wondered why Abby had been so adamant about saving the old grease and sweeping the ashes into a barrel every day. Now she knew. And was glad she'd followed suit for, with the addition of what she contributed, both she and Goody Smithfield netted a barrel full of jelly-like soft soap that would last throughout the next year.

When the complicated procedure was finally completed, Goodman Smithfield obligingly rolled Catherine's barrel down the dusty path to her home and set it just inside the front door, convenient for scooping out a handful when one wished to scrub trenchers or do laundry outdoors. Although Catherine was glad to have learned how to accomplish yet one more necessary task in the New World, she was completely exhausted when the sun finally set on that long day.

The next morning, she was awakened by an excited hue and cry from outdoors; the two ships everyone had been anxiously watching approach were sailing into the harbor. Other ships had arrived since Catherine had come to the New World, but she had never run down to the pier with the colonists to welcome the new arrivals. Today she did.

It was a sunny May morning with fluffy white clouds overhead. Talk amongst those who breathlessly waited on shore centered around what supplies the ships might have brought. The winter months had been harsh and everyone's store of foodstuffs and general household items were running perilously low. Unless the traders could extricate something edible from the Indians soon, everyone would have to wait until harvest-time to replenish their food supply. Women on shore wondered if the ship brought letters from home, or fabric, new clothing, coffee and tea, or perhaps exotic spices; men wondered if there would be new tools, or perhaps a cow or goat to purchase. In the past year, Catherine had worn holes in the soles of her boots. Entertaining the hope of purchasing a new pair today, a few coins jingled in her apron pocket as she stood on shore gazing out at the tall ships in the harbor, their hulls brightly painted red, yellow, and green. Atop the tall masts, red and blue silken flags snapped in the breeze. Joyous cheers erupted from the throng on shore when the first longboat reached land and the new arrivals stepped onto solid ground.

Caught up in the exultation, Catherine surged forward along with the other excited settlers.

After waiting a lengthy spell for the ship's merchant to set up his store in a longboat near the water's edge, she did purchase a new pair of sturdy brown leather boots and two lengths of fabric, which she meant to stitch into gowns for herself. If she were with child, she also meant to fashion tiny garments for her precious infant to wear.

That night, as she lay in bed thinking over the events of the day, she could not help but be reminded of her own arrival in Jamestown nearly one year ago. She cringed when she recalled her supreme disappointment when she'd learned that Noah hadn't waited for her, that he'd married another and the couple already had a babe on the way. Although a very great deal had happened in the past twelve-month, she thanked the Lord now that at long last everything had been set to rights and she and Noah were finally man and wife.

Weary, she settled the bedclothes in readiness to sleep. But sleep did not come. The tight knot of anxiety in her midsection simply would not let her rest. Despite Adam's dire warnings about Noah, she'd stubbornly clung to her childish notion that she loved him, and he loved her. Now, she wondered, after all she'd gone through to be with Noah, had she only been successful in deceiving herself? Doubts and unanswered questions about her new husband troubled her waking hours and were now also disturbing her sleep.

CHAPTER 27

Throughout the rest of that long week, Catherine found she could not push down the unanswered questions in her mind regarding the different-sized arrowheads. In addition, something else she discovered one day also troubled her. Moving a few items around in the shed, she found a large, bulky package, which she assumed belonged to Noah. Inside were a dozen ax blades, several pouches of the purple glass beads, and five or six glossy pelts that she thought were beaver. How, she wondered, had Noah come to be in possession of such fine pelts? And why would he trade them with the Indians, since most animal skins the settlers owned came *from* the Indians? Assuming that Noah meant to take the package with him on his latest expedition and, in his hurry to depart, had left it behind, she decided to take it indoors so he might remember it for his next trip.

Every time the sight of the beautiful beaver pelts spread out on the board table caught her eye, the pesky voice in her head told her something was amiss. She recalled that before the men left this time, they all again bemoaned the fact that they had nothing to trade with the Indians. Since no ship had arrived bringing fresh supplies suitable for trading, this mission was turning out merely to be one of good will. That and to remind the werowances of each tribe of their previous pledge to bring two bushels of corn per man to Jamestown's communal storehouse.

Fresh doubts about Noah began to assail her. What was he keeping from her now and why?

When the second week passed and Noah still had not returned home, Catherine again made the trek to Sabbath services alone. Afterward, as she stood outdoors on the green visiting with her brother and Abby, and Jack and Nancy, whose girth was increasing as her pregnancy progressed, she found herself standing near John Fuller. When her brother and his party headed toward shore where Adam's dugout was moored, Catherine turned toward John.

"Good afternoon, John."

Smiling, he greeted her. "Mistress Colton."

"I wonder if I might beg a moment of your time, sir."

"Of a certainty." He gazed at her expectantly.

Catherine cast an anxious glance over one shoulder. "P-per-haps we might walk. I shouldn't want our conversation to be overheard."

"As we both live on the same side of town, it will not appear improper if we walk that way together."

She smiled tightly as they set out. Once they were a good distance from other colonists also walking that direction, Catherine began to speak, though she kept her eyes glued to the tops of her new boots, first one peeking from beneath the hem of her gown, then the other. "I would like to ask you a question in the strictest confidence, John."

" 'Pon my honor I shall never reveal a word that passes between us."

"I do trust you, John." She gazed up at him. "What I would like to know concerns the night of my . . . my late husband Victor's accident."

"I clearly recall the events of that night."

"What I would like to know concerns my present husband, Noah. Could you tell me who was dispatched to fetch him into town that night?"

"Indeed. It was Deputy-Governor Argall's servant lad. I happened to be visiting Argall that afternoon when Jack arrived to tell us of the accident. My being there that day is quite likely the only reason I was drawn into the matter. I recall Argall telling Jack that if the accident involved Indians the best person to consult was Noah Colton. He summoned his boy at once and sent him to fetch your husband, that is, your present husband."

"But what did the governor say to the boy? Did he tell him *where* in the woods the accident had taken place?"

"No. None of us, that is, neither Argall nor myself, yet knew where the accident had happened. Jack merely said his friend Victor had sustained an arrow wound and that we should come at once. It was not until we entered the forest that we discovered precisely where Victor was when he was shot. Until then, we had no idea."

Filled with apprehension over what she'd just learned, Catherine managed to school her features into some semblance of normalcy as she thanked John for speaking openly with her. After extracting one more promise from him not to repeat a single word of their conversation to anyone, she left him standing at the crossroads gazing curiously after her as she hurried the rest of the way home alone. It would not do for Noah to see her walking with another man if he had returned to Jamestown whilst she was at services that morning.

Unable to calm herself as she nibbled at the small meal she'd prepared, Catherine quickly put everything away and hurried into the forest to her Special Place to think.

Was her imagination running away with her, or did Noah truly have something to do with Victor's death? Again and again, she went over what she recalled of that fateful night, coupled with what she'd just learned from John.

She was certain she remembered exactly what Noah had said the night she opened the door to admit him. He said he hadn't been anywhere near the stream. And yet, if what John had just told her was true — and she had no reason to disbelieve him — when Noah arrived at her door, he did not know the accident had happened near the stream, for no one had yet told him. He did not even know *what* had happened, or why he had been summoned.

Her insides churned as the turmoil within her grew. *Dear God, had she stumbled upon a horrible truth?* Noah had threatened many times to kill any man who touched her. But she'd never thought he meant it. Would he have actually taken Victor's life? Noah was married to Charity at the time; therefore he could not also marry her.

But marrying her did not seem that important to Noah, the persistent voice in her head reminded her. He would have been content to come to her in the dead of night, or whenever it suited him.

Tears filled her eyes as she buried her face in her hands. Her dream of a rosy future with Noah was fast turning into a nightmare.

What must she do now?

What *could* she do?

The answers to her questions were always the same. Nothing. Were she to say anything to anyone regarding her suspicions, they would no doubt call her a disgruntled wife bent on revenge against her husband over some trifling matter. Or they'd point out that on the night in question she'd been so distraught she had no clear recollection of what anyone said.

Was that the truth, she wondered? Was she mistaken about what she'd heard?

No! No, she was not mistaken! She clearly remembered what Noah had said when she opened the door to admit him. He grew defensive and declared he hadn't been anywhere near the stream! However, since the other men present that night were talking amongst themselves near the hearth, she was the only person in the room who had heard what Noah said, so any sort of investigation into the matter would come down to her word against his. And her words would always be that of a hysterical woman.

A weary sigh escaped her. She truly did not want to accuse her own husband of murder. And even if she did, he likely would not be convicted due to a lack of proof. That Noah had in his possession a quiver full of different-sized arrowheads would be easy to explain . . . for Noah. All he'd have to say was that he traded for them with Indians from different tribes, which was probably true; therefore he'd be telling the truth! So, once again, the crux of the case would boil down to what she *thought* she heard him say when he arrived at her home that night. Her word against his, since no one else had heard what he said.

Hugging her knees as she sat on the moss-covered ground in the shade of a tall tree, it was becoming increasingly clear to her that there was no good answer to this puzzle. The only course open to her now was to keep her suspicions to herself . . . and her mouth shut.

Drawing in long, deep breaths, she tried to calm her fevered thoughts. But seconds later, the insistent voice in her head began to pick at the problem again. It was possible, she told herself, that Noah had been in the forest that day, and he might have indeed seen what had happened . . . and if that were true, then he would have indeed known where the accident took place . . . by the stream. Noah maintained he had learned from the Indians how to see without being seen. So it was possible he could have been there.

Cogitating on that scenario, she finally decided it was the only explanation that made sense. Noah had been in the forest and had seen Victor fall to the ground, shot in the shoulder and the leg by swift-flying arrows — from bows belonging to Indians, not Noah. He had not committed a crime himself; he had merely witnessed one.

It was not until much later, after she had retraced her steps and returned home, that she began to wonder why Noah had not told the governor he had been in the woods that day and had witnessed the crime. And, if he had been in the woods and witnessed the crime, then why had he been so quick to declare to her that he hadn't been anywhere near the stream?

Nothing made sense anymore.

CHAPTER 28

Noah returned home a few days later, hot, tired, hungry, and in an ill humor. The first thing that set him off when he charged into the house was the sight of the six beaver pelts spread out on one of the board tables in the common room.

"What in the hell have you done?" He whirled to glare at Catherine, who had been outdoors pulling weeds from her corn patch and hurried up to the house when she spotted the three traders emerging from the forest.

Her smile fell. "I thought you forgot to take them with you. The day you prepared for your trip you lamented the fact that you had nothing to trade. I found the bundle in the shed. I thought you must have forgotten—"

"Meddling!" He flung his helmet to the ground, shrugged out of his breastplate and let it clatter to the floor behind him. "No man likes a meddling wife!"

"Noah, I wasn't meddling. I thought you had forgotten. There are beads and ax blades and —"

He stormed into the second bedchamber and came right back out again. "Where are my clothes and the rest of my things?"

Suddenly, a sharp pain stabbed Catherine's middle. *"Oh-h!"* Clutching her stomach, she slumped onto one of the ladder-backed chairs before the hearth.

Appearing not to notice her discomfort, angry strides carried him across the room. "Answer me! What have you done with my things?"

The pains in Catherine's midsection were so intense she could not draw breath. She had recently missed her second monthly flow and was now certain she was with child. She had hoped when she told Noah, he would be pleased.

"Noah —" she gasped. "I'm pregnant."

He stared at her for a long moment. Finally, he said, "Well, I confess I was beginning to think ye were barren. Or that ye were swallowing some tisane behind my back to prevent conceiving."

She raised her head to stare up at him. "Why on earth would I do that?"

An arm swept the room. "Why on earth

would you do this?"

His anger over such a silly matter struck her as funny and a nervous giggle escaped her.

"And now you're laughing? Catherine, have ye gone daft?" Both fists parked on his hips, he stood glaring down at her.

"I cleaned out the second bedchamber a-purpose. Two ships arrived after you left and I thought we might invite a man and wife to share our home. Your clothes are in our room. The rest of your things are in the loft. Reverend Buck admonished us to be charitable toward the newcomers. He asked for volunteers."

"So, ye volunteered our home to strangers, did ya?"

"No, I wouldn't do that without consulting you."

"And my pelts? What part do they play in this?"

"I told you, I found them in the shed along with the ax blades and beads. I thought you had forgotten to take them with you."

"So a ship has arrived." He moved across the room and began to gather up the beaver pelts. He next noticed the handful of beads she'd placed in the center of the other table, the one where they took their meals. He scooped them up also. "What are these doing here?"

"They are for Lanneika."

"The Indian girl's back?"

"No. I found those on the floor when I changed the rushes last week. I'd been paying her with the beads I dropped the day I fell from the ladder. You recall."

"Indeed." His eyes narrowed. "I also recall those were my beads." His mouth pursed as he walked back toward the table, which held the pouches of beads Catherine had brought into the house from the shed. He poured the beads in his hand into the bag, then stalked past her into their bedchamber.

Catherine rose to follow him, though she moved slowly, fearing another sharp pain might strike her. "Noah, I will soon need help. I won't be able to haul water from the spring or even bring in logs for the fire. Another woman around would be a great help to me."

Standing in the doorway of their bedchamber, she watched him remove his doublet and soiled shirt and change into fresh clothing.

"Are you going somewhere?"

"Are the ships still in the harbor?"

"Yes, both of them. Very few of the settlers have found homes on land." She moved into the room and slowly knelt down beside the bed to retrieve her valise from beneath it. "I've no idea if there are any indentured contracts left, but if you'd like to take the money along —"

When he held out his hand, she gave him the pouch.

Back in the common room, he slung the rich beaver pelts over one shoulder and left her standing in the doorway, watching him stride toward the fort and the pier beyond.

Several hours later, a bit past sundown, Noah returned carrying a large bundle beneath one arm. Straggling a few steps behind him was a girl. Catherine stared at the poor thing. She was slight, stood no more than five feet tall, and was thin as a rail. Her face and arms were streaked with weeks of filth no doubt accumulated during the long hard months of her shipboard journey. Her mousy-brown hair hung in greasy tangles about her dirt-smudged face. The threadbare garment she wore hung on her skeletal body like a flag tattered to shreds in a high gale.

Having deposited his heavy bundle on one of the empty board tables, Noah turned to address his wife. "Ye said ye needed help."

Catherine was still staring at the girl.

452

"Where is her husband?"

"No husband. She's a servant. I bought her contract. She's indentured to me for a full seven years."

"Y-you . . . bought a . . . girl?"

He shrugged. "Man or woman I'm still entitled to my fifty acres."

Catherine said nothing.

"You said ye needed help."

Catherine turned back to the girl standing mute inside the doorway. "What is your name?"

"Lyd-jah."

"Lyd-jah?" Catherine frowned. The girl's accent was so thick she could barely understand her. "Are you saying your name is Lydia?"

The girl shoved back a hank of hair hanging before her face. "Tho's rot, mum."

Catherine flung an exasperated look at her husband.

"Well, get her cleaned up," he barked. "Plain to see, she needs washing and something to wear."

Catherine's lips thinned. "I stand a good five inches taller than she, Noah. Not a single one of my gowns will suit."

"Well, find her something."

Catherine rummaged around and finally turned up an old bodice and tattered skirt

Nancy had left behind, both more suitable for the rag pile than to be worn, but for now she supposed they'd have to do. She led the girl outdoors with a bucket of water, a rag, and a handful of soap jelly and told her to scrub her face and arms till there wasn't a speck of dirt left on them.

Going back inside, she said, "I'll make a place for her in the loft."

"Put her in the spare room."

"But there are still upward of two hundred settlers in need of a home, Noah. We've plenty of room here for —"

"Lydia gets the spare room and there's an end to it."

Later, Catherine prepared their evening meal while Lydia stood mutely looking on. Occasionally Catherine assigned her a simple task, such as carrying the filled trenchers to the table or placing clean spoons beside each plate. Otherwise, the girl appeared at a loss regarding anything to do with cooking.

In their bedchamber that night, Catherine could no longer contain her questions about their new servant.

"What was her crime? She would not have been sentenced to transportation if she had not been convicted of a crime."

Stepping from his breeches, Noah climbed

into bed wearing his shirt, which is what he usually slept in. "Didn't ask. Whatever her crime, it doesn't signify to me. You said you required help. She's female. I assume she can cook and clean."

"Methinks you presumed a great deal," Catherine muttered as she lay back on the bed.

"I picked the prettiest of the lot."

"What do her looks have to say to anything?"

"The other women were snaggle-toothed hags. Couldn't abide looking at that every day."

Catherine's eyes rolled upward. "I thought you meant to purchase a male servant so he could work our land. Actually, I thought you meant to purchase two indentures. Both men. They could quickly put up a bark hut and go to work at once clearing the land. It's too late for a tobacco crop this year, but there's plenty of time for a decent corn crop, if you planted it right away."

When Noah didn't reply, she added, "We also need vegetable seed — turnips, peas, carrots. I noticed the ship's merchant had a variety of seed packets for sale."

He turned his head on the pillow to look at her. "You went to the pier?"

"I needed new boots. In a year's time, I've

walked holes in mine."

He turned back over. "I also bought new boots today, a couple of new shirts, and a few other necessities. My beaver pelts fetched quite a good price."

"So we still have money left for a male servant?" For answer, she heard only silence. "We could go down tomorrow and —"

"Not certain now I want to be planter," he muttered.

She sat up, staring at his backside in the darkness. "It's what you've wanted all along!"

"I am ill-suited to hard labor. My pelts fetched a good price," he said again. "Apparently fine English gentlemen covet fine beaver hats. Ship's merchant said he'd pay a premium for all the beaver pelts I could provide."

Catherine's eyes widened. "Are you saying you now mean to become a *trapper?*"

"Didn't say that. Trapping's also hard work. Curing the skins . . . no, never said I mean to become a trapper, not in the . . . purest sense of the word."

"You are not making sense, Noah."

He turned over, one arm reaching for her. "And you, my dear, are being far too inquisitive. Suffice to say there are other methods of obtaining pelts and skins. Come,

Goodwife Colton, since you refuse to go to sleep, you may as well take care of your husband." Raising himself up on an elbow, he began to tug at her night rail.

Catherine did not resist. She knew his rutting would be over quickly, and it didn't matter to him if she enjoyed it or not, or even took part.

"Well," she murmured once he'd rolled off of her, "I suppose if you mean to become a trapper, we shall have plenty of wild game to eat. Are beavers edible?"

"Go to sleep, Catherine."

Though she was plagued by doubts over this new twist in her husband's plans, Catherine had little time to ponder the matter. Showing Lydia how to perform even the simplest of tasks took more and more of her time each day. The girl was not terribly bright and didn't seem to know one end of a broom from the other or, when one was placed in her hands, what to do with it. Catherine ached to ask a few questions about her background, but, because she was afraid of what she'd uncover, she refrained. Young girls sentenced to transportation could be guilty of crimes ranging from something as simple as stealing an apple or orange from a street vendor to picking pockets or . . . worse. Catherine just hoped she and Noah were not giving this criminal a second chance to commit the same crime again.

A few mornings later, when Catherine realized the ships had still not left the harbor, she mentioned that fact to Noah.

"Since you did not use our money to purchase a second indenture, I thought we might go down to the pier and see what else the ship's merchant has to offer."

"Why, do you require something?"

"We have a baby on the way, Noah. And we also have another mouth to feed. I gave Lydia my old boots to wear, but I understand that, as her employers, it falls to us to clothe her. Yes, it would be fair to say I require something, quite a number of 'somethings.' "

"Very well."

Though Noah had already dressed for the day, he retreated into their bedchamber and emerged some minutes later wearing his new pair of puffed burgundy breeches, white linen shirt, and matching doublet with gold buttons he'd purchased for himself the day he came home with Lydia.

Whilst he was changing clothes, Catherine took Lydia to the corn patch and set her to work pulling weeds from amongst the new bean and squash shoots. When she returned to the house, she found her husband awaiting her in the doorway.

"Your new finery looks quite splendid. I expect I'd best change my clothes." She hurried to put on one of the gowns she usually reserved for Sabbath wear.

The sun was already high overheard, and, though it was a warm day, the pleasant breeze wafting inland from the river cooled them. Catherine realized as they walked that this was one of the few times she and Noah had gone anywhere together, other than to Sabbath services when he was in town. They passed other settlers, some also headed to the pier, others returning home with their purchases. Noah seemed to know everyone by name and called out greetings as they passed. It occurred to Catherine that away from home, her husband's demeanor became considerably more charming and affable, especially toward the ladies, which, before they married, was the way he used to be with her. Everyone liked him, and they all returned his friendly greetings. She was also aware that they received many admiring glances. They did make a handsome couple, and, despite her recent misgivings about her new husband, she felt proud to be walking beside him.

As they neared the walls of the fort, through which they had to walk in order to reach the pier, she asked Noah if he needed any new traps or special tools for his new trade as a trapper.

"No," he replied breezily, "I have everything I need."

Catherine wondered where he kept his traps. She assumed he'd use different-sized traps for different-sized animals, and she'd seen nothing of the sort in the shed or the second bedchamber. But she did not pursue the matter. Instead she asked him what he meant to do with their land now that he'd abandoned the idea of becoming a planter.

"Sell it at a premium, of course. Land hereabouts will soon be gone. New settlers arriving with the notion of making a fortune in tobacco will be willing to pay a high price for land when they realize there's none left. Mark my words, Catherine, land grants will soon become a thing of the past."

"I confess I hadn't thought of that." Though she thought it might be a good many years before all the land had been allotted. No one yet knew how far west land in the New World stretched. She'd heard tell of a mountain range somewhere in that direction, but no one had ventured far enough inland to actually see it. "I intend to purchase some of the seed packets today that I saw last week, if any remain."

"What do you want more seeds for?"

"Noah, the four of us have to eat."

"Four of us?"

"Must I keep reminding you that I am with child? And now we have Lydia. The food stored in the loft will not last forever. It must be replenished. And we must replenish it before winter sets in." She chose not to tell him that Adam owed her another winter's worth of provisions. Now that she'd married Noah she wasn't certain Adam would honor the agreement; nor was she certain Noah would accept it. "It's imperative that you clear at least a portion of our land, so we might plant more corn and a variety of vegetables."

He grimaced. "I doubt I will have any spare time for clearing land. Besides, you know very well I am ill-suited for common labor. We'll not starve. Jamestown's storehouse is full of corn."

"The corn in the storehouse is meant for newcomers and those settlers who have nothing! The rest of us are expected to grow our corn. We cannot plant amongst the trees, Noah. The land must be cleared."

Just then, they stepped through the fort walls and could hear the sound of excited

461

talking and laughter coming from those colonists gathered around the ship's merchant's makeshift store in the shallop he'd dragged onto land, it filled to capacity with wares the man had brought from England to sell. A cow tied to one end of the boat mooed, and noisy squawks came from a nearby crate filled with chickens.

Feeling a surge of excitement well up within her, Catherine exclaimed, "Oh, Noah, look! It is very like the county fairs we used to attend as children!"

She twined her arm through his as they walked, but in no time he reached to untwine it. "I have business to take care of, sweetheart."

"Noah, I need some money!"

He dug into his pocket and handed her some coins before he disappeared into the crowd.

Feeling somewhat chagrined by being so quickly abandoned, Catherine approached one end of the longboat and snatched up the few remaining seed packets she spotted and paid for them. She was fingering a length of blue worsted stuff when she heard a familiar voice behind her.

"Would the lady like a length of that fine fabric?"

"Adam!" She turned, a bright smile lighting up her pretty face.

"Allow me to purchase that for you, my pet."

"Oh, I shouldn't."

"I insist. Consider it a belated birthday gift. I daresay I've missed the past, oh, eight or nine."

Brother and sister laughed as Catherine told the merchant how much she needed, and Adam paid for it.

"Is Abby with you?"

"Indeed, she is just . . . there." They strolled that direction and the three commenced to talk. Adam mentioned he'd just bought yet another indentured contract and the crate of chickens.

"The entire crate?" Catherine exclaimed.

"Adam, do let us give Catherine one or two," Abby urged. "I recall there are several roosters near the old place. She and Noah can have fresh eggs every day."

"That would be lovely! I have some joyful news to impart," Catherine added. Beaming, she told them she was certain she was with child.

Delighted, Abigail hugged her sister-in-law. "I do wish our families could visit one another. Eli is getting quite big now. I long for him to know his dear aunt Catherine."

"Perhaps when my little one comes along,

things will change between our menfolk."

"Are you here alone today, Cat?" Adam asked.

She shook her head. "Noah is also here . . . somewhere." Glancing about, she spotted him engaged in a heated debate with Ed Henley. No one had to tell her what the two men were discussing and who would emerge the winner in the controversy. She turned back to her brother. "I had wished to purchase a cone of sugar and some oats today, but I . . . unless Noah turns up, I shan't be able to make it home with a fifty-pound bag of oats."

"Adam can carry it."

"My new manservant will carry it," Adam retorted and they all laughed.

On the way home — the new servant trailing a few paces behind with the fifty-pound bag of oats slung over his shoulder — the threesome continued to visit.

Adam, carrying a chicken tucked under each arm, asked if Noah had managed to clear any of his land yet.

"No." Catherine sighed. "He has decided to become a fur trapper. He was quite pleased with the price he received for his beaver pelts."

"So, he's trapping beaver, is he?"

"I suppose so, though I confess I wasn't

aware he'd set any traps. But I did see the pelts and they were quite beautiful."

"Trapping requires patience. And then there's the curing."

"Oh, I don't believe he means to do the actual trapping, or even the curing, himself."

"So he's taken a partner, then?"

"I . . . don't really know." Catherine was growing confused. She'd have to question Noah further so she wouldn't sound so dense when telling people about her husband's new occupation. "How is Nancy feeling?" she asked Abby. "You have my permission to tell her my good news."

"Nancy is doing very well and she'll be thrilled by your news, I'm certain."

When they reached the house, Adam sent his man to the loft with the bag of oats while he deposited the chickens in the coop where he and Abby had previously kept theirs. He then headed up to the loft and the two men emptied the heavy bag of oats into the nearly empty barrel. "You don't want rats getting at the oats," he told Catherine when he came back down.

At that moment, Lydia stepped into the house.

"Oh, you've finished weeding the corn patch?"

The girl nodded but didn't speak.

"This is our new servant, Lydia. Noah bought her indenture last week."

"So Lanneika is no longer coming?" Abby asked.

Catherine shook her head sadly. She sorely missed the sweet-tempered Indian girl and did not feel Lydia would come close to filling the gap left by Lanneika.

Before they all bid one another good-bye, Adam leaned down to kiss his sister on the cheek. "I don't mean to be a down-pin, sis, but you'd best keep a close eye on what your husband is up to."

Catherine nodded assent, then turned toward Lydia. "Let's go see how you did with the weeding, shall we?"

That evening, after Noah returned and Catherine sent Lydia to the spring for water to wash the soiled trenchers, Catherine exploded.

"Noah, she pulled up all my new bean and squash plants! Said she couldn't tell the difference between them and the weeds! The girl will simply not work out. I insist you take her back and trade her for a grown woman, one with a strong back who knows how to cook and clean."

Noah looked at his wife as if she'd sprouted another head. "I have no intention of trading Lydia off. It would look as if I cannot manage my own servants!"

"Well, you are not the one doing the managing! And, besides, what difference would it make what anyone thinks? The girl is inept and, for the most part, worthless!"

"Well, you claim to be a teacher; so teach her. You taught Lanneika and she didn't even speak English. It's no wonder the girl knows nothing, having been plucked straight from the London street."

"Gutter, more like," Catherine muttered, realizing again that trying to persuade her headstrong husband to see things her way was a useless waste of breath. Noah was strong-willed and obstinate, and Catherine was fast learning that arguing with him served no good purpose. There was only one way things would be done in their household. His.

CHAPTER 29

The following week, a load of supplies was delivered to the house. Noah oversaw the unloading of the crates and told the men where to put them. Most of the heavy crates were stored in the shed; a few were hauled to the loft. Noah told Catherine the supplies had been sent from England for trading with the Indians. Sure enough, the very next day he set out on another expedition. Only this time, Catherine noted, he went alone, and said he wouldn't be gone long.

However short his time away, Catherine felt she'd been granted a respite from her husband's increasingly foul temper. That afternoon she put Lydia to work washing soiled linens, making sure the girl understood that all the wet things had to be spread out over the bushes to dry, otherwise, in the humid clime, their clothing and bed sheets would soon become moldy.

Looking forward to her plans for the

afternoon, Catherine snatched up two fair-sized baskets and headed for the woods. The last time she was there, she'd been excited to stumble upon a patch of wild strawberries all but hidden from view in a pretty clearing amongst a stand of tall trees. The luscious berries should be ripe for plucking now.

Easily finding the strawberry patch, she quickly filled one basket and was starting on the second when she was startled out of her wits by something zinging past her left shoulder. Her head whirled that direction but when she saw what lay only a few feet from her, she sprang to her feet with a cry of alarm.

Inches from where she'd been kneeling on the ground was a large coiled-up snake, now dead, its head pinned back against its body by an arrow still shuddering where it struck.

Catherine flung a wild gaze about, searching for the Indian whose sharp eyes and swift action had saved her life. From out of nowhere, Phyrahawque stepped into the clearing, a longbow in his hand.

"Sassacomuwah."

Gasping, Catherine nodded assent. "Yes, the snake is dead." She relaxed the veriest mite. "Thank you."

She relaxed a bit more when she saw the

granite-hard angles of his handsome face soften. The Indian walked toward her, his piercing black eyes never leaving hers. "Welcome," he replied haltingly.

Catherine managed another smile, one hand still pressed to her heart as she gasped for breath. "You gave me quite a fright."

"No mean fright you."

"I am very grateful you were nearby."

Standing before her, Catherine could see tiny flecks of light glittering like diamonds in the depths of his black eyes. When he took yet another step closer to her, she instinctively drew back with fresh alarm. But he was only reaching past her to lean his longbow up against a tree. Without speaking, he bent down and began to scoop up the berries she'd scattered when she sprang to her feet and knocked over both baskets.

When she saw what he was doing, she knelt to help. At one time they both reached at the same instant to drop handfuls of bright red berries into the basket. Feeling his hand brush against hers, a tremor shot up Catherine's arm. His tawny skin felt smooth and warm to her touch.

Kneeling so closely beside him she became aware of his scent — musk mingled with the wild, clean smell of the forest. His aroma so delighted her, she found herself drawing long deep breaths of it as she and the mighty Indian warrior worked silently beside one another picking berries.

Catherine couldn't help stealing shy glances at his nearly naked body, noting the outline of his bulging thigh muscles and the sinews of his long tapered legs. Her gaze lingered on the sculptured perfection of his shoulders and bare chest. Draped around his neck today was a cord of leather strung with some type of beads. Gaining a closer look, she realized they were not beads at all, but the pointed teeth of wild animals. Moving his head as he reached here and there for berries, she became enthralled by the graceful flow of his long, silky black hair. She felt an almost compelling urge to touch it but of course, didn't dare.

When they completed their task, both stood up. The Indian was so tall that the top of Catherine's head just barely reached the middle of his chest. She lifted a guarded gaze to meet his, but relaxed anew when she saw no menace in his pitch-black eyes. Instead, she thought she detected a curious wistfulness there. Smiling tentatively, she reached to take the basket, knowing full well that in so doing her fingers would again brush against his. When the expected con-

471

tact came, she saw a flicker of something cloud his dark eyes. He allowed their touch to linger a moment longer than necessary before he withdrew his hand and turned to quickly snatch up his bow.

"Thank you for helping me, Phyrahawque."

He gave a nod as if to say, "Of course." Then he bent down and carefully picked up the dead snake by the arrow still impaling its body. Carrying his prize over one shoulder, he disappeared into the dense woods surrounding the clearing.

When Noah had not returned by nightfall, Catherine knew she'd be sleeping alone that night and that her husband probably wouldn't be. But she didn't care. Noah's touch no longer excited her. In the three months they'd been married, he'd never once made love to her as he had that first night he'd lured her into bed — the night she'd burned for his caresses, only to have him cruelly pull away and leave her wild with yearning. Since then, his lovemaking had been quick, rough, and selfish. A fleeting thought about the Indian warrior Phyrahawque came to mind. How would he make love to a woman? she wondered.

She pushed the wayward thought aside

and again turned to ruminating on her marriage. Her dream of a happy life with Noah seemed to be dying for a second time — the first time when she saw that he'd married another and now, as she was fast realizing that being married to him was not the life of unfettered bliss she'd always dreamed of. The bitterness growing between them disheartened her, but she felt powerless to quell it. She did not know how to reach him anymore, and every time she tried, it seemed only to anger him further and to widen the gulf between them. More often than not, when he was home, he was sullen and moody. He had a way of turning the smallest disagreements into insurmountable obstacles, almost as if he had no desire for peace or harmony between them.

It frustrated her that he seemed to have no idea what it took to live day-to-day in this wild new land; that one's food must be grown and that hard work was not a choice, but a way of life. She had purposely not mentioned the fifty pounds of oats she'd purchased, for she knew he would ask how she managed to cart such a heavy bundle home, and she didn't want to anger him by confessing she'd allowed her brother to help.

It amused her now to recall how surprised she'd been when Noah actually asked about the chickens in the coop, but she'd adroitly avoided an argument by telling him, and not untruthfully, that "chickens were in that coop when Adam lived here."

Wondering what they would eat this winter was a constant source of worry. Every night she prayed that Adam would make good on his word and again provide the bounty he'd promised for yet another winter, most especially this one, since by then, she'd be huge with child.

The babe growing in her belly was the only thing that made her marriage to Noah Colton worth the trials and upsets she was enduring. She prayed that nothing would take that happiness from her.

Noah did not return for the next two days, but because both were rainy, she suspected he was snug somewhere in an Indian maiden's hut with agreeable company and plenty to eat.

When the rain let up, Catherine knew she'd best tend to the weeds in her corn patch, which would have grown a foot or more the past few days. She knew better than to allow Lydia anywhere near either her herb garden or the cornfield, so she put the girl to work indoors. It had pleased Catherine to at last find something at which Lydia seemed adept. Sewing. During the rainy days, the pair had cut out garments for themselves from the lengths of new fabric Catherine had bought from the ship's merchant. She felt confident that Lydia would soon turn the vast array of cut-out pieces into finely stitched garments.

Rummaging around now in the shed for her hoe, something glinting in the ray of sunlight that spilled through the open doorway caught Catherine's eye. Curious, she moved past a dozen or more of Noah's crates to reach those in the back. When she saw that the lid on one had been pried up, she peeked inside but at once drew back with alarm. Muskets. But the top layer of firearms was clearly missing. That there were several more crates of the exact same size told her this was not the only one containing muskets. Glancing about, she wondered what might be inside some of the other boxes. Spotting another crate with the lid also slightly ajar, she climbed over the boxes of muskets to look inside. It was full of bags marked "Gunpowder." An empty place in that crate told her some of the gunpowder bags were also missing.

Her heart pounding, she sank down onto one of the sturdy crates. Surely Noah had not taken muskets and gunpowder to trade with the Indians! So far as Catherine knew, the governor's strict mandate against giving the Indians anything that might be used as a weapon had not yet been lifted. She clearly remembered Argall saying at the meeting that night that the men shouldn't even take hatchets or ax blades to the Indians anymore. It was still far too soon after Powhatan's death to be certain what the Indians might do. Giving them firearms at this juncture was not only foolhardy, it was dangerous. Not even Noah would be that thoughtless.

Sighing wearily, she pulled herself to her feet. Once again she was faced with a dilemma. Should she question Noah about her discovery or let it lay? To even mention that she knew what was in some of the boxes would invite an argument.

Making her way around the obstructions, she picked up the hoe and headed to the corn patch.

Apparently whilst she was weeding, Noah returned, for when she entered the house later, she found him there.

"I did not see you return," she said swiping a hand across her brow, now damp with perspiration. The heat mingled with the wet earth had caused the humidity to rise, making the day far warmer than it might otherwise have been.

Seated at the board table, Noah was enjoying a mug of cool ale, apparently talking idly to Lydia, who sat with her back to the door at one of the other tables, industriously stitching away.

"Was your . . . expedition satisfactory?"

"Fair." Noah drained his cup and without another word, rose and exited the house.

Catherine watched him leave. "Well, then, I shall wash up and see if I can't find something for us to eat," she said to his disappearing backside.

After washing her hands and splashing cool water on her face, she put on a fresh bodice and returned to the common room. "Lydia, I need you to help me make dinner. Will you go to the loft, please, and bring down a trencher full of cornmeal?"

When Lydia seemed not to hear, Catherine repeated the summons, speaking a bit louder this time. Lately, she'd begun to wonder if the girl was hard of hearing rather than obstinate. Perhaps the child's ears had been boxed one too many times. Either way, she definitely lacked manners. Catherine had never once heard her say "please" or "thank you."

But a few minutes later, after Lydia had climbed the ladder to the loft, Catherine clearly heard the girl scream. Still screaming at the top of her lungs, she scampered back to the ground. Her pale blue eyes were round with fright as she pointed toward the loft.

"They's wild animals up there! Don't make me go back, mum, don't make me!" To Catherine's astonishment, the girl burst into tears.

"Lydia, dear, calm yourself. Sit on the stoop where there's a nice breeze." She urged the trembling girl forward and, after settling her in the opened doorway, turned to ascend the ladder to the loft herself.

Emerging onto the planked floor, she gazed about and finally saw what had so frightened the impressionable servant girl. Pelts. Apparently Noah had brought them up when he returned, and Lydia, sitting with her back to the door, had not seen, or perhaps even heard him enter the house and climb the steps to the loft.

Catherine walked toward the slanted end of the low-ceilinged room where Noah had piled the stack of animal skins. The manner in which the setting sun shone through the loft window must have lit up the eyes of one of the pelts, which Catherine noted was a beautiful silver fox complete with head and tail. It, she assumed, was the "wild animal" that had so frightened Lydia. She bent to stroke the soft fur. No doubt it would fetch a handsome price. What, she wondered, had Noah traded for the skins? And how could she persuade him to tell her?

Because Lydia rarely said much of anything — at all, ever — Catherine didn't expect her to bring up the matter of the "wild animals" in the loft at dinner, and Catherine didn't either.

But when she and Noah were alone in their bedchamber that night, she did bring it up.

"Tell me about your expedition, Noah. Was this trip on behalf of Jamestown, or on your own . . . behalf?"

His gaze cut 'round. "My purpose was to establish myself as a fur trapper with the Indians, that is, as a . . . fur trader."

"Ah, and were you able to trade for any furs?"

"A few."

She removed her bodice and hung it on a peg. "Tell me a bit more about how your fur-trading business works."

He whirled around. "Why are you asking so many questions?"

She stepped from her skirt and turned to hang it on a peg. "I am merely showing an interest in my husband's new business venture."

"I fail to see where the details of my transactions concern you."

"On the contrary, Noah." She moved toward the bed. "Everything you do concerns me." Drawing on her night rail, she sat down on the bed. "Let me see if I have it straight. You trade something with the Indians for the furs, which *they* trap, and *they* cure, then you sell the furs at a premium, which becomes the profit *you* receive for your efforts. Is that how it works?"

He eyed her suspiciously but said nothing as he unbuttoned his jerkin, shrugged out of it, and hung it up.

"The beaver pelts you stored in the loft this afternoon are beautiful. The silver fox is especially stunning."

His eyes narrowed. "Meddling again, I see!"

Reining in her temper, Catherine schooled her features to remain calm. "I am often in the loft, Noah. I was there only this evening as I prepared our dinner. I am also often in the shed."

"And what is that supposed to mean?"

"It means, husband, that I am curious to know what you traded for the pelts in the loft."

"That is also none of your concern."

She could see that he was growing angry,

and, because she didn't really want to provoke him, she decided to change her approach before their argument got out of hand. "Noah —" she began in a less challenging tone, "I know exactly what you traded for the pelts."

"You know nothing," he muttered, sitting on the one chair in the room to remove his boots and stockings.

"The muskets and bags of gunpowder in the shed are not yours to trade."

"Who says I traded muskets and gunpowder?"

"Noah, I saw the opened boxes and noted that items from each were missing. Despite your claim to the contrary, I know the weapons were shipped here to be distributed amongst the settlers, not the Indians."

Exhaling a sigh, he looked like a child who had been caught misbehaving. "We traders are not properly compensated for the risks we take. The few shillings we're given for our efforts aren't nearly —"

"You agreed to the compensation when you became a trader. You must have thought the payment worth the risk."

"Didn't think much about it then." He leaned back in the chair. "I agreed to trade for a lark. I had nothing else to do."

"I understand how you feel, Noah. Which

is one reason I hoped you would give up trading. Although, even if you feel you are not being properly compensated, you must agree that what you are doing now is wrong." She felt she was making headway. He actually appeared to be listening. She waited for his reply. When he said nothing, she continued. "Noah, none of the supplies in the shed belong to you. True, most were sent from England for the purpose of trading with the Indians. But not the muskets, or the gunpowder."

"All of us do a bit of . . . trading on the side."

"Ah. The packages you used to conceal here with me?"

He nodded.

She paused, considering how best to drive home her point without angering him. She'd never quite seen this side of Noah. He was behaving like one of the small boys in her school who, when caught doing something wrong, would hang his head until she began to gently explain that he'd misbehaved. When he understood, she'd wrap her arms around him just to let him know she still thought him a good boy.

"You have other options, Noah. We have plenty of land." Noting his brows pull together, she knew she was treading on thin ice. "I realize you have changed face on that head and no longer wish to be a planter, but there are other things you could do with the land. Victor drew up extensive plans for a mill." She hurried on. "I have the diagram and all his calculations. The land fronts the water, which is perfect for the waterwheel to fuel the —"

"I have no intention of becoming a miller!" he exploded. "I like what I'm doing! Despite the risks." He rose and began to pace. "The Indians trust me!"

Catherine also stood. "The good people of Jamestown also trust you."

He shot her a wicked grin. "Which works quite well to my advantage, doesn't it?"

She was losing ground, and patience. "But you are stealing from them! What you stand to gain from selling those pelts does not belong to you!"

"Well, I don't see it that way! You are faulting me for finding an easy way to turn a profit and make a decent living for you . . . and . . . and our child!"

"Do not bring our unborn child into this!"

"Keep your voice down! We are no longer alone in the house."

Catherine's nostrils flared as she felt her anger rise. "Lydia is sound asleep. She snores as loudly as you do, and it begins the minute her head hits the pillow. Besides, even if she heard us talking, it would mean nothing to her. She doesn't hear half what I tell her, and the half she does hear, she doesn't understand. Although I am beginning to think she is not as dim-witted as she lets on."

"You've developed a sharp tongue, Catherine, and I do not find that quality the least bit attractive. I much preferred the other Catherine, the one who —"

"Never said boo to a goose? I admit I have changed, Noah, but so have you. And I much prefer the old Noah. You are being dishonest and deceitful and what you are doing is wrong!"

"What I am doing is my own business!"

"Well, do not ask me to support it."

He snickered. "I will not ask it, my dear, since as your husband, I am in a position to *demand* it. Since you stand to benefit from the fruits of my trading, that makes you as guilty as I." He took a step closer to her, his blue gaze ominous. "You will say nothing to anyone about this, do you understand?"

"I understand only one thing, Noah Colton. You have deceived every citizen in the New World. You are a thief and a traitor to Virginia and to the king of England. You are a traitor, Noah . . . a traitor to the Crown!"

His face contorted with rage as he lunged toward her, throwing her backward onto the bed, his body on top of her, both hands pinning her down. "How dare you accuse me of —"

"I am accusing you of nothing," she ground out, struggling to free herself. His weight felt especially heavy on her belly. "I am speaking the truth!"

He grinned wickedly. "I like it when you struggle, my love." He bent to cover her mouth savagely with his own.

Not returning the kiss, Catherine managed to free one hand and pushed against his shoulder. "Noah, stop!"

"Stop?" He raised himself off her a few inches. "I am your husband! You do not tell me to stop!"

"You will hurt the baby!"

He snatched her wrist and held her down. "Then we will make another one."

Her nostrils flared. To fight him was useless. "Then take me." She ceased to struggle. "Get it over with so I may go to sleep and forget that I —"

A split second later, he rolled off her.

Casting a puzzled gaze at him, she sat up. "I said I'll not fight you. Do what you must."

"I find I no longer want you." He stood up to remove his breeches. "I am like any man. I want what I cannot have. When it is so freely given, I find I do not want it."

Still sitting on the edge of the bed, she straightened her clothing. "You have taken me before when I was not struggling."

"I took you because you were here," he spat out, moving to hang his breeches on a peg. He blew the candle out, returned to the bed and crawled in. "Move over so I may go to sleep."

"I do not like being told what to do," she replied petulantly, stung by his admission that he took her merely because she was there.

"Move away. You are on my side of the bed!" He straightened his long leg out and gave her a swift kick on the rear. The unexpected blow sent her flying to the floor. She landed with a hard thud and for a moment lay crumpled on the rushes, too stunned to speak.

"Get up," he ordered. "And come to bed."

Catherine slowly began to rise, using the shaft of moonlight shining through the opened window as a guide to tell her where in the room she was and where the bed and chest were located. Suddenly a large dark object obscured the light. The object sprang at her and yanked her to her feet.

"I said get up!" He flung her from him

again, only instead of landing on the floor, her upper body and midsection slammed into the wall, knocking the breath from her. Gasping for air, Catherine sank onto the straw-covered floor of the darkened room.

"Fine. Sleep on the floor."

Panting for breath, Catherine waited until she heard Noah's even breathing before she pulled herself to her feet and crawled into bed beside him. In the darkness, the words of the London minister whose teachings were meant to prepare her and Lucinda for marriage sprang to mind. The clergyman had said that when a man beat his wife, it was likely due to *her* evil disposition and shrewish temperament.

Dear God, was she being a shrew tonight by confronting Noah? She didn't think so. Just this past Sunday, Reverend Buck had said that according to the Church, women were forbidden to discuss religion or anything of a serious nature with their menfolk, as such topics would tax their delicate brains and overset their emotions. *Rubbish!* thought Catherine. True, she had become emotional discussing Noah's misdeeds, but it had not taxed her brain!

Suddenly a small voice inside her head reminded her that one clergyman — she could not recall which — had said it was the *husband's* unkind and churlish speeches and *his* rash furiousness that caused most domestic discord! Which clearly said that not *all* the fault for their marital discord lay at *her* feet!

Still, the Church did uphold a man's right to strike his wife, and Noah was certainly within his rights to demand her obedience. For all she knew her brother Adam also raised a hand to Abby. Catherine had seen him every bit as sullen and moody as her own volatile husband. If her mother were alive today, Catherine knew she would instruct her daughter to meekly submit to her husband in all things. But . . . a silent sob rose within her . . . Noah's churlish speech tonight had hurt her deeply. Yet she had vowed to love, honor, and obey him. She clearly knew now that to *not* do so only invited his wrath.

Dear Lord, she prayed, *please help me curb my temper and be meek and mild when addressing Noah. And dear God, please, please do not let my baby be dead.*

Chapter 30

When Catherine opened her eyes the next morning, the bed beside her was empty. Apparently Noah had arisen early and already left the house, giving her no idea where he'd gone or when he would return. As the memory of their heated argument rushed back to her, she realized again that trying to talk sense to him was useless. However wrong his actions were, she should never have brought up the matter of the pelts or what he traded for them. All she truly cared about now was the safety of the babe in her belly.

She rose hesitantly to her feet, fearing that some damage may have already befallen her unborn child last night, when Noah sent her reeling to the floor and into the wall. Spotting no blood on her gown or the bedclothes beneath her, she thanked God that overall she felt well and healthy, except for the bruises on her arms where his fingers had roughly grasped her.

Upon entering the common room, she saw Lydia already seated at the board table busily stitching on the blue worsted skirt she was making for herself.

"Have you eaten something, Lydia?"

No answer.

A wave of irritation washed over Catherine, and suddenly feeling weary of trying to make a proper home for herself, her foul-tempered husband, and a non-responsive servant, she snatched up a piece of cold flatbread, dug out a handful of the strawberries from the pipkin on the table and, without uttering another word to Lydia, exited the house.

The day was bright and sunny, the sky overhead cornflower blue. Not looking toward the shed, in case Noah might be there, Catherine headed straight for the woods and her Secret Place.

Tramping through the forest, she munched on the bread and berries, thanking the Lord over and over again that she felt good and strong and had no pains in her middle . . . although her ribs and rump felt somewhat sore.

Once she'd reached her Secret Place, she sank onto the soft carpet of lush green moss before her favorite oak tree. Hugging her knees, she gazed out over the glassy water. Feeling tears began to pool in her eyes, she pressed her forehead to her knees and wept.

Dear Lord, what would happen once Noah's thievery came to light?

Would he be hanged, or at the very least, locked in the pillory that stood at the far end of the church green? Though infrequently used, its very presence loomed as an ever-present warning to the citizens of Jamestown. Surely the missing muskets and gunpowder would soon be noticed and commented upon.

Dear Lord, please, please tell me what to do.

She did not hear the soft footfalls as someone entered the clearing. But hearing the snap of a twig nearby caused her head to jerk up.

"Lanneika!" Fresh tears pooled in Catherine's eyes. "Oh, Lanneika, I am so happy to see you."

The petite Indian girl lowered herself to sit cross-legged on the ground before Catherine. "Not look happy."

A shaky smile flitted across Catherine's face as she sniffed back her tears. "I've missed you terribly."

"Trader-man hurt you?"

Catherine didn't know how to answer. Yes,

Noah had hurt her, but perhaps she deserved it. On the other hand . . . so far as she knew, both she and her babe were safe, so, no, he hadn't hurt her.

Lanneika's black eyes were gentle. "Cat-e-wren come home with me. Trader-man no hurt you there."

Catherine smiled.

"I take care of you . . . and babe when it come."

Catherine's face registered surprise. "You know I am with child?"

Lanneika nodded. "You" — she held both hands up, palms outward and made a sweeping motion that encompassed Catherine's entire form — "shine more. Like sun."

Unable to contain the emotions welling within her, a sob caught in Catherine's throat.

Lanneika wrapped both arms around her friend and began to slowly rock back and forth. The motion had the effect of stilling the turmoil roiling inside Catherine. In moments, her tears subsided. When Lanneika's arms fell away, Catherine saw teardrops glistening on the Indian's girl's straight black lashes.

"I've missed you so much, Lanneika."

"Come to my home now, yes?"

Catherine was tempted. Oh, she was

tempted. How easy it would be to run away, to simply disappear into the forest, to have her baby and to raise him in peace and harmony, to never again have to endure another loud, irrational argument with Noah. But . . . she couldn't. Gazing into Lanneika's eyes, she shook her head sadly. "I cannot. I must return to my own home."

When she rose to her feet, Lanneika did likewise. Catherine moved one step away from the pretty Indian girl, then stopped and turned around. "I love you, Lanneika."

The small Indian's girls chin quivered. Curling her brown fingers into a ball, she placed it over her heart. "I . . . love . . . you, Cat-e-wren."

On her way back through the forest, Catherine felt comforted not only by Lanneika's gentle presence but also by her words, which confirmed that she was indeed still with child, and her baby had not been harmed.

Though Noah's admission — that he'd made love to her not because she was his wife and he loved her but because she was there — still stung, she realized it did not really matter. Perhaps Noah had never loved her, certainly not as she loved him. She had heard that love often abandoned a marriage, but she wondered if it often vanished so quickly. And was she being selfish to wish that something tolerable remained to take its place? Shared purpose, respect, or at the very least, friendship? Now it seemed that her only hope lay with their child. To have a dear little babe to love and care for would, indeed, make her life with Noah bearable. Therefore, the important thing was the safety of her baby. Having seen more of Noah's dark side last night, she knew now that when provoked, he not only became angry, he turned violent. Henceforth, it was imperative she not say anything to him that would arouse his anger. Whatever the cost to her own feelings, she had to protect her baby.

Catherine kept her resolve for close on a fortnight. Noah made several trips into the woods, telling both Catherine and Lydia that, if anyone asked, they should say he was in the forest checking his traps. Always he returned in a day or two with another pile of shiny beaver pelts or other plush animal fur.

Lydia finished the garments she was making and, after much coaxing, agreed again to return to the loft when Catherine asked it of her. Catherine began to relax a bit, thinking that by not saying anything to

Noah about his fur-trading business, they'd settled into a truce of sorts. She still worried that his scheme would come crashing down upon them, but for the nonce, all seemed well.

Until the afternoon he returned home from one of his trading trips and burst into the house in a full-blown rage.

CHAPTER 31

"What have you done?" he shouted at Catherine the second he barged into the house.

She looked up from the pot of vegetable stew she was stirring. "Nothing, Noah. I've done nothing."

Grabbing one arm, he yanked her around. "What have you done with my muskets and gunpowder?"

"I haven't done anyth—"

"Where did you hide them?" he yelled. Then, spotting Lydia near the board table holding two empty trenchers and spoons, he shouted, "Lydia, get out of here!"

The command was delivered in a tone plenty loud enough for the girl to hear. With wide round eyes, Lydia darted from the house.

"Noah, please —" Catherine attempted to wrench from his grasp.

He grabbed her other arm and backed her

into the corner beyond the hearth. "You and I were the only ones who knew about the muskets and gunpowder. Now everything's gone! What have you done?"

Catherine had never seen him so angry. "Noah, I haven't been in the shed except to get my ho—"

"You're lying!" He slapped her across the cheek.

The sting caused her to cry out. "Noah, stop!"

"Tell me the truth before I —"

"Please, calm yourself," she gasped.

"Calm myself! I find an easy way to turn a profit, and now you've ruined it! Where did you put my crates? You've hidden them somewhere!"

"Noah!" Tears pooled in Catherine's eyes. "I've done nothing. *Please . . . believe me!*"

He flung her from him. "You're a lying bitch, and if you don't tell me the truth, I swear I'll kill you!"

Landing on the floor, Catherine feared for the safety of her child, so she drew up her knees in an attempt to protect her middle.

"Get up!" He kicked her backside with one foot.

She coiled tighter. "Noah, stop! You'll hurt the baby!"

"I'm sick of hearing about that damned

baby." He grabbed a fistful of her hair and yanked until she raised her head.

"I'll get up! I'll get up!"

He jerked her to her feet. "Get up and show me where you've hidden everything!" With an impatient shove, he pushed her toward the door.

Catherine knew better than to resist. With Noah in the lead, they both headed around the side of the house toward the shed, but just before reaching the stack of firewood, the edge of her long skirt caught on a bramble. She bent down to loosen it.

"Hurry up!" Noah shouted over one shoulder.

"My skirt is caught, Noah!"

Muttering something that sounded like, "Damned useless female," he spun around to grab Catherine's arm and yank her forward.

The bramble held fast, and instead of being able to take a step, Catherine's body lurched forward and landed with a hard thud against the stack of rough-hewn sticks of firewood. The sudden impact knocked the breath from her. With a gasp, she crumpled to the ground clutching her middle.

Noah seemed not to notice. "Damn you! I'll find the crates myself!" Without a backward glance, he disappeared into the shed and some moments later, into the woods.

No one had to tell Catherine her baby was dead.

When Lydia stole around the corner of the house and found her mistress lying on the ground, she ran at once to fetch Goody Smithfield. The older woman helped Catherine into her bedchamber where they peeled off her blood-soaked skirt and undergarments. Although feeling as if she might lose consciousness at any moment, Catherine managed to tell Goody Smithfield which of her herbs to bring from the loft and how to prepare and administer them. The older woman did exactly as instructed. For the next several days, she also came by to check on her.

That week Lydia learned how to cook.

For days, Catherine lay alone in bed, hardly speaking to either the servant girl or to Goody Smithfield. She did her best to eat what was put before her, but inside, her soul felt numb. Over and over in her mind, she retraced the events of that horrible afternoon. The injury was so devastating she feared she might never conceive again. Some days she could not halt her tears and they flowed unchecked. Other times her anguish was so deep, no tears would come. How, how, how could she ever forgive Noah this?

When he finally did return home, he said little, did not ask how Catherine or the baby fared, or mention the missing muskets or gunpowder. The two women hardly dared speak to him, or to one another.

One evening, as the three were finishing up their evening meal, they were surprised when Deputy-Governor Argall and the other two traders, Tidwell and Sharpe, stepped to the threshold.

"So, yer home." The deputy-governor looked in, addressing Noah.

"Come in, Argall; Sharpe, Tidwell. Lydia, pour the gentlemen some ale."

The deputy-governor pulled one of the ladder-backed chairs up to the table and sat facing Noah. The traders slid onto the bench opposite Catherine.

Her breath grew short even before the older man began to speak. *Was it all to come to a head now?*

"I'll get straight to the point, Colton." Argall's tone was somber.

Noah flung a nervous glance at Catherine who sat mute, the little bit of color that had returned to her face having now drained from it.

"I've received some disturbing reports from a couple of planters over by Henricus. Seems a band of Indians armed with muskets been raidin' homes and barns over that way. One man shot dead and his wife raped. Couple other planters injured though they're still alive. Barely. Soon as I received the first report, I came for ya', but yer girl here said ye was out checking yer traps. The boys and I took the liberty of carting away all the crates of muskets and gunpowder been stored in yer barn."

Catherine's eyes fluttered shut.

"Ought ta' lock that shed up, Noah," Tidwell remarked.

"Wish ye had," Argall chimed in. "A good many muskets were missing and a whole box of gunpowder gone. Some sneaky Indians must 'a broke in durin' the night and made off with 'em."

"Well." Noah spoke up quite strongly. "I daresay I never heard a thing. Did you, Catherine?"

Her lips tight, she merely looked down.

"Of course, I've been away from the house a good bit lately."

"So, how does yer trappin' fare?"

"Quite well." Noah nodded. "I wonder I did not hear about the Indians raiding farms or —"

"I thought it best not to publish the news. No need to pitch the settlers here into a panic. All the same, I want you boys to head over to Henricus, camp out north and west of there, move around a bit. Watch; see what ye can learn. If ye hear anything suspicious, get word to the planters at once. I don't want any tobacco fields burned or anyone else killed. Don't need to remind you this is serious business. All the planters are armed now. The boys and I distributed the muskets and gunpowder to every man on every plantation up that way." He paused. "If ye'd 'a been at home when we come for 'em, I'd 'a wanted ye ta' come along."

After the men talked a bit more, deciding when to set out for Henricus and what to take with them, they rose to leave. Near the door, Argall paused. "Oddest thing, Colton," he mused, "them Indians that stole from ye, they knew exactly which crates held the muskets and gunpowder. From the look of it, they didn't tear into a single other crate." He shook his head. "Them Indians are a crafty lot."

Catherine could no longer remain silent. Since she was not carrying a child and did not believe she could ever conceive again, she had nothing now to fear from Noah.

When they were preparing for bed that night, she prepared her mind to speak.

"Noah." She kept her tone calm. "Surely you will now give up conducting 'private' trades with the Indians."

"You heard Argall." He addressed her without looking up as he removed his jerkin. "We're to go to Henricus."

"I am referring to the future, when you return to Jamestown. A man has been killed, Noah, by an Indian to whom you gave a musket."

He whirled around. "You have no proof of that. The Indians have been stealing weapons from us since Captain Smith's time."

Catherine inhaled a measured breath. "Noah, I saw the crates in the shed. Muskets and gunpowder were missing. And now you have a pile of pelts in the loft for which you traded something."

"Have you seen me leave here with weapons?" he challenged. "It would be impossible for me to carry half a dozen muskets and bags of gunpowder into the forest . . . on foot. You have no proof of anything."

Catherine's ire rose. She knew he was lying, but other than what she'd seen in the shed with her own eyes, he was right, she had no proof. Even the deputy-governor believed the Indians had stolen the weapons.

Noah had so completely gained the trust of everyone in Jamestown that not a one of them would suspect him of wrongdoing. It would be the same as with Victor's death, her word against his.

"A few months ago, all you could speak of was becoming a planter. You now have your hundred and fifty acres. You could earn quite a good living planting tobacco."

His mouth twisted with annoyance.

"You could hire someone to help you clear the land. The planters would gladly share their knowledge with you." When still he said nothing, she went on. "Noah, we have to eat. Which means we have no choice but to grow our own food."

"There is plenty of grain in the store-house," he grumbled.

From her place on the bed, she sprang to her feet. "That corn is not yours! It is for new settlers to see them through until their first harvest!"

He remained calm. "Governor Yeardley didn't see it that way."

"What are you saying?"

"Yeardley told me, Sharpe, and Tidwell, to help ourselves."

"That was because you had no land! You have land now! You are expected to farm it. You are well aware of the ordinance commanding every settler to plant and harvest his own corn."

"Argall does not plant corn."

"And what does that mean?"

"It means the deputy-governor and I have a good deal in common; seems we are both ill-suited for hard labor."

"You are not making sense, Noah." She glared at him.

"If you must know, I intend to become governor myself one day."

Shock registered on Catherine's face. "I do not think that a good idea, Noah. For a certainty, all your lies and deceptions would come to light."

He angrily lunged toward her, but she successfully sidestepped him to press her body against the back of the door. He stood near the bed glowering. "You are a woman," he spat out. "Who would listen to you?"

"Nonetheless," she countered, "you are as ill-suited to be governor as apparently you are for hard labor. A governor must be above reproach."

"So you believe Argall is above reproach, do ye? Apparently ye do not know it was he who kidnapped your friend Pocahontas afore she wed John Rolfe."

"I . . . confess I did not know that," Catherine faltered. "Still the New Virginia

Company must trust him, otherwise they would not have appointed him."

"And the colonists trust me. *I* am the man Argall turns to in time of crisis. Not Sharpe or Tidwell. I know more about the Indians than any man since John Smith. Argall has a fine house and servants. But I have something he doesn't. A wife. The Virginia Company investors will take kindly to a family man becoming governor. Argall is a mere ship's captain who issues orders." He grimaced. "Which I obey."

Catherine shook her head with dismay.

"As my wife, you took an oath to obey me," he gloated, "therefore when I issue an order, it is *your* duty to obey. And I hereby order you to behave in a seemly fashion, befitting the wife of a governor. To your credit," he added, "you handled yourself quite well this evening."

"I said nothing this evening."

"Precisely." He crossed the room to extinguish the pine-knot candle.

In the darkness, Catherine slowly walked to her side of the bed and climbed in. Lying abed, she softly addressed him. "Noah, what has changed you? You are not the same man I knew in England. The Noah I knew, the clergyman's boy, would never lie or cheat or steal. What caused you to turn against the goodness your father instilled in you?"

She heard his snort of derision. "Your brother, for one."

She sat bolt upright. "You cannot blame your actions on Adam!"

"He cheated me out of what was mine."

"My father paid your passage over. The land he received for doing so belonged to him. Upon his death, it rightfully passed to Adam. I've compensated you with the land I inherited, therefore that score should be settled. Adam is not to blame for your lies or your thievery."

"I have committed no crime. Now, cease badgering me and go to sleep. I've a hard day's travel ahead of me."

She said nothing further. As usual, trying to make her husband see reason was useless. She did not believe he would ever be appointed governor. He was arrogant and irrational, and Adam had been exactly right about him. His scheme to become governor was yet one more method to avoid doing his share of honest, hard work. Her only hope for their survival this coming winter was the bargain she'd struck with Adam. Beyond that, she had no notion what was to become of them.

CHAPTER 32

July 1618

Noah left early the following morning for Henricus, leaving Catherine feeling at loose ends. Physically she was pleased to find that each day more and more of her strength returned, although she had not yet resumed any of the heavy work, hauling water, or bringing in logs for the fire. Those tasks fell to Lydia, who during Catherine's convalescence had been forced to take on more and more of the household responsibilities. Catherine was pleased to see that Lydia now often began a task without being told to do so. She was an early riser, and, now that she knew it was necessary to build up the fire as soon as she arose, and how to prepare their morning meal, she quietly and efficiently did so.

That afternoon, after the women straightened up indoors, gathered Noah's soiled garments, and changed the rushes on the floor, Catherine decided to venture into the woods. The weather was glorious, and she felt her Secret Place calling her. She hadn't been there in over a fortnight, not since the day she saw Lanneika.

Once she'd made her way to the cove, she sat down beneath her favorite old oak and wrapped her arms around her drawn-up knees. After inhaling several deep breaths of the fresh, clean air, she began to feel the peace and serenity of the forest soothe the wounded places in her soul.

She did not wish to spoil the lovely day thinking about Noah, about what he had said last night, and certainly not about his wild scheme to become governor. But the agony she had suffered at his hands and the anguish over the uncertainty of their future continued to weigh on her mind, and, try as she might, she could not thrust her worries aside.

All her life she had wished to be wed to Noah Colton, and, now that her dream had come true, she found the reality more akin to a nightmare. Beneath Noah's lighthearted exterior there lurked an angry man; the merry twinkle in his blue eyes masked a dark demon within. His quick temper made him difficult and unpredictable to live with. Every time she thought about their lost babe, her eyes filled with tears. She did not know how long it would take before she could forgive him. But in her heart she knew she must try. With a heavy heart, she vowed to cease thinking about his shortcomings and try instead to be thankful for what they had, a good solid home, which had withstood the harsh winter months and a number of spring storms. They had land, even though he chose not to work it. For now, there was plenty of food in the loft, so she needn't worry for a while on that score. And although she did not regard Lydia as a friend, the girl had finally come around to fulfilling her intended purpose, which was to be a help to Catherine, and for that, she was indeed grateful.

She sat pensive for a long moment, gazing out over the pool of clear blue water, enjoying the damp earthy smells that surrounded her. Suddenly she decided to dip her toes in the water. The day was exceptionally warm, and there was no one about to chide her for being reckless.

She hurriedly peeled off her shoes and stockings and, lifting her long skirts, padded barefoot toward the water's edge. Beneath her bare feet, the dark-green moss felt soft and cool, the pleasant sensation bringing a smile to her lips. Reaching the water's edge, she reached one toe out, then, feeling her other foot slip from beneath her, she plopped down hard on the moist ground.

"Oh!"

A burst of embarrassed laughter escaped her. She realized she hadn't felt laughter bubble up inside her in weeks, perhaps months. Not since the first days of her marriage. Fresh tears welled in her eyes. *No!* She would not give in to self-pity. Turning her focus to the water lapping over her bare feet, she noted it was also beginning to wet the edges of her skirt. She reached to tug it out of the water, baring her legs almost to her knees. Inching along on her rump, she dangled her legs deeper into the cool clear liquid. But, of a sudden, she felt her entire body slide into the pool!

"Oh-h-h!"

Submerged in the water all the way to her neck, her skirt billowed out around her like a sail as her feet desperately sought purchase on the slippery sandy floor. She stretched an arm toward the bank for something to grasp hold of in order to pull herself out of the water. She wasn't afraid; she did know how to swim, though if she'd intended to bathe, she would have removed more of her clothing. It was merely the unexpectedness of finding herself in the water that unsettled her.

Her erratic splashing sent droplets of water onto her face and into her eyes, and when she raised a hand to brush the wetness aside, more water trickled down her face. Squeezing her eyes shut, she reached blindly toward land but this time her hand touched something soft and warm. At once, her eyes sprang open. Tilting her head up, up, and up, she was surprised to find a pair of twinkling black eyes gazing down at her.

"Lanneika!"

The petite Indian girl began to giggle. "I pull."

Having something to hold onto gave Catherine the leverage she needed. Grasping her other arm, Lanneika managed to drag Catherine's upper body onto land. Drawing a knee up, Catherine climbed the rest of the way out of the water. Her water-logged skirt and petticoats felt as heavy as a ship's sail following a storm at sea. Though she'd pinned her hair up that morning, it had escaped its moorings and hung like a heavy wet blanket down her back.

Her breath labored, Catherine murmured, "I hadn't meant to take a swim today."

"S-swim?" Lanneika sat down beside her.

Catherine grinned. "Bathe. Wash self."

Lanneika laughed. "How you clean self with clothes on? Better to take clothes off when go in water."

Smiling, Catherine shook her head. "I must look a fright."

"Look wet." Tilting her dark head to one side, Lanneika studied her friend. "Baby gone," she said softly.

Catherine's chin trembled. She bit her lower lip to halt the tears that seemed always behind her eyes. She nodded tightly.

Lanneika rose to her feet. "Cat-e-wren too wet to go home. With me, come." She extended a small brown hand.

Which Catherine took, allowing the smaller girl to pull her to her feet.

Tired, distraught, and fighting her soaked garments with every step, Catherine took no notice where amongst the trees they exited the clearing. After trekking through the thick woods for what seemed like a long distance, she at last begged Lanneika to stop and allow her to rest. They perched on a fallen log, Catherine twisting about to wring water here and there from her sodden skirt.

"I'd best take my petticoat off," she said, and stood up to do so.

Taking the soggy garment, Lanneika began to twist rivulets of water from it. "Like when we do wash."

Catherine nodded. "Yes, like when we do the wash."

They set out again, Catherine feeling considerably lighter without the waterlogged petticoat clinging to her legs. Carrying it over her arm, Lanneika led the way deeper and deeper into the woods.

Catherine soon realized it would have been quicker for her to simply make her way home than travel deeper into the forest. She had no idea where they were, and, on her own, she'd never be able to find her way back. They came upon a sparkling stream where a handful of Indian children were splashing in the water, their mothers sitting on the bank looking on.

"Here I bathe," Lanneika told Catherine, who took that to mean they must be drawing near her village.

Instead, Lanneika directed her straight into the mouth of a huge dark cave. For an instant, alarm gripped Catherine, but she immediately dismissed it. She trusted Lanneika completely. Both girls' voices echoed as they walked hand in hand in the darkness.

Emerging from the tunnel into the light, they walked only a short distance before coming upon what seemed like the densest thicket of tall trees Catherine had ever seen.

Once past the stand of trees, the Indian girl's face brightened. "Home," she said.

A few steps more and Catherine again gazed with awe upon the second Indian village she'd seen. Here, as in Werowocomoco, rows of neat bark houses squatted in shaded comfort beneath the impenetrable canopy of thick, green leaves. The houses were long and narrow, their rounded shape reminding Catherine of loaves of bread. Most had the bark roofs, and even the sides rolled back to let in both light and the cooler air wafting through the trees that surrounded the village. As in Werowocomoco, she marveled over how clean and orderly everything appeared. Beside each tidy house was its own thriving garden, the green corn stalks as tall as she. Beneath them, squash vines were loaded with fruit while vines heavy with beans climbed every stalk. Colorful flowers lined narrow paths leading to each house. Here and there, small, naked children ran and played, caught up in their laughter and games of make-believe.

As she and Lanneika walked through the center of the village, Lanneika nodded and spoke to every woman they passed. That Lanneika was well-liked was evident. And Catherine, as Lanneika's companion, meant that she, too, was regarded in a friendly, albeit curious, manner. She noted several of the Indian women eyeing her warily. Although enjoying the unique experience, Catherine's footsteps were dogged by the fear that she really shouldn't be here. Noah would be furious if he knew.

When they reached the largest and longest of the bark houses, Lanneika surprised Catherine by walking straight into it. Inside, it took a few moments before her eyes became accustomed to the dim light. The house felt surprisingly cool inside and was deathly silent. Glancing about, Catherine spotted a hand-stitched tapestry, beautifully decorated with beads and shells hanging on one wall. Ornaments handmade from feathers and dried herbs hung on another. Several gaily painted earthen pots sat about.

Entering an adjoining chamber, she noted a number of straw mats on the floor, each topped with furs of small animals, squirrel, marten, and beaver. Further down the tunnel-like house, she saw a stone oven and assumed that was where the family prepared their meals. It appeared only she and Lanneika were in the house.

"Take off wet clothes," Lanneika said. "I rub dry."

While Catherine peeled off the damp sleeves of her bodice, stepped from her dripping skirt, and removed her shoes, Lanneika produced a handful of soft turkey feathers and proceeded to feather-dry Catherine's arms and legs. Weariness from the long trek through the woods must have shown on her face, for Lanneika soon bade her lie on her stomach on one of the surprisingly soft mats while Lanneika knelt beside her to feather-dry her long, wet hair. Then, with a type of hog-bristle brush, she gently smoothed the tangles from her hair, which felt so pleasurable Catherine soon drifted off to sleep.

Sometime later, she awoke with a start and became aware of a lightweight blanket covering her naked body. She also became aware of the delicious smell of food being cooked nearby. Because she heard voices, she surmised they were no longer alone in the house. Just as she was wondering where Lanneika might be, the girl appeared carrying a soft doeskin garment.

"You wear."

Holding the blanket close about her, Catherine glanced at the dress. "My clothes are not yet dry?"

Lanneika grinned impishly. "Nice you look in this."

Catherine let Lanneika drop the doeskin garment over her head. When it slipped down over her nude body, her hands skimmed over the smooth soft skin. The loose-fitting dress had no sleeves and fell to just below her knees, ending with a fringe that tickled her bare legs.

Catherine grinned self-consciously. "I feel . . . a bit naked."

"Look beautiful. Look like me now. Except for hair. Sit. I braid."

Catherine complied, and, when done, Lanneika appeared quite pleased with her handiwork. She gave Catherine a pair of moccasins to put on her feet and, taking her by the hand, led her to where the rest of her family was gathered just outside the house.

In a flurry of Indian words, Lanneika introduced Catherine to all the tawny-skinned people, her mother and sisters, several Indian braves, and a handful of younger boys and girls all related to Lanneika in some way, and all with names Catherine knew she would never remember. Phyrahawque, she noted with a flicker of disappointment, was not amongst them. But perhaps he had his own home elsewhere in the village, complete with a wife and children. Lanneika had never commented on her brother's marital status, and until now, Catherine hadn't wondered about it.

"Cat-e-wren *netab!*" Lanneika announced proudly. Turning to Catherine, she said, "I tell them you friend."

The Indians gazed at Catherine pleasantly as she and Lanneika sat down on the ground.

Catherine's gaze was drawn to the eldest of the women, Lanneika's mother, who sat a bit apart from the others on a cushion of luxurious furs. She was dressed in a white doeskin garment with ropes of pearls and colored beads hanging around her neck. Her long hair, shot with strands of gray, was held back from her face by a leather band ornamented with feathers and intricate beadwork. Though her weathered face bespoke the beauty that was once there, her features appeared serene now with the wisdom of old age. Catherine thought her beautiful, though she could also see the tiredness in her eyes that age also brings. Still, it was easy to see where both Lanneika and Phyrahawque came by their good looks.

"Your mother is beautiful," Catherine said to Lanneika, who smiled and nodded.

After all the children had been called over and told to sit down, three or four Indian women began to stream from the opening in the bark house carrying earthen bowls of steaming hot food which they placed on the ground. Another Indian maid handed around wooden trenchers similar to the ones Catherine used. After Lanneika's mother had said a few words, which, Catherine assumed, was a prayer of thanksgiving for their food, they all began to eat. Like any large family, they talked and laughed amongst themselves as they ate.

Catherine thoroughly enjoyed the tasty meal, which consisted of a type of roasted meat she couldn't identify, steamed squash, beans, and fluffy wedges of hot corn bread, washed down with a fruity-tasting juice served in gourds. Afterward, they all ate handfuls of sweet, juicy berries.

While eating berries, Lanneika directed Catherine's attention toward what appeared to be a canoe with four pairs of legs beneath it headed toward them.

"Phyrahawque back from river."

"Oh." Catherine watched as the Indian braves knelt, to place onto the ground the dugout they'd been carrying upside down over their heads. Then the braves, unclothed except for a scrap of leather stretched across their loins, drew closer. Near the doorway, one dropped the basket he'd carried slung over his shoulder. From the smell of it, Catherine assumed it contained the day's catch, which the family would eat tomorrow.

The others greeted the latecomers, and,

amidst much laughter and good-natured teasing, they too settled on the ground. It was only then that Phyrahawque seemed to notice Catherine's presence, his piercing black eyes casting sidelong looks at her.

"Cat-e-wren fall in water. I bring home," Lanneika explained.

Phyrahawque nodded, then turned his attention to the food before him.

After the men had eaten, the children eagerly bounced up to play and most of the women dispersed. Catherine noted that most everyone in the village sat on the ground before their houses, enjoying their evening meal. Rising from the center of nearly every bark rooftop was a lazy rivulet of smoke. To Catherine the atmosphere of the village seemed tranquil and idyllic. Jamestown sometimes felt the same way to her, but only when Noah was away, she admitted sadly.

The peaceful Indian village, so different from anything she had known before, suddenly made her think of Pocahontas, who'd spent her childhood in just such a place. How different life in London must have seemed to her, how offensive the clamorous noise, dirt, soot, and fog. A veil of sadness crept over her. She, too, would soon have to leave this beautiful place and return to her own home . . . though she was sorely tempted not to. The sun had already dipped behind the treetops and the first twinkling stars of evening now pierced the dusky sky.

She turned to Lanneika. "I really should go now."

The girl's brow furrowed. "Stay till sun again in sky."

"Oh, no. I mustn't stay the night."

"Trader-man not there."

Catherine blanched. How did Lanneika know that? But, then, how did the Indians know most of what they did?

"Trader-man no hurt you here."

Catherine inhaled a sharp breath. She hadn't told Lanneika any events of the past few weeks, and yet the perceptive Indian girl seemed to know everything.

"Stay for singing. I dance for you."

Catherine's interest rose. There would be dancing? Oh, she truly did wish to stay for that. Perhaps it wouldn't hurt to linger a while longer. Noah wasn't home, after all.

In minutes, everyone began to gather on the greensward in the center of the village. Several braves built a fire. Others produced rawhide drums, gourd rattles, and flutes made from reeds. Enthralled, Catherine sat beside Lanneika, her blue-green eyes taking it all in. When groups of Indians got up to dance, Catherine clapped her hands along with them. Once, she stood up and joined hands with the others to form a circle, stamping her feet as they did in time to the music.

She couldn't help noticing Phyrahawque amongst the dancers. He was not only the tallest of all the braves, he was by far the most handsome, his shoulders the broadest, his muscled arms and legs the strongest. Deferring to his height and regal bearing, all the other men stepped aside to let him pass. Women grinned self-consciously and ducked their heads. When he danced, Catherine noted the eyes of every female following Phyrahawque. And no wonder. His lean body was beautifully formed, his movements fluid and graceful. Catherine heard a good bit of whispering and giggling amongst the younger women as they lustfully eyed Phyrahawque.

"Lanneika," she finally asked, "does Phyrahawque have a wife?"

Lanneika's dark eyes twinkled merrily. "No. Many wish he choose them."

Catherine watched him dance. She admired the magnificent Indian warrior's good looks, as did all the women. She was surprised when, right in front of her, Phyrahawque stopped dancing and extended a hand. At Lanneika's urging, Catherine let him pull her to her feet and join him in the center of the ring. Her cheeks flushed, Catherine did her best to keep up with the quick movements of his moccasin-clad feet. The rhythm of the drum was infectious. Pulsing up from the ground, it seemed to ignite a fiery passion within her. Apparently the drums had the same effect on others, for she couldn't help noticing when several pairs of pretty girls and lusty young braves slipped away hand in hand into the night.

It was definitely time to go home. She leaned toward Lanneika. "I should change my clothes now. I'll need you to walk with me back to Jamestown."

"Phyrahawque take you."

CHAPTER 33

Catherine was unprepared for the exhilaration that filled her when Phyrahawque lifted her up and onto the back of his huge white stallion. He flung himself up behind her and, without a word, slipped one strong arm around her midsection, his other hand expertly grasping the reins. As his heel spurred the mighty steed into action, Catherine aimed a glance at Lanneika, who stood smiling in the shadows in front of the large domed house.

Skirting through the trees just beyond the village, the night smells of the forest hung on the air like rich perfume. From her perch high above the forest floor, Catherine drank in the heady sensation. Behind her, Phyrahawque ducked on occasion to avoid colliding with a low-hanging branch. His muscled chest grazing her back sent tingles of pleasure coursing through her, a feeling that in a sad way reminded her of the first time

Noah had kissed her. How odd that being near Phyrahawque could arouse the same feeling of longing within her. Even before they reached the mouth of the cave, her body beneath his strong forearm burned with fire. Though she fought it, her breath began to grow short and her heart to pound like the Indian drum she could still hear in the distance. Because the darkness inside the cave was so very dark, she wondered that Phyrahawque could see where he was going.

"I . . . can't see a thing," she finally said, tilting her head to look up at him.

"Nothing to see," he replied, his response in flawless English.

Catherine chuckled at his humor, which caused her stomach muscles to tighten. His arm tightened about her middle.

"No want lose you."

She didn't want to lose him either. She reached to lay a hand on his arm, then just as quickly, jerked it away.

"No move hand," he said, his warm breath ruffling her hair. "Feel nice."

Catherine slowly replaced it. Beneath her fingertips, the Indian man's skin felt warm, smooth, and hairless. She fought an urge to snuggle closer to him. *Dear God, what was happening to her?*

Emerging from the other side of the cave, the horse cantered briskly along a narrow trail lit by the moon and a splay of twinkling stars overhead. When the trail ran out, Phyrahawque slowed the steed's pace, letting the horse pick its own way through the trees and underbrush. Night sounds filled the stillness. In the distance, an owl hooted. Small animals rustled through the tall grass.

Catherine chewed fretfully on her lower lip, all too aware that she was alone in the forest with a mighty Indian warrior, a warrior even her husband feared.

"You much safe with me," he said softly, as if reading her thoughts.

She relaxed as best she could, considering the manner in which his nearness was affecting her. "I am not afraid of you, Phyrahawque. It's just that I-I'm a married woman . . . and I . . . I . . . ," her voice trailed off.

After a pause, he said, "Cat-e-wren spirit not in harmony with trader-man."

Catherine flinched. Though Phyrahawque and Lanneika's English was broken, what they lacked in words, they easily made up for in perception.

She felt compelled to reply. "I haven't a clue what grievance you have against my husband, but please accept my apology for

527

whatever he had done to offend you."

"Crenepo cannot say sorry words for man."

It was true. Regardless of what Noah had done, she knew she could not apologize for him. "Well, then, please know I am truly sorry for his misdeeds."

"You not one at fault."

They both fell silent before Catherine again spoke. "Lanneika told me you learned English words as a boy."

She felt his head nod. "Half sister teach me many moons ago. She go often to white-man camp."

Catherine started. The only Indian woman she knew who'd frequently visited the Jamestown settlement was Pocahontas. "Are you saying your half sister was . . . Pocahontas?"

Again, he nodded. "She your friend."

"Yes, she was my friend." His admission stunned her. But then, Powhatan was rumored to have had as many as a hundred wives. If they each gave him only one child, then the children could each have nearly a hundred half brothers and sisters. "Is Lanneika also half sister to Pocahontas?"

"No. Matoaka and I have same father. My mother, Lanneika's mother, same. We no have same father."

Catherine shook her head to clear it. How did they ever keep up with who was related to whom?

"If you are related to Pocahontas, then why are you not part of the Powhatan tribe?"

"Mother much-favored wife of Powhatan. He make her weroansqua of own tribe."

"So, your mother is the leader of your tribe?"

"No. Mother not warrior. I leader now."

Phyrahawque's place in the tribe was as Catherine suspected — he was the werowance.

Too soon they reached the edge of the forest. Phyrahawque reined in his horse a few paces before they entered the moonlit clearing. Regret filled Catherine as she realized her wonderful day with the Indians had drawn to a close. Dropping the reins, he slid off his horse then reached up for her. Their eyes locked as she placed both hands on his strong shoulders. He caught her about the waist and swung her easily to the ground. When it seemed his hands lingered a few seconds longer than necessary about her waist, Catherine's breath lodged in her throat. Catching sight of the wistful longing in his black gaze, she lowered hers.

"Thank you for bringing me home, Phyrahawque." She moved away from him, one hand smoothing the wrinkles of her skirt into place.

"Per-haps —"

She glanced over her shoulder. "Yes?"

"Per-haps I see you in forest."

She nodded. "Perhaps." Ducking her head, she darted away from him, nervously aware of the small, secret smile on her own face.

Catherine lay awake a long time that night, thinking over the events of the day. The peaceful life the Indians led in the forest, their serenity and easy laughter amongst their family members, was exactly the sort of life she yearned for. Was exactly the sort of life she'd come to the New World to find, complete with a loving husband, home, and children. It was not wrong of her to want such a life; it had just astonished her to learn that Noah did not want the same thing when all along she'd thought he did. Phyrahawque was right when he said her spirit was not in harmony with Noah's.

Oh, how she wished now that she hadn't clung so stubbornly to her childish notion that she and Noah loved one another, that she'd opened her eyes once she came here and been able to see him as he truly was.

Now, she realized, she had only been in love with the memories of Noah she knew as a boy. She did not know Noah the man at all. And, she had to admit, albeit sadly, she did not love him any more than he loved her. Indeed, there was no harmony between their spirits, and she doubted now there ever could be.

For two long, lonely days, Catherine found her thoughts drifting again and again to the pleasurable hours she'd spent with the Indians. She thought about Lanneika's smiling face and her sweet nature and, of course, about Phyrahawque — his kind, gentle nature; the loving way he spoke to his sister and his mother. But she also thought about how his muscles rippled in the firelight as he danced, how her insides burned when his arm was clasped about her middle. How . . . how *something* made her want to kiss him. Always, her vivid imaginings ended in waves of longing for — oh, how wanton her thoughts had become! Clearly, she was powerfully attracted to the handsome Indian warrior. But . . . she shouldn't be! It was wrong. True, she no longer loved Noah, but she was still married to him; she was still his wife. She worked to push all thoughts of the handsome Indian warrior from mind.

But . . . it was no use.

Even now, two days later, the thought of being with him set her heart pounding with desire. She'd been drawn to him from the moment she laid eyes on him, the afternoon he came for Lanneika and she'd found his piercing black eyes looking straight at her. And then again the day he walked into her house looking for Lanneika, or perhaps, for her? Though Phyrahawque knew she was married to the hated trader-man, he had always been kind to her. He had danced with her, said he did not want to lose her and that *perhaps he would see her in the forest*. As the days passed, Catherine near swooned every time she recalled the look of longing on his handsome face when he'd said those words.

Every day since she'd visited his village, she fought the urge to run into the woods and search for him. With Noah still in Henricus, she reasoned, there was no one to stop her, or question her whereabouts once she returned home. Perhaps if she saw Phyrahawque again, just once, in the bright light of day, she wouldn't feel the same way about him. Perhaps the strong pull she'd felt towards him that night in the village was the result of the sensuous beat of the drums, or even the moonlight. Perhaps, taken altogether, the strange, overpowering yearning she now felt was the result of some sort of magical spell the Indians' music had cast upon her.

Surely, that was it. Or . . . perhaps . . . it was not.

Perhaps she was drawn to the magnificent warrior because of his strength, his virile manliness, and then, of course, there was his handsome face, which drew her like no man she'd ever met before. Not even Noah. Or, perhaps it was his honor. For, indeed, he was honorable. He had been alone in the dark of night with a white woman, one he thought "beautiful" — for Lanneika had said her brother thought her beautiful — and yet, he had behaved in a respectful, trustworthy manner. He had not accosted her. He had not been the least bit forward or inappropriate. He had been a perfect gentleman. One she longed with all her heart to see again.

On the third afternoon since the day Catherine visited Lanneika's village, she could no longer resist the urge to run into the woods. Soon after she and Lydia finished their midday meal, she scooped up a basket and announced she was off to pick berries, though she knew full well she might not return with a single one.

She had just reached the strawberry patch where Phyrahawque had killed the snake when, from somewhere behind her, she heard the soft neigh of a horse. Breathless with anticipation, she whirled around. Was he here?

Yes! Yes, he was here!

She spotted his enormous white steed nibbling grass amongst the trees only a few paces from her. Phyrahawque hovered near the horse, his smoldering black gaze intent upon her, his bare chest heaving with the same pent-up desire pulsating through Catherine. Compelled by a force she did not understand, she flung her basket aside and ran towards the magnificent Indian brave whose arms opened at once to receive her.

"Phyrahawque!"

She melted into his embrace, every inch of her longing for him, her body already aching to take him inside her. His lips found hers, and as the kiss lengthened and deepened, Catherine forgot all else and gave herself up to the intoxicating desire that consumed her.

In moments, Phyrahawque scooped her up into his strong arms and carried her to a secluded place where he had already prepared a bed of soft skins. His black eyes never left hers as he gently laid her down. Bracing himself beside her on one elbow, he gazed deeply into her eyes, then slowly reached to untie the strings of her blouse and gently pushed it aside. His dark gaze slid lower to rest upon the sight of her bare breasts.

"Beau-ti-ful. White."

Smiling, Catherine reached up to caress his tawny cheek, her slim fingers tracing the smooth planes and angles of his face. One fingertip slowly outlined the sensuous curve of his mouth.

"I want you," she murmured, her breasts rising and falling with each ragged breath she drew.

"I want you," he mouthed.

Again and again he kissed her. With one long tapered finger, he traced a fiery path from her neck to her breasts and back again, sending tingles of pleasure through her.

She arched her back, her fingers splayed across the strong, hairless mounds of his chest, then inching down, down, down toward the roll of leather holding his breechcloth in place. A low moan escaped him when her hand brushed against the bulge already visible beneath his breechcloth. He was every bit as aroused as she.

She reached to unbutton her skirt and,

with his help, slithered out of it. She tossed off her shoes and rolled down her stockings, then lay back, naked to the waist, only her pantalets covering her lower body. She saw the puzzlement on his face when his eyes raked over the odd garment.

"I can take them off."

"No."

One brown hand moved slowly across her flat belly covered only by the thin white cloth. He moved to caress the curve of her hip. Slowly, tantalizing her as he did so, his hand moved down, down, down the swell of her thigh to the knee, then back up the inside of one leg. Catherine's eyes fluttered shut as she relished the tingling sensations his touch inspired within her. And he'd not yet touched her bare flesh *there.* His hand teased her lower belly, coming nearer and nearer to her soft, feminine center.

"Please . . . touch me," she gasped.

"Soon."

He lowered his head to kiss her again, one arm pulling her body against his, the other caressing her back and buttocks, gently molding her to him. Catherine draped one leg over his back, both arms twined about his neck. He rolled her on top of him; then pushed the last remaining article of clothing from her. Naked, she lay atop him, each of them drinking in one another's essence from a long, deep kiss.

Without interrupting the kiss, he rolled her beneath him while one hand gently massaged the soft, moist place between her legs.

"Phyrahawque," she gasped, feeling his fingers stroke her silky wetness. Her arms around his shoulders tugged him closer. Beneath him, her body writhed with desire.

Soon, she felt the velvety end of his manhood gently probe her hot, pulsating center. The hard length of him teased her, the tip kissing her, pulling away, then thrusting, but not yet entering her.

"Take me, take me," she gasped, feeling she would die from sheer longing.

"When I certain you want me."

"Oh, Phyrahawque," she moaned. "I want you. I've wanted you since the moment I first saw you."

He covered her mouth with his again, and finally, with a low groan, he entered her, the hard length of him pushing up, up, up, igniting the most exquisite tremors of pleasure she'd ever known. As his thrusts drove deeper inside her, low moans of ecstasy escaped her.

As they both gasped for breath, he broke the kiss, and, lifting his head, his eyes closed and his strong chest heaved as he gulped for air. In moments, Catherine became aware of a place deep, deep inside her. A white-hot flame like nothing she'd ever known began to build and grow stronger and stronger and stronger until she thought she would explode inside. Phyrahawque's thrusts drove deeper and deeper, until, as one, they reached the pinnacle of their passion together. Wave after wave of tremors washed over Catherine. She had never felt *anything* like this before.

A growl escaped Phyrahawque's throat, then with a shudder, he fell limp on top of her, his breath hot against her cheek. Catherine's body also began to relax as weeks and weeks of pent-up tension drained from her. Her eyes fluttered shut as she lay beneath him, vitally aware of his shaft of hardness still buried deep within her.

Opening his eyes, he smiled down at her, then, placing a hand at her back, he rolled her toward him as he lay on his side. Gathering her closer, he pulled her against his chest and began to drop feather kisses on her forehead, her nose, and both cheeks. When his lips again covered hers, his tongue explored the soft cavity of her mouth, tracing her teeth, caressing and sucking on her tongue. Catherine again felt the tingle of response in her belly. Within her body, she became aware of his manhood growing hard, this time inside her.

He began to move, slowly at first, in and out with long languid strokes, pulling nearly all the way out, then thrusting deeply into her. Her breath again grew ragged with desire. Draping a leg over his back, she rocked along with him as his thrusts grew more insistent. As before, she marveled when once again he found that place deep inside her that brought her senses to a near fever pitch. In seconds, her longing matched his. Then together, in one dizzying burst of raw pleasure, their desire exploded. When simultaneous moans of ecstasy escaped both of them, Phyrahawque hugged her so close she thought he might smother her.

She became aware of their bodies, moist with perspiration. Damp tendrils of her hair clung to her forehead and shoulders. Her breasts pressed tightly against his moist chest. Locked in one another's arms, they may have drifted off to sleep; Catherine couldn't say for certain. In what seemed like a long, long time, he at last drew out of her and sat up. Catherine's eyes fluttered open as she rolled onto her back, one hand reaching to caress the strong muscles of his arm, now clasped about a drawn-up knee. Gazing at her over one shoulder, he reached for her hand and pulled her to her feet.

"Wash now."

Catherine did not question what he meant. She simply did as he did, bent to gather up strewn garments. He scooped up the mat of skins they'd been lying upon. His white stallion followed behind them as Phyrahawque led her, naked except for the clothing she held before her, through the dense trees to her own Secret Place and the pool of clear, cool water.

"Oh!" She smiled up at him with delight. "I've been here before."

He nodded, the mischievous grin on his face reminding her of Lanneika.

Hand in hand, they slipped into the water, Catherine's smiling eyes never leaving his. Once they'd gained the gurgling center of the pool, his head disappeared beneath the surface. Catherine relished the feel of the gentle waves. Stretching her body out, she swam a few strokes, luxuriating in the feel of the water lapping over her bare body. She laid her head back, letting the cool water soak through her hair. Suddenly, Phyrahawque's dark head popped up only inches away, his silky black hair mingling with her flaming tresses.

His eyes smiled as he reached for her arm and drew her into the circle of his. She saw that he carried a handful of sea moss. He laid her on her back and as she floated before him, he rubbed the moss over her chest and belly and down her arms, then rolling her over, he rubbed her back, down her legs, and up between them. Turning her head slightly, she watched him dive to the bottom and come back up with another handful of moss, which he used on himself. She relished the clean, fresh feel of her skin as she watched him wash his own body. Once clean, he again reached for her and drew her to him, the water lapping between them as he sensuously molded her soft nude form to his lean muscular one. The feel of his naked hardness against her belly instantly aroused her.

From sheer happiness, Catherine flung both arms up and lay back on the surface of the water, her torso laid bare before him. He licked her from neck to navel, trailing his tongue lower and lower, and lower still. Catherine shuddered with a longing more intense than any she'd ever felt before. *Would she never get enough of him?*

As his lips sought and found hers, she wrapped her arms around his neck and slid down the length of him. Twining her legs around his back, she felt his hardness slip inside her. Locked together, he twirled her around and around in the water as she rode him, one of his arms supporting her rump, the other treading water at his side.

As his thrusts deepened, she again felt his hardness awaken that special place deep within her, and with one final thrust, they both flung their heads back and cried out their pleasure as they climbed that intoxicating crescendo together, then welcomed the blessed release that shuddered through them.

When the hours of pleasure with Phyrahawque drew to a close, Catherine at last made her way home. Being with Phyrahawque that day had changed her forever. Never, not in all her life, had she known such joy could exist between a man and a woman. Never had she imagined her body could feel such exquisite pleasure, such magical sensations. Surely this magnificent Indian warrior had cast a spell over her, one she hoped she'd never, ever, awaken from.

The next afternoon, she again raced into the forest and found him waiting for her, this time in her Secret Place. They again made love in the water, then lay together on the mossy bank, their arms and legs intertwined as they murmured soft words of affection to one another. Phyrahawque had brought along a basket of wild berries and rye bread, and after their lovemaking, they enjoyed the simple repast.

Catherine laughed when he squeezed a berry and dribbled the pink juice over her bare breasts, only to sensuously lick it from her with long languid strokes of his tongue.

Another day that same week, they climbed partway up a tree, and, when both were comfortably seated in the crook of a sturdy limb, his arms holding her securely about her waist, her legs draped over his, they talked and talked. Catherine asked him about Pocahontas and his boyhood in Werowocomoco. Though his English was broken, and he confessed to having forgotten many words his half sister taught him, he managed to tell her much about the early days when Captain John Smith first came to their shores, and Pocahontas made frequent visits to the settlement.

He told her about the day the Tassentasses arrived and how curious all the Indians were about the light-skins and their floating island, which he later learned was a huge ship. He told of their astonishment at the exploding fire-sticks the Tassentasses carried and their huge cannons that snorted fire and smoke.

He said he was a few years older than

Pocahontas, but, because she was their father's favorite child, her pleas to accompany the older, more experienced warriors to the settlement to study the light-skins was granted. Then when she began to return with knowledge of their language, he said he was the most anxious of all the braves to learn the new words and she gladly taught him.

He told Catherine about the night the light-skins' storehouse burned, and Pocahontas and her warrior-escorts had come running back to Powhatan's village to report the loss. Then, the next day they carried bushels of corn and dried venison back to the fort so the settlers wouldn't starve. He said when the light-skins came, it appeared they did not know how to grow their own food, or how to hunt, or even take fish from the river and that the Indians tried to teach them.

"Lanneika taught me how to plant my corn," Catherine said. "And when to do so," she added with a laugh.

She told Phyrahawque the reason the early settlers did not know how to farm or hunt was because most of them were high-ranking gentlemen who, in England, did not farm. "They had servants who did the work for them. It has only been in later years," she added, "that the Virginia Company has sent farmers and laborers to these shores."

"You high-ranking woman?" he asked.

Catherine shrugged, choosing not to answer the question. His status amongst his people was far and away higher than hers amongst the English.

Phyrahawque told her the Tassentasses had given Powhatan their word that they would not be staying, that they would leave once they'd learned more about the area and had drawn their maps.

"I expect you wish the English had made good on their word and left you in peace," she said softly, feeling sad for the Indians over her countrymen's deception.

"I not wish you to leave." He hugged her to him and tenderly kissed her.

Their talks were often interrupted by intimate kisses and soft caresses. Catherine reveled in his touch. With Phyrahawque, she felt safe and protected. He seemed to care how she felt and whether or not she was happy and comfortable. Always, he seemed to be thinking of her, and it filled her with a joy she'd never known before.

One day that week, he took her on horseback to his village and, once there, told Lanneika to find again the doeskin dress Catherine had worn the night she visited. When she'd put it on, he lifted her onto his white stallion, and they rode off into the woods, Catherine straddling the horse behind him this time, her arms wrapped about his middle, her bare legs hugging the horse.

She found riding horseback in such a fashion exhilarating! The wind on her face and in her hair felt glorious! Never had she felt so free! The wind sweeping past them cooled the bare skin of her legs and whipped her red-gold hair into a scarlet banner that flew straight out behind her. Her heart thundered in her ears as Phyrahawque urged his steed faster and faster. The speed at which they skimmed past trees and brush and once flew over a small gully thrilled Catherine to her core. Throwing her head back, she relished each and every sensation, giving free reign to the laughter and joy that bubbled up within her. She'd never felt so glorious in all her life!

When Sabbath day came that week, Catherine toyed with the idea of not going to services and instead running into the woods, but she decided she'd best go to church since she didn't want Noah, when he came home, to question why she hadn't attended services.

The sermon that day included prayers for the many settlers who'd succumbed to swamp fever the past week and for those unfortunate ones who were still suffering. Catherine squirmed when the reverend issued yet another heartfelt plea for those who had room in their homes to take in as many settlers as they could. Many still did not have permanent lodgings. When the sermon concluded and everyone streamed onto the sunny greensward, Adam and Abby approached Catherine and insisted she come home with them.

"Who knows when Noah will be gone again," Abby said. "We'll have a nice meal. Nancy would love to see you. She's as big as a cow these days."

Catherine smiled. She'd dearly love to visit with Nancy, but the pull of the forest and Phyrahawque was far stronger. Eventually, however, she acquiesced, sending Lydia home alone and walking with her brother, Abby, and the Morgans to Adam's dugout on the riverbank.

Though she didn't really expect to see Phyrahawque as they floated up the James, she couldn't help scanning the woods beyond the shoreline for a sign of him on his magnificent white horse.

"You seem distracted, Cat," Adam said. "Are you feeling well?"

"Indeed, I am quite recovered."

"You look wonderful," Abby put in. "Your loveliness has returned tenfold. You are positively glowing!"

Catherine ducked her head. Was her new-found joy so very evident on her face?

Once they'd arrived at Harvest Hill, the Morgans went to their own home while Catherine enjoyed the delicious meal Abby and her brother's servants had prepared in their absence. Catherine played with little Eli, hugging his small squirming body and laughing with Abby as they tried to make sense of his coos and gurgles. Then Abby walked with her to Nancy and Jack's snug little cottage not far from the main house.

"Look who I've brought to see you!" Abby called when they caught sight of Nancy and Jack outside their tidy little wattle-and-daub home.

Nancy squealed her delight, and the two girls embraced, Catherine exclaiming on Nancy's girth when she drew back.

"I declare I am carrying twins! Runs in my family, it does."

"Oh, my!"

"She'll have her work cut out for her if that's the case," Abby said. She told Catherine Adam would take her back to Jamestown when she was ready to leave.

Nancy proudly showed Catherine around

her modest home, then took her out to the flourishing kitchen garden where row after row of corn and all manner of vegetables grew.

"Jack stays busy all day in the fields, so I am often here alone, although Margaret and Abby have taken to stopping by regularly. I think they fear I may explode one day with no one here to assist!"

Both girls laughed. Catherine was near bursting to tell Nancy of her adventures the past week, though she didn't dare whilst Jack was present.

"Do you feel up for a short walk, Nan?"

"Indeed. I'll show you the orchard. We have apples and pears. The peaches are ripe now."

The orchard beyond Nancy's home was beautiful and, more importantly, secluded. They wandered amongst the trees, Catherine enjoying the cool breeze wafting off the river and the pungent smell of the ripe fruit. They both picked a peach and bit into it. Finally, Catherine could keep still no longer.

"Something has happened, Nan, something terrible and wonder—"

"I am so sorry for your loss, Catherine. I wept when Abby told me ye'd lost yer babe."

"No. No, it's not that."

Nancy studied her friend. "You are smiling. What could have happened so 'terrible' it makes you smile?"

"Oh, Nancy." Catherine hugged herself and twirled around and around. "I've never been so happy!" She stopped abruptly. "I've met a wonderful man."

"Oh, my!" Nancy sucked in her breath. "What have you done?"

"Everything!" Catherine laughed gaily. "I couldn't help myself. I've never felt this way before. Oh, Nancy, I only thought I loved Noah. I didn't love him at all, not the way I love —"

"Who?" Nancy's eyes widened. "Who do you love? I know of no man in Jamestown more charming than Noah Colton . . . unless it be one of the new settlers just come off the ship."

Taking hold of Nancy's hands, Catherine gazed deeply into her eyes. "If I tell you, I must have your word you'll never say a word to anyone, not ever! Not even if you are tortured!"

"Tortured!" Nancy frowned. "I'm not sure I want to know. Perhaps it's best kept a secret. I'm certain ye'll not let it get out of hand. Think of the scandal. Ye'd have no choice but to leave Jamestown. Ye don't plan to leave, do you?"

"No, of course not." Catherine bit her lip

to keep from saying more. She'd said too much already. She'd never meant to tell Nancy his name. She was just so giddy in love, her joy showed on her face, it spilled from her eyes, and . . . apparently from her mouth. "I'm being silly. It's only my imagination. We've hardly even talked." True. They spent far more time making love. "Forget everything I've said."

"Well, I'm glad to see you're feelin' better."

"I feel wonder— yes; yes, I do feel better, Nancy. Much better, thank you."

When Catherine returned home that evening, she found Lydia curled up in bed, her entire body burning with fever.

CHAPTER 34

On the bed in her tiny chamber, Lydia lay barely conscious. Apparently the girl had contracted the fever some days ago and had only now begun to feel so bad she could not continue her duties. Catherine knew at once what the trouble was and raced to the loft for herbs to stir into a tisane that might bring down the fever.

She sat with Lydia throughout the next several nights, nodding off on occasion even as she kept a silent vigil at the girl's bedside. Getting virtually no rest, it took all the energy she could muster to prepare sufficient food for herself and bowls of nourishing broth for Lydia. Each time she went outdoors for more logs, the sight of the diminishing stack behind the shed filled her with dread. If Noah didn't come home soon, where would she get more wood? Lydia hadn't said a word about it last week, and Catherine had been so preoccupied with her own . . . activities, she hadn't once looked toward the woodpile.

She plastered the girl's chest with a pasty mixture of crushed yarrow blossoms and bathed her fevered brow again and again with cool water. On the third day that week, Lydia's fever finally broke. When she opened her pale blue eyes, they were clear.

Catherine smiled down on the girl lying limp as a rag doll on the bed. "You've given me quite a scare."

"I be fine, mum." That said, her eyes glazed over, and once again she fell into a fitful slumber.

Still fearful, Catherine watched her sleep. Lydia had grown so thin that even if she recovered, Catherine knew it would be a long while before she regained enough strength in her small body to be of use to anyone. At length, Catherine tiptoed from the room to go and lie down on her own bed.

The next morning, when Noah barged into the house, he found both women sound asleep. The fire that usually burned low in the hearth was a pile of white ashes.

"Catherine." He shook her roughly. "Get up! Fire's gone out and I'm famished."

Catherine rolled over. "Is Lydia — ?"

"Asleep, the same as you are. I leave the

house, and the two of you become lazy slugabeds!"

"Lydia's been ill, Noah." Blinking herself awake, Catherine got to her feet. "I'll prepare something to eat."

When Catherine saw that the fire had indeed burned out during the night, she asked Noah to take the shovel to the outdoor oven and bring back some live embers so she could build it up again.

He grumbled but did as she asked. While he was gone, Catherine looked in on Lydia, who was still sleeping. She then went to bring in the last few logs in readiness to get the fire going and prepare their breakfast.

"We have no more wood, Noah," she announced briskly when she came back inside carrying the last few logs. "You'll need to cut down a tree and split the limbs —"

He looked up, a scowl on his face. "Where have you been getting wood from?"

Her lips pursed with annoyance. "If you must know, John Fuller brought the last stack, before you and I married. We've completely used it up."

Noah muttered an oath.

Over the simple meal of corn pudding Catherine prepared, she again brought up the matter of the firewood. "Unless the deputy-governor has been providing you traders with firewood as well as corn, you have no choice, Noah, but to roll up your sleeves and —"

He slammed his trencher onto the table. "I'll take care of it, Catherine. Lord, you've become a nag."

She clamped her mouth shut and said nothing further, not even a half hour later when he swaggered out the door whistling a merry tune, his new red beret perched jauntily on his head.

Instantly, the thought struck Catherine to race into the woods in search of Phyrahawque. She had missed him fiercely all last week. But she quickly changed her mind. It would be far too dangerous now with Noah about. Instead, she took a basket into the corn patch to pick whatever ears had ripened overnight. Lanneika had warned her not to let the golden ears sit too long on the stalk lest the raccoons get at them.

She was plucking corn from the last row of stalks when a flicker of movement through the trees caught her eye. Phyrahawque! Her eyes widened. She flung a quick glance over one shoulder in search of Noah. Not seeing him, she lifted her skirts and darted into the woods.

But it wasn't Phyrahawque.

"Lanneika."

"Phyrahawque worry. He say I come see. You all right? Not sick?"

Wearing a sad smile, Catherine said, "I'm not sick, but Lydia has been ill with the fever, and Noah returned home this morning."

"I tell Phyrahawque." Her shiny black eyes alert, she cocked her head to one side. "You look —" She paused, a smile playing at her lips. "I now go."

"Tell Phyrahawque I miss him terribly."

Lanneika grinned. "He miss you."

Indoors sometime later, a disturbance caused Catherine to look up from her work in time to see Ed Henley's flatbed wagon rumble to a halt outside. Noah sat on the platform beside Ed. Behind them the wagon was piled high with sticks of wood. In seconds, Noah brushed past Catherine into the house, hurried up the ladder to the loft and came back down carrying a shiny beaver pelt draped over one arm.

"Got you some firewood and me a dozen jugs of ale," he said with high satisfaction.

Catherine's lips thinned as she returned again to work.

Following services that next Sabbath morning, Deputy-Governor Argall stepped to the podium and announced that every able-

bodied man was hereby pressed into service
to help construct bark houses for those settlers who still remained homeless and, when
that task was complete, to dig a new water
well.

Catherine could not hold back her own
secret smile of high satisfaction.

Twice that next week while Noah was
laboring with all the other men in
Jamestown, she managed to sneak off to
meet Phyrahawque in the forest. The threat
of discovery made their time together all
the more precious. For both of them, it took
no more than a look, a touch, or the simplest
of kisses to ignite a passion within them they
both found irresistible. They clung to one
another more tightly than ever before, loath
to part lest they not see one another again
for many suns.

"I dream of you every second we are
apart," Catherine murmured, her arms
clasped around his neck, her warm breath
fanning his bare chest.

"You Phyrahawque's woman now." He
kissed the top of her auburn head.

"I have been yours since the moment I
saw you," she replied dreamily. "I wonder
that I can live without you."

He pulled away, his black eyes pinning
hers. "You mine now," he said solemnly.

"Your home with me now in forest."

Catherine gazed up at him, her breath ragged as she chewed on her lower lip. *Dear God, how she wished it could be so!* When she was with Phyrahawque all her worries melted away, and she felt more free and happy than she'd ever felt in her life. "If only I could be with you . . . forever."

"Come." He grasped hold of one hand as if to take her with him right then.

"No." She shook her head. "No, I . . . I cannot."

But the idea stayed with her. Especially those evenings when Noah came in, hot, tired, and irritable from having spent his entire day toiling at a loathsome task.

"I refuse to go back tomorrow."

"You have no choice, Noah." They were seated at the board table finishing up their evening meal, it being the first Lydia had prepared since her illness.

"I've neglected my trading," he mused.

Catherine's heart lurched. Were Noah to resume his daily excursions into the woods, she would have no choice but to cease seeing Phyrahawque altogether. A prospect she did not wish to consider. Ever. Despite the fact that occasional pricks of guilt over her shameless behavior did assail her, the immense love she felt for him meant it took precious little effort for her to successfully push the guilt aside. She could think of nothing powerful enough to erase the enormous love she felt for Phyrahawque. Beneath his strong, stoic exterior she now knew him to be the kindest, most tender-hearted man she'd ever known. Nothing short of being struck dead by a lightning bolt from Heaven could keep Catherine from his arms now. She loved him that much.

Noah lingered longer than usual at the table that night, downing mug after mug of Ed Henley's strong brew. When at last he staggered into the bedchamber, Catherine had already retired and lay dreaming about her few stolen hours that day with Phyrahawque. Her dream was shattered when Noah roughly dragged her toward him. He hadn't touched her since she'd lost her baby.

She stiffened now. "Noah, please!"

"You're my wife, and I have my needs!"

Knowing it was useless to resist him, she gritted her teeth against the inevitable. Her eyes squeezed shut as he jerked her night rail above her waist and heaved his drunken weight on top of her.

Two weeks later, she was alarmed when her menses did not come on schedule. Her alarm turned to panic when the second month came and her menses didn't. Ordinarily, she'd have been thrilled to know she was with child. Now fear and worry seized her. Having believed she could never conceive again, she'd been careless with Phyrahawque, not asking him to take the necessary precaution to avoid conception, such as not spilling his seed within her, or herself chewing up a handful of carrot seeds, which she'd been told would prevent a woman from conceiving. Worse, still, she could not say for certain who the father of her child might be. Phyrahawque or Noah.

CHAPTER 35

September 1618

She also could not decide whether or not to tell Noah she was pregnant. Since she never knew when he might be away from Jamestown, or for how long he'd be gone, if she waited until later to tell him and he hadn't been home for several weeks, he would very likely accuse her of infidelity. On the other hand, were she to tell him now and the child was Phyrahawque's, she would die if Noah became angry over some trifling matter and harmed this baby.

Still, since Noah had so recently been at her, recent enough that he could easily recall the encounter, it was likely he would accept the child as his. At least until the baby was born. In her heart Catherine knew the child was Phyrahawque's, conceived out of the deep love she and the Indian warrior felt for one another. With all her heart, she wanted this baby even more than the last one because it was Phyrahawque's, and she knew it would be beautiful and much loved by both herself and its father. Nightly she prayed that God would help her get through the next seven months and bring this child into the world alive and healthy.

In the end, she decided it was safer to tell Noah now, though she was not prepared for the scowl of anger he turned on her.

"I've hardly touched you!"

"Well, apparently you've touched me enough. Besides," she fabricated, "they say that abstinence makes a woman more fertile, so I expect the weeks I was . . . ill, and you were away rendered my body more receptive. In any case, by my reckoning, the babe will be born sometime in the early spring."

Later that night as they lay in bed, he again brought up the matter of her pregnancy. "I have decided the fact that you are to have a child will bode well for me. A babe will increase my consequence as a family man."

"I don't understand," Catherine murmured sleepily.

"My bid for the governorship." He sounded irritable that she hadn't followed his reasoning.

Though the room was pitch black, Catherine did not need light to detect the familiar twitch of annoyance at his mouth.

"For the selfsame reason, I've also decided you should start up your school again. The Virginia Company investors will look favorably on a family man whose wife is the only teacher in the colony. I expect Argall to be removed from office soon. Rumblings against him are increasing daily, especially since the uprising in Henricus."

"But that was your fault," she pointed out.

He sprang up in bed, his body twisting toward her in the darkness. "A vile accusation from my own wife! Don't ever say such a thing again!"

She quickly remembered her vow not to overset him. "I'm sorry, Noah. Clearly, I am wrong. You are far and away the most qualified man in Virginia to be named governor."

"Well —" He appeared mollified. "I daresay your judgment is improving. Pray, let it continue. Now, I expect to see children seated at the board tables in the common room at once. I plan to have my list of grievances against Argall ready to hand to Lord De La Warr when he arrives."

Catherine had some difficulty convincing Noah that since everyone in the tidewater area, except himself and the other two traders, were at this time of year busy harvesting their tobacco crop in readiness to ship the leaves back to England, now was not a good time to start up her school.

"Even in the beginning, I let it be known there would be no classes during harvest. Perhaps I could hold a short winter session, although, if you recall, I dispensed with that last year due to harsh weather."

At his growl of disapproval, she added, "Very well, I shall post a notice on the meetinghouse door just as soon as harvest is over and leaf-fall upon us. The children can come for a month or two before and after Christmastide — at least until the snows become too heavy for them to get here."

Once again, Noah appeared mollified.

Because Jamestown's new freshwater well had now been dug, and every new settler now enjoyed a semblance of shelter in his own bark hut, Noah had the leisure to spend a good part of each day making secret treks into the woods with items he absconded from the crates in the shed. Catherine noted with chagrin that the pile of pelts in the loft teetered higher and higher. She, on the other hand, was forced to stay close to the house. Though she longed with all her heart to see Phyrahawque, she feared he might not now find her body as beautiful as he once had.

In late September, Nancy gave birth to twin girls she named Jean and Jane. Catherine gave out the news she was again with child.

"I am so happy for you," Abigail gushed. "I told Adam the day you visited with us that I believed you were with child. You looked positively radiant that day, as you do now!"

On one especially warm November day, Catherine looked up from her work and noted that the leaves on the trees were ablaze with color — fiery scarlet, brilliant orange and glittering gold. Not a cloud in the sky marred the expanse of azure blue overhead. The day was so glorious it took her breath away. Tears of sadness gathered in her eyes as her heart ached to share the beautiful day with Phyrahawque. They would lie on their backs on the ground, his silky black hair interlaced with hers as they stared up at the sky, their hearts bursting with love for the peaceful world around them . . . and for one another. She nearly choked with longing as she realized she'd lost count of the days and weeks since she'd last seen her beloved Indian warrior. He did not even know she was carrying his child.

One day when Noah left the house early,

she could resist the pull of the forest no longer, and soon after the midday meal, she set out for the woods. But instead of finding Phyrahawque in her Secret Place, she again came upon Lanneika, who in grave tones told her that Phyrahawque had been forced to gather an army of warriors and travel to the place where the tribe usually lived during the sleeping time, when the snow fell.

"Warring tribe strike. Phyrahawque fight to protect."

Her heart thudding with fear, Catherine listened with horror to Lanneika's tale. She could not bear the thought of something dreadful happening to Phyrahawque.

Lanneika tried to comfort her friend. "Phyrahawque strong. He be safe."

Lanneika said that Phyrahawque had decided the tribe would not move north this year, as was their usual custom. "He want to be near you," she added softly.

Catherine smiled sadly. Did she dare tell Lanneika she was certain she was carrying her brother's child? Perhaps the Indian girl already knew. She said nothing, but before leaving she made Lanneika promise to get word to her the minute her brother returned. "I will pray for him every day," she added.

That night over supper, even Noah had

heard about the warring Indian tribes.

"It's said an entire village was wiped out, houses burned and everyone dead, including women and children."

Catherine gasped. "I pray that to be an exaggerated account."

"What do you care?" he scoffed.

"The Indians are human beings, God's children, the same as you and I are."

"Well, the news pleased Argall. Said if the Indians killed each other off, it'd make our lives that much easier."

Catherine cringed. She hardly dared think that Phyrahawque could have been involved in such a massacre. Or worse still, that it was his village that was decimated. She worked to suppress her horror. "Well, we have plenty to keep ourselves occupied here. With winter close on, we shall be needing more firewood, and a mud bank needs to be built up along the outside walls of the house."

"A mud bank? Whatever for?" Noah pulled a face.

"It helps ward off the chill. The chinks in the walls must also be filled. You've plenty of time now to take care of things, Noah. We also need a good deal more food to set aside for the winter months. The woods are full of wild turkey and other game, rabbits and deer. I understand it's easy enough to take fish from the river. We desperately need food, Noah," she said again.

"When I am appointed governor," he replied, his cocksure tone telling her he had no intention of soiling his hands hunting or fishing, "all our needs will be amply provided for."

"But we cannot be certain you shall be appointed governor. We really must see to our own needs."

As the days passed and Noah didn't lift a finger to take care of anything, Catherine felt she had no choice but to approach Adam regarding the bargain they'd struck when she bought the house from him.

On the following Sabbath, Noah — dressed in his finest scarlet satin doublet with shiny brass buttons and froths of lace at the cuffs — sauntered amongst the colonists, shaking hands with the men and doing the pretty for the women. Catherine quietly moved to stand by her brother.

"Noah appears in fine fettle today," Adam observed.

"Yes, he can be quite charming when he wants to be." Catherine cast a chagrined look at her finely turned out husband, now laughing with several men and a comely woman. She recalled the day, not too long past, when she, too, had been taken in by his easy charm and lighthearted banter. He was without question a fine-looking man, but knowing his true personality as she did now turned all his fineness to dust.

"There are many who say he'll be our next governor," Adam mused.

Catherine nodded.

"You do not seem particularly pleased. The appointment should make your life a good deal easier."

"I don't believe anything would make my life with Noah . . . easier."

Adam looked concerned. "Something's troubling you, Cat. What is it?"

She inhaled a long breath. "I am sorry to have to make such a request of you, Adam, but the truth is, Noah is so confident he will be appointed governor that he is doing nothing now to provide for our needs. Over the summer, I managed to grow a bit of corn in the field that Jack and Victor cleared, but we've eaten it, and now there is none left to grind or save. I fear our circumstances are fast becoming dire."

Adam turned an indulgent smile on his beautiful sister. "If you are wondering if I mean to make good on my promise to provide provisions for you this coming winter, I've just been waiting for you to ask.

I wasn't certain Noah would allow it, if you must know."

"Well, I have every intention of allowing it!" With a sigh of relief, Catherine thanked her brother profusely.

The day Adam and Jack and a couple more men from Harvest Hill appeared at their door saying they'd rowed two flatbed rafts downriver loaded with a dozen barrels of dried pork, venison, and vegetables, Catherine did not bother to consult her husband. She knew the task of replacing the empty barrels in the loft would take nearly the whole of the afternoon. Furthermore, she did not expect Noah to offer to help.

Adam left two of his men behind to begin hauling the empty barrels to the ground whilst he and the others returned to the river for full ones.

Eventually Noah came into the house and, catching sight of the men in the loft and the ropes dangling from the rafters, demanded, "What the hell is going on here?"

"Come into the bedchamber, Noah, and I shall explain." Catherine hurriedly told him about the bargain she'd struck with Adam when she bought the house. "As you know, my brother is a man of his word."

"And I am not?"

"I did not say that."

"Well, you sure as hell implied it!"

"I implied nothing of the sort. I am merely trying to see to our needs for the upcoming winter. We must eat something until you are appointed governor . . . and all our needs are amply provided for," she added, unable to disguise the sarcasm in her tone.

His face contorted angrily. "What do you want from me, Catherine?"

"A peaceful life, a family with children, and a husband who is happy to do what is necessary to provide for us."

"You have that!"

"No, I do not have that."

"Well, I want a wife who appreciates me, and I certainly do not have that!"

Catherine wrung her hands. The last thing she wanted was to quarrel with him. Drawing an uneven breath, she admitted, "I — I am . . . not happy, Noah."

"You have nothing to be unhappy about," he argued.

She said nothing.

He persisted. "You could be happy if you'd accept that I know what is best for us and that I am doing what it takes to provide for our future."

Despite her resolve to remain calm, his words irked her. "I could be happy only if

I'd never come to know you as you truly are!"

"And what does that mean?" he demanded.

"You are not the man I thought you were, Noah. You lie, and cheat, and steal from anyone you can!"

"You are a dreamer, Catherine. This is a new world, and the old rules do not apply. A man does what he must in order to survive."

She worked to calm herself. "I fear you will one day take something from someone who will fight back."

"Are you threatening me?"

"Of course not. I am a woman. Who would listen to me?"

He smirked. "That, my dear wife, is precisely what I am counting upon."

With that, he brushed past her and the men working in the common room, and exited the house.

November turned to December, and though her heart wasn't in it, Catherine made good on her word to start up her school again. The notice she posted on the meetinghouse door emphasized the fact that *all* children, English and Indian alike, were welcome. A part of her hoped that if a few Indian children came to the house each day, she might learn what was truly going on with the warring Indian tribes. It had been weeks since she'd last seen Lanneika, and she was now beside herself with worry over Phyrahawque. Many were the long endless nights she lay awake, unable to sleep for worry about him and his people.

It didn't help when Noah brought home fresh rumors about the warring Indian tribes — rumors that sent icy fingers of fear down Catherine's spine.

Noah was now spending several hours each evening going door to door, visiting with the settlers and collecting support from those who agreed that he should, indeed, be named the next governor of Virginia. Although the colonists' opinions would carry little to no weight, Noah hoped if a town meeting were called when Lord De La Warr arrived, the colonists would be angry enough with Argall to voice their opinions and freely speak out in favor of him. He'd had Catherine write a letter outlining all his qualifications and kept one copy with him in readiness to present to the Virginia Company representative as soon as the emissary arrived from London. The other copy he'd sent back on a ship carrying tobacco leaves to England. Even when word eventually reached the colonists of the death of Lord De La Warr, who had been en route to Jamestown to investigate the allegations against Deputy-Governor Argall, Noah's hopes remained undimmed.

"Argall is as good as gone," he told Catherine one evening as they sat before the fire, Catherine mending one of his shirts, he doing nothing, Lydia alone in her room.

"Why do you say that?" Catherine didn't look up.

"Amongst De La Warr's private papers was a warrant for Argall's arrest. I am most certain to be named Virginia's next governor," he gloated. "The colonists all agree that the bulk of Argall's mandates were calculated to increase his own wealth with little or nothing left to benefit the colony."

Not unlike you, Catherine thought to herself but did not voice aloud. She had no confidence whatever in Noah's bid for the governorship, despite his staunch belief to the contrary. Her thoughts and worries these days centered solely on the well-being of Phyrahawque and the people of his tribe. As yet, she still knew nothing concrete, and it was becoming increasingly difficult to get through yet another long day with no word regarding her beloved.

"I am also talking up your school amongst

the settlers," Noah said. "You may have quite a few new pupils this term."

"Hmmm."

"It is time you raised your fee."

"I have no set fee. I merely accept whatever a child's parents feel they can spare from their own store of supplies."

"Well, I intend to keep a reckoning of everything they bring, in order to be certain no one cheats us."

How very like him, Catherine thought, to want to be certain no one cheats him, when with a clear conscience he would readily steal from them anything that was not nailed down.

On the day designated for classes to begin, five students showed up. A few days later, two more came. Catherine found that, despite the uneasy state of her mind, she once again enjoyed the diversion. Laughing with the children and listening to their chatter and constant questions kept her from endlessly worrying about Phyrahawque.

One bleak rainy morning in late December, when five of Catherine's seven pupils were already seated around the board tables, their hands folded primly before them, their expressions expectant as they gazed up at her, another rap sounded at the door.

Opening it only a crack lest a gust of icy air chill the entire house, an audible gasp escaped Catherine when she came face-to-face with the imposing figure of Phyrahawque. She was so shocked, she had to cling to the doorjamb to keep from fainting dead away.

"Phyrahawque," she mouthed, staring up at him. She was so thrilled to see him she very nearly threw herself into his arms. Blinking back the tears of joy that welled in her eyes, it took all the restraint she could muster not to. Opening the door wide enough to admit him, she noted he was not dressed in his usual manner. The days being exceptionally cold, his entire body was covered in warm doeskin. His black hair hung long and loose; draped over his shoulders was a plush white bearskin. An Indian youth of about nine or ten stood beside him.

"Bring boy to learn." Phyrahawque maintained a steady composure, though his piercing black eyes probed Catherine's for answers to questions he did not ask.

She saw his gaze drop to her middle. From the furrow of concern that flitted across his brow, she knew he longed to ask how she fared.

"W-what do you call the boy?" she managed, her eyes filled with longing as she gazed up at him, nearly overwhelmed by the ache in her heart to know everything that had happened since she last saw him.

"Taquitock."

Phyrahawque all but pushed the reluctant youth forward and, in his own language, told the boy he would return to collect him in a few hours. Catherine knew exactly what he'd said, and it was she who nodded up at Phyrahawque.

Though she spent the morning listening to the children recite their lessons, her mind whirled with ideas about how she might manage a few stolen moments with Phyrahawque when he returned for Taquitock.

It was several days before an opportunity presented itself. Once again the fire in the hearth had nearly gone out overnight, and when Taquitock and Phyrahawque appeared on the doorstep that icy cold morning, Catherine seized the moment to ask the boy if he'd accompany her to the woodpile. Grabbing her shawl, she wrapped it tightly about her shoulders before she hurried from the house, Phyrahawque a few paces behind her.

Once beyond the shed, while Taquitock bent to scoop up several logs, Catherine turned a wide-eyed gaze on the tall Indian warrior.

"I've missed you terribly," she whispered. "Lanneika told me months ago you were fighting. I've worried myself sick about you!"

Phyrahawque smiled into her upturned face. "You beautiful." One brown hand reached to lightly caress her swollen belly. "Mine."

She nodded, the love in her heart causing tears of joy to spring to her eyes. "I wasn't certain you knew."

"Lanneika tell me many moons ago."

Catherine blinked back her tears. "What am I to do, Phyrahawque? What am I to do once our child is born?"

"I tell Taquitock no speak; listen to trader-man's words. Come for me if trouble."

Catherine dared not stay too long away from the house. Noah was indoors, still snug in his bed.

"Perhaps Taquitock could stay a bit longer each day. I desperately need help. Noah helps me with nothing, and Lydia is . . . not strong." She cast a glance down at the few remaining sticks of firewood scattered about. "I desperately need firewood and always water from the well."

Phyrahawque nodded. He motioned for Taquitock and in plain English told him to do as the teacher-lady said.

Catherine grinned. "So the boy does know words."

"He know many words. Lanneika teach." When Taquitock was out of sight, Phyrahawque leaned down to brush his cool lips against Catherine's. "I bring wood for fire."

"Thank you." She exhaled a breath of relief, more for knowing that he was alive and safe than for the firewood he promised to bring. "I am so happy to see you." Though she did not yet know the outcome of the Indian wars, Phyrahawque was alive and safe and that was all that mattered.

He drew her into a quick embrace and in a husky voice said, "Phyrahawque love you . . . and babe."

His sweet words warming her, Catherine hurried back into the house, where the Indian boy was carefully sliding his few spindly logs into the fire. In moments, Noah appeared and scowled when he saw the Indian youth.

"What's he doing here?"

"He's the new student I was telling you about. I told his father just now he must pay something for Taquitock's lessons. He said he'd bring firewood tomorrow."

"The father understands English?" Noah's brows drew together suspiciously.

"I cannot say for certain," Catherine

hedged. "I did a good bit of pointing and gesturing. I hope he understood me." She smiled. "I guess we'll see tomorrow."

The next morning, a commotion in the yard drew both Catherine and Noah outdoors where they saw two strong Indian braves nearly finished unloading and neatly stacking pieces of wood from the pair of sturdy *travoises* behind their horses. That Noah had accompanied her to the shed caused Catherine's breath to catch in her throat until she saw that neither of the naturals was Phyrahawque. She thanked the men when they finished their work, and without incident both she and Noah returned to the house.

"I didn't recognize either of those savages," Noah said. "Has your new student indicated what tribe he's from?"

Catherine shook her head. "Actually he hasn't said a word since he came. I have a feeling he may be mute."

"What makes you think that?"

"Because he hasn't said anything. The day his father brought him, he pointed to the boy's ear and nodded, as if to say the boy could hear, then pointed to his mouth and shook his head, as if to say he couldn't speak."

"Hmmm."

Catherine was relieved when Noah didn't pursue the subject. She was also greatly relieved to have a fresh supply of firewood for the winter months and also that Taquitock lingered each day to bring fresh logs into the house and to fetch water from the new well, located a good distance away from the house.

She kept a sharp eye on the boy and couldn't help noticing that his alert black eyes were often fixed on Noah, though not in an overt manner. Still, it never escaped Taquitock's notice when Noah came in from one of his excursions with an armload of pelts, which he secreted in the loft.

Catherine asked her husband one evening when he planned to sell the skins.

"As soon as the next ship arrives. The one carrying orders for Argall's dismissal," he added with a sly grin. "I expect we shall be removing to the governor's house before too very long. Those pelts will purchase a good many luxuries."

Catherine thought it odd that none of the colonists questioned Noah's new occupation as a fur trapper. After all, he was never seen hauling into town any of the animals he professed to have trapped, and he certainly spent no time curing skins, which so far as she knew was a lengthy and complicated process. It occurred to her that perhaps Deputy-Governor Argall knew of the perfidy and perhaps, for a share of the profits, was turning a blind eye.

She also wondered how Noah was managing to keep his own accusations against the deputy-governor from reaching Argall's ears. She shuddered to think what would happen when Noah's thievery and deception came to light. Would he be tried and sentenced to hang? What would be *her* fate if her husband was killed for stealing from the colony, and she was left alone to raise an infant? Especially if her infant was . . . not white. Always, her worries made her sick to her stomach.

With a sigh of regret, she thought back over the nearly two years she'd been in Jamestown, and realized that since she'd been here, she'd been embroiled in one deception after another, beginning with her own unintentional one when she boarded the ship in England and told the captain her surname was Fielding. Since her marriage to Noah, the deceptions had piled one on top of another. And now with the babe in her belly, she was forwarding yet another. Would the lies and falsehoods never end?

By far the most worrisome thing on her mind these cold winter days was what Noah would say and do once she'd given birth, and it was plainly evident her babe was Indian. If it had skin darker than her own, or straight black hair instead of soft golden down, or even the russet color of her hair, then what? Noah's rage knew no bounds. Certainly he would threaten to kill Phyrahawque. But would he? Could he? Would he threaten to kill her? Would he kill the baby?

Always the questions in her mind traveled in circles with no answers in sight. Should she throw herself on her brother's mercy? Would he take her in once he knew she'd committed adultery, with an Indian no less, and that since then, she'd been lying to everyone? She loathed deception, but for now it seemed she had no choice but to continue the one she was forwarding, that Noah had fathered the babe in her belly.

Many evenings as Catherine sat before the fire pretending to listen to him brag about his qualifications to be named governor, Catherine's thoughts were centered on all the things she and Phyrahawque had spoken of those many long months ago. He knew she was unhappy in her marriage. Once he had wisely said that if she wished to feel the sunshine, why did she continue to sit beneath a shade tree? Phyrahawque's wise counsel came again and again to her mind.

She tried to imagine what her life would have been like if she had not married Noah. She had met both Lanneika and Phyrahawque before she walked down the aisle with Noah. If only she had opened her eyes to the truth about him earlier. If she had known that he was no longer the lighthearted, easygoing boy she'd known in England but was instead an angry, heartless man, she would never have married him. It broke her heart now to realize that her refusal to listen to Adam's warnings about Noah may have led to Victor's death. She had no way of knowing the truth of what happened that day in the woods, but knowing Noah as she did now, it was not a stretch to believe that it was he who let fly the arrows that eventually took Victor's life.

Was it jealousy that drove him? Envy? Hatred? Or, was it because Noah simply wanted to possess her, to — as he'd once said — have something other men wanted. Whatever his reasoning, it baffled her. Also sad was the fact that there were people who truly loved Noah. She had loved him once, and she assumed Charity had. And he had a little daughter who would grow to love him, if given the chance. So far as Catherine knew, since Noah had left the Benson plantation and moved into Jamestown to wed her, he hadn't so much as seen his baby daughter.

She realized that, of the many deceptions she'd been embroiled in, the worst one was that of self-deception. All along, where Noah was concerned, she'd been deceiving herself. Her refusal to see the truth had had the effect of keeping her own happiness at bay. She had no idea now how things would turn out; all she knew for certain was that as each day passed, she longed all the more for the safe, secure haven of Phyrahawque's arms.

The question was . . . did she truly have the courage to leave her own people and live amongst the Indians in order to be with him?

CHAPTER 36

January 1619

"I believe Lydia has an admirer," Catherine told Noah one evening after the girl had gone to bed. She and Noah sat by the fire, Noah smoking his pipe, Catherine hand-stitching a baby garment. For days, she and Lydia had both been working on small things, especially now that Catherine had dismissed classes until the blustery winter weather let up.

"What makes you think she has a suitor?"

"She has lingered behind after services the past several Sundays. Twice I have seen a young man walking her home, but he doesn't come all the way to the house; he leaves her near the communal oven."

"Well, I shall bring that to a halt!"

"Oh, leave it be, Noah. I would not have told you if I thought it would make you angry."

"She's mine for the full seven years of her

indenture! I won't have it!"

"Noah, please. I'm certain it's harmless. The poor girl needs something sweet to think about. Surely you didn't think she would stay with us the entire time. She's young, and there are so few women in the colony, hardly any unattached. Surely you expected she'd marry one day."

"You are too soft, Catherine."

"And you have other things to think about. A ship will arrive soon and you will be named governor, remember?" She had learned of late that to remind him of his high-flown ambition effectively diffused his anger over very nearly everything. She had begun to hope he would indeed be named governor for it might even diffuse his anger with her once her baby was born.

In bed that night, he reached for her, which to her relief he hadn't done in quite a spell. But she didn't want Noah's attentions now. She didn't want anyone but Phyrahawque. Fearing for the safety of the child in her womb, she especially did not want Noah's rough handling of her tonight.

"Noah, please. The baby."

"I have my needs, Catherine! You are being derelict in your duty!"

"It will only be for a short while longer."

"By my reckoning, spring is more than a

short while longer."

"It's possible I was off by a few weeks. I have never carried a child to term. I don't want to risk injuring it this far along."

"Damn you," he grumbled.

Long into the night, an odd noise awakened Catherine. Turning over, she realized Noah was not in bed beside her. She heaved her heavy bulk upright but only had to take a few steps toward the door to realize what was taking place.

Noah was with Lydia! The girl's alarmed cry must have awakened her. Her eyes rolled skyward. What should she do? She paused to listen. Judging from the sounds coming from the other bedchamber, the vile deed was already done, and were she to interfere now, Noah would no doubt lash out at her and hurt the baby. She could not risk that. Fearing he would soon sneak back to bed, she decided her best course was to simply crawl back in bed and pretend she'd heard nothing. She would figure something out on the morrow.

The next morning, stealing a quick look into Lydia's bedchamber told her the girl had fled. All her things were missing. In her haste to leave, she had not drawn the front door completely shut. The fire in the hearth was again a mere pile of ashes. The house was not only frigid, but ice crystals had formed on the sides of the pot hanging on the spit.

"Noah!" Catherine shook her husband awake. "Lydia ran away in the night."

He sat up, brushing sleep from his eyes, his blond curls tousled. "Damned female. Now what am I going to do?"

Catherine parked both hands on her hips. She knew exactly what he meant, and she was tempted to inform him she knew exactly what he'd done last night. But she wisely refrained.

"What you are going to do is let her go," she said. "If you brought her back, she'd only run away again. Apparently she is determined to be with her young man, and there is nothing you, nor I, can do to stop her."

Nonetheless, Noah set out that day, determined to track the girl down. After all, he maintained, he'd been cheated out of seven years of service still owed him on her indenture — for which he had paid handsomely. With Catherine's money.

Alone that day, Catherine again fell to worrying over her situation. She'd been counting on Lydia being there to help stave off Noah's anger when her child was born, or at the very least, to go for help once his fury exploded, as she fully expected it would. She also desperately needed help with the household chores. She was already unable to make it up the ladder to the loft to scoop food from the barrels for their meals. With Lydia gone, she would have to think ahead each day and ask Taquitock to fetch things for her when he was here, or somehow persuade Noah to help.

Her bulk was increasing at such a rapid rate she knew her calculations had been off by a month or more. The child was definitely Phyrahawque's, no doubt conceived the first time or two they'd been together . . . when Noah was in Henricus.

She also knew she'd need help delivering the baby, for that was something she certainly couldn't manage alone. But if the midwife were a white woman and her child was not white, then what? The color of her child's skin alone would attest to her crime.

The following Sabbath, although Noah was in high spirits, Catherine felt especially low. Afterward, when Abby and Nancy approached her on the green, it took all the will she could muster to paste a smile on her face.

"You don't look well, dear," Abby began. Her eyes dropped to Catherine's bulky middle. "From the look of it, you could deliver any day now."

Catherine gulped back her tears.

Nancy reached to embrace her friend. "Everything will be fine once yer free of the burden yer carryin'."

When Catherine's chin trembled afresh, Abby asked, "What is it, sweetie?"

"I . . . I'm afraid."

"Abby and I 'ave both had children," Nancy said in a soothing tone. "I had two. We came out of it alive."

"It's not that. It's just that . . . what will I do when the time comes? Especially if there's no one to send for help?"

"Lydia has not come back?"

Catherine shook her head. "Noah thinks she and her young man are somewhere in the woods, that friendly Indians took them in."

"I understand your concern," Abigail said, patting Catherine's cold hands, which were clutching her worn cloak about her ample middle.

"Would you like me to come and stay with you?" Nancy asked.

"Your infants are still suckling. It would be too much for you."

"How about Mary?" Nancy asked Abigail. "She knew exactly what to do when my time came."

"Mary?" Catherine looked from one to the other.

"Of course, why did I not think of that?" Abigail turned to her husband. "Adam, you must bring Mary in to stay with Catherine until her baby comes."

"Mary?" Catherine murmured, thinking she'd never heard anyone mention that name. "Who is Mary?"

Abigail laughed. "None of us could pronounce her name, so we all took to calling her Mary. She is very capable."

"She knew exactly what to do when my time came," Nancy said again.

"You might have seen her when you visited. She's Indian, an older woman from the same tribe as the young girl I sent you last year when you needed help with Victor."

"Oh. *Oh!*" Alarm spiraled through Catherine. "You mustn't tell Noah that Mary and Lanneika are from the same tribe."

"Was there some problem, dear?"

Catherine glanced over one shoulder lest Noah be standing near enough to hear. "No, but their tribe is one with which Noah seems to have a grievance. You've nothing to fear, it's just something between him and
—"

"I'll not say a word, sweetie. At any rate, Adam and I rarely have occasion to speak with Noah. Nancy, be sure and tell Jack not to say anything. There" — she turned back to Catherine — "it's all settled."

That afternoon, as planned, Adam brought into town the Indian woman they called Mary. Catherine gave her the second bedchamber, telling Adam she'd like her to stay both day and night, at least until the baby came. She did not worry for Mary's safety or virtue, as her stout build and stern features would more likely inspire fear in Noah than lust.

"She generally takes one day off a week," Adam told Catherine. "Spends it with her family in her village. However, I'm sure she'll comply with your wishes." He turned to say a few words to Mary, and the Indian woman nodded as if she understood.

"Does she speak English?" Catherine asked, walking beside Adam back through the house.

"She hardly speaks at all." He grinned. "But, she seems to understand English. Abby says she's quite efficient and, considering her age, works quickly."

Noah wasn't home when Mary came, and when he did return that evening, he hardly seemed to notice the Indian woman's presence.

"I need help, Noah," Catherine began,

thinking she'd have to convince him to let her keep Mary. "I can no longer climb the ladder to —"

"Fine, fine; just keep her out of my way."

When Taquitock came the following afternoon, Catherine saw he and Mary exchange a look and knew that by nightfall Phyrahawque would know she was no longer alone in the house with Noah.

A fortnight later, word came from Kiccowtan that two ships had been spotted on the far horizon. From then on, Noah was oblivious to anything but plans for his own bright future.

For the next several days, bad weather and a heavy snowstorm kept the ships from the bay and Noah and the two women cooped up indoors. Catherine was aware of the Indian woman's alert black eyes following her everywhere. As Adam had indicated, Mary rarely spoke, but she efficiently obeyed any request Catherine made of her. Catherine gratefully let the Indian woman take over all the cooking and cleaning while she rested and waited, as calmly as possible given the circumstances, by the fire.

During the inclement weather, Noah paced. On the first day the snow let up, he vanished. Once during that day, Mary quietly addressed Catherine. "I see you one day. In village. You Phyrahawque's flame-haired woman."

Catherine turned an alarmed gaze on her. "Mary, please do not ever mention that in front of my husband. It is true, I am Phyrahawque's woman, and, because of that, I and my baby, Phyrahawque's baby, are in grave danger."

The Indian woman nodded and said nothing further.

On the day the two ships finally sailed into Jamestown's harbor, an emissary from King James himself stepped ashore, carrying an edict demanding that Captain Samuel Argall, deputy-governor of Virginia, return immediately to England to answer charges leveled against him by the investors of the New Virginia Company. The same edict stated that in Argall's place, Captain Nathaniel Powell would serve as deputy-governor until Sir George Yeardley arrived to resume his former position.

When a runner came to the house to deliver the news to Noah Colton, he was livid and, without a word to his wife, left at once for the pier. Fearing her husband's volatile temper, Catherine, who felt her time was drawing near, seized the moment to take the only precaution she had thought of to take — hide his musket and sword. Once she'd located the weapons, she gave Mary explicit instructions to take both to the loft and hide them as securely as possible.

When Noah returned home that evening he was still in a rage. "How dare they?" he demanded of Catherine, as they sat down to an early supper. "Not a man I spoke with today can understand the reason behind Powell's appointment, or Yeardley's. Nothing was accomplished under Yeardley's rule. Why put him back in office? It makes no sense!"

Catherine tried her best not to get caught up in Noah's tirade for his agitation was only adding to her discomfort. Her birthing pains had begun in earnest that afternoon, and she wished to keep the news from him as long as possible.

"Powell has no experience and even fewer qualifications. He is lacking in every area deemed necessary to hold office! Something must be done!" He slammed a fist onto the table.

Catherine jumped. "Noah, please; calm yourself."

"Calm myself? How am I to stay calm in the face of such idiocy? My future hinged on this appointment. Now all is lost and all my brilliant wife can say is: calm myself!" The veins in his neck popped out as the color in his face deepened.

Catherine worked to steady her own frayed nerves. "Where is Argall now?"

"Already on board ship."

"Well, at least you should be able to sell your pelts. That should make you happy."

"Pelts be dammed!"

Suddenly an anguished cry escaped Catherine, and she clutched her middle. Warm fluid seeped from between her legs, soaking her undergarments. *"Mary!"*

Beside her in an instant, the Indian woman helped her into bed. Catherine heard the front door slam shut and knew Noah had left the house. His absence provided her with a modicum of relief during the grueling hours that followed. More than once, Catherine was thankful for Mary's presence as she had never given birth before and had no idea how painful and intense the experience really could be.

Mary worked quickly and efficiently. When the trying ordeal was finally over and she'd cleansed and snugly wrapped the newborn infant — a boy — in a warm blanket, she placed the tiny bundle into Catherine's outstretched arms. Tears of joy swam in her eyes as she gazed down upon the most beautiful baby she'd ever beheld in her life. When one tiny brown hand clasped hold of her finger and held on tight, Catherine's heart filled to overflowing with a love more intense than any she'd ever known.

Through tear-filled eyes, she gazed up at Mary. *"Go!* Tell Phyrahawque I need him. *Now!"*

CHAPTER 37

Although exhausted from her hard labor, anxiety over what would happen next kept Catherine from drifting off to sleep, that and the squirming little bundle she held in her arms. Gazing down into her baby's sweet face, she knew the time had come to make the most important decision she had ever made in her life. Without a doubt, she loved Phyrahawque and now his precious child with all her heart. And she knew he loved her, and that he'd welcome her and their baby with open arms. Still, she wasn't entirely certain she had the courage to leave her own people and go to live amongst the Indians.

Perhaps, said a small voice in her head, *Phyrahawque would not come.*

No, she thrust the disturbing thought aside. He would come. He was the kindest, most honorable man she had ever known. Their time together and the many long talks they'd shared had given her a deep insight into his character. He was a wise man and an extremely capable leader. His people looked up to him, and every last one respected him. Unlike Noah, Phyrahawque was not a cruel man. With Phyrahawque as her mate, she knew she could have the peaceful life she had always wanted. Many times Phyrahawque had told her their spirits were in harmony, which greatly pleased her. She recalled something else he had said to her, that passion taken together with joy would always give one the courage to take action.

It was the answer she needed. A peaceful life was the dream that had brought her to the New World. She had found her way here, but she had not found the sort of life she wanted in Jamestown because she'd mistakenly believed it would be possible with Noah. She had deceived herself by clinging to the memory of the love she once felt for a fair-haired boy she used to play with in a grassy meadow.

Though she had managed to find a peaceful place in the midst of the tangled woods here, she realized now she must also find a peaceful place to dwell within the tangle of human emotions. The passion for the life she truly wanted was still alive within her.

And her love for Phyrahawque, and now for their son, gave her the greatest joy she'd ever thought possible. Her passion and the joy she derived from her love for them would indeed give her the courage she needed to leave her people and go to live with her beloved amongst the Indians.

In addition, she realized now that more than anything she must protect her son. It occurred to her that she had no idea what the whites would do when it became known she had lain with an Indian; it was possible they would kill her child! She could never risk that! In order to protect him and ensure his future well-being, she truly had no choice but to be with Phyrahawque. Even if for some reason Phyrahawque rejected her, Lanneika never would. Her child would always be a grandson of the mighty emperor Powhatan and, among the Indians, considered royal. To grow up with his own people he would never have to face the prejudice and ridicule Pamoac and Tonkee did when they first came to her school. Catherine, herself, could teach him, as well as all the other children in Phyrahawque's tribe . . . in *her* tribe. And she need have no fear that Noah would ever find her. Phyrahawque and his tribe had eluded all the traders' efforts to find them. With Phyrahawque, she and their son would be safe forever.

It was not as if she would never see Adam and Abigail, or Nancy and her babies, again. She would do as Mary did, leave her Indian family from time to time to visit with her English kin. One day, if Phyrahawque wished it, she would proudly present him to Adam. She and Phyrahawque and their son would be a happy, loving family. Snuggling her precious child closer to her, she smiled into the pitch-black eyes gazing curiously up into hers.

Enthralled with this precious little person, Catherine carefully studied one miniature feature after another. His smooth, satin skin was indeed a beautiful shade of mocha. His eyes were almond-shaped and as dark as a moonless night. His little nose and mouth were perfect, as were his ears and the tiny fingers and thumb on each hand. Most telling of his parentage was that his perfectly shaped head was covered in thick, straight black hair. To Catherine's touch, it felt as soft as silk. Just like his father's.

She lay quietly studying her newborn infant for what seemed like a long while. Then, hearing the front door open and the heavy footfalls of her husband headed across the common room toward the bedchamber, her heart lurched with fear. Terror seized her as she pulled the baby's blanket down over his head.

The door to her chamber creaked opened and Noah stepped inside. His blue eyes were curious as long strides carried him to her bedside.

She raised an apprehensive gaze to meet his.

"A boy?" he asked, his tone hopeful.

She nodded tightly, a small smile on her lips.

As Noah reached one hand toward the swaddled babe, Catherine inhaled a sharp breath and drew the child closer.

Noah's brows pulled together. "Am I not allowed to see?"

"Of — of course." Slowly, carefully, she peeled the blanket away from the baby's face, clearly revealing the color of his skin and hair.

Noah's eyes widened with horror. "You lying, whoring bitch!" His upper lip curled with revulsion. "I did not father *that!*"

"Noah, please!"

He'd already flown from the room, leaving the bedchamber door wide open in his wake.

"I'll kill that savage!"

She heard him rifling through his things

in the common room in search of his musket.

"I've been humiliated at every turn today!"

As he tore through the house, she heard
things tumbling helter-skelter.

"What have you done with my musket?"
he shouted. And a second later: "Where's
my sword?"

She heard him thunder up the steps of the
ladder to the loft, then the sounds of crates
and barrels being knocked about.

Dear God, she prayed, *please do not let him
find the musket!*

In minutes, she heard him race back down
the stairs again. Then, suddenly, as the front
door of the house flew open, a gust of cold
air swept into the room.

"You bastard!" Noah shouted.

At once, the scuffling sounds of two men
fighting in the other room reached Catherine's ears. Grunts and thuds punctuated the
brawl as first one, then the other fell, then
sprang up to lunge again at the other.
Catherine held her breath, hoping against
hope that Noah had not found his musket.

Her heart froze when she heard the one
sound she'd feared most, the explosion of
gunfire. She next heard what sounded like a
chair splintering and one final thud. Then
everything fell silent. Catherine lifted her

head, her face ashen with fear. *What had happened?*

She held her breath, then seconds later, let it out when Phyrahawque stepped to her doorway, carrying in his arms a plush white bearskin pelt.

"I heard a shot!"

"I no shoot him." Phyrahawque moved toward her, the love shining from his black eyes as soft as a caress.

"You fired the shot?"

He nodded assent. "I take fire-stick from him, so he no shoot me." He stood gazing down upon her and the newborn infant in her arms. "Boy?"

She nodded, and he smiled, his white teeth a striking contrast to his dark skin.

"I take you and boy home."

Tears of joy streamed down Catherine's cheeks, flushed with love and relief as her outstretched arms reached for her beloved. "Thank God you came."

Phyrahawque bent to tuck the warm bearskin rug about her and the baby, then scooped them both up into his arms. As he whisked them through the house, Catherine caught sight of Noah sprawled on the floor in a far corner.

"Is he . . . dead?"

"He sleep." Phyrahawque's black eyes

directed hers toward the gaping hole in the roof.

"Oh, my!"

"If rain come tonight, he drown."

A nervous laugh escaped Catherine as she tightened one arm about the tall Indian's neck, her other clasping their sweet child to her breast. Phyrahawque's arms tightened about her, making her feel safe and protected.

Outdoors, he gently laid her onto the warm bed of soft skins he'd prepared on the sturdy *travois* trailing behind his huge white stallion. He settled the plush bearskin rug around them, then expertly secured the load with thick leather straps.

The full moon overhead lit up the trees with a silvery glow as Phyrahawque's steed flew through the forest carrying his flame-haired woman and their newborn baby home.

Crisp cold air ruffled Catherine's hair as the sturdy *travois* skimmed over the forest floor. She could not help wondering what would have been the outcome if she had instead given birth to a pink-skinned, russet-haired babe. But even with Phyrahawque, she could have a flame-haired child one day, a little girl, perhaps. Anything was possible.

For now, she was truly on her way to a New World and the new life she had always dreamed of, one filled not with lies and deception, but with peace, harmony and love, which is exactly what she had come to the New World to find.

AUTHOR NOTES

Apart from telling Catherine's story, I wanted also to depict what life might have been like in early Jamestown. While I made every effort to be as accurate as possible in citing actual persons and historical events, it is likely — considering these events happened nearly four hundred years ago and no one is alive today who can verify anything — that I erred in placing someone in Jamestown between 1617 and 1619, when, in fact, he was elsewhere at the time.

In my research, I discovered many discrepancies involving times and dates of historical events in the early 1600s. Especially difficult to pin down were the exact dates of deputy-governors' terms. Some, like Captain (later Sir) George Yeardley served more than once. Yeardley was deputy-governor through April and May 1617, and again from March through December 1619. During most of the time *Deceptions* takes place

— except early in 1619 when Nathaniel Powell was named Argall's replacement before Yeardley again took office — Captain Samuel Argall was deputy-governor. After being investigated for wrongdoing, Argall was removed from office. For Noah to allude to Argall's nefarious activities does indeed coincide with historical fact.

Scholars also differ regarding the Virginia Company Headright System — when it went into effect, the amount of land granted, and to whom given. Some sources state that women could own land, others dispute that claim.

I found discrepancies in the spelling of Indian words, and words commonly used by the settlers. Since a dictionary did not exist in the early 1600s, people sounded out words when writing, therefore inconsistencies in spelling became the rule rather than the exception. For instance, the word the Indians used to mean Englishmen I found spelled Tassentasse, Tassautessus, Tasentasse and Tassantasses. The word "Powhatan" was spelled Powhatan, Powatan, Powhatam, and Powhaten.

The Powhatan empire or federation actually referred to all the tribes under Pocahontas's father's rule. The English took to calling the chieftain himself Powhatan, rather than Wahunsunacock(e), which was his given name. Most history books maintain that upon Powhatan's death, his brother Opechancanough succeeded him. However, some historians claim that another of Powhatan's brothers, Opitchapan, ruled for a time and that he continued the peaceful relations between the Indians and whites, which Pocahontas's marriage to John Rolfe established in 1614. Four years later, when Opechancanough took over, it was he who engineered the deadly massacre of 1622 when hundreds of colonists were killed.

As for Indian words I used, some are from the antiquated Powhatan language, a sampling of which appears online and in Captain John Smith's writings, but again, discrepancies exist in spelling. Most of the Indian names, as well as some of the tribal names I used in my story, I made up.

Regarding the types and numbers of animals present in early Jamestown, one source stated there were only six horses in the entire colony, and not a single cow until 1624, but Smith mentions the presence of "cattle" in his writings, and he was there in 1607! However, as late as the mid-1800s the word "cattle" also meant horses. A coach driver was called a whip if he could drive his cattle (meaning horses) within an inch. For the purposes of this work, I chose to have an assortment of livestock present in 1617 — goats, horses, cows and even an ox.

The exact time of Pocahontas's death is also disputed. Some historians declare she died at the inn where her party was staying the night *before* she and her husband boarded the *George* for Virginia; another that she became ill on board ship that first night and passed away the following morning. Still another states she became ill several days into the voyage, thus forcing the ship to return to Gravesend where she was taken ashore and soon passed away. Most sources agree that a hasty funeral was held at Gravesend.

The date John Rolfe returned to Virginia following his wife's sudden death is not firm. Some sources put his return in June 1617, only a few months after Pocahontas died in March of that year. Others maintain he did not return for several years. All agree that their infant son Thomas was left behind in England and the boy never again saw his father. Most sources agree that when John Rolfe did return to Virginia, he eventually married a colonist's daughter named Jane (or Joan) Pierce and that he died of unknown causes in 1622, although not during the massacre.

Thomas Rolfe eventually returned to Virginia in 1635 and he did inherit many thousands of acres of Powhatan land. Thomas visited his mother's people from time to time, but married an English girl named Jane Poythress. Among their descendants were noted Virginia statesmen, lawmakers, educators and ministers.

I chose to go with Pocahontas's death as occurring the morning after the Rolfes' ship, the *George,* departed for the New World. I do not know whether or not there were other ships in the convoy that left England that day — sometimes as many as nine ships sailed to the New World together. I invented two fictitious ships; the *Inverness,* upon which Catherine Fielding and her maid Nancy Mills make their voyage to the New World, and a second ship I called the *Hampton.*

More important to my story than the exact time of Pocahontas's death was what Catherine's meeting with the Indian princess meant to Catherine. Though her interaction with Pocahontas was brief, it made a lasting impression on her, becoming the basis of her lifelong love and compassion for the Indian people.

Once Catherine reaches the New World, I

gave her the occupation of teacher, which does not deviate from historical accuracy since early colonial schools did exist. They were called "Dame Schools" because the teachers were women who held classes in their homes where children aged six to eight learned to read, write, and cipher.

Within my story, Noah's deplorable behavior toward Catherine is understandable given the time in which they lived and the prevailing attitudes toward women and their place in society. However, judging by today's standards, Noah is a selfish, manipulative brute who does not respect women. He did not love Catherine; he wished only to possess her. If you ever find yourself in such an abusive relationship, please seek help. Please understand that if a man mistreats you in the way Noah mistreated Catherine, you are only deceiving yourself if you believe he truly loves you.

I thoroughly enjoyed researching and writing *Deceptions*. I hope you enjoyed reading about Catherine's life and her adventures in early Jamestown, and will want to read my next book also set in colonial America.

BIBLIOGRAPHY

Brown, Ralph A., and Marian R. Brown. *Impressions of America.* New York: Harcourt, Brace & World, Inc., 1966.

Coddon, Karin, ed. *Colonial America.* Farmington Hills, Michigan: Greenhaven Press, 2003.

Collier, Christopher, and James Lincoln Collier. *The Paradox of Jamestown, 1585–1700.* New York: Benchmark Books, 1998.

Dow, George Francis. *Everyday Life in the Massachusetts Bay Colony.* New York: Benjamin Blom, Inc., 1967.

Earle, Alice Morse. *Home Life in Colonial Days.* Originally published, New York: Grosset & Dunlap, 1898.

Gunn, Giles, ed. *Early American Writing.* New York: Penquin Books, 1994.

Hakim, Joy. *The First Americans.* Oxford University Press, 1993.

Hall-Quest, Olga Wilbourne. *Jamestown Ad-*

venture. New York: E. P. Dutton & Co., 1950.

Hawke, David Freeman, ed. *Captain John Smith's History of Virginia.* New York: The Bobbs-Merrill Co. Inc., 1970.

———. *Everyday Life in Early America.* New York: Harper & Row, 1989.

Hoffer, Peter Charles. *Law & People in Colonial America.* Baltimore: The John Hopkins University Press, 1992.

Holler, Anne. *Pocahontas: Powhatan Peacemaker.* New York: Chelsea House Publications, 1993.

Hoobler, Dorothy, and Thomas Hoobler. *Captain John Smith: Jamestown and the Birth of the American Dream.* Hoboken, New Jersey: John Wiley & Sons, 2006.

Kupperman, Karen Ordahl. *The Jamestown Project.* Cambridge, Massachusetts: Belknap Press of Harvard University Press, 2007.

Lange, Karen E. *1607: A New Look at Jamestown.* Washington, D.C.: The National Geographic Society, 2007.

Lizon, Karen Helene. *Colonial American Holidays and Entertainment.* New York: Franklin Watts, 1993.

Middleton, Richard. *Colonial America: A History 1565–1776.* Malden, Massachusetts:

Blackwell Publishing, 1992.

Moulton, Candy. *Everyday Life Among the American Indians.* Cincinnati, Ohio: Writers Digest Books, 2001.

Pearson, Lu Emily. *Elizabethans At Home.* Stanford, California: Stanford University Press, 1957.

Price, David A. *Love & Hate in Jamestown: John Smith, Pocahontas, and the Start of a New Nation.* New York: Vintage Books, 2003.

Pobst, Sandy. *Life in the Thirteen Colonies: Virginia.* New York: Scholastic Library Publishers, 2004.

Sakurai, Gail. *The Jamestown Colony.* Danbury, Connecticut: Grolier Publishing, 1997.

Stevens, Bernadine S. *Colonial American Craftspeople.* New York: Franklin Watts, 1993.

Taylor, Dale. *Everyday Life in Colonial America from 1607–1783.* Cincinnati, Ohio: F&W Publications, 1997.

Terkel, Susan Neiburg. *Colonial American Medicine.* New York: Franklin Watts, 1993.

Thompson, John, ed. *The Journals of Captain John Smith: A Jamestown Biography.* Washington, D.C.: National Geographic, 2007.

Vaughan, Alden T., ed. *America Before the*

Revolution, 1725–1775. New York: Prentice Hall, 1967.

Warner, John F. *Colonial American Home Life.* New York: Franklin Watts, 1993.

Web Sites:

Powhatan Language & the Powhatan Indian Tribe. http://www.native-languages.org/powhatan.htm.

Smith, Captain John. Generall Historie of Virginia: 1624. Glasgow, 1907. http://www.historyisfun.org/.

Rediscovering Jamestown. http://www.preservationvirginia.org/.

ABOUT THE AUTHOR

Marilyn J. Clay grew up drawing pictures, reading voraciously, and writing stories. After graduating from college with degrees in Art and English, she illustrated children's textbooks, owned a graphics design studio in Dallas, became a fashion illustrator and a creative director for a fashion magazine, and served as University Editor for The University of Texas at Dallas. For sixteen years, she published *The Regency Plume,* an international newsletter focused on the English Regency. She has had six Regency romance novels published, three translated to foreign languages, and designed Romance Writers of America's RITA award statuette. *Deceptions* is Marilyn J. Clay's first novel set in colonial America. She now stays busy writing novels, reading voraciously, and painting pictures. For information about Marilyn's novels and artwork visit: http://theregencyplume.tripod.com/